THE BEST
AUSTRALIAN
STORIES
2 0 1 0

THE BEST AUSTRALIAN STORIES 2010

Edited by
CATE KENNEDY

Published by Black Inc.,
an imprint of Schwartz Media Pty Ltd

37–39 Langridge Street
Collingwood Vic 3066 Australia
email: enquiries@blackincbooks.com
http://www.blackincbooks.com

ISBN 978-1-86395-495-2

Contents

Introduction

Cate Kennedy

When reading takes up a large part of your time and attention, it's inevitable that its subject matter is also going to take over a large part of your consciousness. The stories I read in search of the ones that make up this collection did more than occupy that mental acreage. They re-surveyed it, subdivided it, and sometimes even built on it. Through the cold months in 2010 I collected short stories in boxes and sacks from my post-office box, lugged them home and approached those waiting stacks like a wine buff might eye a new shipment of Shiraz. Some of them I read in clichéd 'editor' pose: by the fire in a big armchair, a cup of tea in reach. But as more stories kept arriving and the stacks kept growing, they began to co-opt more of my life. I kept a pile by the bed and read at least five a night before going to sleep. I read dozens in trains, and in airport departure lounges waiting for delayed flights, and I knew I was onto a good story when I'd pull it out again in the plane and even in the taxi once I'd arrived back on the ground. I read them late at night as the winter really set in, so totally absorbed in their small universes that at 2 a.m., when I rose to get more wood for the fire, the freezing stillness of the outside world woke me with a cold-steel shock of reality.

As I worked my way through individual submissions, literary quarterlies and anthologies, the stories that stayed with me found their way to a particular pile and I re-read these memorable pieces several times each. I had to – I had over a hundred in there and I knew I'd soon have to make some difficult decisions. It's been said that a writer can't really know how to write a story until they've written it, and in a way the same is true of a selection process. I did not set out looking for anything particular to reward in terms of craft or subject-matter in these stories – I didn't know what I'd find or how it would affect me, I just approached each one hoping to be surprised and moved. Short stories, as Richard Ford said once, are daring little instruments, and they dare you to define them. But there is little to match the pleasurable exhilarating rush, for my money, when we know we are in the hands of a writer with authority. Their power is like a kind of charisma – we allow ourselves to be willingly, absolutely persuaded. They make an arcing sweep of their brush and suddenly a whole scene is painted in, a whole prior, plausible life suggested. They deliver an exchange of dialogue that we know is not really 'lifelike,' we know it just possesses the cadence and feel of real talk, but somehow we believe it, and we believe in those people. A writer with authority takes their story events in a direction we could never have predicted but which still feels perfectly right and satisfying, and we're with them every step of the way.

Part of our willing surrender to this authority is admiration for its skill, because there's nowhere to hide in a short story – we writers only have a few thousand words with which to win your heart, and if we have no skill or nothing to say it is immediately apparent. A short story, that miracle of compression and distillation, can't carry any dead spots, clunky machinery or hairline fractures without these flaws being thrown into cruel relief. So when an author pulls it off – manages the highwire act of conjuring up a memorable, revelatory world in just a few pages – we absorb every considered word with faith and gratitude.

The other part of this authority, though, lies in choices which are not about craft so much as instinct. It would be a mistake to call these instincts 'unerring,' because the very process of writing is sometimes a dogged struggle to work out why our attention is so caught on something from life, something we feel compelled to try to make coherent. Before we can write it for someone else, we need to write it for ourselves. This intuitive, hesitant process, as an author steps out irrationally onto the wire, putting one word after another without fully understanding why or how, is the real test of intent. Writing tutors are fond of quoting Forster's famous 'only connect' directive, but we forget that was only half the quote. 'Only connect the prose and the passion,' he said, 'and both will be exulted.' The stories that made my shortlist, from the longlist of excellent pieces, stayed with me not only because of their technical prowess but also this harder-to-define quality; they tempered something passionately felt into an unexpected revelation that worked its way into my own thinking and stayed there. Stories that galvanised with their energy, and left me feeling – yes – exultant.

It was only at this point my editorial *imprimatur* began to emerge, such as it was: as I read and re-read stories full of admiration not just for their authors but also for the short story form itself, and the way it's capable of containing such huge diversity and vibrancy. From the longer, more intricate plots of Nam Le and David Francis, both dealing in their own ways with the tumultuous, helpless love of family and all it asks of us, to Josephine Rowe's lyrical and elliptical 'Brisbane,' which takes only 500 or so words to cartwheel across that highwire in a bravura display of delicacy and distillation, this contrast stands testament to the form's capaciousness. Joshua Lobb's ambitious 'list' story, Ryan O'Neill's hilarious sequence of book reviews and Gillian Essex's 'One of the Girls,' which unspools a tale from one breathless, wondering sentence, all demonstrate this vibrancy of form and the unexpected ways a story can be told. Some stories I wish I hadn't read late at night before attempting to sleep – David Mence's 'The Cliffs' and Chris Womersley's 'The Age of Terror' both spring to mind, and both drive a splinter under the skin with their depiction of dark and complex self-justifications. Some voices – and this is the great yardstick of a skilfully rendered character – followed me out of the room, still talking, pulling at my arm, demanding to go on being heard. Mike Ladd and Michael McGirr's stories, both so deceptively, achingly simple, found a bruise where I didn't know I had one. A few years ago in his introduction as editor to this anthology, Robert Drewe mentioned the 'wow' factor in selecting stories; for me this year it was more like the 'ow' factor – a tender spot revealed, which reminded me that the greatest technical ability in the world is nothing until it is leavened by compassion.

It feels a little reductive to single out stories for praise just because they are different from each other, when their other qualities are so much richer. Suffice to say even selecting with the balance of prose and passion in mind still left me with many more excellent stories than I could include, so the final cut here is shaped to my tastes and my idea of balance and depth. There are still thirty stories in the box – enough for a whole second collection – which do not appear here and whose omission weighs heavily on my conscience. I hope those stories, too, find their way into publication and the wider audience they deserve.

In a synchronicity you'd dismiss as too stagy and heavy-handed for a work of fiction, the day I handed in my final selection for this anthology, after being awash for months in a tide of submissions, the river in my part of the state rose three and a half metres and broke its banks. Gullies which had been dusty holes for the better part of fifteen years were suddenly billabongs full of astonished, gratified frogs; dry, bare paddocks were inundated, roads closed and the river became a deep, noisy flood. The exultant feeling of waking to that glittering world of water and selecting these stories now feels inextricably linked to me. And that river – cutting and shaping new banks, moving with momentum and unstoppable purpose, slaking a drought-stricken landscape – well, there's a metaphor for new stories you couldn't make up.

My thanks to Denise O'Dea, and to everyone who submitted their stories this year. It was a pleasure and a privilege.

Cate Kennedy

Once Removed

David Francis

Way out the back where the wedding bush grows and mosquitoes breed in the gullies, there's a weatherboard house with bay windows, the place where my English grandmother died. But it sat on her farm at Moorooduc then, among the bracken and ti-tree, pardelotes nested in the sandy cliffs, when my grandmother slept in the four-poster bed, and I dreamt there were bears in the hall, marauding. Suddenly there was no more snoring and I could sleep. She'd gone to be with her Jesus.

The cottage was moved by my father, in slices on trucks, and patched together in the Tindervick bush, set on a rise facing north. Its bay-window eyes staring out to the Pakenham Hills, as if watching for fires. I was shipped along with it, ostensibly in one piece, back to my parents on the same stretch of land, to this big brick homestead that stands among the whining cypresses, where my mother now lives alone. Where magpies fly down the chimneys, her black and tan dog lying in wait to hunt them down, land them stunned and breathless on the hardwood floor. My mother waits too, giddied by the prospect.

Now I stand at the door with my rolling Hartmann luggage, the rented white Prius in the lantern light behind me like something from another galaxy. I'm back for the first time in years, staring through the stained-glass kitchen door, watching her armed with a broom and a fly swatter, disappearing deep into the dining room, where the walls are four bricks thick and bees swarm in the unused chimneys. Ants invade, my mother slaughters armies of them, showing off piles of the dead to occasional visitors.

Unseen, I open the door to the vague smell of compost, the frantic yelping of the dog. But this time it's not a bird being hunted. A brushtail possum, terrified, scratches its way along the picture rail. It pisses with fright on the portrait of Aunt Emma Charlotte, over the pastel of me as a boy. My mother doesn't notice me; she's mesmerised by the leaping dog and the possum as it plummets down onto a table, smashing plates. It hurtles out past me into the Gippsland evening, the dog a dark blur behind it.

'Hello,' my mother says, the broom over her shoulder like a rifle. 'How was your trip? Did you get yourself an upgrade?' Her words are eclipsed by a distant barking, but my mother hears nothing, deaf as the sideboard, deaf as the night. I'd give her a hug but her body would stiffen like a bird's, afraid I was trying to accomplish something unnatural, something American and intimate. So I nod and smile, but don't answer – her interest is more in her questions and the noises she hears inside her head. I just wonder how she's heard of upgrades.

I lean my bags against the door as she returns to her kitchen, irrigating ants from a cupboard, wiping them up with an ant-speckled washcloth, as though she's already forgotten I've arrived. Since her stroke, her memory of moments just passed has become more elusive. She refuses to wear her hearing aids. And I'm back in the silence with her, to the place that's been here all along, the comfort of things unchanged. Just the faint rustle of wood ducks nesting in the chimney, cooing again now that the house is still, the house that coos as if it's calling out. A place for the shelter of species, provided they stay hidden.

A letter lies on the table already set for tomorrow's breakfast. The writing, angled and childlike, addressed to *Those Whom Are Concerned,* signed at the top and the bottom, *Sharen W.* The tenant in the house out the back: Sharen Wills. My father, Remy's, tenant. Remy as in Remington, although my mother says it's short for Remedial. He thinks the house is still his because his little mother died in it. But he lives five miles away now, in a sad-looking cottage in a place called Blind Bight. Stuck there with his girlfriend, Kim, ever since my mother threw him off the farm.

I pick up the letter uninvited and my mother pretends not to watch me read. She guides a trail of golden ant poison along the ledge.

I do not know how much you know but I can only assume you are naive in the field. That is of the situation of Remy and myself and I will not be harassed by Remy who is bulling me to leave. I pay the same for my horses being here as anyone else but I don't get the use of the faculties.

I glance up, my mother's eyes upon me now. 'She's illiterate,' she says, 'poor little thing.' Sharen Wills, whose rent provides my mother's shopping money.

I feel there is a stigma because of me and Remy. Also I have been attacked by those three black Clydesdales in the back paddock. None of this is safe for me here but I will not leave under these provisions. I will get my own solicitor. I will not be railroded.

'Hell hath no fury.' My mother trails off as she hands me a dustpan, a load of dead bees and ants, spoils of the sweetness she leaves on the jam jars, as lures.

I head outside and empty the carnage of insects on a lavender bush, stand on the tiled veranda, and watch the purple remains of the evening, the glint on the windows of the distant clapboard house. The house you can see from Station Road on the way into town or from the window of the shearer's quarters, or from here, out across the lagoon paddock.

The phone rings shrilly and I run back inside, see my mother under her jigsaw lamp, leaning over a Wysocki lighthouse puzzle, the phone going unanswered, a message being left on the machine.

'Ruthie, it's Sharen. I need to talk before I do something stupid.'

My mother lifts her head. 'She grows marijuana out there,' she says, 'in tubs in a horse float.' She returns to sorting pieces of sky.

I stand by the black rotary phone on the desk, the small jug of familiar pens and broken pencils, and I think of the letter, *the situasion with Remy,* how I don't want to deal with Sharen Wills, whose number is fifth on a list on the wall, after the fire brigade and the vet, my father and Dr Hopkins. My mother, who dreads the phone and resents others using it, turns the television on so loud it sounds like a plane is landing on the roof. She goes on searching for jigsaw edges.

I pull my rolling suitcase along the carpeted hall, let it rest outside the fancy bathroom. The original Victorian tiles, the bath with its iron-clawed feet. I brush my teeth with the toothbrush that waits for me here in a small pewter goblet, squeeze the remains of my miniature Qantas toothpaste. I look in the mirror, a jetlagged ghost of myself. *I need to talk to someone before I do something stupid.*

My mother remains in her jigsaw world. On the television screen, the clever blue eyes of the new prime minister, but I'm listening again to the message on the dusty answering machine, wondering what my father's done to Sharen Wills. Only the dog observes me, from its roost in the cushions along the back of the couch, as I dial the number, a call that rings and rings, goes unanswered. Overcome with an old desire to escape this house, and to know what's really going on, I steal out into the night and start up the silent Prius. I glide through the shadowy paddocks, scraping along the overgrown track down towards the windmill, rabbits scurrying in the headlights. As I open the lagoon paddock gate, I shoo away dark horses approaching to sniff the soundless car, heavy part-Clydesdales I don't recognise. The whoop of what might be an owl up above me, mosquitoes drift about my face, the cacophony of crickets. I try to remember why I don't live here. Is it the noise or all the silence?

I notice the lights from the house out the back, bay windows appearing as beacons through the trees, the house of my first night terrors, where my mother discovered my father in bed with Kim and ordered them both away. The house where my parents' marriage ended.

A dark hump appears in the headlights, a car abandoned in the field. It hunkers low in the grass on bare axles. An old Mitsubishi sedan with its tyres removed, brimming with trash and what looks like a chair leaned up against the door. Beyond the car, the garden fence, and the yard that was once tidy emerges as a carnival of corrugated iron, engine parts and overgrowth, a rusted clothes-line whining. There were once hibiscus, black-eyed peas and black-eyed Susan, a twelve-foot passion-fruit vine.

I park the hybrid under a eucalyptus near the fence and wend my way among rusted fenders and a sunken laundry trough to the sagging carport, and knock on the brown waterlogged door of my childhood. A shout from inside and then footsteps; the door opens a crack. Then the face of a woman with creased smoker's cheeks and turquoise eyes, her hair in a tangled nest. Nipples pressed through a long Cold Chisel T-shirt stretched down to bare, slender legs.

'You must be Daniel!' she says, suspiciously. 'A chip off the block.' She is nervous, speaking more with the urgency of speed than the drawl of a stoner. 'Excuse this dreadful mess,' she adds. She clasps her shoulders, blames 'the boys' for the maze of laundry on the floor, but there are no signs of boys just the smell of cannabis. In a kitchen I barely recognise she offers me coffee. She's probably only my age but looks like she's done it harder. I glance away from her angry but curious stare, down at a floor now bereft of linoleum, to a sink where leaning plates and angled saucepans tower precipitously. The kitchen where my grandmother once stood with the sun beaming in on her delicate English face, pouring tea and placing scones on a silver tray, baking her special rice pudding.

Sharen Wills' arms are tanned and her hands are shaking as she plugs in a kettle. She announces, 'The Landlord and Tenant Act of Victoria requires twenty-four hours prior notice for a visit from the landlord.'

'I'm not your landlord,' I say. 'Just making sure things are okay.'

She puts the kettle down. 'I'm having trouble with your father,' she says. No mention of the letter.

'We've had trouble with him ourselves.'

'He appears on a horse at the window at all hours and I rarely wear clothes in the house.' She looks down at herself, the cotton clinging to her narrow body and I wonder if I'm supposed to find it appealing. She offers me a cigarette.

'He hasn't ridden for years,' I say. 'He can barely walk.'

'He'd crawl if he had to,' she says. 'He's at the door at midnight

… and when I don't answer he pulls out my marijuana by the roots.'

I imagine her in tight-fitting, camel-toe jeans. 'It's his mother's house,' I say. I don't tell her the whole five hundred acres, houses and all, are now in my mother's name, after he was sentenced to life with Kim. *Now I've got two bitches in my soup*, he once told me on the sly. I look over at this woman pouring me coffee and wonder if there aren't now three. *A rat gets caught in its own trap*, my mother says of him.

'He wants me out of here,' says Sharen, hugging a cup of coffee between her breasts. 'He wants to move back in here; he wants to die in his mother's house. But I want to die in his mother's house too,' she says.

I'm not sure what to say. My father, almost eighty, thinks he's my age, despite the fact his hips are fusing. I look at the squalor of plates and piles of paper, a place I wouldn't want to live or die in. My grandmother's quaint English furniture left in this woman's hands, and the last time I visited, my father on his death bed in the Dandenong Hospital, pale in one of those paper gowns, pneumonia and congestive heart failure, a shriveling man in a narrow metal cot. But he still thought he was virile, working the nurses, wheezing, flirting, something to live for. Bright young nurses in robin's egg blue attending, the glint in his wrinkled farmer's eyes. He offered them trips down here, said he'd take them out riding, as if he could still get on a horse. Half-dead and still handsome.

'I'll take him to the tribunal,' says Sharen. 'How dare he try to evict me after all I've been through?' She looks over at me, gauging loyalties, more defiant than tearful, angry at these unexpected visits, the skulking, or maybe angry that he skulks no more, that I'm not moving to comfort her. I don't need to tell her he's always been a hands-on husband, women pressed against the fridge, my unsuspecting girlfriends bailed up on the hall-stand, that Lipman woman emerging with him from the haystack in the middle of the night while my mother slept alone up in the big house, the lantern standing dim above the roses.

Nervously, Sharen lights a second Marlboro. 'I've had him up to here,' she says, the cigarette in her nail-bitten fingers cutting across her throat.

I wonder where she's really had him up to. I lean on the ledge and try to summon my lawyerly training – her claim could only be against my mother, since she's the one who now owns all this, but Sharen Wills has no cause against my mother, except perhaps a bifurcated empathy. Still, I recognise a stake laid out on the grease-stained living room floor. A black oil patch where someone dismantled an engine, take-away food containers adorning my grandmother's inlaid mosaic table. Furniture from some ancestral home in Norfolk.

'Are your horses still here?' I ask. The pair of plump Anglo-Arabs out in the couch grass. Last year one of them foaled unexpectedly and my father went ballistic, ordered them off the place, but they kept reappearing, mare and foal and other stray horses, munching on his precious grass that really belongs to my mother, grown for the cattle he thinks are still his.

Sharen has a hand on her hip, reminding me she pays her rent. I've heard how she visits the big house, speaks loud enough so my mother can hear, charms her in front of the Aga stove, brings treats for the dog and drinks Earl Grey tea and partakes of stale Teddy Bear biscuits, laughing. Sharen Wills isn't stupid. She probably helps with the crossword, places difficult pieces into the blue miasma of a jigsaw sky.

'I'm working as a psych nurse at Dalkeith.' She's trying to impress me. She has an income; she specialises in old people. She will not be *railroaded*.

'Why didn't you just tell Dad to piss off?' I say.

'How could I?' she asks. 'He's the landlord.'

'But you tell him to piss off now.' I've heard how she has my father agitated, taunting him in her T-shirts, shouting epithets out these curved bay windows. *I'll have your balls for breakfast.*

Nodding, feigning tears, 'I have no choice here,' she says.

'Did he ever touch you?'

'Not really.' She's suddenly defensive, almost shocked. 'He just chased me around.' But I'm not sure I believe her. He can barely walk. Maybe he's touched her in ways she's not even sure of. Despite the charm he's predatory, under his guise of playfulness. I watch her and pretend to drink her tepid coffee, thoughts of my buckled-up father before the Tenancy Tribunal, fending off assertions, an old man accused of shuffling around his own mother's furniture, brandishing his cheeky smile in some fumbling pursuit, then yanking out her marijuana as his only vengeance. A man possessed by lust. It's not his reputation I care about; that's long lost and gone. It's him on the dock of some petty assembly, collapsing, carted away without a chance to limp down the end of this short, dark hallway and climb alone between the sheets of his mother's four-poster bed.

'You'll kill him,' I tell Sharen Wills.

She stares past me, out into the bay-windowed night, as if the pleasure would be all hers.

*

I drive back past the dark, abandoned car, through the milling horses then along the grass track to the big house. The night is clear, the garden lantern turned on for my benefit. When I open the door to the kitchen, my mother doesn't ask where I've been – she's used to her men disappearing at night. She stands like a twig in pyjamas, heating her wheat bags in the ancient microwave with her mottled sun-spotted hands. 'Hello, Foozle,' she says with curious enthusiasm, a nickname I've not heard in thirty years. The dog still in its perch among the pillows.

'Do you have everything you want?' my mother asks, her blotchy terracotta cheeks, her small bird face with small bird eyes. Eyes that could pierce holes in steel. But she doesn't wait for an answer. Wheat bags in one hand, she slinks up into the dark hallway with a goodnight wave over her shoulder, heading for her narrow bed. She says the bed spins when she lies down in it. She forgets she suffers from vertigo and what the doctor called *left-side neglect*, a skewed awareness of one side of her body, the effects of a stroke.

I roll my luggage further up the hall, glimpse Aunt Emma Charlotte's portrait in the shadowed dining room, her face streaked with possum piss, which gives her a thin damp smile. From behind my mother's bedroom door, I can already hear her wireless blaring – 3AW talk and oldies, the throaty roll of Burl Ives from her rickety bedside table.

I no longer sleep in the meatsafe, with its hooks in the tongue and groove ceiling and the freezing bluestone floor, or in my old room in the shearer's quarters, festooned with dusty horse-show ribbons; I sleep in the Senator's Room, named in honour of a television show once filmed here. The light unveils the familiar ornate moulded roses on the fifteen-foot cobwebbed ceiling, a fresh rent where chunks of plaster have fallen, a dark hole up into the cold slate roof. The room is still decked out as the master suite of the television senator's house. The familiar blue floral wallpaper, the only wide bed in the place. My parents once had their two single beds parallel parked in here, separate and unequal. In a house where men find it hard to survive.

I heft my bag up onto the re-covered chaise and wonder which came first – was my mother unwilling to share her bed with him because she realised what she'd married, or was it that she didn't share herself and he went elsewhere, to sleep in the campervan or his mother's house out in the bush? I imagine my conception here, forty years ago, my mother looking up into the cobwebs, a vague disgust in her eyes, or maybe just wondering what all the fuss was about. The irony of them still strangely in love even now, a love so fraught with disappointment it manifests as acrimony.

On the mantel, a sepia photo of my mother swinging wide at a polo ball, her body clinging like a monkey to the side of a horse at a flat-strap gallop. Her childhood clock on a small, varnished table beside the bed. Its hands dead parallel at 9.15 p.m. Branches scratch the corrugated roof, up where possums gnaw the electrical cables. A vague smell of burning, as if the whole house is quietly smouldering, the slow combustion of oak beams plundered from vessels shipwrecked off the coast.

I undress to the lilt of Burl Ives. Out in the windmill paddock I can hear horses; one begins to canter, followed by the thunder of elderly geldings galloping, pummelling the dark sandy earth. I get into the senator's bed, the same cream sheets unwashed from last time, the stale smell of my own night sweats, but also the smell of wheat. Against my leg, a wheat bag of my own, heated and carefully placed by my mother. I try to sleep but am wide awake. The spurned look in Sharen Wills' bright blue-green eyes, a kind of stricken ferocity that's never quite left my mother's. Sharen Wills who will not leave *under these provisions*.

I hold the warm wheat bag against my body and listen to the burr of talkback radio, the groans of the cypresses. I dream I'm clambering up through the hole in the plaster, crawling through attics crammed with rows of wooden coat-hangers, leather hand-bags hanging from hooks like small curing pigs. Possums, eyes wide with beady judgment. The sound of a distant explosion and I'm wide awake. Two a.m. on the bedside clock. The muffled noise of my mother, her bedroom door shoved open against the carpet, her quick jolty steps out onto the windswept veranda. A sound so loud even she heard it.

I pull the curtain and watch her out there, her nightie blown against her narrow body, her wild night hair pushed back from her face, glaring into the distance. Flames rope up from a fire at the edge of the bush. Within seconds I am joining her in my boxers and T-shirt, our eyes glued on the flicker of orange. 'Is that the house?' I ask.

'I hope so,' she says, rubbing her favourite spot below her hairline, pretending to be inured to the sight of fires, how things here start and end in flames – like the time there was a fire in the Station Road paddock and she searched for my father so he could help. She found him out there in bed with his girlfriend, in the house that now seems to be burning, lit like a candle on the horizon. In a wind like this with the trees so dry – I watch my mother hug herself, knowing this could incinerate a thousand acres and the town.

'Don't let the bush burn,' she says, as though it's up to me. The remnant vegetation, native plants and species, bandicoots and mallee firs, the bush is a place of Aboriginal significance. Not to mention the field where those big dark horses live. I know how horses get panicked by flames, run through barbed-wire fences.

I'm already back in the house, dialing the Country Fire Brigade, the number on the list taped to the wall, above my father's number at Kim's, above the vet and Sharen. 'A fire on Rawson's place, the end of Hopetoun Road.' I talk as if I'm not from here, and now I'm pulling on clothes, running cross-country, wondering if the whole place might just combust in the wind, the bush and the houses, cattle and horses trapped in dry carpets of grass, feathery fetlocks catching like torches.

Down at the windmill, fumbling with the latches on gates, I realise it's not the house that's gone up, but the car in the field. That's what exploded. The great shadows of the heavy horses circle it like spectres, a dance of retreats and advances between the bounds of their fear and fascination. I leave the gates wide open and call out with my father's cry: 'C'mon, c'mon.' One of them turns but not for long, back to its wary appraisal, the orange and crack of the flames, the floating of embers to sniff in the air, while the small house on the rise lies dark as the night, feigning innocence. The car wrapped in flames and the fire-engine wail bathing the thick night air.

I race near as I dare to the blue-orange heat and stamp fire that spreads from the vehicle through the midsummer grass. The horses circle behind me, quizzical, mesmerised, nostrils flaring at the smoke, as if daring me closer. But it's too hot here and the sparks make me wary of another explosion. The sound of the crackling. I pull off my coat to thrash the ground where a flame is causing a new patch to smoulder. Luckily the growth is so short from grazing that it doesn't just flare up like broom straw. Then, at my feet, a piece of my grandmother's headboard, an ornate hacked-off corner, and at the base of the flames I see more – a dining room chair, the spindly leg of a bridge table thrown onto the bonnet. An outrage whips through me like the earth quaking. Pieces that survived the passage from England haven't survived Sharen Wills. I stare at the top of my grandmother's mirrored armoire, cast out like a demon in flames, but it's too hot to lunge in and salvage anything. Embers float from my grandmother's bedhead chopped into sections, from the bed where she died with *The Book of Common Shrubs* on the now-burning end table, her small round specs on the still-open page. When she was alive and this house was as it should still be.

I turn from the bonfire and make out a shape in the dimly lit bay window, not fifty yards between us. Sharen Wills, gazing at her accomplishment. She who will not be *railroded* is railroading us. The sight of her makes me want to snatch a burning chair leg and set her alight, but I'm saved from myself by the fire-engine lights turning up into Hopetoun Road, like an ambulance arriving for the already dead. The siren turned off now, just the hissing of vinyl car seats and sparks from lost antiques.

I slap my jacket at another scorched swath of grass as the truck rattles silently over the cattle grid and sweeps its lights across the paddock. The arch-necked horses canter off and I'm left here alone with my face lit by flames and the charcoal smell in my nostrils. Up in the truck cab it's Bobby Gennaro. We once played tennis as boys, when my mother allowed me to mix with the townies.

'You know it's a total-fire-ban day,' he shouts at me, jumping down from the running board. He seems invigorated by the blaze, and I sense the divide between us. The two young volunteers unwind the canvas hose. No one asks why a car is on fire in the middle of our paddock; they know weird shit happens out here. My tears are caused by the smoke but my anger is gilded with shame. I might have fled eight thousand miles from this place but it's a feeling as old as the corduroy coat I flail at the grass. Yes, I'm a Rawson. And they haven't even noticed the furniture yet. But a new hissing sound and a gust of the high-pressure shoots on the windshield and a burning chair goes flying, charcoaled pieces of French-polished wood. Bobby Gennaro aims lower and smiles to himself as if he's hit the jackpot. He hoses the flames that light up the delight on his face.

'Fucking Sharen from the house,' I shout, as though it has little to do with me, 'she's pissed off at my father.' But my voice feels like kindling in the wind. They know Sharen, surely, the way she shows her tits and midriff, and they must talk about my father, *the Eccentric Millionaire from Tindervick*, despite the fact he now owns nothing. And despite the fierce sprays of precious water, sparks still fly from Sharen's old burning car and his burning heirlooms, sprung from the house he rented to her regardless, when my mother called him a loon for leaving it furnished. My mother who knew Kim wouldn't be enough, that he'd keep a keen eye on his dead mother's stuff and his hands on his slender new tenant. My frail mother, still out on that far dark veranda, smelling the wind for embers, hosing the remains of her garden or hosing down the cypresses in case this gets away and rips through the rye grass towards her. And I'm out here with the nearly doused fire, water sizzling on the white hot metal of the car, attempting to contain these inherited feelings, and ignore Bobby's stifled amusement. They'll dine out on this, wake their wives as they walk in their doors in the early morning: 'You shoulda seen what that Sharen Wills did to old Remy Rawson.'

A remnant of my grandmother's English bedspread blows against my leg, brittle and disintegrating, the bobbles singed and loose on the fringe. A bed that should have been mine. The dividends of my father's charm: my grandmother's inlaid vanity attached to the trunk like a cancer and the sight of Sharen Wills watching through the smoke from the quaint bay window, taunting me while my father sleeps elsewhere. The busted-up mosaic table.

I glance back at Sharen Wills with my watery eyes but turn away in disgust, drawn back to the smouldering aftermath, the last sprays of high-pressure water on the rusted black chassis, a blistered piano stool lodged deep in the back window, its legs reaching out like the haunches of a deer, the shapes of these snickering, adrenalised men in the beams of their truck lights. In the steam and ashes, the remains of the small, incinerated rocking horse. The silver mane and real leather bridle. My grandmother rode it as a child in the Cotswolds, and then rocked me on it in this strange country she called the *Frightful Antipodes*. The rocking horse is blackened, the painted wood sooty and blistered in the rubble. I move in to retrieve at least something, kneel down to the memories of her pretty English face, *ride a cockhorse to Banbury Cross*. But the remains of the plaything are sodden and the wet, disintegrating feel has me moving away through the smoke.

With charcoaled hands, I tread through the dark towards the house, past a wheelbarrow, to the figure now gone from the window. I am deliberate, climbing the chicken wire. My father, who cares less for belongings than for the chance at a woman like this, and I, who've been striving so hard to divorce myself from this ridiculous history. But it's me who is pounding the green-panelled door. I don't shout her name, just beat on the wood, unsure what I'll do if she answers, or if she doesn't. Then I realise it's not even locked and I burst in, and there she is in her washed-out glory, through the frosted glass doors in the sitting room. The stale smell of her pot and adulterating rubbish now mixed with the remains of fresh-split mahogany. She's had a busy night.

Sharen in bra and panties slouches in a modern rocker-recliner in a room bereft of my grandmother's things. The axe that's done the job leans against the wall like a casual assistant. Despite me, she watches out the bay window, as if it's all on television, the young fire fighters and their brightly lit truck, all framed with a bottlebrush foreground. Staring out like I'm not even in this entry hall. Her arms are tanned and slender, wrists I could snap in my hands; her fingers loose on a cigarette, legs crossed to support the ashtray in her brazen lap. I want to snatch her up from her tacky recliner, drag her outside by a fistful of stringy chestnut hair, across the hardwood floor, her bare heels furrowing through the chips from my grandmother's dining-room table.

'How dare you,' I say.

She turns, recalcitrant. I move into the naked room, bear down on her.

'Don't touch me,' she says, fending me off with her cigarette, stabbing wildly at the air, her expression still snide but strangely playful.

As I grab the cigarette, it burns into my palm. I let out a yelp that surprises us both, stamp the fag end into the floor and I can see her suppressing a smile.

'I don't want to touch you, believe me,' I say. She leans forward in her small dark bra, shows me what worked for my father, but her ashtray falls to the floor. 'You're not that appealing,' I say.

'Ridden hard and put away wet?' Her laugh is brittle and mocking but I stand over her with a desire to hurt that unnerves me, to give her what she wants.

'They were my grandmother's antiques,' I say. 'Shipped from England in the twenties.'

'Don't talk to me about your family's history,' she says.

It's all I can do not to strike her. 'I'm not my father,' I say. 'And I don't want to go where he's been.'

She looks up at me with something stubborn and primal in her bloodshot eyes. 'I'm not going anywhere,' she says.

'Yes you are.' I'm behind her now, at the back of the recliner, pinning her narrow hands to the arms of the chair, hefting it up with her in it, moving over the room as she yells about lawyers and the rights of tenants and how I don't want to do this, but I'm already out in the entry hall and it feels like this is the right thing to do. I think of my grandmother's rocking horse as I hiss with exertion in the doorway and step into the chill of the night, Sharen screeching and spitting. She bites the arm of my coat as

I use her as ballast to thrust her outside; she tries to square her legs against the door jamb but they don't quite spread that wide.

'I don't care what you did with my father.' I rip my sleeve from her teeth, empty her out of the chair and down the bluestone steps. Sharen Wills ends up splayed in a scant-clad heap with her own broken chair on the path of my childhood. She looks back at me like a victim of some horrible crime.

'You *are* like your father.'

Firemen run through the darkness, the fastest one almost hurdles the fence.

'You wish,' I say.

The breathless young firemen are already there. One kneels at her side and she's sobbing. It's a volunteer's dream, this on top of everything else.

'Take her with you,' I say. 'Get her off the place.'

'I'll tell them what Remy did.' She curls her lip at me as she's helped to her feet.

'Tell them what you like,' I say. Inside, I close my grandmother's door behind me and lean my back against it. Just don't tell me.

In the sitting room echoing with what has just been, I shake with a rage that wants to trash what's left but there's nothing – a *Women's Weekly* and an empty Tindervick Pizza box on the floor, a wicker laundry basket draped with socks. I punt it clean across the room at a wall bereft of pictures. The Munnings print, thoroughbreds with dust rugs over their loins, is gone. A feeling wells up inside me I've not felt since I was seventeen and pummelled my father, bloodied his angular face and then left this farm for the first time. My stupid fucking father. And now I'm back here, back in time, in this sad little house, ridding us all of Sharen Wills. The sting of her cigarette welt in my palm, her teeth marks on my forearm, and out the same bay window, her narrow shoulders draped with a blanket, escorted by firemen across the paddock to the truck. Their shadows like tribespeople travelling through.

No sign of the black horses, just the silhouetted figures climbing into the cab of the fire engine – then, at the edge of the spray of truck lights, a frail shape in the dark. My mother in her cream nightgown like a sheet in the wind above the grass. A skeletal woman out after midnight, hugging herself in the smoky air now dissipating in the breeze. I walk toward her, past the remains of the broken recliner, climb the fence and move through the paddock. She's moored to the earth by my father's oversized boots, monitoring the fire engine as it bumps off through the night, her shiny button eyes tracking the taillights down Hopetoun Road.

'That's something accomplished,' she says. Her face shines with a translucent pleasure, as if a lost territory has been retaken.

In the dark, the burned-out vehicle appears like the carcass of a gutted beast, smoking and sizzling, my mother shivering with victory, her nightie blowing against her ribcage. We watch the red lights recede towards town.

'She'll be screaming bloody murder,' I say.

'I doubt you hurt her,' my mother says, quietly phosphorescent, like she's Eleanor of Aquitaine, betrayed but undaunted. 'I was your witness,' she says. Her hearing seems strangely acute in the smoke-scented breeze.

'How much did you see?' I ask.

'You poured her out like a load of wood,' she says proudly. The smile. 'But you didn't hit her, did you?' She neither looks at me nor waits for an answer. 'Remember that time with your father, after he threw the hammer at you?'

'I didn't hit her,' I say. I had my father pinned against the fridge and punched him until his Roman nose was broken and his cheeks were scraped with blood, and I pinned Sharen Wills' narrow hands to the arms of that now-busted chair and she disappeared, cradled between men in a truck. I wrap my mother in my jacket and place an arm about her bony shoulders, an unlikely liberty. We move to inspect the steaming remains, the dregs barely visible in the unlit night, just a dark hump and the faint sibilant hiss of water dripping on hot metal. It's too dark to be reminded of the rocking horse.

'She burned all of Granny's furniture,' I say.

My mother exhales dismissively. 'That spindly little English stuff, you could barely use it anyway.' She always despised my grandmother's gentility, the fact that she was so spoiled and pretty, not to mention religious, that she pledged her modest fortune to American evangelists. A malady equated with madness.

We turn away from the carnage and trudge through the paddocks, back up to the main house. 'And the Munnings was gone from the wall,' I say.

She looks up, squinting. She loved that painting, the fine shapes of well-bred horses. She'd always had her sights on it, but my father insisted it stay on my grandmother's wall. 'Your father is a sloven and a slut,' my mother says, then stares ahead as I wonder at her unlikely choice of epithets.

'Would he have insured it?' I ask. 'Any of it?'

'Don't be ridiculous,' she says. 'And don't worry, you'll end up with all this.' She stares across the spread extending flat and black as bitumen before us, shrouding me in an old unholy alliance, me the lucky one. Schooled as a boy not to care for my father, her disillusionment placed like a bounty at my feet, advising quietly how his side of the family may have been pretty but they weren't that bright, letting me know on the QT that his parents were actually cousins. 'That's why they left England.'

My father, the only surviving son of runaways, charming, square-jawed. I could beat him at Scrabble before I was ten, or I would have if I'd bothered to play him. I was too busy doing crosswords with my mother, measuring up to her vocabulary, while he was already out chasing skirt. My mother too tough for him to compete with, on a horse, at cricket or cards. A polo player, she rode jumping horses in England at the Royal Windsor Show, studied agricultural science at Melbourne University, played tennis like Margaret Court, came second in the Australia-wide bridge pairs with Gill the cook. My father who'd begged my mother to marry him until she gave in. 'He wouldn't leave me alone,' she once told me, 'so eventually I said "yes" just to make him stop.' My mother proceeded to split me – prodigal son and surrogate husband. My father sought his approval elsewhere. He knew there was no competing here.

The creak of the windmill above us where the three gates meet, and again the hoot of that unseen owl, the weight of this old conspiracy, my arm around the matriarch – part-parent, part-child, her confidant. I glance back in the direction of the newly emptied house and feel the onslaught of misgivings.

'Bobby Gennaro was amused,' I say.

My mother allows another huff. 'You scared them all off,' she says. She treads carefully through the longer grass, past the concrete trough in the centre paddock. 'I'm just glad that woman's gone,' she says. 'Good boy.' But I wonder if that woman will be back.

'We'll get Al to clean up the mess,' my mother says, forgetting that Al's as old as the Empire. He's worked here so long he can barely cut wood to keep her in logs for the stove. He could no more clean up that burned-out wreck or the squalor in Sharen Wills' kitchen than run for government.

I imagine Sharen at the fire station telling her woes to the boys over a smoke and a beer.

'I should call the police,' I say.

My mother laughs. The laugh she uses when she hasn't heard, in case what I said is supposed to be funny. In lieu of a response she motions at the dark billowed shapes of the heavy horses in the distance, grazing in their fresh paddock. 'We should just change the locks on the cottage,' she says and I realise she's heard all along. She's reminding me she doesn't approve of involving outsiders; she'd have preferred we fought the fire ourselves.

'We also need to keep your father out of that house,' she says. 'Once he gets wind of all this he'll want to move in there with bloody Kim.' My mother seems to be gaining momentum. No longer a wavering stick in white cotton, she steps through the grass erratically, plotting like old times. She must have her hearing aid in. 'Next thing you know he'll be dead and we'll be left with *her*.' She holds course for the lantern in her garden on the distant hill, where her dog is shut inside and barking.

We head along the old tractor path and she hitches up her nightie and starts telling me stories. 'Remember at Monomeith we had those Dutch people.' She talks as if I were alive then, on the farm where she grew up. 'They used our chairs as firewood. Too lazy to go out and chop their own.' This is why we were taught to hate the Dutch.

My mother pulls free from my arm at the stile by the chicken coop and climbs unassisted. If she falls we both know she'll shatter a hip. Balancing on top in the night breeze she looks down at me.

'When I was a kid,' she says, 'we used to ride our ponies bareback and help spot bushfires from up on Two Bays Road.' She shields her eyes as if we're in broad daylight. 'The firemen gave us canvas knapsacks of water and we'd spray the remains.' She goes to step over but stops. 'I was good at firefighting,' she says.

I feel a strange desire to defend the dignity of this old woman, who stands resilient up in the dark like something immortal. 'No sign of fires from up here,' she says, the recent one perhaps already shot from her memory while its implications adhere to me like the soot on my fingers, a charred rocking horse and a lost Munnings, my mother up there as if she might just float away. I love the life that's returned to her eyes. 'You're the reason I stay alive,' she says, then boldly steps down to the ground.

She walks on ahead through the wood chips by the chopping stump, leaving me this side of the fence, split in pieces of my own – the part that yearns to be here with her, to stay like this forever, and the part that needs to disappear into a city far away.

Harvard Review

One of the Girls

Gillian Essex

My bed's covered with clothes and I'm still not sure what to wear because it was only yesterday she rang and first I thought I hadn't heard it right that she wanted me to have lunch and listen to a band with her so then I had to rearrange things and I didn't even think about what to wear but I don't want to embarrass her though now it's too late so I settle for the skirt because at least it's black and I don't look so fat in it and then the doorbell rings and it's Emma and I haven't even put make-up on but I ask her if I look okay and she says fine without really looking then on the way I don't know what to say because it's been a while and she looks at the road because she's driving so I just gaze out the window then she asks me where I want to eat but I don't know so she picks somewhere and orders but I pay for it and then I eat most of hers as well as mine because all she's done is play with it just like when she was little and she gives me that look and it makes me try to hold my stomach in when we walk into the pub and she introduces me to the band and they're all flat-bellied skinny girls and I think about how bands always used to be boys except maybe the singer but I call out hello to the girls then one of them comes right over and shakes my hand then Emma leads me over to a battered leather couch facing where the band is setting up and she tells me that this'll be comfortable for me as if I'm old or something but I think the stools off to the side might be better though I sit on the couch anyway and try to pull my skirt over my knees and think about how it would have been better if I'd worn jeans like everyone else here and I hope the band won't be too loud then she asks me if I want a drink and I do really but I tell her no because I'm off alcohol now and then I think I should have asked for a lemon lime and bitters but I don't even know if pubs do that anymore and she says she needs a drink so she goes to the bar and I think she'll come back but she perches on a stool and doesn't look my way again and I wonder if it'd be okay to get up and join her but it looks like she's chatting up the barman and at first I think she could do better than that but then I think it's a start and anyway maybe she's just relieved there's someone else to talk to besides me so I stay on the couch and wonder how long it's been since I've been in a bar and if all pubs are like this these days with fake wood panelling and mirrors and stainless steel fittings and metal furniture apart from the couch and hardly anyone here to listen to the band but it's only three o'clock on a Sunday afternoon and it's sunny outside and perhaps when they start to play people will come through the large doors that open onto the street and I suppose that's what the band's for but it looks like they're being paid in drinks instead of money by the way they're knocking back red wine in beer glasses and I wonder if they'll even be able to play and then in walks this woman and I think she's one of the girls because she's thin and she's wearing faded and ripped jeans and a T-shirt with writing on it and her hair's got different colours in it the way they do it these days only mine's the same colour it always was except my roots are showing and she greets the girls in the band like they're all mates and hugs Emma but then she comes over to the couch and she says this must be the mothers' couch only I think she's said 'the mother's couch' but then she sits beside me and from close-up I see she's got wrinkles but they're covered in make-up and she looks fantastic and I wish I'd put mine on and she says you must be Emma's mother but I just nod and wait for her to go away because I'm hoping that Emma will come back and then she tells me she's Sophie's mother and I don't even know which one Sophie is because I didn't catch their names but Sophie's mother points out the girl who's adjusting the mike and it's the one who shook my hand and she tells me that Sophie's the lead singer and I think that'd be right and

I look at Emma and think she must be just the groupie if that's what they still call them and then Sophie's mother tells me that Sophie's studying law but I didn't know you could be a lawyer with a ring through your nose and she says she didn't really want her to be a lawyer and I think why not and then she tells me that she supposes Sophie chose law because she's always been surrounded by lawyers and I guess if Sophie's parents are lawyers then that's how come Sophie's mother can afford to look so good and then she says she's worried about whether Sophie will have enough time to study with all the band practice she's doing but she tells me Sophie's just won a medal at the uni so I guess Sophie does all right and I just think about how Sophie's mother hugged Emma like it was the most natural thing in the world and Emma didn't even flinch or not that I could see and then Sophie's mother tells me Sophie's going off to work in an orphanage in Cambodia as soon as she's finished her degree and then she wants to work in human rights and I think oh God she's going to save the world as well and I wonder if Emma would have turned out better if I'd managed to stay with her father because then she wouldn't have been so angry and we would have had more money not that she's turned out badly it's just she hasn't worked out what to do with her life yet and she's never even had a boyfriend or not that I know of but I haven't been much of a role model there and I wonder if it's because of me but then Sophie's mother says she doesn't want Sophie to go overseas and I think why wouldn't you because I would have liked to and I think it would be great if Emma got to go like for me and then suddenly the band cranks up and Sophie's voice sounds like she's channelling Janis Joplin and yet she's so tiny and she plays the guitar as well and now the girls are singing songs they wrote themselves about women taking control of their lives and I don't know where they could have got that stuff from being so young and Sophie's mother's sitting there and she's mouthing the words like she knows all the songs by heart and she says she goes to all their gigs as if it wasn't obvious and I think Emma must too because Sophie's mother talks about Emma like she knows her really well and I didn't even meet Sophie until today and all the time Sophie's mother's been talking I haven't said a word but I suppose I'd better say something so I say you must be very proud of your daughter and I ask her if Sophie got her talent from her and she says God no so I say from your husband then and she laughs in a brittle kind of way and tells me that she hasn't got a husband and then I say are you a lawyer and she laughs again only this time it's more like a sob and she tells me she just works for a law firm that's all well actually she just files and cleans up a bit and makes them coffee but all the lawyers look out for Sophie and I wonder how Emma might have turned out if people like that were looking out for her or even if I'd just encouraged her more but there was always work and bills to pay though I suppose that's just an excuse really because I wanted to try and have a life before it was too late but then almost before I noticed she'd grown up and then she was gone and if I'd known it was going to be so quick I would have waited and we could have had more of a life together and perhaps if I'd taken her to music lessons she'd be on the stage like Sophie and I'd be the stage mother and now Sophie's mother is talking about how she and Sophie are close like sisters and I wonder what that would feel like and I ask how old Sophie was when her father left but she says there never was a father and then she starts to cry and she says that she was married once but she lost the baby then her husband left her and had babies with someone else and she was so upset she persuaded a friend to help her have one too but he wasn't too keen at first because he was worried about the legal stuff so she got a lawyer to draw up some papers and the lawyer took pity on her and he was the one who gave her a job because she didn't have one and wasn't qualified to be anything except a mother and now all the lawyers in the practice are good to Sophie but you know how lawyers are she says only I don't and I think that was some friendship she had but then she says she used a turkey baster to get herself pregnant and I didn't think people really did that but Sophie doesn't know because that was part of the deal and I think that anyone who tried that hard deserves to have a daughter like Sophie even if it is a bit weird so I put my arms around Sophie's mother because she's still crying and I tell her she must have been a good mother because Sophie's so clever and she cares about people but then Sophie's mother says she's really scared because she doesn't know what she'll do when Sophie goes overseas and what if the band becomes successful and goes on tour and she can't go with them and then she tells me she's on anti-depressants and the doctor keeps putting up the dose but it's still not working and she supposes that's why she's crying and she does it all the time and then I notice that Sophie and Emma are staring at us and I see the pub's filled up with people so I move my arms but I keep holding Sophie's mother's hand between us on the couch and I give her a tissue to wipe the mascara streaks off her face and then Sophie comes to the microphone and welcomes a new band member to the stage and it's Emma and she goes to the microphone and starts to sing and it's just backing vocals but I'm so proud and I have to let go of Sophie's mother's hand so I can clap but not too loudly and then Sophie's mother stops crying and says I didn't know Emma could sing and then I start to like her better so I tell her that it's time she started thinking about herself and that there's lots of things she can do now that Sophie doesn't need her so much but when I say this she looks kind of panicked and I think she must be scared of being alone and perhaps I should tell her that it's not so bad when you get used to it but then the band's packing up and Emma comes over and asks me what I think and I tell her the band was great and she was fantastic and I would have said more if I could have thought of better words but there's a look on her face like what I said's enough and then later in the car Emma thanks me for coming and she says it was good that I could keep Sophie's mother out of their hair because Sophie thinks her mother's embarrassing and she wishes she wouldn't come to the gigs but they noticed that I seemed to be getting on all right with her and she asks me what we were talking about but I just say stuff because I know that's what Emma would say and I don't think she really wants to know and then she tells me that the guy at the bar owns the pub and he encouraged her to sing otherwise she would've chickened out and that's why she had to have a drink because he told her it would help and that she should pretend I wasn't there until after she'd sung and then I start to think differently about him too but by the time she's said all this we're back at my place and I ask her in and she hesitates then shakes her head but then just as I'm getting out of the car she gets out too and she tells me how glad she is that I came to hear her first gig and she says she hopes I like Sophie because she and Sophie are an item but they can't tell Sophie's mother because she'll freak and she tells me she's going to Cambodia with Sophie and all the while she's looking at my face and I try to keep it the same but I tell her that I think I like Sophie a lot and going to Cambodia with her is a good idea and then she walks right round the car and gives me a hug and tells me I look great and she likes my skirt and she thanks me for lunch and says that maybe next time Sophie can come too and I say of course she can and then with a wave she's gone and I go into the bedroom and pick up the pile of clothes on the bed and carefully hang them in the wardrobe and then I catch sight of myself in the mirror and there's this little smile on my face and I sashay into the kitchen and make myself a cup of tea.

Brisbane

Josephine Rowe

And she had this way of swivelling her head round like an owl to talk to you as she drove, except not like an owl because the skin of her neck creased up in folds and she looked so old when that happened, though she wasn't, not then, and Luke would lean over and say Watch the road, Mum.

And what I'll remember of this time is split vinyl and continental breakfasts, fights about who gets the passenger seat, a wallaby cracked over the head with the jack handle and none of us talking till Lismore even though we know she's done the right thing.

We pull in silent to the motel, a low, sandy-brick L shape, with all the doors facing onto the car park and the car park mostly empty, mostly dark. Our room is number seventeen and there is a TV that only gets two stations and one double bed which my brother and I fall into fully clothed with only our shoes kicked off. But something wakes me a few hours later and I panic, forgetting where I am. I go over to the window on shaky legs and see her from the back, standing out by the road. A blonde in denim pedal pushers and white tennis shoes, standing in the light of the motel sign, like the ghost of 1967. Ghost of her younger self, holding a slim beer bottle down by her hip, fingers round its throat like she wants to swing it at something.

In the dark of the room I find the bar fridge and take a bottle of cola from inside the door. Luke lifts his head from the pillow and says Eli, don't you drink that. Those cost like four times as much as they do in the shops, and I say Shut up I'm not going to, and I go back to the window. Try to stand the way she does, the bottle dangling loose from my fingertips. Like I don't care if I drop it. Like I don't care about anything. She stands like that for a long time, just looking out at the road like she's waiting for someone to come pick her up.

In the morning there are flecks of rust-coloured hair dye in the bathroom sink, and Luke takes one look at her and says That's not going to change anything, Mum, because he's older and sharper than I am but he still gets a slap for it, so we're all silent in the car again, all morning, and I wish the radio still worked.

When we get to Brisbane, she's telling us, you won't even remember. And I don't know if she's talking about Dad or the slap, or the wallaby or Victoria or that she was ever a blonde, but in any case I know she's lying, cause she's got her lips pressed into a pale line and her eyes fixed hard on the road.

Small Room

Armadillo

David Kelly

The three of us sit in the orange bucket seats in the foyer of the Newcastle Children's Court. My arse is numb and my sister's hair needs a wash. Her husband has two ugly sweat stains descending out of the armpits of his air-force uniform. He's flown halfway round the world to get here, but I don't know where from. He won't talk. Each time I try, he masquerades as a dead airman, head down, shot clean through the sides.

I think he suspects.

To our right an old woman appears out of a utility room and cranks open a small table like it's an ironing board. She might be a fortune-teller, or a laundress, but instead of a crystal ball, or an iron, she re-emerges carrying an electric kettle, canned coffee, and a sign.

Coffee and Care. A Volunteer Service. A Donation Would Be Appreciated.

I give her a moment to arrange her table.
'May I have a cup of black coffee, please?'
She nods.
While she levels out a plastic teaspoon of ash-fine coffee, I imagine her wondering how such a polite young man ended up in a place like this. Maybe she thinks I'm a court reporter, or a lawyer. Or maybe, because she doesn't ask anything, it's like in prison where it doesn't pay to ask.

'I bet you've seen it all here, huh?' I say, giving her space to display the care quota of this transaction.

'You could say that,' she says, counting her tea bags.

I wonder what secrets she keeps buried beneath her blouse. I want to grab her and tell her about mine – the one lurking beneath my shirt – how I used to walk like an ape because of the rashes, an unfortunate consequence of the aluminium-rich roll-on the doctor prescribed for my hyperhidrosis. How the doctor said injections of botox into my glands, or surgery to remove them, would stop my excessive sweating. But both options were expensive: too expensive on my wage.

I imagine telling her about my invention called *Armadillo*.

You can't see this, I'd say, making a slow turn with my arms out-stretched, *but beneath this average, long-sleeved, collared shirt, left casually open at the neck, I'm wearing three T-shirts that I've cut deep Vs into, that when pulled on, stretch open to the sternum.*

And here, I'd stop my slow spin, and adopt a carefree attitude; slip my hands lightly into the tops of my trouser pockets, and tilt my head.

This means I can wear my outer shirt unbuttoned without revealing my collection of undergarments below. Thereby presenting a completely fresh and relaxed look no matter how close I am to the point of nervous collapse.

Well how about that! I imagine her response. *How did you ever think of such a thing?*

It wasn't easy, I'd say, and go on to describe my first failed attempt. How I'd scissor-snipped a V from one collarbone down, and then back up to the same spot on the opposite side. How the V speared obscenely past my belly button, like an outra-geous leotard. How I understood why male acrobats grow huge moustaches and cultivate their chest hair, because on me, the modified T looked awfully feminine.

At this point she would titter, but then realise the extent of my painful journey, and would lean past and give my sister a fierce glare. *Don't feel too poorly. The ones that end up here usually deserve it.*

Thank you, I'd say. *You are very kind.*

And the Armadillo name? I imagine the old lady asking. *Where did you get the name?*

The idea came from the cotton edge of the V rolling over on itself from the scissor cut, which is what armadillos do when they're threatened. Right? And also because of the words, arm – armour – armadillo. See?

Without Armadillo to mop up the sweat, I'd say laughing. *I'd look like a contestant in a wet T-shirt competition, but without the tits.*

She hands me my coffee without a word.

Holding the Styrofoam cup I donate twenty cents and walk to the windows. I watch myself in the reflection, blowing lightly and making black wrinkles.

I used to blame my sister, but now I blame the government. They move young couples from one military installation to the next all over the country, and expect them to cope. And then they separate them. There are others here standing about in defence-force uniform. One middle-aged couple sits next to a belligerent-looking teenage boy, and I can see another mother and father combo arguing with a girl in the car park. Both fathers look like they've flown back in the same plane as my sister's husband.

I remember my first visit to my sister's house, stepping out of the car and being enveloped by the sound of gigantic bowling balls rolling across the sky searching for pins, and the fighter jets coming in low overhead. Seeing a white horse in a paddock across the road watching, ears twitching, first one way, then the other, sending me coded signals.

My sister lived in one of six modern bungalows backed onto bush. None of the dwellings had front fences, as if fences were rude.

I checked the house number and pressed the buzzer.

'Hey,' my sister said, like we'd seen each other the week before, instead of the years since Mum's death.

'What's with the planes?' I asked, by way of greeting.

'There's a bombing range in the bush out the back.'

'Jesus, isn't that dangerous?'

'Dummy bombs.' She looked at me like I was stupid. 'They're doing target practice.'

The house was floored in white tile that sounded hollow beneath her heels. The air in the house was three degrees hotter than outside and smelt strange. Milky. There was a framed picture hanging on the living-room wall of a toddler with a faraway smile.

The rest of the pictures were of fighter planes in formation, and men in blackface and camouflage. I recognised her husband grinning down.

'How long is he gone for?'

'Three months,' she said, sighing. 'He'll be back in another two.'

We walked into the kitchen. There were open bags of rubbish about the bin. The combination of heat and smell pushed me to the kitchen window. The sink was stuffed with dirty dishes and dotted with baby bottles half full of curdled formula.

'Do you mind if I open the window – let in some air? I'm really hot.'

'Just a bit – I can't stand the sound of the jets.'

I forced my hand through the vertical blinds for the window latch. Through the glass I saw a flurry of guinea pigs being herded by an invisible force into the corner of their pen. I couldn't see anything scaring them.

'Guinea pigs,' I said, feeling the breeze seep into the room. 'They're spooked by something.'

'Snakes from the bush. One killed the dog.'

The breeze started shuffling the vertical blinds like cards.

She was standing by the dining table when I saw the rope, taut like a tightrope walker's practice wire, stretched between one of the table legs and the knob of a nearby closed door. I decided it must be an indoor clothesline she'd rigged up. Leaning against one wall of the dining room was the skeleton of a child's bed, down on its side and missing the mattress.

'Can I make a cup of tea or coffee?' I asked, because it didn't look like she was going to offer.

'I don't drink tea or coffee,' she said, looking at me as if she was making an important point. 'I have to sleep.'

'What do you give visitors?'

'I don't have visitors.'

'Well you've got one now!'

She dismissed me with a fairy wave of her hand. 'You're my brother,' she scoffed.

I tutted and turned, made a real show of leaning my tailbone back against the sink, buying myself time.

There was a photo of our mother magnetised to the freezer

door, taken before her diagnosis. She was smiling a ghostly smile and I remembered the last thing I said to her.

'Yes,' I had cried, on my knees beside her bed. 'I promise to look after my sister.'

'Isn't it funny that we should end up in the same part of the world?' I said, pushing the memory aside.

Silence. I changed the subject.

'Where's your little boy?'

I expected to hear her say the words *day care.*

'Sleeping in his room.' And then she looked at the closed and tied door.

All of a sudden, over the hot stink of milk and rubbish, I could smell myself.

Mum, help me.

'Why do you have rope tied?' I asked carefully, without alarm.

'To stop him getting out.'

My sister pressed her ear against the door like it was a game.

'Why?' I wanted to add, but my sister, she closes down like a nuclear power station in meltdown mode if she senses criticism, and I won't be allowed in. It got worse after Mum died.

'Is he awake?' I asked.

'I can hear him now.'

'Can I see?'

My sister suddenly acted like a sulky guard at a border crossing.

'Oh, go on, darling,' I said, remembering how sweet-talk sometimes worked with her. Or it used to. 'He's your gorgeous son, and my lovely nephew, and I've never met him before.'

She loosened the knot and peered in through the slight gap. It worked.

'Yup, he's just lying there with his eyes open. You do that for hours some days, don't you sweetie?'

I looked in over her head, expecting to see a tangle of coloured mobile strings and hanging felt animals, but saw only empty shelves and bare walls. My sister unravelled the rope and pushed the door open. The stale sweet smell, even more concentrated, flumped out.

A little boy, naked except for a disposable nappy, sat on a foam mattress under the window. No curtains, sheets, picture books or toys. Nothing. His blond hair looked clean enough and he seemed unharmed: until I looked closer. There were small, grey curls all over the mattress and carpet. Not shit, but until I lifted my eyes to the window, unidentifiable. The window ledge was scalloped, where he'd been sucking, biting and spitting. The curls about him were wood and paint, like something a dog would do, but the dog was dead, bitten by a snake. The little boy turned his face up in our direction, and with eyes closed, sucked air noisily in and out of his nose as if to get our scent. My shirt stuck to my sides as if I was being vacuum-sealed.

*

I must relax. I should sit down. I return to the spot beside my sister.

'Can you smell me?' I whisper.

She is wearing a blue satin dress which could've been worn to a graduation ball. The fabric clenched in her armpit, the one closest, shows a gunmetal-coloured half-moon, where she's also shed water. There's something vaginal about underarms. As kids together in the backyard, I remember placing two fingers over the junction of a cocked elbow, pressing down, raising up a fleshy mound with a crease down the middle.

'Pussy,' we'd giggle, with that knowing unknowing.

She takes her time to turn and face me. She rarely meets my eyes anymore.

'No.'

'Good,' I say.

Feigning tiredness and careful not to spill my remaining coffee, I stretch out my arms and erase any false vaginas lurking beneath my long sleeves.

'Where did your husband fly in from?'

'It's top secret.'

'Come on, sissy,' I say. 'East Timor, Afghanistan or Iraq?'

'Loose lips sink ships.' She almost spits it.

'I thought he was air force,' I say, scrambling away.

*

A lawyer, weighed down with files, walks into the lobby, talking on a mobile phone about his house renovations. How much guilt do lawyers have? Why isn't he dripping? He must have his own version of Armadillo. I wonder what it is, and whether it's better than mine. But of course he can afford the operation to remove his sweat glands. That must be it.

He stops, introduces himself. He is their solicitor. When I say my name he looks at me as if he can smell me. He's read the file and knows it wasn't any neighbour peering through the curtainless window who dobbed. He knows I'm the one, and wants to know why I didn't do more to help my sister before they took her child away. I want to tell him I tried, but it did no good. *She's in denial,* I imagine saying, *and not the river in Egypt.* Crack a stupid joke, as if it's not so bad, or that I never promised my mother.

He says the hearing won't be until after lunch and that we may as well go and get something to eat. We go to McDonald's drive-through and then along Parkway Avenue to Bar Beach. On the promenade, in our nice clothes and with bewildered expressions, we must look like guests who've just discovered the wedding has been postponed. The horizon is partially obscured by ships waiting to access the port: I count twenty-three, and try to get a handle on myself.

My underwater arms, stimulated by cheap coffee, break through the last of Armadillo's barricades. It's like I'm bleeding. Liquid snakes down my sides and under my belt, finds its stride and runs down my legs. My shoes fill up. It pours over the leather edges and worms towards the shower drain where small kids hop from foot to foot, washing off sand and ocean water. My sister and her husband are oblivious, heads down, chewing their burgers like cud. I am diminishing, emptying out from within. The bloom spreads out into the ocean, turning the waves yellow: golden traitor yellow. It's a toxic spill and the ships on the horizon jostle in an effort to contain it to just this part of the coast.

The Salesman

Paddy O'Reilly

Marly sat on the front veranda, waiting. Shaun and Azza had been working on Azza's car all day, driving Shaun's ute to the wrecker's for parts, taking Azza's black V8 for spins around the streets, steering the big car back through the hole in the fence to lean in and bury their heads under the bonnet like stupid long-legged emus. It was past six o'clock, though you wouldn't know from the heat. The house was cooked. Even the fridge was moaning. Marly was desperate for a beer.

She leaned back in the veranda armchair and wiped the sweat from her face with the back of her hand. Chances were that the boys had stopped in at the pub on their way home from SuperCheap. They'd be standing at the bar, promising each other just one beer before they headed back. And that meant she was stuck. Shaun had insisted they rent this crappy house, miles from anything except other crappy houses, because it had a ready-made hoist and pit in the yard and he'd be able to make a few extra dollars fixing mates' cars. Six months later and all anyone had ever paid was a slab. A half-empty slab by the time the guy had driven off.

She pulled her phone from her pocket and played with the buttons. No credit. No one had texted or called. Out in the front yard the dog yawned and stretched out in the patch of dust he had claimed as his own when Shaun brought him back from the swap meet a couple of months ago. Marly didn't get the idea of a dog. They didn't do anything for you. They didn't do anything at all except eat and sleep and shit. Cable had chosen one corner of the yard for shitting, and it happened to be on the route to the letterbox. The rest of the yard was littered with things Shaun had been going to fix but had never got around to. They'd all ended up in front of the house, waiting for the big day when he'd load up the ute and head off to the tip. Except that Marly knew from experience a trip to the tip meant a trip to the tip shop. The actual amount of rubbish around the house stayed the same – it only changed shape and degree of uselessness.

'Excuse me, madam, am I speaking to the mistress of the house?'

Marly shaded her eyes and squinted at the dark man standing beyond the fence. 'Whatever you're selling, we don't want it.'

The man was short and slender, with small hands holding a blue clipboard and feet encased in shiny black shoes. He shook his head.

'I am not a salesman, madam. I am not here to sell you a single thing.' His face was perfectly proportioned, like a doll's face. His skin was a rich burnt-toffee colour. He had eyes like a girl, runny dark brown with thick lashes and an upward tilt on the outside. He was as beautiful as a girl. Maybe he was a girl. Marly had seen plenty of sex-change people on TV shows. He might once have been a girl and now he had turned into a beautiful man pumped full of hormones with a prick made of sewn-up bits of skin and flesh.

'Madam, I wonder if I might have a glass of water. I'm very tired, and thankfully this is my last street for the day, but I still have to walk through the reserve to get back to my car. It's very hot. Very hot indeed.'

She could see the glisten of moisture on his upper lip. His white business shirt was stuck to his dark chest. What would be the harm?

'You can come and wait on the veranda in the shade and I'll get you some water. But don't you come near me,' Marly said, certain that this honey-dark man with his girl eyes would bewitch her somehow into kissing him. 'You sit on the steps there. My husband will be home any minute.'

As if he had heard her, Shaun's tune rang out from the mobile.

'Azza's shouting us pizza for tea. You want capricciosa?'

He was slack in plenty of ways, but no other boyfriend had been as attentive as Shaun. She would never do better than this – a man who thought about what she might want, who asked, who had not once in eleven months raised a hand to her.

'With double cheese and, hon, don't hang up – I've got no credit. There's a guy here, he wants to sell us ...' She paused. What did the Paki want to sell them? He was sitting on the veranda steps in the shade, elbows on his knees, shirt sleeves rolled up and hands hanging to his ankles. The blue clipboard and a canvas shoulder bag she hadn't noticed before lay behind him on the peeling floorboards. 'Yeah, anyway, bring home some beer, will you? And don't take long.'

The dirt from the veranda would ruin Pran's grey cotton pants but he was too exhausted to stay on his feet. The streets in this neighbourhood were desolate and confusing in their sameness. On his map the courts and crescents wound around each other like snakes. Spindly wilted gum trees stuck out from burnt-brown nature strips, and house after house had nothing but broken toys and rubbish in the yard. No shade anywhere. In some yards the carcasses of dry weeds stood higher than Pran's head.

About every third house his footsteps would detonate an explosion of barking. Mongrels, most of them, but occasionally a Rottweiler or a pit bull would push its brutish head through a hole in the fence and stare at Pran as he passed. Three streets ago he had seen a weatherboard Church of Christ, surrounded by gravel and beaten-up cars. The windows of the church were boarded up.

Yet despite the dusty quiet of the hot streets and the empty yards, everyone was home. That morning in the office the team leader had told Pran and James that the area rated eighty per cent unemployment, so not to turn up their noses like that. 'This is where the sales are. You won't do any good in Toorak. They've got everything they need. This is where you'll make some money.'

The team leader had been right. Pran had overtaken his personal-best daily sales figure by eleven o'clock, and doubled it in the afternoon. He'd been about to take a short cut through this street and cross the reserve to his car when he saw the blonde on the veranda. She wore a faded yellow singlet and blue

satin boxing shorts, and sat on an old stuffed armchair. Strapped
to the stub of her leg under the left knee was a metal prosthesis
with a running shoe fitted over a rubber foot. Her right foot was
bare.

Pran knew he'd make a sale here.

It took a while for the cold tap to run cold water. Marly used
to catch the warm water in a basin, let it cool, then pour it on
the two-dollar punnet of pansies she'd planted in the square of
dirt outside the back door, but they died so she didn't bother
anymore. She waited with her hand in the stream of water,
enjoying the sensation of the water cooling down. She thought
about the pipes running underground that kept the water cool,
and she wished there was some way they could use that to cool
the whole house. On days like this, when the mercury rose above
thirty, the flat roof sucked in the heat and it was five degrees
hotter inside than outside according to the thermometer Shaun
kept on the kitchen wall.

'It's only out of the tap.' She handed the glass to the dark man,
who was mopping his brow with a white handkerchief.

'Thank you very much.'

'You're not here about God, are you? Or Jesus? I'm not religious.'

'No, madam. I am Hindu. Our gods are many and we do not
proselytise.'

In rehab, when she was learning to use her new metal leg
after the accident, the man working with the other physio in the
room had said he thought his disability was a message from the
Lord Jesus. 'He made me this way and I don't dispute it,' he'd
proclaimed, waving around his stumpy arm with its fused fingers. 'I see it as extra rungs on the ladder to heaven, given to
me free and clear as compensation for this damn flipper and
the bits that I haven't got.' The physio strapped a harness to the
man's torso and helped him to ease into the contraption that
took the place of his missing legs. 'I just hope,' the man said,
'that this fancy new equipment doesn't deduct from my extra
allocation of grace.'

The Paki man drained the last of the water and placed the
glass carefully beside the veranda post. Cable had finally stood
up and shaken the loose dirt from his bristly brown coat. He
wandered across the yard to sniff the feet of the new visitor.

'What kind of dog is this?' The man leaned backward, away from Cable who, she had to admit, stank.

'It's a bitser. You know, bitser this and bitser that.'

The man tilted his head to the side for a moment as he thought. From this angle he was even more beautiful. Marly thought he should be a model or a TV star, not some loser walking around the suburbs trying to sell stuff.

'What is it you want to sell, anyway?'

'I tell you, madam, I am not here to sell you anything. I am here to give you something for nothing. I know it sounds unbelievable, but it is true.'

'Yeah, sure it is. And will you stop calling me madam? My name is Marly.'

'Pleased to meet you, Marly. My name is Pran.'

He held out his hand and she reached over and brushed her fingers against it, expecting to find the skin moist with sweat, but the hand was dry and cool.

He nodded at her leg. 'I am very sorry to see you have a disability. It must be hard to get out and about.'

'It's not so bad. When I put on jeans you hardly know it's there.' She thought again about the man whose flipper and missing limbs pushed him up the rungs of heaven. Her leg would hardly count for a single rung. When it first happened, she thought the men would run when they saw it, but she'd found the opposite. She used to say to her girlfriends that having half a leg had ended up being a bloke magnet, in a weird way. All of them falling over themselves to prove they were cool about it. 'Because it's discreet,' one of them had said. 'If you've got to have something wrong with you, it's good that it's discreet.' Marly knew what he meant, but it was more than that. Hep C was discreet. Having a bra stuffed with padding because of cancer was discreet. This was something else. And at that point it was better to stop thinking about it because it started to feel creepy.

'How long have you been in Australia?'

'Strange that you should ask. In fact, today is the anniversary of my arrival, seven years ago. I came as an undergraduate student at Monash University, then completed an MBA. Now I am looking for employment in my field.'

'You must be pretty smart, then.' Marly's sister always talked about wanting to do an MBA. Marly was going to heap shit on her now. Get an MBA and you can walk the streets selling door-to-door.

'So Pran, let's cut the crap. What are you selling?' Marly collapsed back into the soft lounge chair at the other end of the veranda from the man. It had been two years since the accident but she still leaned to her good side when she stood too long, and the aching would start in her hip and shoulder. 'I told you my husband was coming home soon, right? He's got a mate with him too.'

Sometimes she thought she and Shaun had a psychic bond. Like before, when she was playing with her phone wishing she had credit and he'd called. Now he and Azza turned the corner into the street, the ute so bright and gleaming that its red shine reflected off the fibro walls of the houses either side.

'See? Here he is.' In a movie she would leap off the veranda and run in slow motion toward the ute, her hair streaming behind, white dress fluttering in the breeze. But these days all she could do was stump around. The rubber foot connected with the ground at an odd angle, and she could feel it jar through her body with every step.

The boys pulled into the yard, eased themselves up out of the low car and stood staring at Pran for a moment. Azza snickered. He turned his head so Shaun and Marly could see his face but Pran couldn't. *Paki*. Azza made the word shape with his mouth and Shaun smiled and looked away.

'Good evening.' Pran stood and extended his hand, grateful that this would be his last sticky, grimy handshake of the day. The first thing he did when got home each night was to take a long cool shower with antibacterial soap. Too bad if there was a water shortage. He needed to get clean after walking streets like these.

Neither of the men offered a hand in return. The tall one with the shaved head turned to the woman on the veranda.

'What's he selling?'

She shrugged. 'Did you bring the beer?'

'Here, gimme the slab, Azza. I'll put it in the fridge.'

Pran watched the bald man heft the slab into his muscular arms and cradle it like a baby as he leaped onto the veranda and opened the screen door with his foot. It slammed behind him. The other man lifted two large pizza boxes from the cab of the ute and walked up the steps past Pran, the thick smell of the pizza following him and the dog drifting along behind, nose held high as if it was riding the aroma. At the door, the man paused. He balanced the pizza boxes on one bulky arm and brushed his thick black hair back from his forehead with his free hand.

'Why is it always Pakis knocking on the door? Don't they hire Australians anymore?'

Pran laughed. 'Please, take my job. I earn seven dollars an hour.' It was a lie. He was a natural salesman. He made a good living from these people. 'But actually, I am not Pakistani. I am from Delhi, a large city in India.'

'Right. That makes all the difference.' The man laughed and passed through the door, dog following, leaving the screen door jammed open against a buckled floorboard.

'Shut the frigging door, Azza! The flies get in.' The woman hauled herself out of the armchair and thumped along the veranda.

'Sorry,' she said to Pran, stepping into the house and pulling the screen door shut behind her.

He listened to the uneven thud of her walking down the hall-way. He would have liked one more glass of water, although when he looked again at the glass it was smeary. Still, he lifted it, tilted it high and waited for the single drop from the bottom to roll the length of the glass and fall onto his parched tongue. He put the glass back on the boards and gazed down the street to where the reserve began. Only a ten-minute walk to his car. The reserve was a patch of bushland that seemed to have been forgotten by the council or whoever created it. Even from here, Pran could see that the wooden barrier at the entrance had been torn out and cars driven in. A mattress was propped against the fence of a house adjoining the reserve and further inside, under the trees, was the glint of broken glass.

'Thirsty, mate?' The bald man's voice came from behind the darkness of the screen door.

'Shaun, don't, please.' The woman's voice echoed down the hallway. 'Leave the guy alone.'

'Come on, mate, don't be shy. We'll shout you a beer.'

'You're very kind.' Pran used the veranda post to pull himself up. He was stiff from the long day of walking. 'I'm not a beer drinker, but another glass of water …'

'I think we can rustle that up for you.'

Pran gathered his clipboard and bag and walked into the house past the bald man who held the door wide with his arm.

When the Indian stepped into the room and smiled at her, Marly's stomach flipped. He had been so serious before, an unsmiling manikin, but now that he had opened his face she wanted to touch his soft brown lips with her fingertips, run her tongue along his perfect white teeth. She felt the heat in her face and pushed herself up from the table.

'I'll find some ice,' she said. 'I think there's a tray in the fridge in the shed.'

By the time she got back with the ice cubes melting in the tray, Shaun and Azza were sitting at one end of the laminex table with the half-empty pizza boxes in front of them, while Pran perched on a chair in the opposite corner of the room near the stove.

'He doesn't eat meat,' Shaun said through a mouthful of pizza.

'But I am most grateful for you offering it to me.' Pran was holding his glass at chest height. He raised it in a salute to the men at the other end of the room. Shaun had filled it halfway with whisky. The Indian was so slim Marly thought that much whisky would probably knock him out.

'Here, let me fix that up for you.' She took his glass and emp-tied half the whisky into another glass, then filled the Indian's glass to the brim with water and ice before handing it back. 'This should cool you down a bit.'

'You are very kind.' He lifted the glass to his lips and sipped at it.

Marly watched closely. The whisky was the cheapest you could buy. She couldn't drink it without drowning it in Coke. But the man's angelic face didn't flinch. He lowered the glass to his lap.

'I see you have a plasma television.' Pran nodded at a screen visible through the doorway into the lounge. It was a fifty-inch model Shaun had bought when they got the government bonus last year.

'Brilliant for watching the footy.' Azza spoke to Marly, as if he couldn't bear to speak directly to the Indian. 'Right, mate?' He said this to Shaun.

'That's why I bought it.' Shaun reached for the pizza box and passed the second-last piece to Marly before taking the last piece, rolling it into a tube and stuffing it whole into his mouth.

Marly took a bite and chewed on the salty, meaty, oily slice. She loved pizza. Sometimes eating was almost as good as sex, like now, with the capricciosa sitting warm in her belly and a mouthful of fizzy sweet beer to wash it down. That Indian guy didn't know what he was missing.

'They say that next year all the football will be on pay television.' Pran took another delicate sip of the whisky and water. This time Marly thought she saw his jaw clench as he swallowed.

'Got it.' Shaun reached behind and pulled a roll of paper towelling from the bench. He tore off four sheets and passed the roll to Azza before wiping his mouth and hands and tossing the used towelling at the bin in the corner. 'You're here to sell us Foxtel, right?'

'No, sir.'

'That other one, then. Optus, or Star, or whatever it is.'

'Sir, I am not here to sell you a single thing.'

'Fuck, he's really starting to piss me off now.' Azza spoke to the ceiling.

'Your name is Azza, I believe you said? Where are you from, sir?' Pran seemed unperturbed. He swivelled a little on his seat to face Azza.

'I'm from Thomastown, mate.' Azza had gone quite still.

'And your family? They are from Thomastown too?'

'They're from Lebanon. Not that it's any of your fucking business.'

Pran nodded and took another sip of the whisky.

'So come on, give us your spiel.' Shaun rocked back on his chair and rested his thonged feet on the edge of the kitchen table like he was getting ready to hear a story.

'I have no spiel. All I have for you is a free offer. No obligations, no payments, no commitments.'

'Go on.' Shaun was enjoying himself. Marly remembered the time he got the Mormons in and toyed with them for an hour and a half. She'd been drinking that night and so had he, and the evening was blurry – but the Mormons had never pressed charges, even though she'd found a piece of tooth in the glass on the floor the next morning, and it wasn't Shaun's and it wasn't hers.

'Do Hindus believe in God?' Marly interrupted. If she could break the chain, tonight might end differently.

'We have many gods, which are manifestations of a single reality. We believe in reincarnation, and in karma. What you choose to do in your life determines your destiny in this life and the next.'

'Sounds like that chick in the crystal shop.' Azza tipped back on his chair like Shaun and took a swig of his beer.

'Take your feet off the table, boys. It's not nice.' Marly tapped her nails on the tabletop. The Indian's clean white shirt and his polished shoes were flickering like soft candles in the corner of the room.

Shaun and Azza were so surprised that they lifted their feet and dropped their chairs back to the floor.

'Jesus, Marl, where'd the manners suddenly come from?' Shaun reached across the table. He picked up a tube of toothpicks from the bench. He offered them around the table, but Azza and Marly shook their heads. The room was quiet as he rooted around the back of his mouth and brought out the toothpick to examine it. The tip was bright with blood, like a thin match.

'So.' Shaun rubbed the toothpick between his thumb and forefinger, twirling it up and down the length of his thumb pad. 'So, Pran, mate.'

'Yes, Shaun?'

Marly couldn't believe how relaxed the little dark man was. Either he was stupid or he had some secret weapon.

'Pran, I don't think we'll be taking your offer of a free set of steak knives.'

'I am not trying to offer you steak knives, Shaun.' Pran lifted his canvas bag and brought out a pamphlet. 'I am giving you free of charge six months of—'

'I said we don't want it, mate. The thing is—'

'Mr Pran, what did you mean by manifestations of a single reality?' Marly knew Shaun and Azza would be cursing her for interrupting their entertainment, but she wanted to know. Maybe this calm little man had the secret. The secret of being happy, or of not always wanting to be someone else, somewhere else.

'You see, the Baghavad Gita says that there is a single essence that underlies all existence. You might call it the soul. "The soul dwells in every living being, and in every part of every living being; it dwells in the hand and the foot, the skull and the mouth, the eye and the ear."' Pran watched Marly move her lips as he spoke, as if she was trying to make his words fit into ones she might understand. 'But for us in this world, it is only necessary to do one's duty.'

'You're giving me a headache, Pran.' Shaun finished his beer and lowered the bottle to the table. 'I think we're done here.'

'But I want to hear more. This is interesting.' Marly nodded at Pran and he saw the tension in her tight forehead. 'Come on, Shauny. Let him tell us a bit more.'

'Yeah, Shauny,' Azza whined in a mock falsetto, 'let's hear what the Paki has to say.' His voice dropped to its normal register. 'But you've gotta ask, if they've got it all worked out where he comes from, what's he doing here?'

'Come on.' Shaun leaped up from the table, his big body causing the room to tremble. 'We'll walk you to your car, mate.'

'I'm fine, thank you. It is very near.' Pran thought about the reserve and its bits of glass and discarded car parts. Outside it was getting dark. The bush in the reserve would be dry and still and shadowy. He wasn't sure whether a path led straight through to the street where his car was sitting. Perhaps it would be wiser to take the long way around.

'Nope, I insist. Where is it?'

'Really, I don't want you to bother.' Perhaps these men thought they could attack him, take money from him. As if he would be stupid enough to carry money around a suburb like this. Pran eased his clipboard into his canvas bag and shook it until the clipboard had dropped completely inside. 'Unless you feel like a walk. Company is always pleasant.'

'That's us, pleasant company. Right, Azza?'

'Right.' Azza stood and hitched up his jeans. 'Let's do it.'

Before he headed for the door, Pran turned and dipped his head to Marly. She was looking at him as if she felt sorry for him.

'What you are suffering in this world' – he waved his hand at Marly's prosthetic foot, but his eyes were trained on her face – 'will serve you in the next life.'

'Great, 'cause it's not doing her much fucking good in this one.' Shaun laughed as he positioned his big hand on the back of Pran's neck and guided him out of the kitchen.

*

Marly was waiting in the chair on the front veranda when the boys walked back through the hole in the fence. Neither of them looked at her. As she followed them into the house, a creased sheet of paper eased out of Shaun's back pocket and fluttered to the floor. He didn't notice until Marly had stooped to pick it up, then he turned and tried to snatch it from her. She stared at the printed sheet with Shaun's scrawled signature at the bottom.

'What's this?'

Shaun tried again to nab the paper from her fingers but Marly held on.

'A minimum of two thousand dollars over twenty-four months? Are you fucking kidding? As if you don't watch enough TV already. How did he get you to sign this?' She threw the paper onto the kitchen table and as she did she noticed Azza thrust his hands in his pockets, but not before she had caught sight of the rusty brown stain on his palm.

'Oh, no. What did you do to him?' She pictured Pran's melty eyes swimming with tears of pain, his soft mouth squeezed into a grimace. 'Where is he?' If they'd hurt that beautiful man she was going to kill them.

'He's all right, okay? I lost it for a minute, tapped him on the nose.' Azza pulled his hand from his pocket, spat on it and rubbed it against his jeans until the reddish stain was off his skin.

'That's blood.'

'He's all right. We said we were sorry. He drove away in his fucking Honda coupe. Now shut up.' Shaun slammed his fist on the table. The dog bolted out through the back door.

Marly stood uncertainly in the doorway. Shaun was glaring at her, daring her to say a single word. She'd never find out how the Indian had got him to sign the contract.

'I'm going out front.' She took a beer from the fridge and stumped down the hallway to the veranda on her graceless steel leg. The streetlights were on. She could see the shadows of trees in the reserve. On the other side, somewhere, was Pran, flying along the freeway in his Honda coupe with two thousand dollars of their money. Money they didn't even have yet. Two years of their lives signed away. Everything had turned upside down. She tried to remember what he had said about the essence. Something about hands and feet. Or skulls and ears. Or something.

Griffith Review

Paleface and the Panther

Robert Drewe

Anthony's skin was so white, almost translucent, you could see
the veins fanning out from his temples into his rusty curls. The
vulnerability of those electric-blue wires shocked me; sometimes
his skull looked like a physiology poster. At the same time, the
eggshell frailty of an orphanage or illness seemed to cling to his
body. When he had his shirt off for the bath or beach there were
those eerie neon veins again, beaming out from inside his chest.

I tried to paint him a few times but I find children difficult.
They come out either too sentimentally cherubic or Hollywood
demonic. In oils Anthony looked like a changeling, with a wily
old face. And I couldn't resist the veins – maybe I overdid the
cobalt. Anyway, the paintings met with strong disapproval from
the Miller sisters, pale redheads too, who maybe had Renoir and
innocence and velvet suits in mind, and they were destroyed
before I could reuse the canvases.

Even in real life he didn't appear a normal West Australian boy,
neither tanned nor sunburnt, not freckled or peeling, more like a
vitamin-D-and-protein-deprived European waif from yesteryear.
Just off the boat, as they used to say. Dickensian poorhouse. But
he wasn't sick or poor, just pallid and thin. And he was actually
a fourth-generation Sandgroper, and only half orphaned, and
now that a temperamental flush masked his veins, and his curls
were unravelling in the summer humidity, he was the image of
my father.

It was Anthony's birthday party, and in the cricket game taking place in a municipal park of buffalo grass sloping down to the river, a match he had insisted on, he'd just been clean bowled for the third time in a row.

It was torture to watch. He was trying out his new Slazenger cricket set, my present to him: a cricket bat, ball, pads, gloves, stumps and bails which came in a nifty PVC bag with the Slazenger panther emblem leaping in full horizontal stretch the length of the bag. It was expensive but I'd wanted to give him something sporty and manly, something we could do together and maybe shift the gender balance a little. Make him not so milky-pale and veiny. He was always surrounded by women and I felt guilty for not paying more attention to him in the past couple of years when I was living it up. Painting hard, yes, but also playing hard. The usual recreational activities.

Anyway, if his flushed cheeks and boisterous eagerness to test the cricket set this afternoon were anything to go by, he loved the gift.

But now he was clean bowled again, and he refused to leave the crease. Even as he flailed around, his glowering, determined face – my father again – seemed to say, Are you all mad? Why should he go out? What idiot would swap batting for bowling or, even more ludicrously, fielding? Batting was the whole point, wasn't it? It was his birthday and his new cricket set and he was the most important person here, especially today of all days.

Not surprisingly, the fifteen party guests fielding in the park this January afternoon were losing concentration and patience. Of course the birthday boy had been allowed to bat first. Uncle Brian was bowling underarm, and had substituted a tennis ball for the hard cricket ball – and, what's more, had bowled him out three times already.

All over the park, young fielders were flopping down on the ground and sucking twigs and peering longingly towards the river or the party table that Anthony's mother and aunts were setting up under the peppermint trees. The kids had given up on having a turn with the bat and now they wanted to swim or eat; at this rate there'd soon be an uprising. Oblivious to the general restiveness the three Miller sisters were drinking their customary spritzers and laughing while they blew up balloons and tied them to the trees' branches, special balloons that said Happy 8th Birthday Anthony!

I was wicket-keeping. Because I wanted him to succeed, and I wanted the cricket set to be an appreciated gift, I was torn. But eventually I said, 'You're really out, my man. Give someone else a turn.'

He swung at another slow underarm ball from Brian, and missed again. I trudged uphill after the ball while he thumped the grass in frustration. But he still didn't give up the bat.

Unusually for a Perth summer afternoon the sea breeze hadn't arrived and the day gave off a sullen chalky glare that stung the eyes. In the river below us, other shrieking children were bombing and diving off the jetty – non-party guests having a better time than us – and becalmed yachts lolled in a deep-water bay as smooth as oily glass. Ageless impressionist subject matter. You've also spotted the scene in a hundred atmospheric summer photographs: skinny show-off boys caught mid-air, spread-eagled jetty and water. Even at my age I envied them. Already my shirt was sticking to me from all that trudging after the missed balls. The buffalo runners had an annoying way of gripping the ball and stopping it from rolling back down to me.

'Don't be a bad sport,' I told him. I was feeling disheartened as well as hot. Anthony was ruining the party mood. As I threw the ball back to Brian, I said, 'Don't bowl any more until the spoilsport walks.'

Brian looked for direction to the women with the spritzers and balloons. In the shade of the peppermint trees the Miller sisters had taken off their sunhats, revealing three different hues of red hair in gradations from vivid orange-peel to mercuric-sulphide pigment to dark rust. They had cigarettes going, too, which interfered with their balloon-blowing efforts, and every now and then one of the women would gasp and giggle and her half-inflated balloon would escape, spinning, blurting and farting crazily over their heads.

The dark-rusty one, Liz, Anthony's mother and my stepmother, glanced at us. 'I hope you've got sunscreen on, Ant,' she said.

Brian looked back at me uncertainly. 'Show him again how to hold the bat.'

Jesus, Brian was being avuncular. He was twenty-eight, married to the youngest Miller sister, Jeanette, and in our occasional dealings the seven years he had over me seemed to give him the advantage. But in the matter of Anthony, I felt I had the upper hand. Brian was only Anthony's uncle by marriage, and even less related to me, not my family at all. Anyway, I had deaths on my side. Two deaths gave me the edge.

'Here we go again,' I said. I gripped Anthony's narrow shoulders and spun him side-on to the bowler. The panther emblem was stamped on the bat as well. I twisted the bat handle around in his hands. 'This is your last ball,' I said. 'Keep a straight bat. See that panther on the bat? It should face your right leg. Defend your wicket. Take it easy. Don't swing like a dunny door.'

He squirmed free of my hands and shuffled back to his incorrect stance. If he swung the bat from there he'd not only miss the ball again but knock his wicket over. His eyes had an oddly familiar shine. My father's old Dewar's glint, his Johnnie Walker midnight-aggressive glint.

'Go shit-fuck-shit away!' Anthony growled. 'I don't have to take any notice of you!'

My God, he needed a smack. 'That's not even proper swearing, Paleface,' I said as I walked off.

*

When I arrived at the restaurant, an outdoor seafood place in the Fremantle fishing harbour, he was already seated. An unusual choice for Anthony, I thought; not fashionable, overly marine-themed, with a table of bluff Yorkshire accents and porky pink skins on one side of us, a tidy arrangement of Japanese on the other. There was the usual network of wires strung above the tables to discourage seagulls, and several pleading Please Don't Feed the Birds signs. The tourists were ignoring these deterrents and hurling their chips into the harbour, where diving and wheeling gulls enjoyed uninterrupted and raucous access.

I'd suggested the lunch at my stepmother's behest. 'What's he doing with his life?' Liz moaned. 'Can you find out and give him some advice, put him right?' According to her, Anthony had abruptly left Angela and their two children, tossed in his partnership with Fairhall Burns Corrie, turned vegetarian, and was 'living with some hippie witch in a mud hut up in the hills.'

I think she thought I was more in tune with low-life ways. Painting and bohemia and all that. It sounded like an early midlife crisis to me, a middle-class cliché, but at this stage Liz was phoning me in tears every night with news of Anthony's latest New Age transgression.

'He's killing me. I don't understand him any more. He's acting all superior to everyone, angry and touchy-feely at the same time. The hippie witch must have some eerie power over him.'

I heard deep raspy breaths; she was drawing heavily on a cigarette and even over the phone she sounded old and needy. I pictured the almost-empty bottle of white wine close by.

'What's all this guru stuff anyway?' she went on. 'Numerology, astrology, holistic blah-blah, tantric mumbo-jumbo. A thirty-seven-year-old lawyer doesn't need all this hoo-ha. I certainly don't need all this hoo-ha! Bruce would be rolling in his grave. What are we going to do?'

We? I didn't need any hoo-ha either. But I felt sorry for Liz. She was no storybook evil stepmother. Sally and I had hardly begrudged her marrying our father. She hadn't pinched him from Monica, our mother; Bruce had been a widower, after all. And for a few years we were still sort of numb, and kept to ourselves while Dad grieved alone and left us to our own devices. Then, as a widowed parent herself – after his death five years later – she'd always been amiably haphazard and not the least bit maternal. I think that's why we didn't overly resent her when we were younger: she wasn't vying for our love. Sally and I had each other and it suited us that she was affectionately distant, not in competition with our mother over anything, and allowed our sad reverence for her to remain undisturbed.

Her focus was completely on Bruce, her husband whether living or dead. As soon as Anthony was seven, she'd sent him off to boarding school, to far-off Guildford Grammar. She'd married late, at forty, the eldest Miller sister and the last to go, and for the fact of being married at all she was grateful to Bruce every day. If he was no longer there, she wanted to be alone with his memory; his memory and the remains of his wine cellar.

But we? What could I do? Anthony was a grown man and, by Perth's standards, already a successful one: a commercial lawyer, yachtsman, weekend tennis player (of minimum ability), and the owner of two storeys of heritage sandstone, a pool, a tennis court behind a disciplined plumbago hedge and, from the second-floor bedrooms at least, three river glimpses and a misty view of the Darling Ranges. He was responsible for his own actions.

Anyway, maybe he was doing the right thing. I was sorry for his kids, but Angela was a provincial Anglophile snob with a cleanliness obsession. The sort who washed your beer glass the minute you set it down, who made you feel unkempt and grubby in her company.

Maybe Anthony had seen the light.

How would I describe our half-brotherly relationship? We were like long-time acquaintances. Beyond our father we had little in common. Our political views collided. Anthony was conservative and well-off, and I was neither. He was a law graduate and I was basically self-educated. There was a thirteen-year age difference and no physical resemblance. Whenever we met up, at Christmas or other family gatherings, we didn't converse so much as banter and nod agreeably and earnestly top up each other's drinks.

'How's the art world?' he'd ask. 'Selling any?' He came to my exhibitions because he liked the business–social aspect, plus the chance to mingle safely with a few raffish characters.

Always we acted as brothers. But we were acting. We weren't exactly brothers, and we weren't exactly friends. We were something in between.

But this was an intriguing twist, being called on for advice. Until recently the role of the family bohemian, the black sheep, was mine.

*

Even his handshake was different now, loose and metallic. All those silver rings on his fingers. Another in his left ear. Silver bracelets on each wrist, a necklace of little beads and seeds and stones, and another thin chain with some sort of gemstone pendant banging portentously against his sternum. I'd never seen an ornamented Anthony before – the Old Guildfordian cufflinks used to be his limit.

Add the rumpled natural fibres, a collarless shirt, rubbery sandals (no leather in evidence), floppy drawstring trousers like pyjama pants that didn't reach his ankles, and he'd gone the whole hog, sartorially. Guru-wear, his mother called it. It looked more like grandpa-wear to me – if your grandpa was institution-alised and had got into grandma's jewellery box.

I'd dressed up in a shirt with a collar and, for the first time, I felt like the conservative brother. 'So, what's happening, Ant?' I said as I sat down. The 'what's happening' came out more abruptly than I'd intended. I meant it more as How are you going? but it came out like What the Christ are you doing with your life?

'What do you mean?' he said, frowning. To be honest, he looked well. He'd lost the extra weight he'd stacked on. Of course those childhood veins had long since vanished into ruddy cheeks and freckled temples.

'How are things? What are you up to?'

That frown at least was familiar. Was he going to answer or not?

His cutlery caught the sun as he was arranging his knife and fork at right angles to the table edge.

'I heard you'd gone vegetarian. So, you eat fish then?'

Yes, he ate fish. Apparently his new lifestyle didn't preclude alcohol either, or his liking for good wines, and once the bottle he'd ordered had arrived he began to open up. 'Look, I've embarked on a new journey,' he began, guardedly. His fingers were still fiddling with the tableware. 'Everything in my life has been leading me to this point.'

'Doesn't it always?' I said. But I was trying to be understanding. 'Tell me about your life changes. Who's the girlfriend? Do I know her?' There was a fair chance I did. My gravelly three acres of banksias and grass trees were also up in the hills. 'Are you sure you're doing the right thing?'

Part calming-Jesus, part-lawyer, he raised an admonishing hand. 'Let me show you something.' He held up the wine bottle, pointed to its label, read out its name: Torbreck Roussanne Mar-sanne. Barossa Valley. Its design featured two concentric circles. He tapped them with a beringed finger. His expression, very legal and wisdom-of-the-ages, declared, I rest my case.

'What?'

'That label says it all,' he said. 'It's a personal message to me. It tells me I'm doing the right thing.'

'Really?' I toyed with the idea of the Torbreck wine people not only knowing of his existence but basing their graphic designs and marketing strategies around his changing emotions. 'I thought the label was saying, Please buy this wine.'

Anthony sighed and cast his eyes around the restaurant. 'The thing is, I can get confirmation anywhere,' he said. 'Okay, see those napkin rings on the buffet over there?' Two silver circles stood side by side, intersecting slightly. 'They're speaking to me. They're confirming the rightness of my journey.'

'Do the circles represent you and the new woman?'

He sighed. 'Among other things.'

'Are you going to tell me her name?'

'Does it matter? Sarita. Maya. Parissa. She goes by several names. She's the essential, fundamental woman.'

Fundamental woman. I got the picture. Cuntstruck.

He said, 'We don't have sex, if that's what you're thinking.'

Our plates of snapper arrived then, the fish engulfed by circles of beetroot and orange slices, and onion and pineapple rings. Collage as much as meal. As I scraped the bright geometric toppings off my fish I almost asked whether all this round food was conveying wisdom to him.

I was running out of questions and Anthony, his cheeks already flushed from the alcohol and conversation, was still frowning. I swallowed another mouthful of wine. I was forced to raise my voice over the dour northern English voices and seagull squawks. So, this new life journey, one of tossed-in job and dumped family – a celibate journey, to boot – was being determined by serviette rings and wine labels.

'Ant, I think you need to see someone,' I said.

*

Charged with carbohydrates, the melee of eight-year-olds fled the debris of the party table. For several minutes Brian and I tried to exhaust them by organising a game of Red Rover under the peppermint trees, but the idea didn't take hold.

Weary of manners and adult directions, first one boy then

another broke away from the game and began running up the hill and rolling down again. Soon all of them were rolling and shrieking and somersaulting down the slope. Late-afternoon shadows were stretching across the park but the day's clamminess seemed to have increased. In the heat, with the river so close, this fierce prickly game looked like madness. Over and over, hysterical, they rolled and climbed.

Behind the main clump of boys, Anthony, less quick and agile, dizzy and red-faced, grass sticking to his shirt, picked himself up and staggered up the incline once more. His legs were wobbly sticks. As he climbed he had to avoid the mob of boys tumbling down, and several times he was knocked over. He was no longer in charge of events and the rebellious horde ignored his angry protests and indignant arm-waving. That urgent noise he was making sounded somewhere between shouting and sobbing. Then he got to his feet halfway up the hill, beat his sides with his fists and started to scream.

*

Anthony drained his glass, leaned back in his chair, dropped his hands in his lap, breathed deeply – once, twice – as if willing the dangerous glimmer in his eyes to fade and a suitably serene expression to slide down his cheeks.

'See someone? You mean a shrink?'

'Well, a psychologist or counsellor or whatever.' It sounded lame. He'd lost his father at the age of five. I tended to forget that. I'd been twelve when Mum died and eighteen when Dad did. Being five was probably worse. But at least he still had a mother. 'You might find it very helpful, dealing with old emotional stuff.'

'I have my own spiritual mentors,' he declared. 'And I've never been more emotionally stable in my life. In fact, I'm so calm that I don't even resent your bloody gratuitous advice.'

'Just because you're calm doesn't mean you're not fucked up and don't need help.'

'And you'd be competent to judge that? With your background? A fucking painter who didn't even go to university?'

'Someone with more life experience and common sense than you, brother.'

He raised an eyebrow. The resemblance was extraordinary. It could have been our father, towards the end. When he was bitter and hitting the bottle late at night, and always giving Sally and me strange looks; when he realised he'd remarried too soon, the wrong woman; when he was still mourning my mother.

'Brother? Are you sure?'

'Jesus! Well, half-brother then.'

He was running a finger round the rim of his wineglass so it made an irritating thin scream. Another bloody circle.

'You're sure of that?' he repeated.

I could have whacked his smug hippie-lawyer head. 'What are you getting at?'

Anthony wore a prim smile, as if an old score was finally settled.

'You never wondered why you're short and olive-skinned? How incurious can you be? I hate to be the one to pass on family secrets, but you know your mother couldn't have children?'

For a few seconds I couldn't see. The glare off the harbour, snowy tablecloths, the swirling white ruckus of the seagulls, blinded me. The whole scene was leached of tint and shade. Strangely, I recalled the faint watercolours of Lloyd Rees when his sight was fading at the end of his life. If it were me, I'd have chosen brighter and brighter colours. But his were pale, soft yet urgent paintings that paralleled his life force. Paintings needing to be quickly said before time ran out.

I remembered how stressful my sister always found those get-togethers of the gingery Millers. The insouciant ways of the Spritzer Sisters, as she called them, the blithe, patronising attitude of Liz's siblings towards 'Monica's kids' made Sally edgy and self-conscious in their presence, and savagely mocking later. My shy sister always got plenty of sardonic material from family gatherings but they wore her out and in the end she'd given up attending them. My older, smaller sister.

Anthony was rolling his napkin into a ball. 'Very commendable of them in the circumstances to take you both in. I guess it must have been spiritually fulfilling in its way to snatch you from the tribe. All Monica's doing, I've been told, and he went along with it because of her infertility problems. Complex legal processes involved, health and cultural risks. Made it easier you two being pale, I guess. God knows that community doesn't give up its waifs too readily.'

*

Some of the boys on the hill stopped surging and somersaulting to stare at Anthony and his noise. The sisters glanced up from their spritzers and cigarettes, shook their heads wearily and resumed chatting. Anthony bellowed on. Tired of the hubbub, a couple of boys made for the shade, brushed themselves down, drank some Coke and looked around for entertainment. Then they spotted the Slazenger bag, unzipped it, got out the bat and ball, set up the stumps and quietly began playing.

I joined the game behind the wicket. The bowler bowled properly overarm, using the regulation hard six-stitcher; the batsman struck the ball squarely back to him two, three times. The face of the bat and the panther emblem hit the ball correctly with sharp, efficient cracks.

Down the hill thundered Anthony. His pallor was gone and his curls were damp and stringy. Muddy tear streaks ran down his cheeks and spit frothed on his lips.

'Give everything to me!' he yelled. He raced up to the surprised batsman and snatched the bat from him; he took the ball from the bowler; he grabbed up the stumps. From the bitter ferocity of his glare, I could tell I had betrayed him.

'What are you doing?' I said.

From under the peppermint trees his mother sang out, 'Ant, play nicely.'

For a moment he stood there undecided, with the cricket gear clasped possessively to his chest. Then he stacked it back into the Slazenger bag, picked up the bag and marched off down the park.

He'd gone maybe twenty metres when something apparently occurred to him and he stopped, returned to the party table, collected all his birthday presents – some gifts still unopened – and crammed them into the bag as well. It was a tight squeeze: the panther was stretched to bursting.

Very businesslike then, a grim smile fixed on his face, he strode down to the river. I watched him go, just as grimly. The sea breeze had finally arrived, sweeping through the peppermint trees, and snappy little waves began breaking on the shore. I followed him but I wasn't going to stop him. Surely this tantrum would soon play itself out.

Indeed, the bag must have become heavy because he had to haul it the last few metres across the sand and onto the jetty. Brushing aside skylarking wet children, curious onlookers, he dragged it the length of the jetty until he came to a pontoon just above the deep water. Then he heaved the bag into the river.

All that wood inside it, and the trapped air; it floated easily. A couple of children dived in and set off after it, then gave up. The tide was going out and the Slazenger bag sailed away into the bay and bobbed into the wide river estuary. I reached the pontoon, and sat down along from Anthony, and we watched the bag in silence until it was gone.

Brothers and Sisters

The Great Philosophers

Michael McGirr

I used to sedate my students with a line or two from the great philosophers. When they complained about tests I told them that Socrates said the unexamined life was not worth living. Every afternoon when they went to their lockers I'd remind them to pack their bags carefully, to think of what they needed, to remember that Ludwig Wittgenstein (1889–1951) said that the world was the sum of everything in the case. I learnt as a teacher that the great philosophers need to be tailored for use in the classroom.

I don't see Anton much. We both have a key to the room and Gloria has one as well, which makes a total of three keys, so if something goes missing then we won't need a long investigation. Anton keeps his gear in plastic bags: laundry and toiletries and a few old magazines. He gets up and goes out early. I saw him once in a laundromat on the other side of town when I was spending a day riding trains. I recognised the set of his back against the front window as he was reading the paper. I'd know that back anywhere because I get to study it across the room in the middle of the night when I can't sleep; the green exit sign over the door is on all the time so the room is never dark. We lie under a wash of cheerless green light, not enough to read, too much to sleep. The mattresses are made of rubber and exhale whenever someone turns on them. Cold night or hot, the rubber feels clammy under the sheets. It doesn't matter. We have the day to sleep as long as we do it away from here. Everyone has to be on their way to somewhere by 9 a.m., even if they don't know where.

*

The kids used to sleep in class sometimes and I'd tell them to wake from their dogmatic slumber. Not once in six years did any of them ask what I meant by dogmatic slumber which was just as well because I'm not sure that Immanuel Kant (1724–1804), a lover of routine, knew himself when he turned up the phrase. He was talking about David Hume (1711–1776), a sweet-natured Scot with a philosophy so tart that it refused to guarantee even tomorrow's dawn. The students never got much beyond Athens, I'm afraid. Mainly Plato (428–348 BC), the man who believed only in ideals but who died of lice.

You know the old routine. You ask the kids if an exclusive car is a good car and they say yes. Then you ask them if an economical car is a good car and they say yes. Then you ask them if a reliable car is a good car and they say yes. By now they are getting weary and they want the answer or at least a punchline, which is a shame because I told them that philosophy is the art of living without answers; if you have an answer it only means your question was too small. A reliable car, an economical car and an exclusive car are all good. So what does the word good mean? Hands go up. I've got them. In 2500 years no one has been able to answer what good means. But here are six, then ten, then twelve kids who reckon they've cracked the world's most cryptic code and all it took was two shakes. They only know the answer because they haven't understood the question. I don't understand it either but at least I know I don't know. That's why I'm the teacher. Was.

*

Gloria says this is a good place. Good enough. She's worked in others and this one is okay because most of the men here are like me to the extent they have not been good with money which is the kind of sin you can wash off unlike stuff you do with your body because your body is something you can't get space from, however much it lies to you. Mostly we have done short sentences and have had trouble, so to speak, finding anything on the other side of the full stop. I started with a single room but it was tiny and next to Gloria's office and I could hear the phone ringing in the night with no hope of an answer and then a pause until the machine kicked in and soaked up the messages of men desperate for a place. I was in that room the night Anton called. I recognised his voice at once as he developed a long weary explanation of why he wanted to come back and start again from here. I supposed he was a regular but his voice was warm with confusion, almost seductive in the way it was trying to tease hope from a payphone somewhere. I could have told him that Heraclitus (540–480 BC), said that you can't step into a river twice. I could have told him Plato's version of Heraclitus said it, except one or both of them was wrong because there are some rivers that just don't move and I've been in one. When Gloria said there was a new man coming and if I wanted to move I'd have to share with him I said okay because I'd shaped his character around his voice. In reality, he nods to me occasionally but he never speaks.

*

For five years, my mother was a voice on the end of a phone. She rang at odd hours when she had permission. There was no routine to this. Nanna would bring the phone to the bed and hold it to my ear and mum would speak about the community she was part of and the discipline of body and mind and the great leader she was following and the price we had to pay for wisdom and often enough I had fallen back asleep before she got to the part about how she was doing this for both of us to free our minds and how she loved me but she had found a place where the word love needed footnotes and as she was starting on those nanna would be doing my listening for me.

*

Somebody said that the whole of philosophy was a series of footnotes to Plato and I told the students that the history of podiatry was full of footnotes and only two of them laughed and besides we had to get back to English which is what we were supposed to be doing and the students were only prepared to talk about reality in abstract terms for so long. I told them that the greatest writer who ever lived never studied a word of Shakespeare at school and still did okay and they asked who I meant and I said I meant Shakespeare. We did Plato's parable of the cave with the shadows that get mistaken for reality. I put Plato's question: 'Is that which is holy loved by the gods because it is holy, or is it holy because it is loved by the gods?' Holy means good. Is something good in its own right or good because of its context? Does something start good or become good? Anyway, with the cave and the question of holy, they had touched the surface of two of Kant's three big issues: 'What can I know?' and 'What ought I do?' The other one was 'What may I hope?' I have been thinking about that myself, living in hope of an answer.

*

When I saw Anton in the laundromat on the other side of town I wondered what he could possibly be doing. He mostly wears the same clothes, even to bed, except his shoes which line up under the sink and his jeans which he drapes over the broken central heating, so he can't have much washing. He was bent over reading the paper. When he comes home, he reads the paper in bed. The same paper. The financial pages. He must read every word, studying it, willing it to reveal something. He has never shown a flicker of recognition but I have never expected it. When he taught me I was in a group of a hundred or more.

In my final year of school, Mum returned from the community and put her belongings, what was left of them, in grocery bags on the kitchen floor. Nanna packed them away and put the kettle on and Mum said she didn't drink caffeine any more or touch meat. That was all she said. She didn't read books any more either, I discovered. There wasn't any explanation of what had happened in the community or what they had done or what the great philosopher in charge had taught except I guessed he didn't believe in caffeine or meat. Nanna got herbal stuff and arranged for Mum to see the doctor and, over the coming months, the doctor organised for Mum to have the pension until she could manage a job. Mum asked me once that year what I was going to do after school.

'Study.'

'That's good, darling.'

The following week she seemed to realise she hadn't asked what I was going to study.

'Philosophy, Mum.'

She turned the rings on her fingers like she was trying to adjust the volume on life.

*

I asked the students to find their own beginning to a sentence which ends '... therefore I am.' Rene Descartes (1596–1650), said 'I think therefore I am.' I told the kids that his sentence could be adjusted to include any evidence they believed would support the proposition of their own existence. The best I ever got was 'I fart therefore I am,' a proposition which neatly rejected Descartes' division of body and soul whilst asserting something about the social contract. Then they had to try one which ended '... therefore I am good.' I only gave them assignments I found difficult myself. The hardest thing to do is to start a sentence which ends '... therefore I am not.' The best I got was 'I farted therefore I am not.' I have learnt the answer is 'I take therefore I am not.' I would prefer never to have found out.

*

I have work three days a week helping in the kitchen, which suits me because the kitchen people are allowed back at about two and everyone else has to stay out till four. The idea is that we are supposed to be doing something for ourselves during the day, looking for work, doing a course, getting a flat. Some of the men deliver papers and catalogues, some go into the city and look around, some read the paper right through. Always the money pages. There's plenty of time. Most weeks, somebody gets done for shoplifting. Anton gets back at 5.30, right in time to eat, then sits in front of the news. Some of the men watch four news bulletins every night. It keeps the world behind glass. Gloria deals with residents' personal issues between four and five. She leaves at five. She has kids, I think, or her partner does. She knows everything about us but is private about herself. She discusses our cases on the phone in her room, which you can hear in the hall and the kitchen, but she steps into the front yard when it's personal. She turns her back to the Victorian façade of the house and gestures with her free arm like she is conducting the traffic on the highway on the other side of the fence.

The place used to be a mansion and there are still traces of its former glory: a ceiling cornice beside a smoke detector, a lead-light panel behind a fire extinguisher, a heavy oak door under a plastic sign about evacuation procedures. There's a sheltered portico at the front, around the old grand entrance that isn't used much because it was easier to make a reception area near the side entrance. The men sit here after dinner and smoke and talk. They always discuss money. Somebody always has a new plan to get rich, a new way to beat the system, a better way to swing the odds, something so piss easy that they could never get caught. They've had all day to think about it.

Once a week, we get a free public transport ticket, supposedly to help us move on in life. Nobody is supposed to be here more than four months. I mostly use the ticket to ride around the sub-urbs, to be a tourist in my own town. Other days, I go to the library and read a bit and watch the people getting frustrated with the photocopier and others getting the sleep I don't get at night. I always look through the old books that are being sold: fifty cents for hardcovers and twenty cents for paperbacks. A few weeks ago, they started selling off their set of the Great Books of the World from the reference section. Some of them looked like they had never been opened. The librarian told me that the texts of all the classics were available online and that people preferred to access them that way because they could search for a word or a phrase more easily. Besides, they needed the shelf space. So, every day I started taking home two or three dollars' worth of Plato or Aris-totle or Spinoza or Hegel or Nietzsche, and stored them under my bed with my bags. Nobody else was buying them and there were always more when I went back. Once I woke in the middle of the night and found Anton looking through a volume but I couldn't tell which one; he had pegged the vertical blinds with a peg and was reading by the streetlight on the other side of the fence.

*

My first year at uni, I enrolled in the survey course, 'The Great Philosophers,' run by Anton Barnard (1951–). The lectures ended late, 7 p.m., because the course was popular with part-timers and mature-age students who could only get there after work and this meant there wasn't much social side to the course which suited me at the time. I enjoyed Barnard's style; he hardly seemed to notice the students. His back bent across the overhead projector when he wanted to emphasise a point like he was pulling at something in his garden. Often enough, at least once a session, he put up blank transparencies. 'This is the bit where you have to think for yourself,' he said and left it at that. Some of the students looked at their watches and shifted uncomfortably in their seats. They already had long days and just wanted answers to write down.

It was on my way home after one of Anton's lectures that I noticed Mum behind the large plate-glass windows of the pub near our station. She wasn't a drinker so I wondered what she was doing. I went in far enough to see she was playing the gaming machines. Her back was straight, her head was still.

*

Both Anton's case and mine made the papers. For Anton, it was the humiliation of being one of the most intelligent people in the country and having to get somebody to explain on his behalf that he had an addiction to gambling; that he had stolen money from the Philosophical Society and from the university to support his illness. Indeed, his methods for embezzling from the university were ingenious; he had thought his way through a labyrinth to get the money his habit craved. My story was not so glamorous. I was the teacher whose students were raising money for a trip to Greece, to Athens, to the cradle of thought. I stole that money. I stole from the wallets and purses of colleagues. I stole from the canteen. People knew for ages before they did anything; by that stage it was thousands. It all went to Mum. I supported her. It wasn't that the machines made her happy, far from it. But I knew that sitting in front of the machine was the only place she could stop being without dying. It gave her relief from whatever the hunger was that made her knock on the door of any crazed person with a big idea to sell. She had lived in half a dozen communities, fallen pregnant in one, been seduced by a list of gurus, at least morally. I paid for her to have a more ordinary form of insanity. It cost.

*

After dinner, Anton comes out to the portico in front of the house. I have never seen him here before. He has helped himself to the volume of Wittgenstein from the stack of Great Books under my bed. He has marked a page and, on the page, he has marked a line in pencil. He hands it to me but doesn't say anything. It is the last line of Wittgenstein's *Tractatus*: 'Whereof we cannot speak, thereof we must be silent.'

He nods.

'Good, eh?'

I approve.

'Yes, good.'

Readings and Writings

Outside

Michael Sala

In the morning you get out of bed and place your hands against the glass. Damp forms around your fingers as you stare at the houses and trees leaning out of the fog at the end of the street. When you sleep, the sea rises and presses against your window. With daylight it retreats. The blanket's warmth lifts from your skin and soon it will be gone. Your brother's breath rises and falls at your back. The clock in the hallway sounds like his heart.

—Where are you going? your mother asks.

—Outside, you tell her.

Rodney sits on the stone stairs over the footpath, in a tattered blue bathrobe and a pair of fur-lined ski boots. He plucks a cigarette from his mouth and reveals his purple gums, a blister glistening on his lower lip. He grimaces, as if seeing you has saved him from some terrible fate.

—Hey there, Captain, he says.

You don't stop to talk to him. He smells like piss. Down this street and another that runs for miles, you come at last to the place where dead cars are piled up in rusted hills. Vincent and Jerome are waiting for you there. The three of you stand around with hands thrust into pockets. None of you know how to begin.

—If they catch you, they torture you, Jerome says.

—Like what? you ask.

He glances into your eyes and his tone hardens.

—Like they make you lick a woman down there.

Somewhere in the city at your back, a truck horn blasts. The sound drifts and unravels on a wind that kicks up around you.

—They fucking do, I tell you. Jerome scuffs his feet on the ground. His freckled skin is pale. His cheeks are blushed with cold. It happened, yeah, to this kid I know.

—Who? Vincent asks.

—Just a kid, yeah, Jerome says, staring out to the piles of dead cars.

You decide that if they catch you, if they try to make you lick a woman down there, you will scratch and claw like a frenzied cat, you will do anything to get free. But you know that Jerome often lies. You will ask your brother when you get home.

Jerome picks up a rock and flicks his arm. The rock hits the bonnet of a car and bounces. The crack falls away into the stillness. A rock balances in your own hand, the grainy surface covered with black dirt, as if it has been excavated from a tomb. It is part of a shattered brick, and you think of how Jerome once lost his temper and threw a brick at your head during a fight.

With a swing of your arm, the rock leaves your hand. Your breath comes out in a whistle. The three of you are throwing now, lost in the rhythm, grinning, the emptiness filled with *thonk, thonk, thwat* and laughter, when one stone comes near a window. Your stone is the first to hit a windscreen. The rock fists a hole in the glass and makes the rest puff into shattered white.

—I win, Jerome says, but you don't have time to answer because a car swings around the corner, as dead looking as those that are piled before you, but kicking towards you on the dirt road, and you catch a glimpse of a man with wild hair and steely eyes hunched over the steering wheel, before you turn and run with the others into the trees.

When you come home a police car stands out the front of your house. The radio drones down the street, and you slow, and feel your balls pull up into your guts. You don't stop completely. It would look bad if anyone saw you, and you are already coming up with a plan, an explanation, and emptying your mind, making yourself believe from the outside in, that here is a boy who did nothing wrong.

*

—Where are you going? your mother asks.

—Outside, you say.

Your father has always been there. Now he is not. Your house fills with people and most of them are strangers. Marjorie, who usually sneers at you for kicking balls into her backyard, mops at the tears and mascara blackening the cracks of her face.

—It's on your shoulders now, she says. No helping that. You'll have to be the man in the family.

She is not talking to you. Your brother holds her stare, like the sheriff of some lonely town. Marjorie turns away and hugs your mother again. You head for the front door.

Outside, you begin walking. You've forgotten your gloves but you don't go back. Fingers curl into fists and find your pockets, and you follow your feet along the pavers. You stay away from the cracks. Bad luck in the cracks, worse luck if you fall through.

You think of the last time you saw your father angry. It was the last time you let him down. In anger, he never touched you, and rarely shouted, but his voice, his soft, dark, clinging voice, would come down like a drizzle that seeps into bones; a voice that made you regret everything.

Now you cannot remember that talk without knowing that it was the last one. At the end, he said:

—I feel as if you've learned nothing from me. As if you'll never learn *anything*.

Those words left behind, washed up with the waves. Your father dropped his shoulders and walked off. It was the sense of defeat in him that moved you. And now it is impossible not to wonder whether he knew all along about all those other things you got up to. The delight you took in hiding them.

*

Your brother is the new man of the house. One day, when you are playing in the backyard, he corners you against the back fence. He gives you that empty, appraising glance as if he is not even there, as if you are simply looking at yourself, bound to condemn yourself, then begins punching you. Not in the face or the neck, but the arms, the ribs, the belly, the places where this thing can stay between you and him.

*

The only you place you have, where you can breathe, is outside. As you walk down the steps, past Rodney, he coughs. You keep on walking. He calls your name. You turn to look at him.

—How are you, Captain? he asks.

You tell him fine.

—I know you're a busy man. He smiles when he says this, and when he smiles he looks afraid. I'd like a moment of your time though.

Knees flexed, the cold air settled on your neck, you stare back up at the house. If your brother were there, if you were walking out the door beside him, you would walk on without a backward glance. You would follow him, and he'd toss back comments like scraps to a dog, that Rodney is a fag, that he has a fag disease and should be left to rot. But your brother is not here, and you feel trapped enough by pity to follow Rodney inside.

The house reeks of incense and underneath it a soft, treacly smell like vomit and shit and urine all mixed up. There are all sorts of tablets on his dining table, arranged in packets and dishes between newspapers and stubbed-out cigarettes. You draw shallow breaths and feel your lungs pull at your chest.

—I know how you feel, he tells you. I know how you feel. I have something for you. Have to get rid of some of these things, yes. They'll just get thrown out anyway, you know. Been meaning to give it to you for a while. It's right here. Right here somewhere.

Ash drops from his cigarette as he searches through his book-shelf. You see trails of ash on the table, the arms of chairs, as if these are the places where shadows come to rest. He does every-thing quickly, with a nervous flick of his fingers and a strange womanly toss of his head, and he never quite stops moving, as if he is afraid that he will break apart if he stays too long in one position. He finally pulls free a book.

—My father gave this to me when I was about your age. My father wasn't like yours. This is the only time that he wasn't a cunt. I'm sorry. I'm fucking sorry for putting it that way. Fuck. God. Maybe they all are.

He appears out of breath and winces. He waves something away from his face, the smoke, but it drifts around him like a web, something so thin that it simply reforms around his fingers. He offers you the book. His nails look powdery and brittle against the faded cover. On the front, there is a picture of a boy in a scout's uniform grinning as he bursts out of a forest with a snake dangling from a branch over his head. In yellow, above the coils of the snake, it says *Adventures for Young Boys!*

—This is how I escaped, Rodney says. This is how. It worked for me. Maybe it'll work for you.

—I can't, you tell him. It's yours.

The truth is that you don't want to touch an object that he has touched.

—I won't need it. Rodney offers that thin, scared smile. I'm just in the waiting room, you know.

The book feels moist and you get outside as quickly as possible. The air has never smelled so sweet. In your own backyard, where you are sure that he cannot see, you put the book in the garbage.

*

At the threshold of your house, you pause, like a surgeon about to put his hands on someone's heart. Your mother is crying and blowing her nose, and her grief is like damp that rises from the floorboards into the walls and makes the door swell up and impossible to close.

—It is a terrible thing, Marjorie says, her voice ringing through the house, a terrible thing to do to you and the children. Terrible and *selfish*.

Marjorie comes around too often, as if the space left by your father has pulled in a body of equal weight. Marjorie carries herself like a rock for your mother to lean on, but you think of her as hard and brittle, and the inward tug of her lips makes your gut tighten. She has her dark hair pulled up, so that you can see the wrinkled slab of her neck. They both turn to regard you. Your mother glances at Marjorie and you see a warning in her eyes.

—Well, heavens, it needs to be said, Marjorie says. Don't you think so?

When you are alone with your mother, you think of touching her, but you are afraid that any gesture will disturb her.

—He didn't do it because of us, she says, as if finishing off an argument.

The words hang in the quiet. Your mother will sometimes lie, to make you feel better, like the time your cat was run over and she claimed that it had simply run off. The thing is, you nearly always know when she is lying, but you pretend not to, because it makes you feel better for the lies you have told her. Your mother is staring down the hallway, out to the small, overgrown garden beyond it, but she is not seeing any of it. The long, pale fingers of her right hand move along the line of her jaw, a light, floating motion, back and forth, back and forth, and you know that it is not her hand at all.

—He didn't, she says again. It was never us.

—I know, you tell her.

She looks at you then, startled, as if she didn't even realise you were there, and you hug her, because it is better than staring at her face.

*

After school you ride down to the cliffs overlooking the sea. You climb over the fence and walk on the grass. If your mother saw you, she would have a fit. You stand there, and the grey, dark sea swings from one edge of your gaze to the other. You wonder what he was thinking when he came to this place, whether the bottle was in his hand, whether he was singing in the place deep in his throat without opening his mouth, the pipe clenched between his teeth. This is what they brought back of him; the pipe, black remains in the chute, from the last knot of tobacco he teased to fiery life and slowly drained.

Your mother went to the hospital to see him. They spoke about *him*, but they meant his body. At home with your brother, you stupidly asked if your father would be okay, and at first he appeared not to have heard. When you asked again, your brother's eyes slid across your face. He studied your features, forehead, nose, mouth, as if he were reading a difficult book. He lifted his right hand and dropped it again.

—Don't you *get* it? he said.

*

At the funeral, you felt as if you should have cried, for the sake of everyone else, and that made it harder. Your mother cried, and so did some of your aunts and uncles. You sat there and felt as if you were being buried alive, your brother's face as polished as the fake panelling on the walls of the funeral home, the electric falseness of the organ and all those wooden seats in rows, like an awkward imitation of a swell rolling in from the sea towards the lacquered darkness of the coffin. They did not have the lid open.

*

Now you stand here alone. A breeze runs across your back, over your neck and flows out over the lines of swell rolling inwards, feathering the breaks with spray. The rocks below split the motion of the sea. A hawk hovers nearby. The subtle ripple of its wing feathers keeps it motionless.

They used to say you looked like him, but not these days. Not even your mother. You face yourself sometimes in the mirror, and hold his picture alongside. The same wide mouth with the fine edges, the long, slightly curved nose with an uneven turn at the end. The eyes, sunken, heavy and blue. How much of him is inside you?

*

In the classroom, you sit right at the back. On the first day back, most kids avoid you. Jerome comes up at lunch. His flat eyes flick onto yours then fix over your shoulder.

—Hey, what was the funeral like?

The way he stands over you twists something in your stomach.

—None of your fucking business, you tell him.

He looks stung. You've never seen him caught off balance before, but he recovers quickly.

—You don't even seem upset.

You don't answer him.

—You should be upset, yeah. But you're smiling. Freak.

—Fuck off.

The grin cuts between your cheeks. You don't know how this has happened. You know that he wanted to say something nice, and that you should have helped him.

—At least I had a father to start with, you say.

You push past him and he is a stranger.

—Freak.

He mouths the words to you from the front of the class, then whispers something to the boy sitting next to him. You realise that you hate him.

*

The word has gotten around that you had something to do with your father's death. You know where it came from. Some of the kids follow as you seek out Jerome. And more are coming, as if there is a whisper, an electric current passing through the school, that only other children can sense.

—Take it back, you tell Jerome.

He gets up from his seat and doesn't look at you directly. His chest sags between his shoulders. He straightens and steps closer, the freckles on his pale face livid, his arms limp banners dangling either side of his waist, the fingers curled and rigid. You know that this is all wrong, that he will never take anything back before an audience.

—You always lie, you say in a voice that doesn't sound like you at all. You're a liar.

Jerome shows his teeth.

—So, when is it your turn?

A groan erupts around you, and the other children back off. But Jerome stares at you with his flat, cruel eyes and says it again. You push him, feel the bony lightness of his chest. Someone shouts, Hit him! Go on.

Jerome grabs your shirt at the shoulder, twists the cloth, and you jab your fist at his face, and keep jabbing as he swings you around in a blind, quiet circle as if the two of you are dancing, the other children cheering and cheering and wildly cheering a song they cannot know.

*

The principal runs his eyes across the two of you and asks who started it. Neither of you answers. He slides a finger down his tie, and flattens the tip over his belly. He turns away.

—This won't be taken further, he declares. But even so, he goes on, even so. When matters get difficult, you have to rise to the challenge. You have to move through the hardship and focus on the positives. His gaze never leaves the window, as if he's reading words in the clouds. On the way out, Jerome tells you that he's sorry. You tell him that it's nothing.

There is a huge old fig tree at one end of the schoolyard, past one of the demountables. Two branches come together at one spot that you like. You climb up, hold on, lean back, and stare at the rippled sky, cut through with branches and twigs. You have heard that when you fall asleep with a hand curled around a branch, you'll wake up still holding it.

You always wonder about that idea but never trust it, though you close your eyes sometimes and pretend. The heat of the fight has turned to stiffness. Sweat pools at your armpits. There is a tremor in your lungs, a quietness that makes you feel the blood in your fingertips and the grinding labour of your heart. The bark feels good. Your grip tightens. Eyes shut. The wood creaks around you. Wind stirs at your ankles. You imagine falling.

*

When you get home, you go to the bin. You rummage until, under the stinking weight of a split garbage bag, your fingers touch the thing that you were looking for. You pull out the book and wipe away the moisture. *Adventures for Young Boys!*

Under the covers of your bed, you run the torch over each page, and breathe in the warm, dusty smell. The book doesn't make any sense, but you like it. The stories make you feel as if you are overhearing conversations, as if you are looking in on something that exists outside your own world. Somehow, the ridiculousness of the stories makes your eyes water.

It's not that you believe any of it. And if another boy had given you the book, you would have laughed at him. But it came from Rodney, and Rodney was a boy once, and in the simple words on the yellowed pages, you can imagine him before he knew what it was like to be in a waiting room.

*

That night, you dream that the ocean is washing up over your back fence, waves spearing through the carefully tended features of your mother's garden. You lie in bed, hear the breakers tear at the walls of the house, feel the walls bend and shudder, and then come the footsteps, one after the other, a sodden beat up the stairs, to your door, and your door opens, and you smell something like dead fish and smoke and your father's aftershave.

*

You wake into a cloud-filtered light that binds everything together, like threads left by some monstrous spider. Shivering, you throw on clothes and step outside. A snarl of untended bushes gathers around you. You cannot see the sun, but you know it will be there soon, rising over the fence, unfurling across the rooftops, spilling against dark windows.

The door creaks at your back. Your brother steps out, fishing rod in one hand, bucket in the other.

—Ready? he says. You push your feet into boots and drink a cup of the watery tea he has left on the kitchen bench. You will keep the door unlocked. The next time your father comes, you will try not to be afraid, you will think of how he could make you laugh, and the warm, smoky burr of his songs and you will tell yourself that the dead cannot touch the living. But you can never be sure, you can never be sure. You can never be sure.

Harvest

The Movie People

Fiona McFarlane

When the movie people left, the town grew sad. An air of disaster lingered in the stunned streets – of cuckoldry, or grief. There was something shameful to it, like defeated virtue, and also something confidential, because people were so in need of consolation they turned to each other with all their private burdens of ecstasy and despair. There was at that time a run of extraordinary weather – as if the blank blue sky, the unshaded sun and the minor, pleasurable breeze had all been arranged by the movie people. The weather lasted for the duration of the filming and then began to turn, so that within a few weeks of the close of production, a stiff, mineral wind had swept television aerials from roofs and disorganised the fragile root systems of more recently imported shrubbery.

My main sense of this time is as a period of collective mourning in which the townspeople began to wear the clothes they had adopted as film extras and meet disconsolately on street corners to re-enact their past happiness. I didn't participate. I was happy the movie people had left. I was overjoyed, in fact, to see no more trucks in the streets, no more catering vans in the supermarket parking lot, no more microphones and boom lights standing in frail forests on corners or outside the town hall. The main street of town had been closed to traffic for the filming, and now the townspeople were reluctant to open it again. It's a broad street, lined with trees and old-fashioned gas lights (subtly electrified) and those slim, prudish, Victorian storefronts that huddle graciously together like people in church, and as I rode down the street on my scooter on those windy days after the movie people left, it struck me as looking more than ever like the picturesque period town, frozen in the nineteenth century, that brought the movie to us in the first place.

I rode my scooter to the disgust of women in crinolines with their hair braided and looped; men in waistcoats and top hats: citizens of some elderly republic that had been given an unexpected opportunity to sun itself in the wan light of the twenty-first century. I knew these people as butchers, plumbers, city commuters, waterers of thirsty lawns, walkers of imbecile dogs, washers of cars, postmen, and all the women who had ever taught me in school. They were so bereft that they stayed in the street all day. They eddied and flocked. Up the street, and then down again, as if they were following the same deep and certain instinct that drives herring through the North Sea. They consulted fob watches and pressed handkerchiefs to their sorrowful breasts. The wind blew out their hooped skirts and rolled the last of the plastic recycling bins down the street and out into the countryside, where they nestled lifelessly together in the scrub.

I rode my scooter to the home of my wife's parents. She was sheltering there, my wife – Alice – because the movie people had left. She loved them, see. Not her parents – that tranquil couple of bleached invertebrates – but the director, the key grip, the costume ladies, the hairdressers, the boom operators, most particularly the star. The whole town loved the star. Even I succumbed to it, just a little – to the risky and unpredictable feeling we all had in the weeks he was among us, that he might at any moment emerge from a dimly bulbed doorway or unfold his long legs from a rooftop. We'd never seen anyone so beautiful. He shone with a strange, interior, asexual light; and his head seemed to hang in mid-air, as if there was no body to attach it to – nothing so substantial. Looking at him was like entering a familiar room in which you see everything all at once; and at the same time, nothing.

I rode to my wife and said, 'Alice, darling, he's left now, they've all left, so can you please come home and love me forever; entangle your limbs in mine on the couch while watching television;

comb your eyebrows in the bathroom mirror when I'm trying to shave; go running with me in the gorgeous mornings; and dance guiltily, ecstatically with me to bad disco music in the kitchen?'

But Alice, who now wore the costume of a sexy, spinsterly librarian, trim with repressed desire and lit, at her throat, by Edwardian lace, only sat on her parents' chaise longue embroidering silken roses with inconsolable fingers. Her parents sat nearby; her father, that placid old sinner, was now dressed as a country parson with a monocle in his crooked eye, and her mother peered out at me from the battered piano, which until recently had been nothing but a prop for picture frames. Now my mother-in-law played it with a watchful plink and plunk, with maternal suspicion tinkling over the expanse of her oatmeal-coloured face, and a frill of veil in her ornamental hair.

Other times I visited, the door was opened by a sour maid who informed me that my wife was not at home.

'Is she not at home?' I asked, 'Or is she not *at home*?'

The maid, with a grim, polite smile, shut the door in my face.

The mood of the town improved with the success of the movie. A special preview was held just for us, in the town hall; we sat in the municipal pews and called out the names of everyone as they appeared on screen in a long and lustful litany. Each name we invoked brought laughter and teasing, but really we were all overcome with a kind of bashful pride, as if finally the world had reached a solicitous hand into our innermost beings and, liking what it found there, held us up for emulation and respect. We were so distracted that, afterwards, nobody was sure what had actually happened in the movie. A forbidden love, generally – something greenish and unrequited – one of those glacial *fin-de-siècle* stories in which the tiniest gestures provoke terrible consequences about which no one in polite company speaks.

At the premiere party, the townspeople danced the gavotte and the quadrille; they waltzed among potted palms with a slow, bucolic concentration; and they feasted on tremulous dishes of jellies and aspic. All throughout that strange, orchidaceous, combustible room, women fainted into arms and onto sofas, and a tiny orchestra of men with Civil War whiskers played endlessly into the night as Alice – my Alice – danced time and double time and time and again with the star, who appeared to have flown in especially for the occasion. Her parents nodded and smiled and accepted the nods and smiles of other doting gentry, and Alice flew over the carpets, her face alight.

I demanded of everyone I met: 'Who does he think he is? Just because he's famous, he can dance all night with another man's wife?'

Unlike that decorous crowd, I was insensible of my own dignity. Finally, the man who used to service my scooter (dressed now in the handsome uniform of an English corporal, which made of his red belly a regimental drum) drew me aside and told me that the man Alice was dancing with wasn't famous at all; he was, in fact, Edward Smith-Jones, a man of the law, and selected from among the population as the star's stand-in. Apparently it was obvious to everyone that the entire scene in the stables featured this man and not the star, who was nervous around horses, especially during thunderstorms. So there he danced, lordly Eddy, with another man's wife and another man's haircut, and I watched his hand rest on her supple back and my heart was filled with hatred for the movie people.

When I asked Alice for a waltz she told me, with a demure shake of her head, that her card was full.

I lost my job when my graphic-design firm was asked to move elsewhere. Certain other sectors of the citizenry, too, were politely dissuaded; the Greek fruit shop became a dapper greengrocer's, manned by a portly ex-IT consultant with Irish cheeks and a handlebar moustache. He stood jovially among his gleaming bronze scales, measuring out damsons and quinces. Unless they were willing to wear their hair in long ropes, the town's Chinese population was encouraged to stay off the main street between the hours of eight-thirty and six, and preferably to remain invisible on weekends. The gym was forced to close for lack of customers, and the Video Ezy. The tourists came in excitable herds, transported from the nearest town in traps and buggies. They mistook me for another tourist, and I was comfortable walking in amongst them, watching as my wife strolled in the botanical gardens, her face in parasol twilight; a brass band playing in the rotunda; a British flag afloat above the trumpets; nannies sitting with their neat ankles crossed on benches as children toddled close to duck ponds. Alice walked with her Edward, and her parents followed close behind. She tilted her head this way and that. In the movie she had been one of those extras who almost has a speaking part; the kind they focus on to gauge the reaction of a comely crowd.

When I heard they were engaged, Alice and Mr Smith-Jones, I retired my scooter. I took a job at a printing press, and the tedious hours of setting type gave me finicky time to think things over. On the day of their wedding, I dressed in costume. In the movie I play the role of a man about town; you can see me in the lower right at 20:16, loafing with friends on a street corner while gauzy women flutter behind us, in and out of seedy cottages. Yes, right there – I'm the one watching the dog.

I walked to the church among apple carts and small sooty boys, and there was a yellow quality to the air, a kind of residual loveliness, as if the sun had gone down hours before but stayed for some time just below the horizon. The church doors swung open before me, revealing soft pale heads among bridal flowers. The parson – my father-in-law – trembled on the moment when I should speak or forever hold my peace. I spoke. Eddy and I met in the aisle; he swung and I dodged and I swung. Alice shook in her slim white dress, and roses fell from her hands. I floored Eddy; he pulled me down. We rolled on that ecclesiastical carpet, up and over and around and down, while flustered ushers danced around the edges of our combat. Ed would be on the verge of springing up, a lawyerly Lazarus, but I clawed him back down; I, on my knees, would be making my way altar-ward, only to find him wedded to my foot. The organ began to play. The congregation piped in alarm. An elderly woman keened among her millinery. Finally we exhausted ourselves, and it was me – me! – Alice came to comfort. I knew she would recognise my supplicant heart. Edward was banished, and loped away into the high noon of heartbreak. Her counterfeit father was ready to join them in mock matrimony, and so with a merry shake of his worldly head, he re-joined us instead. The sun set, and the moon rose. We ate ices at the reception, and great silver fish surrounded by lemons, and that night, as she withdrew her slender foot from a slender slipper, my wife shuddered with a virginal blush and laid her head upon the pillow.

There followed a happy time of croquet and boating expeditions; then Alice went through her suffragette period, which I pretended to disapprove of. Things are more settled now. We read Darwin together, without telling her parents, and she's discovered Marx. We take walks in the country, where my naturalist wife sends me scrambling into trees for birds' nests. Things aren't what they used to be, but there are consolations: a certain elegance to the way she stands at open windows, and longer, darker nights now that the town has switched from electricity to gas. But I've noticed in her lately a strange inability to see the resemblances between things: a tennis ball (she plays modestly, in white dresses) is nothing like the sun; a glass of water, she says, has no relation to the ocean; if I comment on the similarity between her neck and a swan's, she turns away. In fact she dislikes the similarity of things even without recognising their likeness, and can't bear, for example, to see a brown short-haired dog on brown short-haired grass.

The rest of the town is like this too. They have a horror of seeing photographs of themselves, even the hoary daguerreotypes they love so much. They've removed all the mirrors from their houses, and the paintings of jaded horses on hillsides, and the china that depicts, in blue and white, the far-flung tale of luckless lovers. It's as if they're allergic to the very idea of reproduction; or at the very least, don't wish to be reminded of it. What a singular world they all live in, in which no thing has any relation to another!

They no longer mention the movie. They no longer watch movies. They expect to live forever. They've taken up laudanum. They seem happy, however – timeless and happy. I watch them all, a little wistfully, in my fraudulent frock coat. Meanwhile, the trees shake out their leaves in the wind, and in the evening my wife walks through the spent garden. Her face is like a flag that says – *surrender.*

Little White Slip

Karen Hitchcock

> One litre of milk is enough for 40 cups of tea.
> —*Presbyterian Women's Cookbook*, 1955

Black and White
She wears this nightie. A crisp, white cotton slip, plain as paper.
It has thin white ribbons for shoulder straps. She wears it with
trousers and ballet slippers during the day. (Telling herself it
looks French.) And she wears it – without trousers or slippers, or
that maternity bra – to bed. She has four, all identical, all filing
through the wash one after the other. With the powder, bright-
ener, softener, bleach. For the Whitest Brightest Whites!

She used to be a little-black-dress kind of girl. Short black
hemlines, short black espressos, short black nails, short sharp
black bob. Elbows on the bar, one knee on the barstool, nightlife
ballet. A real G-string kind of girl. Little black sambuca shots
screaming down her throat, while she waits for Frederik of Den-
mark, William of England, the French PM, to see her, to find her,
to see her: shiny beanpole in the haystack. Tall amongst all that
short.

Cheesecake
Her husband – an industrial chemist – flies to Melbourne for a
weekend conference. Something to do with tempered precipi-
tants and powdered solutions of some lethal substance or other.

She hides her terror at being left alone with the baby overnight, and asks that he bring her back a slice of cheesecake from Acland Street.

You sure you'll be okay?

Just bring me the cake.

The really special Jewish one, baked from a 400-year-old recipe. She had it for breakfast once, eons ago, not so long ago, tumbling out of a club into dawn, sambuca still cavorting with her tongue. The night is long. She lies awake on their bed watching the baby twitch and dream. All the pillows are on the floor so it doesn't suffocate should she accidentally sleep, and to break its landing should it fall. When it wakes she pulls at a ribbon and guides her breast into its mouth. And it closes its eyes and it sucks and drinks, sucks and drinks, milk wetting its lips.

Her husband arrives home at midday, holding two white boxes wrapped in clear cellophane. He stands in the doorway. 'Ta-dah!' he says

She blinks at the bright sun, and at her husband who blocks it inadequately, despite the two, vast boxes.

'What're those?'

'Your cakes!'

'Cakes?'

'The 400-year-old cheesecakes! From that Polish Street! You know … Acland Street!'

'Tom.'

'Yes, honey?'

'I asked for a piece of cake. A *piece*? *One piece* of cake? You do realise I'm going to eat all of that.'

'Sure!'

'But Tom. Don't you see how fat I am?' She runs a hand down her slip, outlining her round belly.

'LouLou' – he balances the boxes in one hand, puts the free one around his wife – 'you're not fat at all.'

'Sure, Tom.'

'You're not! You're beautiful! And you've just had a baby, for God's sake.' He turns around to grasp the handle of his suitcase.

'Sure sure sure sure sure. That's what they all say. And then you wake up and see the words *Barge Arse* listed on the divorce papers.'

He chuckles. His wife is so funny, such a great sense of humour. Ha ha ha ha ha.

She takes the butter-stained boxes – they're heavy, there must be six kilos of cheese in the fuckers – and stands aside to let him in.

'The baby's in the crib.'

Sambuca Dawn

'Well' – she brings the shot glass up close to her eye – 'what exactly is sambuca, then, Doctor Smarty-Pants Chemist?'

So he wasn't heir-to-some-throne, oh no no he wasn't, but his eyes drew lines from the dark points of her nails and her lips and her sambuca and her hem. Dot to dot he traced her out, then coloured her in, buying her drink after drink.

'It's distilled Illicium verum.'

'Illicit whatum?'

'Illicium verum: star anise.'

'Oh,' she said, for some reason disappointed. 'I thought it was made out of liquorice.'

He apologised, as if it were his fault, which for all she knew it may well have been. Who the hell knew what industrial chemists were responsible for? And to compensate – for he was always compensating, bearing responsibility for some flaw in the world: ants in the rubbish, their combined carbon footprint, the inclement weather, a missed opportunity – he set about describing star anise, and the manner in which it was distilled, trying his best to make it sound beautiful, mysterious. Meanwhile, she half-listened, drank her liquor with its floating beans of coffee, and weighed him up as best she could. Tall, clever, appreciative. Nice shoes, wide shoulders, appreciative. His eyes carved her out of the background. She drank drinks he paid for, and watched him carve her.

'It's eighty-four proof,' he was saying, 'so it's rather easily set alight.'

Clean shirt, white teeth, appreciative.

The Club

Laced around the café table, like round and fat beads of prayer: mother, pram, mother, pram, mother, pram. Everyone sweating into synthetic-lace maternity bras. Sweat and milk swelling Hidden Absorbent Pads! Everyone's eyes behind oversized sunglasses. She's not sure who's being talked at. She's not sure who's listening. A particular way of pouting. She blames all this on Posh. The baby is asleep in its Bugaboo pram. Known in Louise's mind as The Ambulator. As in The Great Ambulator. As in The Really Fucking Expensive Ambulator. Lips peel open and relate brands of dummy, bowel habits and crying habits and sleep habits, and Louise stares into her orange juice, reluctant anthropologist, trying not to make nasty slips-of-the-tongue.

Screens 1
She sits at her desk when it sleeps again in its little fits and starts. *Yes, I am back at work … Part-time, of course. From home. Hmm? Yes, still Designing.* Capital D. *Still Web-page Designing.* In front of her shiny new Mac (white, seventeen inches). Another present from Tom. Another noose. Another dare. She's catalogued all their photos. Backed up the address book. Bought lollies from all over the planet (Duchy Mints, Hershey's Kisses, Iranian toffee). She's written letters with too many exclamation marks that she'll never send to people she'll never see.

Today – making an effort, all her slips in the wash – she wears a black chiffon dress (huge, loose) with pearl-button detail and an emerald silk scarf. Shiny black ballet shoes. She loosens the belt again, crosses her legs, remembers varicose veins and uncrosses them. Hair up. Down. She adjusts her scarf and evaluates the weight of her breasts, estimates millilitres, translates into kilograms, or at least milligrams, takes that sum from her outrageous weight. She chews her pen, tightens her belt, too tight. She likes to look good for her desk. The house is silent. She moves her cup of water to the other side of the dictionary, straightens the stack of sticky notes, colour-orders her pens. And her desk likes to look good for her.

It screams and she feels a fleeting relief, then, in its place, quiet panic. What could it be? Hunger, fear, pain, fear, hunger, pain, fear? They say, *It's just wind, dear.* Such a fierce wind; what the fuck is it doing in there?

She sits at her desk when it sleeps again, staring at someone on the screen.

Second Date

'So,' Louise said and smiled, 'is your degree a BS? Or are you just full of BS?' Her laughter tinkled between them.

He smiled, took a sip of Shiraz. 'It was a *BSc*, actually.'

She rolled her eyes. 'BS, BSc, it's all the same to me.' She flicked open her napkin and draped it across her thighs.

'I'm sure it is,' he said. 'And what was your degree again? A BA did you say? A "Bugger All"?'

She looked up, shocked at the sarcasm.

He went on, 'What did the arts student say to the science student after graduation?'

'See ya round?'

'She said, *And would you like fries with that?*' He looked at her, blood behind his cheeks, eyelids lowered, for distance. 'So. Do you have the whole world categorised and reduced or just me? What am I? A character from *Revenge of the Nerds*?'

'I kind of liked that movie.' A man who blushed had always made her melt.

'I'm no philistine.'

'And I have a real job.'

Tom gulped his wine. She looked away and fiddled with her cutlery.

Her fingertips bouncing on fork tines, she said, 'I thought it was really funny when they set up that camera in the girl's change-rooms and the nerds are sitting in their dorm impatiently watching them undress, and finally a girl takes off her underpants and the boys scream, *We have bush!*'

Tom smiled, faintly.

Louise said, 'Come to think of it, these days the line wouldn't be *We have bush*, it would be more like *We have Brazilian!* Don't you think? Or even *We have post-labial-reduction!* Or *We have pre-op-male-to-female!*' She reached for her wine glass, knocked it over into her dinner, her lap, the entire tablecloth. 'Oh God, oh crap, where's the waiter, oh God, oh fuck, I *always* do this.'

He rose with his napkin, crouched in front of her wet dress. 'Here. Let me help.'

Screens 2

Midday soaps, wild crushes, hormones. She is both raw and

permeable. Whether Michael will love Jane is of vital importance at this moment. Now, before the commercial break. She *is* Michael and Jane and them together and all of them, all of these characters who stroll through dodgy sets reading bad lines. She is with them all the way. A cry rips her out of the box and tosses her back into the living room. She lifts the child by its armpits and carries it to the change table, her rigid arms stretched straight out. She opens the nappy and, breathing shallowly, she stares, as at a complex yet unpleasant sculpture she is on the brink of understanding. She looks up into its red, unhappy face. She sets to work, two tiny feet pressed together and lifted by one of her hands, holding the bottom aloft. She says, *You know, if you were older, double incontinence would secure you a nursing-home bed?* Dodgy sets, bad lines. The unhappy face is undeniably sweet – she can see that – but somehow, it is anonymous. She feels this could be any baby. She looks down at her still swollen belly. Ha, she thinks, and I told myself I was eating all those pancakes and guzzling all of that maple syrup for *you*. She looks from baby to belly, baby to belly. It had been in there, it had. Encased in a double layer of specially nurtured pale soft pancake. The child's feet are warm in her hand, warm like shells dug out of white sand on some long hot beach. Ipanema, Kauai, St Tropez. All those millions of dead shells warmed in sand and sun, emitting heat like life.

Ingrid

So Ingrid rings her out of the blue. *Sorry it's been so long since I've called. I've been so busy.* And Louise says she'll make them lunch. *Yes*, says Ingrid, *it must be easier for you to stay at home.*

Ingrid: assistant curator at some regional gallery, never progressing in her career as she was (Louise thought) not that good at curating. They had been friends since university. They strutted round town, shopped, watched movies and ate and drank together until about the time Louise really started to show. Then her pregnancy unmasked something. Ingrid morphed into the beautiful, thin, *sexy* one of the two; she snatched the role and bloomed within it. So that when they shopped, Ingrid would parade around in her still-tiny underwear and tell Louise not to worry, that she knew other women whose bodies didn't change *that* much after birth. *Just some cellulite,* she said, staring at Lou's hips with carefully blanked eyes. Even though it had been Ingrid who – in reality – had the thick waist and the coarse facial features and the short neck and the dry hair. Everyone knew it except Ingrid. (*Don't you think my hair has a celebrity kink to it today?*) Even though it was Ingrid who could never get a date. (*Will Tom be home soon? I want to see what he thinks of my new dress.*) So Louise got fat and pregnant and the world-according-to-Ingrid took precedence; between them it became The World, and bit by bit tiny parts of Louise were crushed, little black ants squashed one by one, leaving unmentionable black smudges of fury – until she'd stopped answering Ingrid's text messages. *Thank God,* Tom said, *I never did like that catty woman.* Then of course he apologised, took her out for dinner, told her repeatedly that she deserved far nicer friends than Ingrid. For months he listened to the endless list of Wrongs Perpetrated Against Her By Ingrid.

Ingrid stood at the threshold in a floral dress that accentuated her thick waist, and she looked Louise up and down, eyes like fat-seeking missiles firing at the pillows above her armpits, the loose lines of her slip.

'Lou! Long time no see!' That fresco smile.

More

She pushes the pram to the café. It's Tuesday. Again. She wades through the heat, sweat dribbling between her thighs, down her legs. She could always not go. But she collects these habits – wading and dragging – until they form currents that carry her. And here she is, wearing dark glasses, rubbing salty water between her ankles, washed up again onto Café Beach. Her child lulled to sleep by the waddle. Everyone orders banana bread and decaf cappuccino. Louise fights the urge to scream: *Just because they call it bread doesn't mean it isn't cake, you fat fucking cows. It doesn't mean it won't keep your cow-arses fat fat fat.*

She nods periodically, watches deflating milk, peers into the Bugaboo at appropriate intervals. She whispers to the waiter, 'One banana ars … I mean bread, please.'

And Then ...

Tom calling from the front door: 'How was your day, honey? ... Honey? ... You here? ... Hon?'

She rolls over, trying to lift her heavy head, trying to get up and out, so Tom doesn't burst in and wake it.

Third Date, In Bed

'So, Tom. Are you by any chance the piper's son?'

'Why, yes, wench, as a matter of fact I am.'

'Why, Tom, that almost makes you an artist!'

'Okay.' He straddles her, pins her arms back into the pillow behind her head. 'Don't say I didn't warn you!'

With Tom

'Once, in third-year uni, I was with this lecturer in his office and we were discussing cyberpunk fiction and we started talking about mutant animals and then phosphorescence and then he made a slip of the tongue. Instead of saying *I could really use a glow-in-the-dark fly*, he said, *I could really use a blow-in-the-dark fly*.'

'Understandable.'

'I couldn't believe it! He didn't even *hear* what he'd said ... So, what about you?'

'Sure! I'd love one.'

'No! I mean what about you have you ever heard anyone make outrageously revealing slips of the tongue that you can remember?'

'Oh ... mmm ... no, not that I've noticed.'

'Well do you think we should hold someone responsible for their slips of the tongue?'

'Hold someone responsible?'

'Yeah. 'Cause isn't it the case that the slips reveal true feelings?'

'True feelings?'

'Yeah.'

'Aren't they just mistakes?'

'A *blow* in the dark? Come on.'

Tom shrugged. 'I've enough trouble accounting for people's actions.'

'My grandmother always said it was the thought that counted.'

'How traumatising.'

From Ingrid

'You look pretty much the same as you always did. You've just got a bit of a stomach now.'

To Tom

'Can you believe that fucking bitch said I look *pretty much the same as I always did*? Even though I'm *nineteen kilograms* heavier than I used to be? Even though I look like a goddamn cow? I was *never* this fucking fat. I was far better looking than her. She is such a bitch. She thinks she's so fucking gorgeous and someone should tell her to wear foundation over those liverspots, and she actually said she thinks she looks like Angelina Jolie? She pulled a picture she'd cut from a magazine out of her bag to illustrate the resemblance? I mean that is just psychotic. Oh gosh, I never noticed Angelina's appalling acne scars and lack of a neck before! And you know, she actually asked me when you were due home because she wanted to say hi? As if you would be disappointed if she didn't hang around to say hi? *Hi Tom. Hi TommyTomTom. Wanna feel my smaller arse Tom-Tom? My boobs don't leak. My bra doesn't have wires. I'm a size ten, you know. Oh you didn't know? Well here, let me rip my top off and show you the fucking tag.*'

And More

She used to read things other than *The Baby Whisperer, Kid Wrangling, Baby Love, Baby Born*. She used to eat things other than cake. Cake. Cake. Cake. Cake. Cake. She used to read, ah, who the fuck did she read? Don DeLillo at uni. She remembers that, vaguely. And she must have read Carey, surely, something about a man with no lips in a mouse suit? What has happened to her memory? She worries. Is it prolactin that has suspended her in this fuzzy, fleshy ever-present? Throughout her pregnancy they watched a DVD on the old MacBook almost every night, in bed, their shoulders rubbing, and she can't recall a single plot.

She dresses the baby and sings, *We're goin' to the café and I'm gonna go cra-a-a-zy, we're goin' to the café and I'm gonna go me-me-mental.*

She dresses herself. Maternity bra. New black cotton underpants. How the fuck, she thinks, can something be full *and* brief?

White slip with black trousers. Ballet shoes. A relapse. She just feels false wearing anything else.

At the café, rocking The Ambulator with one foot. 'Aha. Aha. Really? Fillet steak for only sixteen ninety-nine? Gosh you're cheap, I mean, that's cheap.' Behind her glasses Louise crosses her eyes. Shoot me now, no one can see. She holds them that way until the little muscles beside her nose, and the ones inside her temples start to scream. Muscles she didn't know she had, screaming at her. Like childbirth on minimum volume. Like childbirth shushed with a massive morphine OD. It stops her throat from screaming, *Anyone here do with a Blow-In-The-Dark?* Her foot rocks The Ambulator harder, faster. Sunglasses take aim at her ballet slipper. She uncrosses her eyes. She stops rocking. Who exactly the fuck are these women? These old fucking ugly hags sitting on chairs-de-bistro as if they have massive PVC pipes rammed up their barge-arses. Women – *mothers* – discussing all kinds of inane bullshit. What happened to her old friends? What happened to her? Surely this cannot be better than an afternoon in her own home? Louise imagines her desk and then her fridge full of condiments, the drawn curtains, the vomit stain on the living-room carpet, Jane and Michael pashing on her TV. She thinks of Ingrid in her size tens and orders the banana bread.

She's next to Pam – Pam who lives five houses down and was probably a perfectly nice and perfectly competent PA in her previous life, exactly the kind of person Louise would never have had to deal with except on the rare occasion that she had to deal with Pam's boss – and Pam discusses all the different kinds, and all the different forms, and all the different colours of the shit that litters her miserable excuse for a life. And Louise shovels banana bread down her throat, imagining all the rotting, black, rancid bananas they must have smashed together to make this cake that smells like a fucking monkey's sweaty arse, and she thinks she might choke.

Home

Eyes closed, it sucks on one breast, and milk flows from both nipples. Her gigantic milk let-down: this engorgement of her breasts feels like a huge inflation, followed by a powerful squeeze. It cries and then – nipple in mouth – it rears back from the fierce rush of milk, gagging. Ever hopeful – in this just like its father – it gives the breast another chance. It drinks easily now, burps, sleeps. Louise lays it in its crib and stands by, making sure it keeps breathing. It does keep breathing, for a long time it keeps breathing. Breathing, and mouthing phantom breasts. And then it cries. Without opening its eyes, it screams for more let-downs. But she leaves it and walks to the toilet. If it's crying it's not dead. She sits. Looks with disgust at her thighs flowing over the edge of the seat and then looks down, at the green tiles and at the empty toilet roll lying like a carcass about thirty centimetres from the bin. *Right,* she says into the empty room. *I mean why would you, Tom, put the empty roll in the bin when you can just chuck it on the floor? How idiotic of me not to realise that the entire bathroom is your personal rubbish bin. A bin for me to fucking well empty, day after day after day.* The thought of Tom dropping the empty roll on the floor – brutally, carelessly – is unbearable. She wants to cause him pain. She rips off a handful of paper from the full roll on the holder, wipes herself, stands, viciously pulls up her underwear and, refusing to flush, she goes to feed the kid.

Still More
Louise looks down at her outfit. More uniform than outfit. She looks up and around the table, at the circle of dark glasses. She points to her white slip and says nervously, 'I actually have four of these, you know.' She giggles. She looks from lens to lens. No one responds. They are waiting for the waiter. Louise clears her throat. She is flushing madly and would like to fan her face with the menu, 'Well. You know sweetbreads?' she says, clearly a propos of nothing, voice cracking up. 'I didn't know, but I read that it's an animal's pancreas. But only if you plan to eat it. Because if you're not thinking it's food then it's still called a pancreas. Isn't that weird?' Pam – feeling obliged as she's sitting right next to Louise – says, 'Hmm, yes.' And then quickly launches into a defence of disposable over cloth. That really gets them going.

Tom
He touches her the way he used to; all of her, as if she's his. There are goose bumps on her skin, a ferocious squeeze inside each breast, then the let-down of her milk. They stop and watch

it stream down Tom's chest: thin, white rivulets, the sound of their breathing in the background. The baby starts to cry. Louise whispers, 'It can smell me.'

The Page

Bound to her desk again, trying to produce *something* for her sole client. The commission: a web page for a cutting-edge Asian-fusion women's-wear label called High Tea With Mrs Woo. The site has had the word *Brewing* on it for two months now. That single word – tea-coloured and generously surrounded by undulating fleur-de-lis and promiscuous curlicues – is the only thing that separates her from rank housewife. Louise opens her computer and the nausea blooms again, infusing her like a foul tisane. It happens every time: open computer, nausea blooms. She thinks she's Pavlov's dog, the computer her bell, the nausea her saliva. She thinks everything she feels is just habituated reaction.

Brewing. Brewing. Brewing. Luckily, thinks Louise, the High Tea girls are Asian. Patient. Respectful. They knew this project would take time. They understood. Some of their dresses take an experienced seamstress twenty-eight full days to construct. Intricate wearable origami. The garments are phenomenally comfortable. Within them you are as insect in flower, nestling and hidden. Louise flips through look-cards from the current season and wonders again which piece she should buy, if she had money, if it would fit. She narrows it down to two. An orange silk floor-length halterneck gown or a black wraparound nouveau-kimono jacket. Brewing. Brewing. Brewing. The jacket might hide her gut? She draws a squat Chinese teapot and, in the steam from its spout, imagines a link to the photographs of the collection. The steaming teapot sits on a laden table. There are fortune cookies and bean cakes and tiny teacups with koi. And then she is cut with the frenzied, rasping scream of a baby being tortured in its flannelette swaddle, abandoned, dying. Louise gently closes the computer. Milk. Milk. Milk. One litre of milk is enough for forty cups of tea, or one hungry baby. She pushes her palms together.

Dough

'Honey! I'm home! I bought you that breadmaker you've been wanting for ages!'

Louise walks to the front door, frowning.

'That *what* I've been wanting?'

'The breadmaker! I researched them and I've bought the super deluxe model that bips so you can add sultanas and nuts, or herbs, or whatever you want mid-cycle? So they don't get crushed by the kneading?'

'What are you talking about?'

'The breadmaker! You said they were great and you had to get one, when we went to that kid's ridiculous one-month-old birthday party that time? Remember?'

Louise turns and walks back to the kitchen.

'Louise?'

'The dinner's burning.'

'But I thought you wanted one.'

'Tom,' she says and spins around, blinking at him like she's trying to clear oil from her eyes, 'I was lying?'

All This Came from Their One Little Slip

It is tiny and blind and squints when it looks up at her. Squints through opaque blue eyes that are always searching for her, waiting for her. And Tom's body is so hard and always ready, always waiting for her too. Muscular, masculine, gorgeous, terrifying in its ready waiting. And Louise's body – she peeks down at the flabby contours as she steps out of the shower – is this white dough, risen and soft and waiting also, waiting to be punched down or something. And it seems to her that she is separate from all of them that make up this nice little family.

Among Surgeons, a Fat Gut Is Called an Apron

Jewel from High Tea With Mrs Woo calls. Louise imagines Jewel holding her iPhone against the shiny hair that bobs above her origami clothes. Black on black on black. Luckily Louise has changed, and is sitting at her desk in ballet slippers and red lipstick, so she can pose with fingers draped over her forehead, other hand cradling her Bakelite phone. *Sure, sure. The cascading style sheets are the struggle.* She is sweating. *Yeah, look. It's almost there.*

I should have the mock-up to you by Friday latest. The tone is important. There's only High Tea between herself and obliteration. Only this single-thread page. She shakes her hair like a wet dog, trying to clear the fog, and looks down at what she has. Sepia-toned curlicues are not very Asian, but still. She closes her eyes and pushes hard against her eyelids. She once read this could make you faint. She is, in truth, so tired she could splinter, and fainting sounds like bliss. She walks to the bedroom and stands in front of the wardrobe mirror just to check there's something that   sort-of-looks-pretty-much-like-her-with-a-stomach   really there. *Mother fucker.* She steps closer. She barely fits inside. Breath from her hot lips fogs the mirror and her face disappears.

Check-up

Louise straps the baby's bassinet into the car and drives to her doctor. She's cancelled the appointment three times and is too embarrassed not to turn up. Although she does not need a doctor. What she needs is a new body and a new wardrobe. A new car would be nice – a two-seater convertible. Tom's okay for now, as is the house, but everything else she needs renewed. A doctor cannot help her with this. She skulks inside the surgery, hands her Medicare card to the receptionist, places the bassinet on the floor, baby lulled to sleep by the drive, and takes a seat. She has the first appointment after lunch and is the only patient waiting. She looks at the clock on the pastel blue wall. What does a doctor eat for lunch? Probably lettuce. Mesclun. Radicchio. Mache. Dr Taylor, mid-forties, looking like every other female GP Louise has ever known – sort of mouse-brown and *inoffensive* – calls her in. Louise hauls the bassinet into the room and sets it down again with a sigh. The child is still asleep.

'So,' says Dr Taylor, hands on her knees, and then smiles in that way they do.

Louise raises her eyebrows and tries to smile back.

'How old is the little one now?'

'Three months.'

'And how's it all going?'

'Oh, it's fine.' Dr Taylor has a large, bright-red tomato-sauce stain on her cream cardigan, just above her right breast. Louise can't help but stare.

The doctor looks down, touches the sauce stain. 'I shouldn't wear cream, I do this *every* time. I'm absolutely hopeless.'

And suddenly Louise is crying. 'I'm sorry,' she sobs into her palms, 'I never do this, I never cry in public. I don't know what's got into me, I'm fine, really.'

'You never cry in public? God, you should try it, gets you great seats on the train.'

Louise smiles faintly, tears trek down her cheeks. 'I'm just so tired … and … so bored … I could start peeling my skin for entertainment. What's wrong with me? Isn't this supposed to be heaven on earth?'

'Yes. Well. I don't know about that. But. Well. Are you sleeping?'

Louise shakes her head. 'Barely.'

'How's your appetite?'

Louise snorts and smacks at a thigh.

'Intimate relations?'

Louise blinks at the ceiling. 'The milk.' She waves her hand in front of her breasts. 'And,' she says, waving her hand over her lap, lowering her voice, 'it's dryish.'

'Topical oestrogen will help with that. I'll give you a script. But Louise, do you imagine hurting yourself?'

Louise shakes her head. 'I'm not going to kill myself. I'm just … unhappy.'

'You know, some mothers adore this very-young-baby stage. They love the helplessness or dependence maybe. Or they find every little event – wee, poo, burp, fart, the lot – fascinating. And then there are mothers who only start to enjoy themselves when the kid starts to talk … That was definitely me, I can tell you.'

'Really?'

'*Hated* the first twelve months, every time. Adore them beyond belief now they're in school.'

Louise smiles and closes her eyes. She opens them. 'Can I have some diet pills?'

Dr Taylor laughs.

Tuesday

The cries, and cries, and the cries. She picks it up and it blinks long, wet eyelashes. The lips are pink and smell like sweetest milk. She brushes them against her cheek. The baby is happy to let her do it. It is happy just to feel her. All it wants is her skin and her milk. It's Tuesday, but she cannot face all those struggling-to-be-brave faces. She stays at home in a crisp clean white slip, without trousers. Barefoot and barefaced she feels her soft thighs rub against each other and, for the first time, it does not repulse her. It feels only soft. Soft and baby-powder dry. She potters in the kitchen, her baby in a sling. She makes a tomato sandwich, throws chicken, onions and wine into a cast-iron pot, reads the bread-maker instruction booklet. In the afternoon she lies on the bed with the baby on her chest. She hums an old song: *We'll start at the very beginning, a very good place to start …* She lets it gorge, watches the eyes blink their magnificent lashes, lips against her skin.

'Hey, baby, if you tell me I'm beautiful I'll give you milk till you're ten.' Baby eyes open and look up. 'There's a good girl.'

*

She wakes to the sound of Tom opening the front door, the baby asleep in the crook of her arm. Tom drops his bag in the hallway and calls out, 'Lou? Lou-Lou? … Mmm! Fresh bread!'

Little White Slips

The Eunuch in the Harem

Ryan O'Neill

From *The Sydney Review*, **23 August 1999**
The Grass Cadillac
By Frank Harmer
Porlock Press, 96pp, $22

Reviewed by Peter Crawley

Reading *The Grass Cadillac* is a unique experience. It is the first book of poems I have ever read which does not include a single line of poetry. The collection marks the literary debut of Queensland writer Frank Harmer, a name I spent a good half-hour trying to rearrange into an anagram of Ern Malley, so sure was I that some trick was being played on me. But even Ern, I suspect, would not have tried to palm these poems off to an editor, no matter how gullible. To say that the verses in this substantial volume approach mediocrity would be a compliment. Mediocrity does not figure even on the horizon of this book, though ignorance looms large. Harmer has no idea about what alliteration or onomatopoeia are, and I suspect he thinks that a metaphor is someone who fights bulls.

As an example, let us turn for a moment (though this is being overgenerous with our time) to the first poem in the book, 'The Melting Clock.' The title is apparently an allusion to Dali, and the poem an elegy to a dead dog, or a love letter to a married woman,

I can't decide which. But then, neither could Harmer. The first line is 'Th'e ni'g''ht cas''cades wh''en she's aw''ay / cuck'old, empo'wer ti'll da'y's da'wn.'

This reads like a poem generated by computer, though surely a computer would do a better job. For some reason most of the poems are punctuated in the above manner, with swarms of apostrophes hovering like flies over the dead verse.

Whilst there is nothing that resembles anything so coherent as a 'theme' in *The Grass Cadillac*, the 'poet' himself appears regularly, every two or three pages, like a dog marking its territory. Sometimes he is in the first person, sometimes the second, and sometimes in the third, as 'Harmer.' Unfortunately these three people together do not add up to half a writer.

If the reader can progress past the first twelve poems there is some respite to be had in 'To My Coy Wife,' at thirteen pages the longest poem in the book, and thankfully free of apostrophes. The 608 lines of this epic begin, 'I am comforted by your sock / that I carry into the twilight of luckbeams / held next to my philtrums' and grinds on in the same way, with little rhyme and no reason, reaching its zenith with 'I am filled with hope / that I may dry your tears of semen / so that we may grind as one / labia to labia / in search of the magnificent rainbow of love.'

I will not weary the reader with any more of Harmer's work, though it is tempting to offer a line or two from the accurately titled 'Shitlines' or a particularly rancid image from 'The Belly of the Dead Baby.' After I had finished reading the collection, I considered not writing a review at all, in order to spare a new poet embarrassment. But Harmer is obviously proud of his work and eager to show it off, in the same way a newly toilet-trained child is proud and eager to show off the contents of its potty.

A great writer once said that criticising a poem was like attacking a butterfly with a bazooka. That may be so, but when the poem is not a butterfly, but a cockroach, then I believe that the critic is justified in the attack. If, as scientists believe, cockroaches can survive a nuclear bomb, then Mr Harmer's poems will survive the winter of this review. I can only hope that they may be driven into the dark, under the floorboards, where they belong.

The most attractive image in *The Grass Cadillac* is the photograph which adorns the front cover. The caption on the dust jacket informs me that the bookish-looking man is Frank Harmer himself, and the beautiful woman beside him his wife. If that is so, then I can only congratulate Mr Harmer on his luck and advise him that he would be better to concentrate on creating the patter of tiny feet, instead of iambic ones.

*

From *The Sydney Review*, 6 November 2001
The Dog and the Lamp-post
By Frank Harmer
Joseph Grand Publishing, 204pp, $35

Reviewed by Peter Crawley

[The following review was written one month ago, two weeks prior to the events which occurred at the Newcastle Literary Festival, at a reading of Emma Harmer's poetry. I would like to thank the many readers who sent me get-well cards, and a number of my colleagues who came to visit me in the hospital to sign the cast on my leg. I would also like to thank Emma Harmer for her many visits whilst I was convalescing, and her apologising to me on her husband's behalf. I will not comment upon the night in question here, as the police are currently preparing a number of charges against Frank Harmer. My only regret is that the debut of a most promising poet was all but ruined by drunken, thuggish behaviour. Regarding the below review – which, I would like to stress, predates the vicious assault upon me – not one word has been changed or added.]

I am one of those readers who like to write my name and the date on the inside of books. I underline striking passages and jot comments in the margins. As a critic, such notes often form the backbone of a review. After finishing Frank Harmer's collection of twelve stories, I idly flipped through the pages to see what I had written, and could find only one comment, on page forty-five. 'No tree should have died for this.' This review is an appendix to that note.

Readers may remember Harmer from a collection of poetry published two years ago, which was reviewed in these pages.

Harmer is evidently one of those pathetic species of writers who read their notices. The title of his collection, and the longest story therein, *The Dog and the Lamp-post*, is taken from a comment by Christopher Hampton. 'Asking a working writer what he thinks about critics is like asking a lamp-post how it feels about dogs.' It will come as no surprise to all four of the people who endured *The Grass Cadillac* that this image of Hampton's is the only memorable one on the book. Philosophers have long been telling us that an infinite number of monkeys sitting at an infinite number of typewriters for an infinite length of time will eventually reproduce Shakespeare's plays. This I am prepared to concede. However, I cannot accept that an infinite number of Frank Harmers in the same situation would ever come up with an original line.

Harmer, admittedly, is better suited to the bludgeon of prose than the rapier of poetry, even if the only wounds he inflicts are on himself. His stories follow loners and losers, men often burdened with literary ambition, but without the talent to pursue it. In 'The Reader of Books,' for example, a man reads a novel aloud to his dying father. In what should be an interesting twist, it turns out that the father has Alzheimer's, and the same two pages of the book are read every night. In the hands of another, this might have been a moving piece. But Harmer could rob even a suicide note of its pathos. His characters obliterate the distinction E.M. Forster made between flat and round. Harmer's characters are square: little boxes half full of dull adjectives.

In 'The Papercut,' one of the less boring stories, a man (Harmer's main characters are always men) cuts himself with his wife's Dear John letter. Again, an interesting premise is utterly squandered with uninvolving characters and flat prose. Harmer does not understand that the short story is a *glancing* form. His stories *stare* and writers who stare give us the same sense of discomfort as people who stare. Of the three stories 'The Last Night on Earth,' 'Rusty's Funeral' and 'What ... What ... What Do You Mean? Exactly?' very little needs to be said. They are a mixture of carved-up Carver and hemmed-in Hemingway.

The longest story, 'The Dog and the Lamp-post,' is a thinly disguised diatribe against literary critics, and one critic in particular.

The main character, Paul Rawley, is a reviewer for a Sydney newspaper. He is described as having thick, square glasses, a sparse grey beard, and a round face 'like a bulldog chewing a wasp.' (Here I would direct the reader's attention to my photograph at the top of the page.) Rawley, an impotent drunk 'who looked like he enjoyed the smell of his own farts,' is tormented by the fact that he is merely a critic, and not a 'true writer.' It is this jealousy that causes him to attempt to ruin the career of a flowering literary genius, Ray Charmer. Eventually (C)Harmer confronts (C)Rawley with a gun, and forces the critic to feed on the review, literally eating his own words. To say this disturbing fantasy is the best story in the collection is not to say much. At least Harmer's obvious hatred of critics (and myself in particular) brings the characters lurching to some kind of half-life, and I must admit it was entertaining to see myself caricatured, in the same way it is entertaining, for a moment, to see a child's drawing of oneself. But just as a child's drawing is disposable, so is Harmer's story.

The last three stories in the collection, 'I'm Not Alone,' 'The Web of Blood' and 'With the Dead,' see the writer take a turn into horror. This is a genre that all too easily descends into the juvenile, and the stories here are no exception, though perhaps juvenile is the wrong word for such violent, misogynistic tales. The sadistic climax of 'I'm Not Alone' does not invoke uneasiness or chills, as the best ghost story does, but mere disgust. By the close of 'With the Dead' one begins to worry about Frank Harmer. His writing has by then begun to resemble that of a mental patient, scrawling his sordid fantasies in excrement on the walls of his padded cell.

It may be some consolation to Harmer that the very few copies of his book that are sold will undoubtedly remain in mint condition. I cannot imagine them ever becoming dog-eared. Once the reader loses his place, there is no desire to get it back. Many of my fellow critics say the novel is dead. If Frank Harmer ever writes one, then it surely will be.

*

From *The Sydney Review*, **29 December 2002**
Ariel's Daughter
By Emma Harmer
McGonnigal-Marzials, 16pp, $15

Reviewed by Peter Crawley
Books of the Year #4

The announcement of this year's shortlist for the Alexander Poetry Prize caused something of a stir among the Sydney literati when, beside worthy works by David Malouf and Les Murray, there appeared the little-known name of Emma Harmer and her slim volume, *Ariel's Daughter*. I was one of three judges of the award and can recall clearly the moment I read her first poem. It struck me like a revelation. Though she eventually lost the prize to Murray, I find that it is Harmer's poems that I enjoy more on re-reading, and wonder if we judges made the right decision after all.

The title of the collection is an obvious nod to Sylvia Plath's *Ariel*. In a lesser writer, such a title would be the merest egotism. But it is no exaggeration to say that Emma Harmer's poems are every bit as luminous, beautifully crafted and extraordinarily realised as Plath's. The fifteen pages and twenty-five poems which make up *Ariel's Daughter* are at once an encyclopaedia and an atlas. They seem to contain the world and everything in it.

The first stanza of 'A Pen Is Not a Penis' is a strident statement of intent:

> fuck him who left poor anne hathaway,
> fuck him who pushed sylvia plath away!
> a pen is not a penis.
> when i say this what i mean is,
> A dick is not a bic
> A tool is not a tool.

Not since Greer's *Female Eunuch* has there been such a passionate feminist rallying cry. And yet, Emma's tone soon softens, and she proves herself capable of the most sublime thoughts, as in the wonderful haiku 'Reading':

midsummer morning
alone at the library
just me and this book

Its companion work, 'Writing,' offers a desolate view of the act of creation, one that will be familiar to any writer:

composing cheaply
pen gorges, listless dreary
melody wails, bleak

And then there is the magnificently angry sonnet/limerick, 'Editing,' in which the poet imagines filling up a pen with her menstrual fluid and using it to correct the collected works of Western literature, removing centuries of sexism and misogyny.

It is a difficult task to quote from *Ariel's Daughter*; I am tempted to continue but this would only result in my transcribing the entire collection. In fact, it is only a respect for copyright that prevents me from doing so. *Ariel's Daughter* is one of those rare books which negates the critic. Essentially, it reviews itself. And with that, I will stop writing.

*

From *The Melbourne Eon*, 2 May 2005
An African Honeymoon
By Peter and Emma Crawley
Xanthippe Press, 192pp, $35

Reviewed by James Devine

An African Honeymoon is the first travel memoir to be written by the *Sydney Review*'s outspoken critic Peter Crawley. Though his wife Emma is credited as co-author, Crawley has let it be known (in a furious open letter) that the half-dozen chapters she actually wrote were excised by the 'Philistine publisher.' Crawley has frequently upbraided Xanthippe Press for 'inaccuracies' in its account of the long-running dispute. This seems unfair, for if anyone has been inaccurate, it is Crawley. The very title of his book is erroneous. Mrs Emma Crawley was still Mrs Emma Harmer when she left for Africa with Peter Crawley in the spring of 2003. The two were certainly not on honeymoon.

The events preceding their hasty departure are described (or rather skated over) in the first twenty-five pages of *An African Honeymoon*. Crawley gives little mention to the controversy surrounding the 2002 Alexander Poetry Prize. To this day, his fellow judges maintain that Crawley browbeat and threatened them into including *Ariel's Daughter* on the shortlist. The controversy deepened when it turned out that one of Harmer's only decent poems, the haiku 'Reading,' was plagiarised from American poet Billy Collins. Harmer's flight from her husband, little-known poet and short-story writer Frank Harmer, is dismissed by Crawley in two sentences. Neither does he mention that his sabbatical from the *Sydney Review* was not voluntary, but rather the result of his ecstatic write-up of the execrable *Ariel's Daughter*.

Some of Crawley's more charitable readers assumed this review to be satirical, but on reading *An African Honeymoon* this assumption is swiftly put to rest. One of the revelations of this memoir is that Crawley truly does believe in his wife's genius. In their meandering year-long journey by train (once) car (four times) and plane (twenty-eight times) Crawley evidently wishes to play Boswell to his wife, recording her every comment and opinion with relish. Unfortunately, Emma Crawley is more Dr Pepper than Dr Johnson. She is sweet and bubbly, but too much of her in one sitting will make you feel ill.

When writing of local geography, the people he encounters and the adventures he undertakes, Crawley is on solid ground. Freed of the confines of criticism, he displays a disarming passion to understand Africa and its inhabitants. His description of wandering through an Egyptian bazaar is wonderfully vivid, as is his alarm at finding himself lost in a rainforest in Uganda. This leads to a superb passage in which a group of Ugandan villagers demonstrate a warmth and kindness that obviously moves Crawley, even now. His dissecting of the social mores of UN bureaucrats in Liberia is a small masterpiece of sustained venom, whilst the short chapter on visiting a genocide site in Rwanda is both sobering and extremely poignant. Sadly, we do not have Crawley's impressions of South Africa, Madagascar, Sudan or

Tanzania, as these chapters were written by his wife, and subsequently deemed 'unpublishable' by editors at Xanthippe Press.

I don't doubt that their decision is entirely justified in light of the Emma Crawley that appears in this book. That she refers to Hutus and Tutsis and 'Tu-tus and Whoopsies' is not charming, as her husband seems to believe, but tactless and crass. Her confusion between the two words 'genesis' and 'genocide' when questioning an old woman in Kigali is horrendously embarrassing, though Crawley strives to present it in a humorous light. Another misplaced attempt at light-heartedness, her referring to the Congo as 'The Fart of Darkness' after a bout of diarrhoea there, falls flat. By the time the couple cross the equator Emma Crawley has emerged as a ridiculous figure. With hilarious repetition, everything she encounters in Africa is 'smaller than I thought it would be.' The pyramids, the Sphinx, even Mount Kilimanjaro are described in this fashion by Emma and faithfully recorded by her husband. By the end of the book, one is left with the impression that the continent of Africa measures approximately two metres by six.

The couple's return to Australia proves a relief for them, though arguably more so for the reader. *An African Honeymoon* is by no means a terrible book. In parts, it is beautifully written and admirably perceptive. It is also infuriatingly silly and often dull. Still, I find myself in the position of recommending it, for all its faults, as have several other critics in newspapers and journals. Next time, I suspect we will not be so kind. Peter Crawley should take note that in art, as in life, the honeymoon is over.

*

From *The Australian Literary Review*, 29 November 2008
The Eunuch in the Harem: Criticism
By Peter Crawley
Hazlitt-Ruskin Publishers, 656pp, $55

Reviewed by Penny McFarlane

October 23 marked the second anniversary of literary critic Peter Crawley's bizarre and violent death at his Sydney home. In a recent press release Hazlitt-Ruskin explained that they felt enough time had passed that they could release the first, long-delayed book of Crawley's reviews and essays. Crawley himself was engaged in the editing of the book when his life was cut short. This edition collects all of his important criticism from the *Sydney Review*, the *Age* and the *Sydney Morning Herald*, and the lectures and speeches he occasionally gave at book launches and signings. The title of the collection is taken from a remark by Brendan Behan: 'Critics are like eunuchs in a harem; they know how it's done, they've seen it done every day, but they're unable to do it themselves.' Crawley often jokingly referred to himself as a 'eunuch,' though many women who encountered him in Sydney's literary scene from the 1970s to the 1990s would be able to give the lie to that. (In the interests of disclosure, I should say that Crawley once made a pass at me at a book reading in Melbourne in 1988. At this time the *fatwa* against Salman Rushdie had just been pronounced, and I can still clearly recall a drunken Crawley, at the end of his speech, declaring that he had heard the title of Rushdie's next work was *Buddha Is a Fat Bastard*. In the ensuing storm, only an abject public apology saved his job at the *Sydney Review*.)

Since his death, Peter Crawley's name has become irrevocably linked with that of Frank Harmer. The editors of *The Eunuch in the Harem* have acknowledged this by placing the twenty pages of Crawley's writings about Harmer at the front of the book. The section opens with the review of *The Grass Cadillac* from 1999 and ends with a dismissive footnote in an essay on Tim Winton from 2006.

To give these writings pride of place in the collection is to do Crawley a grave disservice. His criticism of Harmer, whilst amongst his most scabrous, was certainly not his best. For that the reader should turn to the second section, titled 'American Lives.' Here we can find many unique insights into Bellow, Updike and Mailer (who, incidentally, called Crawley a 'Limey asshole' on the one occasion they met, in New York.) Crawley's analysis of the *Rabbit* tetralogy has been reprinted several times to great acclaim in the US, but is virtually unknown here, and his monograph on Bernard Malamud was highly praised by Harold Bloom. It is a shame to note that Crawley's treatment of Australian authors is spottier. Too often his praise is faint and over-leavened with sarcasm. Still, his half-dozen essays on Patrick White should be required reading for anyone with the slightest interest in Australian literature.

However, it was not Crawley the scholar, but Crawley the self-proclaimed eunuch who wrote such guiltily entertaining book reviews for the *Sydney Review*. In the longest section of the book, 'A Pig at the Pastry Cart' (another allusion to critics), Crawley selected the fifty of his reviews he felt were most enjoyable to read. Highlights include his opinion on the Booker Prize-winning *Life of Pi* ('It is so terrible I doubt there would even be a place for it in Borges' Infinite Library') and his devastating, three-word summing up of Daphne du Maurier: 'middle-class, middle-brow, middling.'

Crawley's harsh reviews of Raymond Carver's stories are surprising, considering the fact that the two men were friends, with Carver even dedicating one of his final stories, 'Buffalo,' to Crawley. But Crawley's dismissal of Carver has a refreshing quality in an era when the American has been hailed as the modern Chekhov. One passage in particular is worth quoting in full:

> [Carver] followed Hemingway's idea of the story as iceberg, that is, only the top eighth of life and emotion would be shown, the rest hidden underneath. But in [Carver's] stories, one can't help thinking that the iceberg is more of an ice cube.

Pleasingly, it is Crawley's evisceration of popular fiction that takes up the most space. His dismissal of Stephen King is brilliantly off-hand. 'To me, his novels are more endearing than scary. King is like a child leaping out from behind the sofa and shouting, "Boo!" We don't have the heart to tell him he didn't frighten us.'

As I have said, Crawley's criticism of Frank Harmer is not his best, but it is a sad thing to contemplate that it will probably be his best read. Crawley never envisaged any mention of Harmer in his book. The section 'Thoughts on Frank Harmer' was added after his death. It does not make great reading. The original review of *The Grass Cadillac* was certainly cruel, if undoubtedly accurate. Harmer might even have taken it as an honour to be tarred with the same brush that had spattered W.H. Auden and Seamus Heaney. He was obviously not aware that a review by Crawley, positive or not, would certainly help sell his small book of poetry. Similarly, if Crawley had been aware of Harmer's history of mental instability, I have no doubt he wouldn't have reviewed *The Grass Cadillac* in the first place. The accounts of their first meeting at a poetry reading are various. Harmer claimed he caught Crawley leering at his wife and assaulted him. Crawley maintained the attack was entirely unprovoked, though considering that Emma Harmer left her husband for the critic, many would tend to accept Harmer's account.

Crawley had already handed in his review of Harmer's short-story collection *The Dog and the Lamp-post* before the incident at the festival, though it had not yet gone to press. (Incidentally, he was annoyed that Harmer had inadvertently stolen the title he had wished to use for his book of criticism.) Crawley subsequently claimed he did not change a word of his review, even in light of the broken leg he received. This is true, but it is not entirely to Crawley's credit. As he recuperated in hospital, Emma Harmer, on one of her frequent visits, had informed him that her husband was being treated for schizophrenia. Knowing this, Crawley let stand the reference comparing Harmer to a lunatic daubing filth on the walls of a madhouse. This was a despicably cruel act from a normally kind-hearted man. Crawley could never forgive Harmer for beating and humiliating him in public, and returns to him again and again in his work in the weeks after the incident. For example, in a review of Pat Reid's *The Raphael Cipher* Crawley says, 'Bad as [this book] is, it has had the good fortune to be published after Frank Harmer's *The Dog and the Lamp-post*, ensuring it will not, at least, be the worst book this year.'

Eventually, Crawley's editor and close friend, David Phillips, banned him from making any further references to Harmer in the journal. By that time, of course, a scandal had erupted over *Ariel's Daughter*. The original review, at close to 10,000 words, was rejected by Phillips, the two men almost coming to blows when Crawley realised Phillips had cut 96 per cent of the review. (Phillips later destroyed all copies of the longer review, fearing it would irrevocably damage his friend's reputation.) Even in the shortened form, the review is excruciating, reading like a

400-word chat-up line. And yet it must have had the desired effect, as soon after it was published Emma Harmer fled to Africa with Crawley. Her husband, pursuing them to the airport, was arrested for brandishing a knife at the boarding gates.

It is the great irony of Peter Crawley's life that he courted controversy yet married banality. But there can be no doubt that he was deeply in love with Emma Harmer. Only a man besotted would have carefully recorded for posterity her asinine travel observations in *An African Honeymoon*.

Controversially, Crawley's last, unfinished piece, the wry essay 'Where Is That Great Australian Novel?,' has been included in the collection. I believe that here, at least, the editors made the correct decision. The twelve pages that survive are amongst the best Crawley ever wrote. Sadly, we will never know the answer to the question he set himself. As he was putting the finishing touches to the essay, a deranged Frank Harmer broke into the critic's house. He found Crawley in his study, bludgeoned him into unconsciousness with a glass paperweight, then stuffed the last eight pages of the essay down Crawley's throat, choking him to death.

Peter Crawley once said, pessimistically, 'The good writing about writing will go first, and then the good writing itself.' This collection of good writing about writing has not sold well, and the publishers have scrapped plans for a second volume. I suspect this will be the last we will see of Crawley on the bookshelves, except perhaps in the form of posterity he most detested, that of three or four lines in a book of quotations.

And the good writing itself? Crawley's widow Emma recently changed her name to Emma Crawley-Harmer. Her autobiography, *The Poetess of Sadness* (with its lengthy subtitle, *One Woman's Extraordinary Journey Through Marriage, Infidelity, Madness and Murder*) reputedly sold for a six-figure sum, and was released by Picador last week. While the reviews were overwhelmingly negative, the book has debuted at number two on the bestsellers list, outsold only by *The Dog and the Lamp-post*, now in its seventh printing.

Harvest

The Yarra

Nam Le

Hours before sunrise my body's already soaked with sweat, as though in anticipation of the real heat. Melbourne's in drought. The city a plain of dust and fire. I wake amidst dreams of Saturday sports as a schoolboy, shin guards and box chafing where the sheets have twisted; noise, collision down the pitch as faraway as a deeper dream. There are Tupperware containers at half-time, frozen wedges of orange. Then a sudden switch and charge, players all around me, the rising breathing in my ears – I am sprinting, dread-filled, from here to there, and here the ball is kicked to there, and there it's booted – at the very moment I've chased it down – somewhere else. The sun is on my face and then it is dark. My brother, my blood and bones, confessor and protector, came in last night, he must be sleeping downstairs, and – as always when he comes – I find my hand on my heart and my mind wide open and wheeling.

I get up and wash my face. The water from the cold faucet is warm, and smells of dirt. Downstairs, a reflexive propriety forestalls me looking at the sleeping form on the couch, and then I look. My brother, Thuan, comes bringing no clues where he's been. As always, he lies on his back. His mouth is open, his eyelids violent with their shuddered thoughts, and even under the thin sheet I can see the heavy limbs, flat and parallel as though lying in state. He has a powerful body.

I make some coffee in a plunger – not bothering to keep the

noise down – and take it outside to the back deck. Surrounded by cicada song I sit down, stare out. Something is wrong. Why else would he have come? I wonder where he's been but then why does it matter? Away is where he's been. I think of his last visit three years ago, then Baby's visit a few months later – how quiet and uncertain she was, how unlike his girlfriend from those rowdier times. Before leaving she hesitated, then asked for thirty dollars; I gave it to her and never saw her again.

Against the darkness, other faces from that shared past occur to my mind with stunning vividness. Even closer, thicker, than the dark is the heat. Another scorcher on the way. Somewhere out there a forest is burning, and a family crouching under wet towels in a bathtub, waiting as their green lungs fill with steam and soot muck. I test the coffee's temperature. As often happens at this time of morning I find myself in a strange sleep-bleared funk that's not quite sadness. It's not quite anything. Through the trees below, the river sucks in the lambency of city, creeps it back up the bank, and slowly, in this way, as I have seen and cherished it for years, the darkness reacquaints itself into new morning.

He's there now, I sense him, but I say nothing. Minutes pass. A line of second lightness rises into view beside the river: the bike trail.

'You still got my old T-shirt,' Thuan says. Even his voice sounds humid. He comes out, barefoot and bare-chested, stepping around my punching bag without even feinting assault.

'Sleep okay?'

'If you mean did I drown in my own sweat.'

He's feeling talkative. 'You came in late,' I say. 'There's a fan.'

He pads around the deck, inspecting it. Since he was last here I've jerry-rigged a small workout area, a tarpaulin overhang. I painted the concrete underfoot in bright, now faded, colours. He lowers himself onto the flat bench. Then under his breath he says, 'All right,' as though sceptically conceding a point. He shakes his head. 'This bloody drought,' he says.

'I know, I've been going down there,' I say, nodding at the river. 'Bringing water up – for the garden and whatnot.'

'Why?'

'You know.' He's making me self-conscious. 'The herbs and stuff.'

'I mean why not just use the hose?'

I glance at him. Where has he been that there aren't water restrictions? Then I catch his meaning: who cared about the water restrictions? What could they do to you?

A shyness takes hold of me, then I say, 'I dreamt about Saturday sports.'

To my surprise he starts laughing. He lifts up his face, already sweat-glossed, and bares his mouth widely. Yes, he's changed since I saw him last. 'Remember when you broke that guy's leg? And they wanted us to forfeit?'

I tell him I remember, though in my memory it was he, and not I, who had done the leg breaking. We'd played on the same team some years. For a confusing moment I'm shuttled back into my morning's dream: the brittle sky, the sun a pale yolk broken across it. Then the specific memory finds me – the specific faces – the injured kid with what seemed an expression of short-breathed delight, as if someone had just told a hugely off-colour joke; the odd, elsewhere smirk playing on our father's lips as he came onto the field to collect us, batting off the coach's earnest officialese, the rising rancour of the opposing parents.

'The look on his face,' I scoff.

I wait for Thuan to go on with the story but apparently he's done. He's chuckling still, but the sound has no teeth in it and that makes me wary. I feel tested by him.

'Coffee?'

He thinks about it. Then, as though shoved, he falls back-wards along the bench, twisting his upper body at the last second beneath the barbell. Hurriedly I count up the weight – one-twenty kilos on a fifteen-kilo bar – not shameful, but nor is it my PB.

'Wanna spot?' I ask, making it clear from my tone that I'm joking.

He jerks the bar off the stand and correctly, easily, completes three presses. When he's done he remains on his back, arms gone loose on either side of the narrow bench as though parody-ing one of the weekend kayakers on the river below. I follow his long breaths. For some time he doesn't move or speak, and in the half-dark I wonder if it's possible he's fallen back asleep. All around us the cicadas beat on, their timbre unsteady, deranged by the interminable heat of the night. I settle back too. A strong whiff of sage from the garden. Trees and bushes sliding into their outlines. Buying this place when I came into my inheritance was the smartest thing I ever did – despite its run-down state, subsiding foundations, the light-industrial mills and factories on every side. I couldn't have known then that ten years on, at thirty-three, I'd be living here alone, jobless. I couldn't have reasoned that I'd end up folding each of my days into this early-morning mood, trained on the dark river below, sensing that the mood, though ineffable, was one less of sorrow than of loss – and that what I called my life would be answerable to it. I know this: my brother, when he comes, muddies this mood in me. For this I am glad, as for the fact that we are bound to each other in all the ways that matter.

As though invoked, he speaks up. 'I'll be out of your hair in a couple of days,' he says. Then he gets up and goes into the dark bushes, presumably to take a piss.

*

Physical excellence has always been important between us. As a boy, I remember pushing myself in sports because my brother did – following him blindly into school and street games of every type. Unlike me, he didn't read, or even listen to music; for him the pursuit of physical betterment was its own reason and reward. I remember witnessing – when I was eleven and he thirteen – a push-up contest between my brother and the four Ngo boys. Later, of course, the four of them would be media-tarred as members of that night's notorious 'Asian gang' but in truth they were no gang – they were barely even friends – and famously never on speaking terms. What they were, were brothers. And even back then, in the kids' room at some family friends' party in St Albans, squatting around the prone figure of my brother who was younger than all but one of them, they'd already learned to stick together. The contest carried on. With no clear winner emerging, they progressed to push-ups on their knuckles, then push-ups on five fingertips, then one-armed push-ups incorporating these variants – the Ngos dropping out until only Hai, the eldest, remained alongside my brother. Then Hai collapsed. All of us watched in incredulity as Thuan went on to demonstrate a one-armed push-up, left hand tightly clutching his right wrist, where his body's weight was borne entirely by the thumb and forefinger of his right hand. I was stricken – as much by my brother's single-mindedness as his strength, the fact he must have practised, in secret, for months. (I say this with confidence because it was only after three months, when I'd buffed two coin-sized spots into the bathroom floorboard, that I managed it myself.)

My brother believed that nothing could make you ridiculous if you were strong. His way was to go at things directly; entering a new school, for example, he would do what movie lore says to do upon entering jail: pick a fight – and win. I wondered what he did in jail. Our father, in his own way, failed to beat this into us, and so my brother beat it into me. I thought then I hated him for it but I was wrong. I wanted to know him – I always have. Now I realise it was only when he asserted himself in physical motion – then, ineluctably, in violence – that I came closest to doing so.

I am on the street of my childhood. I am running late, without any time to scavenge through the disused paddock, veer in and out from under lawn sprinklers – even to catch a breather at the bottom of our steep hill. He's by himself, waiting for me. Both our parents at work. I'm late, and when I come in the front door he'll punish me – those are his rules, and they're clear enough. I come in and there he is, right in front of me, his face almost unbearably inscrutable. He allows me time to put down my schoolbag and deadlock the door. I fumble off my shoes. The hot cord bunches up from my gut into my throat, clogging my breathing. I lift my arms to my face and he slubs me with a big backhander.

'Where've you been? You're late.'

I nod, lick my cracked lips, crabwalk quickly into the living room. He follows me to the couch where I hunch my back and bury my face in the dark red cushion. Over and over he hits me, his knuckles pounding the hard part of my head where I won't bruise. The cushion smells of old blood, and spit, and sweat from both our bodies. If I reach behind to feel for the arm, the punishing fist – try to glove it with my own smaller, sweaty palms – he'll twist and sprain my fingers. If I turn to plead, I'll meet his face absent of heavy intent, as if his attention is somewhere else, as if he's bashing my skull to reach something just beyond it. He's utterly without pity and in my stronger moments I envy that. I'm sorry, I tell him. I'm sorry I'm sorry I'm sorry. He drives his knee into my lower back. At the height of panic and pain something comes free in me. Afterwards, I wipe my face on the cushion and try not to track blood, if there is blood, all over the carpet. I search my reflection in the bathroom mirror. If there's visible damage, he'll barter with me, he'll let me off next time, he'll do my chores, buy me jam doughnuts at the tuckshop – so long as I don't dob him in. But only rarely are there visible signs.

'What happened?' Mum asks. She's had a long day and her face is closed and loose.

'Nothing.'

She pauses. 'I'll tell your dad.'

I look at her scornfully. Even she knows that doesn't deserve an answer.

One of the common tacks in media accounts of my brother, I noticed – beyond the routine designation of 'monster' – was to call attention to his inscrutability. None of the other culprits merited such consideration. The Ngo boys, for instance, always looked thuggishly guilty. But courtroom reporters and sketch artists described, artfully and self-consciously, their failure of scrutiny in the face of Thuan Xuan Nguyen; a face typically depicted as 'smooth', or 'mask-like', on someone whose very name rebuffed pronunciation in each of its three syllables. I could understand their frustration. My brother was a person in whom deep faults ran, yet always he seemed to conduct them into something like charisma. All my life I never judged him; to me he represented the fulfilment of my own genomic seed and tatter. I never suspected, after all that happened, at the trial and beyond, that complete strangers might also be capable of my reservation. This is not to defend what he did. This is to say I understood, completely, the media's macabre, manic insistence on the details of that night. The facts of the matter. The altercation and eviction from the nightclub. The first victim chased down and hacked to death by a gang wielding machetes, meat cleavers and samurai swords. The sickening count of wounds on his body. Victims two and three fleeing into the Yarra, carried by the water approximately 200 metres to the west – shadowed alongshore by the gang. One with gashes on his wrists and forearms, three fingers missing below the knuckle, from a presumed attempt to return to shore. Chances are you may recall these details. The sober-faced, riverside TV reports, the strongly worded declarations by members of the mayor's office, the Homicide Squad, the Asian Squad – while in the wintry background, day on day, the grieving families held vigil, wailing in Vietnamese as they proffered incense sticks, lit and let go of tissue paper. You may have even heard me speak, in one of my presentations, about this incident. Most people recognise my brother only through one of his tabloid nicknames: the Meat Cleaver Murderer. He was there on the bank that night. Here's what most people won't know – what I've never spoken about: I was there with him.

*

When it gets light my brother showers and heads out. I laze on the couch in the living room, windows open but curtains drawn, shirtless in front of the rickety fan, rolling a chilled glass bottle of water back and forth across my chest. Otherwise, I try not to move. When the phone rings, it's Mum – one of her friends has just spotted Thuan on Victoria Street. Is it true? Has he come back?

I'm waiting for him when he returns. We have to go visit Mum, I tell him. He stops, then nods, puts his sunnies back on. Outside, the air is so hot it immediately dries out my lungs; I can feel the bitumen boiling through my sandals. This is a killing sun. We walk south, through the Abbotsford chop shops and factories, the streets made slow, strange with heat vapour, the sudden assaultive glare of metal surfaces. People move, then pause in scant shadows. On the main street the tramlines look as though they're liquefying. Too hot to think, let alone speak, we make our way towards the high-rise flats.

'Child?' our mother asks when she opens the door. She's wearing brown silk pyjamas and there's absolutely no sweat on her face.

'Hello, Ma.' My brother touches her shoulder for a second. She reaches up and cups his ear, then turns to smile at me.

When our father died I advised her to sell the house and car and move here – the flat was government-subsidised, located in the heart of a Vietnamese neighbourhood. During that period she was used to doing whatever I said. I see, looking back, it must have been hard going for her – moving from a family home with yard, driveway and garden to living alone in an inner-city warren sentried by closed-circuit cameras. Up urine-doused lifts and down fumigated corridors. Since then, though, she's grown to like it. She likes the proximity to her new circle of friends, to Victoria Street a block away, and – a few blocks behind that – to me. After all that happened, I sometimes wondered how her friendships suffered – I loathed the thought of her being judged by that array of flat faces and slit eyes, besieged by their silent, hostile curiosities – but of course she'd never have discussed any of that with me.

The dining table, predictably and yet astonishingly, is covered with food. Mum comes out of the kitchen with a jug full of mint leaves and cut lemon halves. She pours our drinks, enquires after my herb garden, brings out a colander brimming over with fresh basil and purple mint and coriander. She'll send some cuttings home with me, she says; the residents picked the community garden clean due to the drought. Every now and then, as she speaks, she'll stop to look at my brother.

'You've been in the sun,' she says. She wets a cloth under the kitchen tap and lays it across the back of his neck.

We eat with courteous gusto. These are all our favourite dishes: spring rolls, shredded chicken coleslaw, a plain winter melon soup offset by caramelised salty pork. My brother doesn't talk, so neither do I. The silence becomes the outside wind: up here on the eighteenth floor it's a constant commotion, driving dust and sound through the metal window jambs, shaking the very light. Every so often I see smallish cockroaches stopping, as though disoriented, in the middle of their skitterings. Oblivious, we eat, and before we're done with any given dish Mum carts it off – brings forth a new one. For a moment it's as though we've ducked out from our nearer past; we're back in our St Albans kitchen, nothing to say, waiting for Mum to finish up. Not knowing it would chase us all down – this past still in front of us. Then, she cooked and we ate. Later, she sat down and couldn't stand up again in a Victorian Supreme Court public toilet, her eldest son counted push-ups in his cell, body wet with heft and speed, I stood in front of strangers and spoke them both down into small dots of sense. Later, she sat with her back straight and head bent, I stood in front of people and delivered up her dead husband.

In cold weather you find the dead roaches behind the radiators, under the electric kettle, microwave, fridge, where they group for warmth. When it's this hot where do they go?

'Child is well?' Finally she's seated, facing Thuan. The dishes are cleared and there's a platter of fruit on the table.

'I'm fine,' he says.

She starts to respond, then stops. Her fingers reach out to test the lacquer of a cut lemon face, left open to the air.

'Really,' he says. He sounds like he means it.

'It's so sad what happened to Baby,' she says. She, too, is thinking about death. 'I didn't even know she was sick like that.'

'Baby? What happened?'

'Thank you for coming to see me. I know you're very busy.'

'You don't know about Baby?' I ask despite myself.

Thuan frowns, then reaches over and squeezes our mother's shoulder. 'Ma. Guess what.'

'Where you've been, or what you've been doing, is your own business,' she continues. She says this shyly and forthrightly, a settlement of fact. 'I don't need you to look after me.'

'I know, Ma.'

'And Lan, he is very good. He can look after himself.'

'He is very good,' repeats Thuan, completely deadpan.

'I hear about Lan speaking at universities, at the community centre, and it makes me very happy.' My brother throws me an offhand smile, and in a ritual manner she follows up his smile, almost too sweetly. Turning her attention to me: 'He has become a brave and caring man.'

I get up, go to the window. There has always been a touch of formal drama about my mother, and a situation like this – her prodigal son's return after three long years – is bound to draw it out. Through the wind-rattled window I watch some seagulls, hovering in the air the way seagulls do. The air is runny with heat and bleaches the blue sky.

Mum's speaking again. 'I know I can't tell you what to do. But I'm your mother and I don't want my sons to be angry with each other.'

I turn around. My brother's mouth is slightly open, sly at one corner.

'I don't know how much longer I'll be here. I want my sons to look after each other.' She speaks with care, a prepared grace. 'Your father would want that too. Remember when you were children, you looked after each other.'

In grade three, when my parents found out I was being bullied, they left it to my brother to beat up the malefactor. Recess the next day Thuan climbed out of the concrete playground tunnel from one end, then, a long minute later, Matty Fletcher from the other, smiling with his mouth full and one hand low on his gut. My family used to bring this up at every chance. Now, Mum stops, following the thought to its logical implication. Another track cut off next to a night river. Nothing, during the trial, was so cruel as watching the jury coaxed and coerced by weeks of 'similar fact evidence' alleging Thuan's propensity for violence – until it was all anyone could see of him. She must have been confounded, afterwards, by the new plot of her life – how, whether forward or back, it inescapably led her, as it did both her sons, to that one night – as though it were exactly where we were all meant to be.

'I've been saving some money,' she says.

'Ma.' His insouciance has settled now.

'I need you to come to the bank with me later. To sign some papers. If you have time.'

'Listen, Ma, I don't need money.'

'You're the oldest, so I want you to look after it.'

For a moment no one speaks. In the yellow emptiness behind the window I hear voices, strains of Asian opera riding the hot red wind from a different floor, maybe a different building. The glass-warmed sun on my face. I'm brought back to mornings waking up when my pillow is so suffused with sun, the air through the open window so full of a sense of lost summer, that I clench my eyes closed again, coach those voices at the bottom of my hearing to sing louder, bear higher their meaning.

'Child,' says Mum, her tone finally relaxing. 'You're too good for money now?'

Thuan leans back at the table, slightly embarrassed.

Mum stands up, brushing smooth her silk pyjama top. 'Heavens,' she says, 'it's been so long since I saw you. I'm going to tell you the truth – I didn't know if I would see you again.' Then, with her usual restraint, she checks herself. Smiling privately, as though she's decided she has all the time she needs, she picks up the jug and heads into the kitchen to make more iced tea.

*

'So Baby.'

The lift drops with the sound of metal squealing against itself.

'Two or three years ago,' I say. 'It was an accident, they think.'

He looks straight ahead. 'OD?'

I nod.

'She was still in Footscray?'

'Yeah, probably. I think so. I saw her – she was all straightened out.'

He frowns, maybe sensing my lie. 'Not if she was still hanging out in Footscray she wasn't.' It's the first time I've heard an edge of the old hard tone. 'Jesus,' he mutters. The lift opens, and I follow him through the two security doors back out into the heat.

In the presentations I've been asked to give, I generally concentrate on sociological factors until the inevitable moment I find myself nudged towards the incident. The cops at our door two days later, their duteous, scornful faces, all the scorn sucked into their eyes and the edges of their mouths as if to curb them from asking, What kind of animals are you? That you could do this to your own? These are not, I think, unfair questions. But the people who turn to me for answers aren't looking to my master's in political science, they're looking at my one-of-them face, they're looking at my pedigree of proximity: the fact I'm my brother's brother. Not that I'm one of them, of course. I'm articulate and deferential, I'm charming to just the right degree. It's that they trust me to tell them the inside story. They want to know – beneath the affidavits and agreed facts – *how it happened.* And so when I talk about socioeconomic disadvantage, about ghettoisation and tribal acting-out, about inexorable cycles of escalation, I say these things and I mean them, but even to me they start to sound insincere. What I mean to say but don't – can't – is that everything always starts with a girl, and in this case the girl was Baby.

My brother was nineteen and one night came home drunk, flushed, probably high, and with a girl. This last had never happened before. There was a shadow on his jaw which I assumed was a bruise. After some time the girl said to me, 'I'm Baby,' then turned to him and exclaimed, 'I can't believe you weren't gonna introduce me!' then kissed him, all the while still talking into his mouth. He made some joke and she laughed and I was relieved, hearing her laugh, that it wasn't the cutesy, infant squeaking so many Asian girls liked to perform in front of guys.

'He talks about you *all* the time,' she said, and laughed again.

I decided I liked her.

How long they'd been together wasn't clear. It seemed, from Baby's comfort with him, that it might have been a while. She was my brother's first girlfriend, I think, and I'm not sure why that didn't surprise me at the time. They'd just come home from a fight. I mentally staged it during their telling: Baby's ex had been at the club, an Asian night, stewing deeper and hotter in Hennessy the longer he watched them until, at the final, emptying hour – the music switched off and lights on, bartenders wiping down bars, tallying the take – he'd called up his mates and followed them outside.

Something flew out of the night towards Thuan's head. He ducked, the bottle smashing against a car, setting off the alarm. I knew that club: its main entrance fed onto a cul-de-sac backed in by warehouses, steel roller doors, a multi-storey car park giving out the only light. Under that spotty, gas-like glow, my brother turned around and saw them – maybe a dozen of them. Their movements loose and stiff with alcohol. He had Baby with him, and the four Ngo brothers – that was it. Breath shortening, the great engine of his glands working till he felt again the thick twists of hormones through his body, he fended Baby back against the blaring car, made quick eye contact with the Ngos, for whom he felt himself flooding with a feeling of deep loyalty, and waited. You can always tell the seriousness of a fight by the speed of first approach. Baby's ex feinted forward, then his crew herky-jerked at them, and instantly my brother knew in his body the entire shape of what would follow. The only surprise was the set of strangers who jumped in to help them; it was only later, in the nervy racing-away euphoria, that they were introduced as Baby's friends from Footscray; only later still, well past the point of ready return, that he learned the guy in the red baseball cap – as affable afterwards as he was vicious during the fight – was another of Baby's exes.

'You should've been there,' Thuan said magnanimously, rubbing the sore spot on his jaw. 'We could have used you out there tonight.'

'You did okay,' said Baby.

I studied her closely – this girl they'd all fought over. She had a face struck together by contrasts: the Asian hair – so black it looked wet – offset by almost European features: chalky skin, sunken cheeks, lips in a burnished shade of red that belonged to some earlier, jazz-smoked era. Her body was slight and wonderfully slouched. She had, all in all, the look of a good girl gone a bit grungy. Thinking of their story, I saw her arms lined by light in the alley, locked crossed amid the scudding bodies, the car alarm caterwauling through her skull. Then I saw my brother watching her. He looked the happiest I'd ever seen him.

'I wish I had been there,' I said, and meant it.

That summer, I spent more time with Thuan than ever before or since; Baby liked my company, insisted on it, and my brother was surprisingly acquiescent – especially given we'd never really had any mutual friends. She called him Little T and so, with even less reason, I became Big T. I came to need her, and probably what I needed most about her was him: the emergent, intricate person he became around her. He developed a way of talking to me through her, in third-person – *Look at him – and he reckons he's not on steroids!* She kept him kind to me like that. At Brighton Beach she stripped to a grey bikini. When he caught me staring, he gave me a look that was warning and mockery, shy and full of braggadocio, knowing and forgiving all at once. Do you see what I mean? We lived then in slow-time; the light more viscous, the breath drawn deeper into our bodies. I had a new brother and a new name – how would I not rally to both?

*

When we get back, Thuan breaks the silence and tells me to head inside – he's going to keep wandering. There's no invitation in his announcement so I go in – glad to escape the punishing heat – strip to my boxers, splash water over my face and chest. I think for a droll moment of working out. Then I resume my place on the couch, following the creak of the fan, the odd foolhardy cyclist whizzing by on the track below.

The wind sears my face awake. I'm sodden and sticky. I find myself incredibly aroused. The wind feels as though it's passed through fire. I press my face into the cushion and reach for myself, drowsing into the familiar memory of Baby, that one time. The habitual quickening. She came over to our house wheeling a large suitcase full of clothes to launder. Yes. These trips were timed so both our parents would be out working the night shift. My brother steered and shut her up in his room, not knowing I could hear their every other sound. At the end of the night she unloaded the dryer and folded her clothes into the suitcase.

'Need any help with that?'

'I'll be right.'

'You can carry it down the stairs?'

A flirtatious pause.

'Sure, you can help me bring it down.'

I glided to the window and lifted the hem of the blinds. I was nearly seventeen. They left, as usual, by the small unlit walkway between the fence and my side of the house. And as usual, they tarried in the dark, swaying in and away from each other, whispering, and I cracked open the window to listen in from above.

'So what's the going tip for a bellboy here?' she asked.

Outside, the night was cool and a wind blew full and quiet along the empty street, carrying with it the scent of new flowers, jasmine and hibiscus and bougainvillea. A wood chime sounded from a neighbour's porch.

'Just a quick blow job,' he said.

She spluttered out a low laugh, pushed and punched him. Then they kissed. She kissed him soft and then she kissed him hard, and after some abortive fumblings she spun around and folded herself over the standing suitcase. She wriggled her pants down to her knees.

'Make it quick,' her voice hissed.

He shoved down his own pants and grabbed her pale hips. He leaned and rocked over her. The wheels scrabbled wildly across the concrete but the suitcase stayed upright. From where I was watching, all I could see of Baby was the side of her head, curtained off by her jogging black hair. She nodded and nodded and nodded and I watched. Finally they stopped, remaining locked together, almost statue-like. Then she unbent herself, bobbed her knees in a little curtsey, and reached between her legs with two fingers.

'You,' she said, grinning delightedly, jabbing her fingers at his chest, 'are going to get me pregnant.'

He shushed her and automatically she looked around, scoping the street. Then she looked up – and saw me. I jerked back but didn't dare release the blinds. After an appalling hesitation, she lowered her gaze, then straightened her clothes. She took possession of her suitcase handle. My brother stood there half-slouched and stupid. I ignored him. I watched instead the new self-consciousness in Baby's body – or did I imagine it? – as she walked away, leaning her weight forward, scraping and sledding her suitcase across the street.

'I never want to see you again,' my brother abruptly shouted into the night. 'Take your stuff and get out of here!'

With a wicked smile she turned in our direction. 'I'm never coming back!' she called out. She heaved the suitcase into the boot and slammed it shut.

Something occurs to me from my childhood I haven't thought about for years. After a particularly nasty beating, if I swore to tell our parents – and his bribes and proofs of contrition weren't enough to dissuade me – my brother would threaten to run away. How strange that I now remember this with something like nostalgia. He would stalk to the closet and take out a suitcase and then he'd start packing it, leaving me mute-stricken as I tagged helplessly and furiously behind him, horrified by the thought of being responsible for his loss – and, far more deeply, of losing him. I'd break, of course, and agree to anything if only he agreed to stay. Was this what it was to love somebody? I guessed it had to be.

A few weeks after my brother's open-air tryst with Baby, we received word that the Ngo brothers had been ambushed at the casino. The crew from that nightclub fight was responsible; they'd driven all the way in, we later learned, from Sunshine. The youngest Ngo, Peter, had had two of his ribs broken with a cricket bat. They'd been out with the Footscray crew from the same fight – the one with Baby's red-capped ex – with whom they'd since become mates. Straight away there was talk of revenge, and soon enough there was another fight, at another Asian night, when Red Cap recognised one of the Sunshine boys. This time, knives were produced, and two people cut.

To Thuan and me, none of this, in itself, seemed critical. These fights happened all the time without ever reaching the hospitals, let alone the courts or headlines. The Ngos were known hot-heads. And everyone accepted that the club scene was booby-trapped with grudges and grievances, blood ties and ven-dettas and bonds of blind loyalty. Asian nights had been banned in Sydney for exactly this reason. The shock of what followed in this case lay mostly in the speed and savagery of its escalation. Afterwards, there was a fair bit of carry-on about who could have done what, when, to whom, to excite such action – but I'll confess that, as irrational and unfair as it may sound, and though it can't really be said to have presaged anything, as soon as Baby looked up that cool night, and commanded my eye, and showed me how dangerous her desire was, how matter-of-fact her recklessness – I knew right then I could no longer be shocked by anything that touched her.

For Thuan it was already too late. First, it emerged that she'd been in contact with Red Cap, her ex, all along – that in fact he was her on-again off-again dealer. I saw my brother's face when he found out, felt the shock and deep retreat as though it were my own. He broke it off with her. She contacted me and pleaded her innocence. She was crying, and had never looked more beautiful. It was over, she said; she'd been clean the whole time, she said, and, still believing her, I passed it on. They reconciled. I was wracked with strong ambivalence seeing, even momentar-ily, my brother so vulnerable. A week later, a friend of mine spotted Baby in Sunshine with her other ex – the one who'd picked the first fight with my brother. I confronted her. At first she denied it, then she stopped short. It was impossible to go anywhere in a Vietnamese enclave without being noted – she understood that.

'Okay,' she sighed. 'I went there.'

I didn't say anything.

'I heard …' She paused, reconsidered. 'Him and his mates are planning an attack. A big one.'

'On who?'

'Johnny. My ex. And all the rest of his friends. Your friends too – the brothers.'

We were in her car, on our way to pick Thuan up from some-where, and she spoke straight ahead, into the busy windscreen.

'You know this? You gotta tell them.'

'I *don't* know.' She frowned, chewed at her lower lip. 'I know him. He just wants to be the big man. That's all it was, I just went there to ask him to stop all this.'

'What'd he say?'

She glanced over at me, and there was a small, strange crease around her eyes I hadn't seen before.

'He said he'd think about it.'

'Okay.'

She drove on a while, then, as though resolving some internal question, she swung her head from side to side. 'Big T, he wanted me to beg.'

All my life I've been told I'm not very good at reading people. There is, I think, some truth to this. Baby, in particular, was so changeable that any attempt would usually be offside and out of step. But in that moment, I was inspired by an intense insight to say nothing, to sit still and let her ravelled thinking tease itself out. In my concentration my face must have lapsed into a frown.

She looked over, cringed slightly. 'I guess you already know,' she murmured. 'I don't know what to do.'

'Do you wanna pull over? Talk about this?'

'I would *love* that.'

She pulled into a petrol station and parked by the air pump. Again, I waited for her to speak.

'You're sweet,' she said nervously. She tilted the rear-view mirror down and checked her face. Then she told me how, when she'd gone back to plead with her ex, one thing had led to another. Not like that. But she still wasn't sure how it had happened.

'What happened?'

She paused. 'I don't want your brother to think I'm a slut.' Her voice was small but quickly hardening. 'That's what he called me last time.'

We sat in silence as the car ticked. Slut. The word led me to the image of her bent over a wobbling suitcase, pants scrunched down to her knees. Sand and salt on her wet skin. The lie of the bikini on her body.

'Yeah but you did fuck him, didn't you?' I could feel my heart throttling my ribs as I thought this, and then, unbelievably – as I said it. Now the new word – the new image it called up – landed heavy and wet between us.

Baby jutted out her jaw. She jerked her head in my direction but didn't look at me. 'You can't … Look, it's not like I'm going out with *you*.'

'Right.'

'You can't talk to me like that.'

'Right. It's not like he's my brother. Like the last time you fucked around, who was it that patched everything up for you?'

She inhaled sharply. She said, 'I screwed up.' Then she turned to me, her face gone cunning. 'But what's the deal with you two anyway? What sort of fucked-up thing is that?' Her skin was clenched tight around the eyes, her jaw muscles working her thoughts. 'I don't even know why he lets you follow him around. Almost like he's scared of you or something. Like you've got some-thing on him – the way you've got something on me – 'cos that's what you do, right, Big T? Spy on everyone? Get all the dirt?'

As she spoke, the space inside the hatchback seemed to shrink. It was as though everything real, dimensional, was happening here, inside, while the windows were actually screens broadcast-ing a program of outside movement and colour. In this enclosure I became acutely aware of her smell – sweat from where her body had kneaded the seat, the chemical tang of her shampoo.

Without thinking I reached for her.

She flinched. 'I'm sorry,' she coughed, then, somewhat unsteadily, she undid her seatbelt, leaned forward, and peeled her cardigan off. I realised her cheeks were wet. I didn't know what I wanted. 'Sorry,' she repeated, and offered both her naked arms to me. She was sobbing now, quietly. And then I saw what it was she was trying to show me. The two dark mottled bands around her wrist, and two more around her biceps. The bruises yellow and orange and green, and myself enraptured and repulsed by them. The rot and ripe of them. Most strangely, I felt myself powerfully flushed with a sense that I only much later recognised – and ultimately accepted – as betrayal.

I told my brother a friend had seen her go into the ex's house. I told him to ask her himself. I told him – thinking he'd be happy to hear it – that this ex was gearing up for a major attack against the Footscray crew. I told him my source was unimpeachable.

*

The afternoon, finally, is cooling down when Thuan returns. He catches me half-naked in the kitchen. 'I've washed up in plenty of kitchen sinks,' he assures me. He's carrying a slab of Carlton Bitter under one arm and holding a supermarket bag in the other. 'Meat,' he explains, 'for the barbie.'

'Where'd you go?'

He ignores me, sets the bag down, rips a couple of cans out of their tight plastic trap. When he throws me a beer I realise it's exactly what I feel like. The rest of the cans he tips into an esky. By silent consensus we head outside and sit on the deck. Through the gums and melaleucas, the thick pelt of scrub and sedge along its banks, the river is light brown, slow, milky. This river that famously flows upside down. The day's heat hangs in the air but is no longer suffocating. The brightness no longer angry. We finish the beers, and then the next ones, and the next. I hadn't realised how thirsty I was. He tells me he walked along the river, up to the falls. He saw kayakers there, rehearsing their moves, and uni students doing water tests. He stops, losing interest in his own story. I picture the concrete-capped, rubbish-choked weir, the graffitied basalt boulders, all dominated by the Eastern Freeway roaring overhead. I wonder whether it brought to his mind another river – the same river – running beside and below a different freeway. I wonder whether, when he stares out at this river now, he connects it to that other river a few Ks dead south of here; if he follows it, in his mind's eye, through its windings and loops, through Collingwood, and Abbotsford, and Richmond, and Burnley – to South Yarra.

He throws me another beer. The barbeque is all but forgotten. I'm getting a bit dreamy with alcohol, my mind draggling in the heat.

'So what's going on with you anyway?'

'What?' I say, even though I heard him. I have no idea why I said this. I start to audition sentences to make my answer over but this only affirms the silence. My brother snorts, then hoists his drink in a wry toast. I skol my can, stand up and torpedo it into the bush. I'll pick it up later. A pair of rowers glance at us from the river and wave.

'Jesus,' my brother says, 'I really screwed her up.'

'Nothing you could have done. She was on edge the whole time.' After my last chance, I'm now eager to speak. 'Probably junk too. And those friends of hers – in Footscray.'

'What?' His brow creases. 'Nah, I meant Mum.' He looks at me curiously for a second, then scoffs at himself. 'Though her too, I guess.'

I recall a story Baby told me during her last visit, how a friend of hers in detention had collapsed from withdrawal; the male guards had grabbed her, double-cuffed her, stuck a motorbike helmet on her head for two days so she couldn't 'hurt herself.'

'Mum still going up to that temple?'

He'd come back from jail and I'd fantasised about receiving his confidences. He'd copped the time for both of us – knowing, surely, that I would've done the same. But he hadn't grown more open at all. Nor the couple of other times he'd visited. Only this time seemed different. This was the most communicative I'd ever seen him.

'In Sunshine? I think so.' He doesn't react, so I go on, 'I think once she ran into one of the families there. I heard one of them spat in her face.'

He nods absently. 'And you? You okay?'

The side-stepped directness of his question stuns me. I saunter my arm out along the view. 'What's not to be okay about?'

'Listen,' he says. 'Can I ask you something?'

'What?'

'That stuff Mum said about you doing talks.'

'It's nothing. Just uni stuff.' I feel myself smirking. 'They just need someone with slanty eyes who can speak in their language.'

'What sort of stuff do you say?'

'You know – just whatever they wanna hear.'

'Like what?'

'Like poverty, or language issues. Cultural marginalisation …'

'They don't ask about what happened that night?'

'You mean do I talk about you.'

He shakes his head impatiently. He's working himself up to something and it puts me on edge. 'I mean, don't they ask why? Why I did it? I mean, isn't all the rest of it bullshit?'

'Why *we* did it. I was there too.'

'Yeah,' he says, visibly annoyed at having been interrupted. 'You're right. I forget. I'm sorry.' I wait for him to go on but now I've mucked up his thinking. 'It's all bullshit,' he says again, struggling to recall his argument, and out of some old fraternal deference I find myself looking away. I listen to the frogs gulping for air down by the rushes. The black ducks and reed warblers. My heart is beating harder and harder. I know, of course, what he's referring to – it's the same thing that brings him here each time, then each time strikes him silent: the mind-boggling bullshit of *me*, years on, still with nothing but time, still cashing in, ever more deeply, on *his* time. Those twelve bullshit years piled on the back of a single night's spur of the moment. That night, too, I'd felt the same sick, heady exhilaration talking to him like this – like we were friends.

'You're shaking,' he had pointed out. We'd made it home and both showered; he'd scrubbed his face, I noticed, until it was bright pink. The corners of his temple lined with delicate blue veins.

'I can't piss. My bladder feels heavy as, but nothing comes out.'

He'd frowned, then reached out and clutched my neck with one of his strong pink hands. I knew the strength of those hands. My stomach hitched. He didn't say anything, and at the physical contact I was shuddered back to our surreal, silent trip in the car; the fog descending upon the freeway canyons, the red blinking lights of radio towers blooming like blood corollas in the mist. The streets had sucked us through the city and shot us home.

'If they come for us,' my brother had said to me.

'No one saw us.'

'You weren't there. If they come for us, you weren't there.'

'Hai and Long and Quang saw me.'

'No they didn't. I'll talk to them.'

'What about you?'

'No matter what they say – so-and-so saw you, so-and-so ratted you out. Don't listen to them. You weren't there.'

'What about you?'

He patted my neck, then removed his hand. The absence was a freezing burn. He was my rough flesh, he was rooted in the same soil, his heart and brain fed by the same blood, and never before had I felt so needful of him. He stood up and abruptly grimaced, clutching his right knee. Then his face smoothed over again. 'I don't think anyone who saw me will talk,' he said. 'But it shouldn't take them long. To find out about the Ngos. And then me.'

'You mean Baby?'

He nodded, then let out a short burst of air.

'What?'

'I'm not saying she'll talk,' he said.

'She's the one who called me.'

To this day I remember how, when I told him this, he'd shaken his head and smiled. 'I know,' he'd said, as though unexpectedly amused. 'Everything always goes back to Baby.' Now it is summer, my brother sits with me on the deck of my own house and his face, sweaty and cooked well past pink, confirms itself in that same expression – bemused, sardonic, slightly otherwise occupied.

'Listen to me,' he says. 'I'm glad you didn't have to go down with me.' His tone is flat with finality. 'That was the best thing that happened this whole mess.'

'Okay.'

'That was the opposite of bullshit.'

'I'm sorry.'

He waves it off. The light is dimming now and he turns away, but not before I catch a brief tensile movement in his expression. There's a discipline holding his face together. I'm horrified by the sudden realisation that maybe he's lying to me. 'But see,' he goes on, 'what I mean is this. I was there, you were there. I don't remember hardly anything. I was off my head but still.' He pauses, perhaps suspicious of his own earnestness. Neither of us looks at the other. 'Haven't you tried to think about it, why we did it, and you can't tell what's what?'

I decide, in the brief silence that follows, that he's not actually asking me this question.

'What happened,' he goes on, 'and what everyone else says that happened?'

My face has reverted to its little-brother mask – imploring his censure and contempt, his instruction.

'You'd think you'd remember everything.'

I nod. I approximate a wry sound. Then I venture, 'I do. I do remember.'

He stops to absorb this. Then slowly, and to my great relief, his face slides back into its ironic smile. 'Well, you have to. Otherwise, who's gonna give those bloody speeches?'

*

That night. I remembered that night very clearly. I'd been at a different club. They'd all gone to Jade – another Asian night – and I hated Asian nights. Too many try-hards, too much attitude. I was in the toilets when I got the call. There was a guy next to me pissing with both hands in his pockets. It was one of the most intimidating things I'd ever seen. I was pretty buzzed by that time, and when I answered the phone, Baby's tinny laughing was of a piece with the cackling going on and off in one of the stalls, and then – out in the club – the DJ's chop to a bass-heavy loop, the dewy, overripe smell of teenage girls. I found a quieter corner so I could hear her.

'Swords!' she was saying. Then I realised she wasn't laughing. 'They've got fucking swords!'

Outside, it was drizzling. I ran down the road, past the shawled girls with clopping heels, the corners and culverts reeking of piss, the darkened power poles specked with staples. Overhead, the wet telephone wires gleamed completely gold in the streetlight, like charged filaments, even though my mind insisted on them as black, sheathed in black plastic. I reached the car, which I'd parked at a defunct petrol station – now just a low, flat, broken roof spewing water onto the oil-stained concrete. As soon as I stopped running, I vomited. I got in the car and caught my breath. I called Baby. She didn't answer. I called my brother.

'Fuck,' he panted. 'Fucking fuck.'

'What happened? Where are you?'

He was running, his breath loud and jagged. The wind took his voice. There was no time to explain. He told me where to pick him up, down near the river. It was only a few minutes away. I arrived at the corner of Church and Alexandra. Across the road from the brightly lit car dealership, human shapes were scampering in every direction. They were all guys, all Asians –

some carrying glinting weapons and cudgels. I saw one pull down the beak of his baseball cap over his eyes. Not daring to stop, I slowed the car as I passed, made out what looked like a small pile of dirty clothes on the nature strip. Then I saw, pale and inverted, the telltale hand. There was no blood. The head must have been concealed by a piece of flapping fabric, or maybe the ground fell away. There was nothing to indicate a body that had been smashed and stabbed to bits, but even then I knew that was what I was looking at, and the knowledge rocked in my skull, riled up my blood.

I drove on a bit further and parked on the grassy shoulder, making sure to turn off the engine and lights. I took out my phone, my hands trembling, saw three missed calls from Baby. I tried her again but again no one answered. Then the phone rang. My brother. Where was I? I told him what I'd seen, we had to get the fuck out of there. Not yet. Where was I? Okay, I should meet him on the other side of the bridge. When? Now. Right now.

I got out of the car. The wind had picked up, gusting sideways on my face. I spat and could see my slag sail forever. Behind me the faux-gothic columns of Melbourne High School were upwardly lit. I crossed the road to the riverbank and ran along the bike path, under bare tree boughs creaking and contending in the wind. Some distance ahead of me, windows in condominium buildings glowed in what seemed secret patterns. I ran into the wind. A car bore down on me, its headlights tunnelling through the thickening fog, changing the shape of the road. It passed in a vicious swipe of noise. By the time I reached the body, which had been left strangely unattended, a veneer had been ripped away within me, an innate excuse brought full-blooded to life. I crossed the bridge.

My brother was three-quarters across. He wore an open-necked shirt as though it wasn't the heart of winter, and leaned against a lamp-lit column as though bored, as though waiting for a late tram. As soon as I reached him he spun around without a word and sprinted down some white-glowing stairs that led to the north bank of the river. There was another track down there, squeezed between the Monash Freeway on one side and the river on the other.

I can't tell you what it felt like, racing through the cold night with my brother. On our right the concrete-and-plastic freeway barricade flickering our progress, on our left the river, and beneath us the paved path springing our feet forward and fast. The wind kicking at our backs. At no point did I second guess what we were doing. I spent my life waiting for him to talk me into something and now the wash of adrenaline through my veins urged me on, faster and faster, as though to chase down, catch my own breath. A voice floated across the river. My brother slowed down, then stopped. His face haggard with exertion but steely, the set of his jaw exuberant.

I turned, breathing heavily, towards the voice. Under the high moon, the river was a trough of light and it was difficult to see behind it. Then I saw. There were two black shapes in the shine. In the darkness opposite there were three more shapes. I soon recognised their voices – the three elder Ngos. They spat and swore into the river.

'Who are they?' I asked, pointing to the two black heads bobbing next to each other. 'Is that Baby's ex?'

Thuan nodded. 'And his brother.'

The two of them seemed to roll and ride over each other on the same spot of river. Every now and then an arm would flail up. Their occasional cries made no sense.

'They're pissed as,' I said.

'Swim over here,' Hai sang out. 'I dare you, come on.'

'Jesus,' I said. 'He's got a fucking samurai sword.'

Instinctively I turned to Thuan and saw, for the first time, his fist gripping a meat cleaver. Looking more closely, I noticed his pants gashed above one knee. His sock beneath that knee was discoloured by blood; on his other foot the sock was white. My lungs filled with air.

'Please,' one of the swimmers beseeched. His voice was low and shaky.

Then, as though they'd just made us out, the two of them began to splash their way towards our bank. My brother looked on impassively. A mist was beginning to settle over the water and the faster swimmer side-stroked awkwardly beneath it.

'That's him,' my brother murmured.

The swimmer came closer. His mouth was wild above and

below the water, his eyes blinking non-stop. Vapour sputtering from between his teeth.

'Please,' he croaked.

I watched my brother for weakness.

'He can't swim. My brother can't swim.'

'Don't come any closer,' Thuan said. 'You had your chance.'

'Fuck him up,' Hai shouted from the other bank.

'What chance? Oh God. Oh God, oh God, oh fuck.'

The icy water weighted his clothes, forcing him to kick hard to stay afloat. Behind him, his brother moved more erratically. I could hear him hyperventilating loudly.

'Please,' Baby's ex said. 'Please, he can't swim. He's got asthma. Please, it's enough.'

My brother shook his head.

'She's not worth it, man. Oh God.'

My brother looked at him again, paying new attention. He murmured, 'You don't talk about Baby.'

Baby's ex started moaning. He swallowed some water, thrashed around for a moment. Then, lifting his face and staring directly at us, he kicked in our direction, desperately dragging his body to one of the beams supporting the walking path. He clutched the edge, then tried to lift himself up, his eyes wild and goggly. As soon as I saw him close up – the thick, straight hair, the snub face and buck teeth – I knew him, and I knew that I hated him. Jeers and catcalls wafted over through the mist. Thuan kicked at him but Baby's ex grabbed his ankle. My brother tried to stomp him with his other leg but it was the injured one, and Baby's ex clung on fiercely, fixedly. Hopping in a weird dance, my brother took a handful of his wet hair in one hand, raised the meat cleaver in the other. He looked at it. Then he looked at me and there was an odd new uncertainty in his expression. I drank in that look. It fed my heart roar, my blood rapids. I was filled with strange rage and I wanted to be as big as my feeling. I accepted the meat cleaver from my brother's outstretched hand, fell down in a swift crouch, the ground rearing up at my shins, and felt my arm go back and then forward, the blade biting into the wet jacket, and when Baby's ex released my brother's foot and hung on to the path's edge, I worked the blade at his fingers until they too let go.

They drifted, in a weakening, wordless flurry, back out to the middle of the river. At one point the river raised the legs of the brother, and he lay on his back, head bent forward, looking at the evidence of his body as though in disbelief. To this day people wonder why they didn't swim a few more metres to the west, where they might easily have held onto a leg or abutment of the railway bridge. Or back eastward, to the Church Street bridge. Further east yet, they could have struck out for Herring Island, accessible only by water, and made sanctuary there. As it happened, they stayed in the deep middle of the Yarra. They were drunk, injured, freezing, one asthmatic and unable to swim, and after some desperate horseplay and muffled splashing their eyes went loose and their bodies calm, as though their feet had finally found a shelf in the water, and then they sank, their bodies spinning in slow dark minutes of motion, and they did not re-emerge until two days later when the police divers dragged them out.

My brother bent down at the path's edge. The new silence rendered the brothers' moments-ago breathing clotted and monstrous in its memory. Thuan took off his shoes, dipped them into the slow-moving river, then took them out and wrung the blood and water out of them. He dipped them in, took them out, and wrung them again. Our shoulders touched and pushed off each other as we ran back to the car.

*

'What else do you say?'

'I talk about revenge. Honour. Loyalty and betrayal.'

'That's all bullshit too.'

'Not to me it isn't.'

'Wouldn't you rather just forget everything?'

'I wouldn't change a thing.'

'More bullshit. This is what you want? This life?'

'I'd do it again.'

'Why?'

'For you. Because you couldn't. Because you wanted to.'

'I didn't know what I wanted. It was stupid. Jesus, it's easy for you to say.'

'No it's not.'

'You didn't cop the twelve years.'

'That's why you came back?'

'No.'

'To rub that in my face?'

'No.'

'Sorry.'

'Actually.'

'I would've done that, I would've copped it.'

'Actually, I came back to ask for your forgiveness.'

'What?'

'You heard me.'

'You don't have to. I told you I'd do it again.'

'That's what I mean. I'm sorry I made you that way.'

*

The next morning he was gone. In hot February my brother came back to me, and stayed for only two nights and one day. I haven't seen him since. My life, such as it is, I owe to him. If guilt is for what you've done and shame for who you are, then how could I feel shame? I was a brother, and my brother's brother. Forget, he tells me, but does he taste them in his tap water, the savour of their hair and skin in his herbs? They too were brothers. Melbourne's in drought. The city a plain of dust and fire. The river hasn't water enough to wash the foreign matter out.

I have my work, and my garden, my mother in her glassy lone-liness to attend. I have my mornings. Who knows if he'll come back? I have my dreams, too, which have come to seem coexten-sive with my memories. My sleep is shallow, and my dreams never seem to go all the way down. I step out of my night window and the river wipes the field before me, a smear of silver noise, the great fishes climbing the water by the plate-glass glint of their eyes, in their indigo and orange glows, mastering the dark. I am underneath, plunging as the grey scrim of surface blackens above me. Breathe, lungs, and let me time. We live our lives atop the body of emotion of which we're capable. I follow my dim thought-embryos, I see by my feeling, I sink with my words, for words are shadow, and shadow cannot explain light.

Where've you been.

You started a thought and you could end up anywhere. Like

watching a fire: its false grabs and reachings, its licks and twists, you stared into the guts of it and came out in the nightlight glow of a shared childhood room, the cheap groan of a bunk bed, you're awake and listening to the breath snagging in your brother's nostrils, the low whistle of his open-mouthed sleep, the insideness of his life and its promise of protection from the harmful world outside.

Where've you been. You're late.

He's dragging a suitcase into the street. He makes it all the way out of the driveway, to the cherry tree, before I stop him. The air is full of pollen and sunscreen. He emerges from the concrete tunnel with a rueful smile on his face. He's bent over me on the couch – he rooted in his terrible motion and I in him.

I'm sorry I'm sorry I'm sorry.

I bite the red cushion. I feel his ribs on my ribs. My body an anvil and he's beating something upon it, shaping it into a truer shape, seeking to prove it, the strength, the ductility, the temper of his love.

Brothers and Sisters

Goodness Gracious Hello

Tim Herbert

Roland was feeling lucky on Google, looking for secrets on Facebook, browsing the Web for Mary Jane, the girl who told the world.

Mary Jane Gulliver, still the face he knew, though back then she was a Livermore, a Jannali A-Grader with a lethal backhand down the line, a double-grip on her father's catgut Slazenger. They lived on Binalong Avenue, a battle-axe block with the stump of a chook yard at the back of their quarter acre. Through rusting chicken wire to a few abandoned nesting boxes, a millet bin and a stringy-bark from which Mary Jane and Roland would swing the fence to land on council property: a pair of recently laid tennis courts. A dismount onto unforgiving asphalt and a discernible lump beyond the service line. Roland the only boy who knew the secret of what lay underneath, how Mary Jane had finally resisted the sting of a fly swatter across her legs and grappled with her mother, breaking the plastic handle clean off. The daughter gathered up the parts. In time would pick her moment and give Roland the privilege of bearing witness. A symbolic burial on a molten summer's day.

Roland had his secrets too. The diary he received at Christmas. His big brothers had teased him. A girly thing. In the chook yard, Mary Jane listened and examined as an eleven-year-old boy expounded on the muted floral pattern and the edging of solid brass, like the rivets of the lock and the keyhole too.

But Mary Jane soon found a flaw. She slipped an index finger behind the security clasp, testing the re-inforced cardboard. He can still see her on those sticky afternoons. Feel her. All vibration like those cicadas, the shrill song of the furrowed bark. She would sit alongside him on the stringy-bark branch, peering over his shoulder in her white tennis dress. Skin flushing above the neck to his serious flow of words. When Easter came, Roland's diary was half full of entries. On Good Friday, she led him away. Reckoned there was a nest of Argentine ants inside her father's dilapidated shed. Mary Jane saw the bare globe was fading, so she located a torch, only to lag once Roland's knees dipped to oily concrete.

A searchlight over slaters and dottle beneath Doug Livermore's lathe, Roland probing with an offcut, brushing back the cobwebs while Mary Jane swept up the diary. No need for a key with a wrist like hers.

He searched for hours to find her, uncovering just the diary, flung into the millet bin, the clasp broken with a page torn out. Roland could laugh about it now, the misadventure, the betrayal. He should never have boasted about being a writer, of being taken by the muse, though most of what was contained in his round, legible hand had been gossip from the neighbourhood, snide notes about his illiterate brothers and about the Livermores themselves, how they served up grits and leftovers and home-made ice-cream that tasted like rancid buttermilk.

Mary Jane would have found a reason to justify, always defending her family, making claims. Like the one about her father being a Spitfire ace over Europe. Roland had recorded everything, the shuffling in his seat, the crossing of arms, the baulking at his brazen question: 'Did you really shoot down six Messerschmitts in the war, Mr Livermore?'

In the end it was his daughter who strafed the air and dived low for the kill. Roland's confessional a schoolyard auto-da-fé. Grilled for a song to the lock forward in the football team, to the long-limbed school captain with the beautiful eyes of palest blue. Roland saw all of him in the change rooms at the swimming carnival, the curlicues of pubic hair, the Donatello bottom. Scripted everything in black and white with a pencil sketch of him mounting the blocks of the pool. A boy roiling in the blue deeps as his classmates sent the page around. Grabbing and tearing and soiling until the teacher intervened, but enough for Roland to be·bullied until his last day of primary school.

Mary Jane ended up at a different high school with a quick-silver gang and a glam rock induction. Roland had crept up a gutter pipe in the night, spied through a blazing side window and found Gary Glitter posted up and staring out from every wall of Mary Jane's bedroom. And then at the railway station he saw her, six-inch platforms and electric-blue flares, staked in a huddle of satin-sheen girlfriends, parroting the chorus to 'Hello, Hello, I'm Back Again.'

*

Goodness gracious, hello Mary Jane
Message sent

She had pages of friends on Facebook and Roland was just a novice who was sceptical of this new social interface.

Roland Finkel hello. Goodness gracious Gary Glitter? I should know the song. I've added you to my list. It must be 30 years!

He was Mary Jane's friend again now. His very first friend on Facebook. Mary Jane's wall posts were criss-crossed with numerous links to other websites. He would amuse her by posting the YouTube original of 'Hello, Hello, I'm Back Again.' Gary poking out his fat tongue, baring his chest alongside his prancing Glitter Band in silver suits and a star-shaped guitar. But then that link to a Christian rock website had him reconsider. Stryper. Petra. Sonic Martyr. Blessthefall.

He scrolled through those other icons and profile photos. Mary Jane's friends and family. Even her father was there, a tight smile in an air-force uniform. Roland clicked the publisher's hypertext. All about a poor boy from Tarcutta, who kept his bare feet warm in winter, the squelch of fresh cow pats in a misty pad-dock. A memoir about a Spitfire ace. For Doug had worked through his demons. A daredevil blurb about fear at 10,000 feet above France, of low fuel and a spluttering engine and of several mates not returning.

Roland surveyed a handful of photos but the medals and stripes were thin on the ground. Simply young Doug with a buzz cut and pipe. Such a modest line in honour and glory and Roland felt the hairs tingling. There was regret certainly, to not have believed, but he had only been a kid in that adult zone of repressed urges and sublimation. Instinct and observation, that was the child's metier, though Roland could see his own failing on that score. Never before had he noticed the colour of Doug Livermore's eyes, almost identical to those of the school captain, to Gary Glitter himself – an arresting, pale blue.

Mary Jane had four children. Roland clicked top to bottom. The daughter must be the real rock chick. A photo of her scrambling out of some moshpit for Jesus in a black T-shirt and a dangling crucifix. 'The praise pit was awesome,' said the caption and there was a link to rapture.com. There was no Armageddon prophecy from the twin brothers even if they did share a Mormon glaze, their lips thin and unforgiving. The posts from the twins were in scattergun Gen-Y argot, though Roland got the drift about their epic hangovers, towelheads on Cronulla beach ('Osama don't surf') and digs at their kid brother Anthony, twirling around the lounge room to *Dancing with the Stars*.

Roland scrolled straight to Anthony. Turning thirteen next month. Roland saw a long-limbed lock forward coming to life, though ballroom dancing was this boy's favourite thing. He even had a Yahoo link to an AFL player, the celebrity winner from season five of the television dance show. Anthony Koutoufides. Young Anthony's blog was there too. His own hot-pink heading as infectious as a high five. Mad about Paso Doble. Salsa. Jive. A radiant smile and those blue eyes, not pale but closer to cobalt, like daedal pools of beauty and grace.

Grace. Despite the knocks, Roland liked to think it was still his to carry. A concern that young Anthony might be tripped up, defeated in a family like that one. Unless he was the one to confound them all. Roland was not asking to be godfather. Not guardian or life coach either, though something more daring than acquaintance or guide. To lure Anthony away from the beaten track. Help find his feet among the stars.

You must be friends with Anthony Bassenthwaite to see his full profile

Roland considered the options:

Add as Friend; Send a Message; View Friends

He did not say much on the message. An old friend of his mother's. That was kind of a lie considering he revelled as her enemy for many years after. The claim that his niece was a huge fan of *Dancing with the Stars* was a falsehood too, though Roland expressed a genuine delight about the many coloured fonts the boy splashed across his blog page. Outasight. That was the lad's tagline and Roland wished he had a smart one of his own. Unreal, Anthony. Was that still the patois for a young adolescent?

After three days there was no response. Not from Mary Jane nor Anthony. And then a revelation:

hi roland funny thats our cats name ... well its always been the cats name and this one is roland the third
i didnt tell my mum about your message though ive heard about you before from mum who reckons you are a writer
can you dance too?

Roland was laughing in his chair. He felt exultant. What a brilliant young fellow. The sense of humour, the curiosity about a man more than thirty years his senior. Only a small obstacle in not being a writer, not since those days in the chook yard at least. Roland had to admit that being an architectural draughtsman sounded a bit pedestrian. Maybe he could keep on pretending. After all, Mary Jane seemed to cherish the idea of his being a writer. Roland even suspected some conflation of guilt about that day in the schoolyard, the day when she unveiled that page from his own diary. So he would send a message to Mary Jane. Ask her to join him and Maxy, the retired song-and-dance man, for lunch in the studio. Don't forget to bring Anthony.

Roland was beginning to feel that as the thread played out, everything gathered to heal, that the human world was benevolent at heart and that even Facebook was part of the mystery.

'Hello, hello, tell all of your friends,' sang Gary Glitter. 'I'm back, I'm back as a matter of fact, I'm back.'

The verse was running through Roland's mind when he logged on again that evening. A matter of fact on his Facebook page.

The profile photos were gone. The promise was gone.

Roland has no friends

The Notorious Mrs K.

Dorothy Simmons

Benalla Ensign, 21 October 1871
Benalla Police Court, Tuesday, 17 October, before Mr Butler, PM
Ellen Kelly v. William Frost
Mr McDonnell for complainant, Mr Pow for defendant

Smile away, smile away: smarmy bugger that you are. What I ever saw …

That's it, keep those weevilly eyes slipping and sliding, every which way but mine. Now why would that be? Come on, Bill, look at me. Fine upstanding citizen like yourself, all done up in your best Sunday-go-to-meeting suit: surely you can look a poor widow woman in the eye …

Can't, can you? Not so long, though, Billy boy, not so long since you couldn't keep your eyes off me, never mind your hands. Look at you: hair all neatly combed over your bald spot, pink snags of fingers squeezing your hat half to death: scared, aren't you? Scared your lady customers won't be coming to you for their best topside roast any more, isn't that it? Real butcher's hands that they are too, sawing the mouths off your poor horses, reefing them in to plunge and leap and make you look flash. Jesus, if you'd been on your own two feet that first time I saw you, we'd not be here this day. But you were up on that lovely grey mare, spitting image of my Red's Misty …

Those were the days. Red on Misty and me on my own Nellie,

cantering down the Melbourne road to St Francis's church at first light, and the priest stood smiling at the altar; riding back with a ring on my finger and the whole world shining. Those were the days ... Every man and his dog out celebrating the independence of Port Phillip, the independence of us: singing 'It's a Long Way to Tipperary,' racing the last mile home ...

My own Tipperary man, Red Kelly: and a thousand times the man you'll ever be, Bill Frost. Poor soul, the grog buried him long before I ever did ... but even blind drunk, even when he couldn't have bitten his own thumb, he'd never have come creepy-crawling around like you, Billy boy. What, ten quid and a horse if I'd drop the case? That's all you thought I was worth? Or never mind me, your own baby daughter: ten lousy quid?

Forgotten, have you? Well, I haven't: galloping into our yard, your horse in a lather and yourself the same, couldn't wait to get your hands on me. Soft touch that I was; not like that Bridget Cotter. Hard as nails, that one. Only one kind of screwing for her, screwing a ring onto her fat finger ...

There she is, set down next to you: Mrs Lady Butcher ma'am, with her paisley shawl and her shiny black beads. Did you ever see the like? Mutton, mutton dressed as lamb. Stick a sprig of mint in her gob and you'd never know the difference. *Jack Sprat could eat no fat, his wife could eat no lean ... and so between them both, you see, they scraped the platter clean ... between them both*, hear that, Billy boy? It takes two; tell that to your side of lamb dressed up in her best bib and tucker. As for that poker-faced bitch set next to her, that's the same constipated cow as took one look at me coming down Bridge Street and sent all her good lady friends scuttling across the road, hands over their mouths like I was some sort of contagious disease ...

No surprises, of course. Annie, with your moaning and groaning about what I was in for, did you think I didn't know? That I needed my own daughter to tell me? Look at them: just look at them with their corsets and their net gloves and their lace collars, they're flesh and blood for all that. Same as me. 'Fallen' woman? Tripped is more like it, and I'll bloody trip him ...

Yesterday we had an adjournment. Big word for putting off. Had they nothing better to do? But Mr Pow had witnesses to call. Conjure, more like. Mine have come of their own accord,

I've had no need of adjournment. Get on with it, that's what I say.

The entire congregation's here: gents all shaved and spat and polished, ladies with their frills and fringes, sighing and sucking and shaking their heads. The McBeans, that McCormick woman, Whelans, Halls: that Constable Flood. Now there's another smarmy bugger ...

It's a wonder the ladies would be seen in the same room. The Notorious Mrs Kelly: I could be catching. Like the pregnancy, I hear that's contagious. Jesus, the looks of some of them, it'd want to be an immaculate bloody contagion. As if the Victorian police aren't righteous enough without their womenfolk setting themselves up in holy orders, holier than thou or me or any bloody one.

Steady, Nell, steady. Calm yourself. What's the only difference between you and them? You took a man at his word. More fool you.

How would they cope, with their picket fences and their geraniums and their doilies, how would they cope with snakes and poddy calves and clearing land? Never mind raising a family. Oh, Ned does his damndest when he's there; but most of the time he's not.

It's only natural. A woman needs a man, a man needs a woman. Somebody to have and to hold. To lose him ... cuts the heart out of you.

You carry on, of course. No choice. But a hand with the fencing or the splitting gives you one less thing to worry about; a squeeze of your hand or a smiley word brightens you up; and at the end of the day it's easy to close your eyes just for a minute, let him stroke your hair back from your forehead ...

At least I know how to love. Which is more that this congregation of buttoned lips and boned bodices ever will. A gold band and a cold hand: what they get and what they give. Oh, and reputation. Pass the reputation please. Pillars of the church, every last one of them. No wonder our constables are the miserable mongrels they are, squashed up next to a bloody pillar all night.

I could have been Mrs Frost. Mrs Frost, she'd have had to be a pillar too, swapping recipes and pruning roses, tittupping along the road on some sway-backed lady's hack. Jesus, I wouldn't last a day! No, I'm well out of it. But that doesn't let you off the hook, Billy boy; bad enough that an innocent bairn gets branded bastard instead of you. Still can't look me in the eye, can you? Well, I'll look you, I'll damn well make sure at least baby Ellen gets a fair go ...

A fair go: all we've ever wanted. Same as anybody else.

Adjournment: when was the last time they adjourned sooling the law onto the Kellys? And what sort of a law is it when you give a man a bite to eat and a taste of whisky and next thing the lick-spittle rat's reported you for selling grog? Ah but the Law, the big bloody 'L' Law, the Law's for everybody. Not just for squatters with their long acres. The Law is set down in black and white; it's printed out in the Matrimonial Statute. God help the child, she's yours as well as mine, Bill. The least you can do is provide for her.

Will the first witness for the plaintiff please step up ...

Head up, Annie, love, that's it! Hand on the Bible, tell them the truth. That's it.

Poor soul, struggling along without her Alex, and their first baby dead in her cot. Like my own Mary Jane, all those years ago. You never forget, never. I can still see the wee face, still feel how cold ... but you carry on. You have to.

No point just moping till the boys get home. No point in just giving up the ghost. You'll get no thanks for that. Ask Ned. If the Kellys know nothing else, they know to stand up for themselves because sure as hell nobody else is going to. It's like the song: *Oh, what can a man do when the world is his foe ... but bend the brow bravely and go away far, to follow good fortune, and get home in the war ...*

It's a war all right.

Thank you, Mrs Gunn, you may stand down.

Ma knew it'd be like this. I warned her, I did. You sure you want to go through with it, the naming, the shaming? I've no call to be shamed, says she. I'm a Quinn and a Kelly and proud of it. Dear Ma: the straight back of her, chin up, spark in the eye: no stopping her once she gets that spark. Thought you were on to a good thing, didn't you, Bill Frost? God's gift to women, she'd be so pleased, so grateful ... no. Not my mother. Not Ellen Kelly.

A congregation, Ma called it: and so it is. That Bridget's face would curdle milk. If you didn't know better, you'd think Ma was the defendant, not the complainant. The complainant, Mrs Kelly. Kelly. That's it. The name. When're they ever going to listen to a Kelly? She'd have been better off taking the ten quid.

Maggie says it's our new sister we've to think of, little Ellen, that the child's not to blame for her father. Maggie's Ma all over again. Heart of a lion. I get too agitated ...

Why does everything always have to go wrong? Alex, you fool, why'd you have to get caught? Three years: how am I going to manage for three years? Women can't shift loads and fell trees. What am I going to do?

All Ma wanted was a man about the place again: bit of comfort for her, bit of help with the boys, bit of security. Did everything for him, cooked, stitched, gave him a warm bed; bugger didn't know when he was well off. Damn him to hell for the liar and cheat that he is ...

The nerve of her: I could never speak out like that. But that's her. Any time her boys were in trouble, she was there too, tearing strips off whoever was there to tear strips off. Got them off more than once as well. But I've never seen her so set on winning as she is this time ...

God, I wish Ned was here. He'd make them take notice. To think of him, him and my Alex, eating their hearts out inside those cold grey walls: it's enough to make you weep. Weep: women must weep. Sometimes I think that's all they bloody do ...

Where's your fighting spirit, Annie? That's Ma. Or Maggie: we can't take this lying down, Annie. Too bloody right, goes Ma, that's what got me into this mess in the first place. You have to laugh ...

Dear Ma. Look at her now, chin up, taking in every word Mr McDonnell's saying. Matrimonial Statute: the legal responsibility of the defendant ...

Mr Pow will now open the case for the defendant ...

You wouldn't believe a word of it. The nerve of her, answering Mr Pow back like that: brazen. Absolutely brazen. Contradicting him without so much as a blush! Running that shanty out at Eleven Mile: there's more than sly grog on offer there, that's for sure. Riding astride: if that's not a red rag to a bull, I don't know what is.

Red rag to a Bill. Wait till I get him home, I'll give him Simson's boundaries; it weren't no boundaries he was riding. Wouldn't put it past him to have scuffed his boots on purpose.

Not that you can blame him, really. It's the old Adam; they can't help themselves. Woman like that, flaunting herself: rolls the eyes, flashes the ankle and he's gone. Hopeless. They're all the same. At least this'll teach him, once and for all. Your wild oats are well and truly sown, William, and don't you forget it.

She's showing her colours now. Oh yes, stamp the foot, toss the head! What, swore he'd make an honest woman of you, did he? Don't you shrug your shoulders at me, Bill Frost, you're not done sleeping on that sofa yet …

Reliable witnesses? What reliable witness would be seen dead next nor near Eleven Mile Creek? Her and those larrikin sons of hers, you can tell the way they've been dragged up … that poor Julia McCormick. Face on fire, only telling the story. No wonder she gets palpitations. Not that the sight of blood worries me, being a butcher's wife; but to untie the parcel that's put in your hands and be looking at a set of calves' testicles! Hacked off, balls stuck together, all black blood and flies. With a note to cap it all: *Go tie these to Jeremiah's cock and you'll maybe get a decent shag out of him.* Decent? Those Kellys wouldn't know the meaning of the word.

That judge hit the nail on the head, him with the big nose and dopey looking eyes. Sir Redmond Barry. Offenders, he called them, offenders who oppressed respectable inhabitants. Like me. Or Julia. He said they were murderers every one, that it was the authorities' duty to exact vengeance and instil the fear of God into them. Just so, say I. Just so!

I mean to say, what decent woman would stand up in court and sue for her own bastard? Is it anything but flaunting herself and what she did to get it? A mockery of marriage and decent women, that's all it is. And her a Catholic baptised! How she can walk into church and raise her eyes to the Blessed Mother of God …

There's some cold cuts and a nice bit of pickle for lunch. That leftover potato, I'll make some potato bread. At least you're sure of the potatoes over here, not got the blight to worry about. Six months, they said, for the ship with the mail; what wouldn't I give to see their faces when they hear I'm married!

Apparently her people, the Quinns, they're from the North. Ulster. Maybe that explains it.

It appears to the Bench that men who are so foolish as to give rein to their carnal desires cannot be immune to the consequences of their indulgence. They must expect a penalty for their actions. Clearly, the plaintiff was also in fault for allowing such advances; however, as the defendant is in a position to contribute to the child's support, the defendant is ordered to pay five shillings a week for two years, with seven pounds, two shillings and six pence cost; further, to find two securities of twenty pounds each to ensure fulfilment of the order.

*

'Here's to your very good health, Mrs Kelly. Death to the Saxon!'

'Thank you, my friends, thank you! I'll drink to that!'

'Ma, did you see the look on fat Bridget's face when the magistrate told Bill he had to pay the penalty? I thought she was going to explode!'

'I did, Annie, I did. Wait till she gets him home, she'll have his guts for garters, I'm telling you! Serve him bloody well right, too. As for that holy bloody Mary next to her, snapping the string on her rosary beads, down on her knees, bum in the air, scuttling round, that scared she'd miss one! Jesus, I laughed!'

From the hotel kitchen, the proprietor looked anxiously out at the Kellys. He didn't want any trouble. You had to admire her, Mrs K., hauling that Bill Frost over the coals; he was a slimy piece of work and no mistake. But they were getting through the whisky like there was no tomorrow …

He stepped forward.

'Mrs Kelly … sorry to interrupt …'

'Don't be sorry, nobody's sorry this day! Your good health, sir!'

'The horses. Will you be riding out tonight, or do you want me to turn them out into the paddock?'

'The horses! My poor Nellie: here we've been, feeding our faces, forgetting about our poor bloody horses. No, we won't be riding home tonight.'

The proprietor nodded.

'Right. Will you be seeing to them then?'

'We will. This very minute we will! But a ride, now, a ride:

couldn't you all just do with a gallop? Annie, you mind that very first evening we moved into Eleven Mile? You and me and Ned, racing to the top of Bald Hill and back?'

'Of course I do: a place of our own at last … Ma! Ma, where're you going?'

'Poor things haven't been out all day.'

'But Ma …'

'Mrs Kelly, it's getting dark …'

'A victory ride! Jesus, it's not every day the Kellys beat the law! And haven't we got the Eleven Mile? And the brave boys to work it? Oh, I mind after Ned got his green sash for saving the Shelton boy, him and me galloping flat tack through the bush back of Avenel, his sash flying out behind him like freedom itself … our Ned. Sure he'll be back soon and then the place'll be like itself again! Come on!'

Thundering hooves: curtains twitching the length of Bridge Street. At the far end, a grey mare spun around and reared, ghostly in the evening light. Her rider's dark hair swirled around her face …

*

Benalla Police Court, Tuesday, 24 October 1871, before
Mr Butler, PM

Jesus wept. Here we are again.

Furious riding in a public place.

Have they nothing better to do? Haven't reckoned on our Mr McDonnell, though, have they? Has Benalla been gazetted as a township, if you please? By Law, would it be designated as a Public Place? The Sergeant doesn't please, but he doesn't know either. No more does Mr Pow.

'We've won, Annie, we've won! Again! Wait till we tell Ned and Alex, can't you just see their faces?'

*

Benalla Ensign, 30 January 1872
Death Notices
Ellen Frost, only daughter of Ellen Kelly and William Frost

The Cliffs

David Mence

He comes home in a state.

His hands are shaking and he has a wild, loose look in his eye.

She has sat up for him. She sits in one of the chairs, slightly back from the table, one leg crossed over the other, looking at the fire. She looks up when he comes through the door. He is sodden even through his calf-hide coat and he peels it off with shaking hands and dumps it on the floor behind the door instead of hanging it on the hook like he normally does. He peers at the coals in the fireplace, glowing softly, and the pots and kettles suspended from their chains.

Do you want a drink of tea?

I don't know what I want but it ain't tea.

Alright then.

She takes down a bottle of grog from the split-bark shelf and uncorks the stopper and pours a double dram straight into his iron mug. He downs it in one, opening the back of his throat to catch the rasping liquid, showing on his face only the faintest trace that there is warmth in his gullet.

What kept you?

He sits down heavily at the table and puts his head in his hands. He seems to be breathing heavily but she can't quite tell and she goes to him and stands by his shoulder and runs her strong hands through his lank hair and asks him again why he is late.

Even the women and children.

I beg your pardon?

Even their women and children, he says again.

What women and children?

He prises her hands away and looks her in the eye and she likes not one bit what she sees. He coughs loudly and grabs at his throat as if there is some demon lodged there and then turns and spits on the bare earthen floor.

For God's sake, I asked you not to do that. And coughing like that is going to wake the children. At the mention of the word children his eyes seem to fold in upon themselves again and he looks at the woodgrain in the table as if he were looking at a painting or a sunset or perhaps just a table but devoid of any intellection. She picks up the rum and pours him another half glass and pulls out the closest chair and sits by his side. She sits watching him carefully and after some time she puts her hand over his.

You got to tell me what's going on. You got to share this with me.

I plan to, he says. And I will.

Alright then.

They sit there in silence while the candle gutters and the wick curls over just that little more and the drafts coming in through the holes in the thatch touch them lightly but with enough of winter to give them a chill. She thinks about putting another chunk of redgum on the coals but then from the back there is the distinct sound of a splutter and the child bawling for its mother's teat. She looks at him and then goes to the back where the child is and picks it up and shushes it gently and pats it on the back and as though she had weaved some magic spell over it it quietens again and is fast asleep. She comes back to him and he has moved ever so slightly and is looking directly at her with some sort of queer, puzzled expression.

What is it?

What?

Why you looking at me like that?

Like what?

Like how you are.

I don't know. He looks away.

With a mighty weariness he lifts his feet up onto the edge of the chair so as to unlace them and as he does so he begins to speak. Quiet and indirect but clear enough in manner that she understands he is going to tell her something she should be ready to hear. He asks her if she remembers not long ago the talk going around of the Myall Creek boys up in New South Wales and how they had hung for what they had done and she says yes she remembers that and he describes to her exactly what it was they had done to the black mobs in that area and how they had been caught and hauled into court before a magistrate and how everybody from Botany Bay to Swan River was now making sure that dispersals not be documented lest the evidence be used against them.

What's any of this to do with us? she interrupts.

Can you pack my pipe?

We don't have any tobacco. You know that.

He looks disappointed at that and strokes at his beard and then says, You know what, I would like a drink of tea after all.

Alright then.

She goes over to the billy and fills it with a pail of water standing by the sideboard and swings the kettle out and over the coals. Out of habit she picks up the lid and checks inside the pot and then puts the lid back on.

I got some damper what's fresh from tonight too if you'd like some of that?

He nods and so she opens the sideboard and takes out the damper and unwraps it from the swathe of dirty paper and cuts a section and puts it on a plate with a clump of grey butter. He thanks her with his eyes and pulls the damper apart and swabs it in the butter and chews on it very slowly as if he wants to make the most out of this moment. Before long the billy is singing and she takes the chain and pulls it up onto a wooden stool and, handling it with a bit of blackened cloth, pours a stream of hot water into his same iron cup which still has rum dregs in it. She hands the cup back to him with a large handful of black tea steeping in it. She places the sugar before him with a mottled tin spoon and lets him stir it in himself as she knows how much he enjoys that. Then she sits down again and watches him eat.

When he is done and has pushed the plate forward on the table she says he should go on with what he was saying.

He takes a sip from his tea and looks at her.

It was spoke of a few times but I don't think any of us thought it would really happen. It was just a way for us to vent what we had to vent. I mean, they done some awful things, some things what caused a lot of hurt. And setting fire to all them sheep. That was the last straw. That's what got the talk going: how many more Christian men are we going to have to inter because of them? Will they ever stop or be happy? What'll happen to our women, our children?

So we rounded them up. We had plenty of horses between us. And plenty enough guns. We took them all up the headland where the cliffs are and the seal rocks. You know the place? We had them all caballed in together and was circling round them like dogs with sheep. A few of them started to cotton on and one bloke even grabbed Dawson off his horse and pulled him to the ground and then a whole lot of crows jumped on him and started beating him with rocks in their hands. We had to shoot a couple. Dawson, poor bloke, he's pretty messed up. I don't know, I am no doctor, but I reckon his nose is broke and maybe his arm too. And then next thing we knew we was driving at them in a wall all joined together and headed for the sea. The horses flaring their nostrils and rolling their eyes. The women was wailing and tearing their hair. The children crying and not knowing why they are crying. The men shouting and pointing and their eyes wide and glaring. And all of them going over the edge in one huddled mass, smashing all of it onto the rocks below. We looked at each other with nothing to say or speak of but turn our backs and swallow down what we had done deep and ride home with our guts in our hearts. To our wives and our children sleeping in their beds. And supposedly say nothing. Take our wives in our arms and brush the hair from their foreheads and kiss our children in their cribs and say nothing.

He looks at her and his face is red and wet with tears and his voiced cracked and choking. She sits there a long time. Silent save for a certain low murmur coming from the wind in the trees outside their hut. She fixes a strand of hair back behind her ear. She stands up and stretches, as though she were going to go to bed, and stands by the fireplace.

Was Henty there?

No, but McVea was. And so was Brownless.

Brownless? What's he to do with this?

He works for Henty too. He just don't wear his heart on his sleeve like McVea.

She thinks about that for a moment, lips pursed, as though completing some difficult calculation.

I guess that's the way of things then.

I guess so.

It's a damned shame, she says, a damned shame. But we got a family too you know. She takes up the candle and licks her fingers and gives the wick a squeeze and puts it back on the table to cool and reset. She unwraps her shawl and hangs it behind the door and goes to him and takes his hand and stands him up and puts her arms around him.

You must be tired?

She takes her arms from him and goes to the back of the room where the children are and gently moves them over on the dirty matting so that there will be some space for him and her and then removes her outer garments and stands there in her underclothes, still young enough to have some shape, rubbing at her forearms in the cold.

Come lie down, she says, and don't keep me waiting.

The Age of Terror

Chris Womersley

I am no stranger to the middle of the night, to its creaks and whispers. It is the time when one is most clearly able to see into the core of oneself, a moment I relished when I was a younger and vainer woman but which I now find almost unendurable. And yet, despite a regularity that grows with each passing year, I am still always surprised to find myself lying on my bed at ungodly hours, staring into the darkness. Should I live another ten years, I can imagine spending entire nights awake. Perhaps this unprovoked waking is no surprise; after all, night is where memory resides and, just as a bear lives off its fat during long, cold winters, the elderly are sustained by their memories.

The first thing I do, as my eyes adjust to the gloom, is listen for Graham's breathing. He will be eighty-two next birthday and his health is, as they say, failing. Even now his breath catches like a bicycle chain slipping a cog. But at least he is still alive, thank God. I dread the day, or the night more likely, when I shall have to put a finger to the artery at his neck, the way I once saw someone do a long time ago. I don't even really know what to feel for. A mild throb, I suppose. A pulse. All I recall is the expression on the ambulance officer's face. It struck me at the time how similar he looked to a trout fisherman, feeling for tremble on his line.

The night also, of course, offers the time and space to imagine the things one would still like to do. It is as if a lifetime of regrets, having accreted about my joints and the ventricles of my heart while sleeping, are dislodged and make themselves known: read that damn Proust epic everyone is supposed to read; sail the Mediterranean; learn an instrument. Naturally, there are other, more profound regrets: affairs never pursued; opportunities squandered. Once, forty years ago, a gentlemanly artist cornered me at one of those inner-city parties populated by the absurdly tasteful and made me an offer I could – and did – refuse but have pondered ever since. Every now and then I hear of him just when I have almost forgotten his face and when I do, it never fails to inspire in me a mild shiver of longing. Not that I regret my time with Graham. On the contrary, he has been my saviour in many ways; I could never have done it without him.

Sadly, the middle of the night is also the moment when one is most acutely aware that one will now never get around to accomplishing these undone things and that one must be content with one's *lot*, as it now stands. At this stage of life, the die is pretty much cast. The Italians, bless them, even have a word for it: *caducita*, the terrible chasm between our attempts to construct our lives and the slow ruin of time. In other words: *it is all too late.* Might explain why the Italians have failed to produce much since the Renaissance, aside from Fellini, of course.

Inevitably, at times like this, I think of Peter. I calculate his age had he lived. The kind of man he might have become. Not that different, most likely, from the boy he was, who was not that different from the baby he had been. He would be fifty in April. Still fifty in April, still the same age I calculated last night and the night before. When pregnant, I imagined him as an apostrophe nestled in my womb, a grammatical scratch that unfurled into a letter, then a word, a sentence and finally into a story of his very own, a tale of no small woe. I knew something was wrong from the moment he was placed, like a chunk of bloody meat, at my breast. Graham sensed it as well, although neither of us spoke of it for some months, as if to articulate our worst fears might give them breath, unleash them.

Not that it mattered. When he was six months old I would inhale his milk-damp breath on nights like this, with the light just so and a dim, naive hope of a future. By the age of three, he seemed to have extra limbs; always clumsy, his chin always glistening with drool. When he was five we organised a birthday party. Not one of the brats we invited from the neighbourhood showed up. God how we persevered throughout that dry afternoon; the smattering of family, everyone mortified, striving valiantly to inject enthusiasm into the occasion, still afraid to speak of his strangeness. I remember the sad-eyed Pole we had hired to juggle for the children took Peter's utter indifference to his coloured sticks and balls as a personal affront. I could never determine if I was more aggrieved by the lack of pain the dismal event caused Peter – another 'developmental hiccup'– or by my own realisation of the wickedness of small children and parents who would organise such a boycott. You think you know people, but they always have something hidden away. It's an awful lesson, corrosive, and one I am still glad my son was never equipped to learn.

Graham snuffles and rolls in his sleep. He clears his throat as if preparing to speak, but says nothing. It is not uncommon in recent years for him to talk in his sleep, sit up, stare at me and mumble 'Jesus, Helen, what have you done?' or 'The nursery is burning' or some such nonsense before collapsing back onto the bed. The poor thing even went through a stage of sobbing himself awake. When he first started talking in his sleep, I would tell him in the morning of his outbursts and we would laugh, sometimes uneasily. Now I rarely bother. Let the night have its secrets, is what I think. There is nothing to be gained.

The water glass on the bedside table is empty. With effort, in the manner of the old woman I have somehow become, I disentangle myself from the bedclothes and sit on the edge of the bed. The deflated inner tubes of my breasts dangle against my stomach, long since emptied of their uses: aesthetic, erotic or otherwise. Two bony knees peer like tortoises from beneath my nightie. There is no glory in ageing, but unlike life's earlier difficult periods – adolescence or youth or even middle age – one cannot of course wish it to end. In the en suite I drink a glass of tap water. It is immensely satisfying and I drink again. The tiles are cool beneath my feet. I feel slightly hungry. It is 4 a.m. so I may as well go downstairs, have a snack and struggle with yesterday's cryptic crossword for a couple of hours before the day gets underway.

The stairway is lined with artworks and framed photographs of family scenes, lost places that are recognisable even in the half light: our wedding day, of course, a thousand years ago, in another country; Graham as a young man in Scotland with his mop of ginger hair that would stay with him for life; a black-and-white snap of a baby cousin in a metal washtub. And, of course, Peter on a swing in a park; the photo creamy with sunlight that seems, even now, many years later, to explode from his laughing head. There he is again, the Christmas we drove to Gippsland to stay in a rented beach house minutes from the sea. The best summer we had together. The last summer. Poor Peter. Still everywhere. Perhaps it is true that we are defined not by what we possess, but by what we no longer have. The press had a field day, of course. Dug out a dreadful photo of me from God knows where. Interviewed other parents. Pure hell. Even now, the sound of a newspaper thudding against the front door at dawn releases in me a flood of mild panic. *What now?*

I make a pot of tea, open the kitchen door to the garden, turn the radio on low and settle in to tackle twelve-down, on which I was left stranded last night. *Sailor posted as missing.* Six letters. Radio National murmurs: a boffin talking about a creature called, believe it or not, the vampire squid that lives in the deepest parts of the ocean. This beast apparently has the largest eyes comparative to body size of any animal, but also – thanks to its body being covered in light-producing organs of some sort – the ability to turn itself 'on' and 'off' so as to see at depths where light doesn't penetrate. Quite a handy ability, I imagine, and one I could do with myself should I continue to wake throughout the night. Would cut the electricity bill, at any rate.

Although I grumble about it, there is a special pleasure to be found in the early morning. Indeed, there is something quite benthic about the ground floor of our old house at this time, a sense of existing in a time zone of one's own, far from the ordinary world. The rules might well be different here. One might almost expect to glimpse one of these vampire fish or another bizarre creature that has evolved miles from human sight, far from anywhere, eyeless. Aside from myself, naturally.

Six letters. *Sailor.* It has rained in the night and damp garden smells drift inside. *Posted as missing.* Trees crackle and drip. *Sailor posted as missing*, six letters. 'Missing' the definition, no doubt. Graham would probably be able to do these crosswords far faster than I will ever be able to, but he has more or less given up on them. Says he has run out of use for words. Sometimes there is only so much you can say.

I don't know how long I have been sitting here when I become aware of strange, high-pitched sounds coming from outside. At first I assume it to be an auditory hallucination but the noise, or noises, persist and I am compelled to investigate. I have to admit to feeling quite terrified, but call out nonetheless in my quavering, 79-year-old woman's voice, 'Hello?' The sounds stop for a few seconds before redoubling in vigour. They have the sibilance of a coven of tiny witches, a sound like nothing I have ever heard before and I stand there in the middle of my huge kitchen, barefoot, clad only in a nightgown, wondering what on earth has come to visit me, what creature has at last discovered my whereabouts. Old thoughts, foolish thoughts. The noises intensify again. I am stranded in the middle of the kitchen, the knives out of reach, Graham asleep upstairs, far from any refuge when I realise what it is. Kittens. Of course. Our tabby cat Sally, who has been lugging her swollen belly around for weeks, has finally given birth.

Sure enough, in her basket in the laundry she is lying on her side with her blind brood mauling at her teats. She looks drunk, exhausted, but utters a croaky meow in greeting and allows me to stroke her head. Poor thing. This is her third brood because Graham won't allow me to spay her. Her babies root about in her damp and bloody fur and clamber over each other like wingless bats. There are five of them. Every so often, Sally licks at the fur at her chest before collapsing back again. I know more or less how she feels. The fatigue peculiar to having given birth arrives, like a comet, from another solar system altogether. *Depleted, drained, battered* are utterly inadequate adjectives for it. It needs its very own dictionary entry, its very own *dictionary*. Perhaps the Italians have a word for that as well? More likely the Indians; they pop out millions of babies. That would be one for the crossword setters. *Seven across, five letters. A Hindi word for the exhaustion of having given birth.* Wherever this word exists, in whatever language, they might also have a better one for *pain*.

I fetch Sally a fresh saucer of milk and sit with her awhile. It's starting to get light. Soon Graham will wander in and crouch down to peer happily at the new kittens and smile his smile of quiet satisfaction. Although we will give them away we will most likely spend much of today bandying around possible names for the new additions based on perceived characteristics. Dopey or Killer or some such. Graham's enduring love of animals is one of the things I still love about him, when his ten-year-old self is closest to the surface, like the imp in the bottle.

After ten minutes or so it becomes apparent that one of the kittens is struggling to get its fair share of milk. A black and white one, already smaller than the others. The runt of the litter. The four other kittens shoulder it aside every time it attempts to jam its little face into Sally's fur. Not nastily, just in the way the strong, in their enthusiasm, inevitably take more than they require. The little one has a scratchy cry and makes periodic attempts to snaffle its way in, but eventually gives up. Sally makes no effort to help it. Like a cartoon creation the kitten flops back unsteadily on its bum and stares up at me with cloudy eyes, as if seeking assistance. There is a speck of what I presume to be amniotic fluid on its nose. Again it squeaks. We watch each other for some time, the kitten and I. Occasionally it stares at its brothers and sisters happily gorging away, before turning back to me. It is heartbreaking. Time passes. The little thing utters pitiful cries, almost emptied of sound. Again it attempts to join the family, only to be batted away by a rival paw.

Eventually, I stand up and fetch one of the large ancient cushions from the cane garden chair. Outside it is light. It will be a sunny day, but cold. My favourite kind of weather. I pause a moment in the garden, inhaling the smells. You get to an age where every new day merely reminds you of one already lived and at this moment I am reminded inexplicably of a morning when I was a teenager in the house where I grew up, having breakfast with my parents, the smell of freshly brewed tea, the way mother placed her hand on father's arm when they shared a joke.

Back inside I pick up the tiny kitten. It mewls against my chest, ever hopeful. Even its claws seem soft, malformed, ill equipped for a lifetime of struggle. We have a small moment, draw solace from each other, before I put the cushion on the floor in the corner, place the kitten in its middle, fold it over and lean on it with all my weight. I am sure it struggles, but I am unable to feel it. The cushion is large and doughy. Sally watches me, her ears pinned back for a few seconds before she relaxes and allows her head to fall back in the folds of the blanket lining her basket. She knows it's for the best.

It is only after some time, roused by the sounds of Graham pottering about in the kitchen that I realise my face is wet with tears and the cushion, doubtless damp from overnight rain, has become even wetter. Then Graham appears in the laundry door-way. He beams when he sees Sally's kittens but then turns to where I squat on the floor with the cushion beneath my knees and his expression alters slightly. We say good morning and mutter approving things about the kittens and how well our Sally has done. There is a brief lull in which the only sounds are those of Sally purring and the chirp of birds in the garden. Then Graham asks me, in his special off-hand voice, what I have got under 'there,' meaning the cushion, but I can tell by his face he already knows.

Readings and Writings

Bobby

Suvi Mahonen

Strands of light blue twisted, crossed over, then sank into the expanse of knitted wool only to emerge at the next stitch and repeat the pattern again. They ran in parallel symmetry, converging at the pompom at the top of the cap. Around the circumference of the brim ran a border of yellow on which marched small embossed elephants, each holding the tail of the one before it with its trunk. Fine wisps of dark hair the same colour as Nick's curled out from beneath the edge to cling to its fuzzy surface in places. When we'd bought it eight weeks ago I'd thought it was too small to fit anyone, but Nick had correctly guessed it would be the right size.

The skin of Bobby's forehead not covered by the cap was furrowed as if in a frown. This accentuated his eyebrows, delicate lines of barely there hair on the ledge of his sockets, inclining medially upwards to form an arc at the top of the bridge of his nose. His nose was short, more like a nubbin, tilted slightly upwards at the end like mine; its tip was a little raw, as if wiped by a tissue one too many times.

I ran my finger over the smooth and doughy surface of his swollen lips. Velvety glossed skin a few centigrade cooler than mine. Drooping in loose repose, colour not right, a dusky shade of purple.

He lay in my arms, loosely wrapped in a green flannel blanket, the back of his head resting in the crook of my left elbow. His body was both light and also strangely heavy. I held my arms still though there was no reason to. Looking at him I tried to align our eyes. His lids were parted slightly, a hint of blue between moist lashes. As I sat there, propped with three plastic-covered wipe-down pillows between my back and the bed's head, I kept wanting, almost waiting for those eyes to blink.

Nick sat on the edge of the bed, arm on my shoulder, looking at our Bobby. Afternoon light angled in through the window and cast Venetian-striped shadows on our son's already mottled cheeks. My finger moved downward, tracing his chin, then onwards across his jaw to his left ear, curving to avoid an open patch of sloughed skin. It wasn't the only one. There were two on his right cheek and a large one on the side of his neck, the full extent of its angry margins concealed by the collar of his Peter Rabbit jumpsuit. Made of the softest white cotton, it was the outfit I'd planned for our baby to wear on his first trip back to our home. Across the garment multiple little rabbits sat on their haunches, cheeks puffed with chewing, holding a large carrot whose tip was missing. Sewn into the outside seam of the left shoulder was a tiny blue tag saying this was a genuine item. Matching mitts and booties were still in the bag.

I moved aside a fold of blanket so I could see more of him. His left arm was angled, bent at the elbow, resting on the front of his chest. The embroidered cuff of the suit's sleeve was hitched a short way up the forearm. Between the rim of the cuff and the base of Bobby's closed fist circled a thick, clear plastic band, fastly secured. In the pocket of the band was a slip of paper, words typed on it in small letters. The portion visible to me said, 'Baby of Alicia Rus ...' The bend over his wrist's bony prominence obscured the rest. A vein line, its discolouring more pronounced than that of the skin, ran up the back of his hand to the fourth knuckle dimple. Lifting his hand gently I straightened his four fingers and thumb from their loose clench. The webbing between them was puffy and wrinkled, like he'd been soaking in a tub for too long. Such small and frail digits, even in their waterlogged state, the creases over their joints swollen to mere faint lines. On his distal pads were enlarged whorls. Opaque slivers of flesh were peeling back from around the nails. I closed his fingers again, covering his hand with mine.

We remained in silence.

Me, my husband and our baby.

I was conscious of sounds from outside the room – muffled voices, the ping of a call bell and the diminishing roll of a trolley. But these didn't enter my reverie. The only noise that was real to me was the whistle of breath from my nostrils and the clicking of the clock's second hand. A mere moment in time, yet this seemed like forever.

'Would you like an autopsy to be performed?' Dr Taylor had asked us.

'Is it necessary?' I said.

'It's your choice. But it may help to find out exactly what went wrong.'

'We'll think about it,' Nick said.

Dr Taylor stood there by the side of my bed. His gaze kept shifting between Bobby and the green blanket. From the edge of my eye I saw his hands move to cross each other and rest at the front of his belt. Speckles of blood soiled the cuffs of his white shirt. I wanted him to leave but also needed him to stay. It was as if I believed he would somehow be able to reverse this. He stayed for a few more awkward minutes, then made his excuses and left the room with a final 'Sorry.'

Nick put his arm around my shoulder and we stayed that way with Bobby cradled against my swollen breasts, which were aching with the need to lactate.

'You haven't called my mum yet, have you?'

'Do you want me to?'

I shook my head. Once our families knew, it would be real.

I stared across the room at the wall opposite. Glints of slatted sunlight reflected off the glass that protected a framed painting. A lamb standing on a hill's green slope. Underneath it, against the wall, was an empty cot on wheels. It was the one in which the midwife had brought Bobby back to me once she had cleaned, weighed and dressed him.

I looked back at my son and squeezed his hand gently. His soft nails pressed into the folds of my palm. I turned to look into Nick's bloodshot eyes.

'Can you ask the midwives if there are any nail clippers around?'

'Why?'

'I don't want him to be buried with long nails,' I said.

I started to cry.

Island

Lillian and Meredith

Stephanie Buckle

A new resident is moving in. Room 17 has stood vacant for a week, stripped down to its essentials. Even the steel-framed bed that Mr Karamantzis had occupied was gone. I had ventured in at last, and was having a little poke around, just in case there was anything left of Mr K; but there was nothing, not even a bit of soap. Then Nina came in.

'You're not allowed in here, Lillian, we have a new resident coming.' She shooed me out with her little bustling steps, the spikes of her hair bristling like armour.

I watch them moving the new resident's furniture in – a rocking chair, a queen-size bed. A woman then; men don't have rocking chairs.

But I miss her arrival because the hairdresser chooses that moment to come and cut my hair.

'Oo, you want a bit taken off here, don't you, dear?' she says, craning towards my reflection in the mirror and twisting a fistful of my hair into the nape of my neck.

She tells me she's seen the new arrival in the foyer.

'She's in a wheelchair,' she says, 'a very fancy one. Apparently, she's been in one all her life, can't walk at all. Would that be better or worse than losing your mobility late in life, do you think?'

I watch the tufts of my grey hair falling under the deft snips of her scissors.

'Mr Chesterton gave her a lovely welcome,' she goes on. Mr

Chesterton is the manager. He's a dapper little man who likes to treat everyone like a film star. He kisses my face when he greets me, holding my hand as a lover would.

'What is her name?' I venture. A kindergarten question.

'Meredith,' she says. 'She asked them if she could have the newspaper delivered to her room every morning!'

Meredith. Able-minded and fresh from the world.

I stand in the empty dining room, watching the two Indian girls setting the tables. They have sleek black hair and big fleshy red mouths. The knives and forks and spoons clatter onto the formica table tops. The glasses follow; they fling each one into position as if daring them to break.

'You're too early for tea, Lillian,' one of them shouts to me.

Nina comes and moves a chair away from the table nearest the door. I take hold of her arm, although I know she won't like it.

'What is it?' she says, frowning and peering into my face, as if I might be hiding something.

I must be quick and not think about the words. 'I would like to move to a table closer to the door,' I manage.

'Really?' she says. 'Any particular reason?'

I try for an expression that conveys, 'It's a bit embarrassing to talk about.'

'Well, that shouldn't be a problem,' she says, pulling her arm away. 'There's a space next to our new resident.'

*

Meredith has short, thick, white hair, but her eyebrows are black, and jut across her face like two deft strokes of a Japanese artist's paintbrush. She must be old, to be in here, and yet the skin of her face is extraordinarily smooth. She has the direct and curious expression of someone who is in complete possession of all her marbles.

She eats her dinner with gusto, and between mouthfuls, asks me a lot of questions. How long have I been here? Where did I live before? Why did I come here? (In a blessed surge of spontaneity and whimsy, I tell her it was because I couldn't be bothered to cook any more, which is at least partly true, although Suzie said I should take the bed while it was offered, even if I didn't need it yet, as no one could say how rapid my deterioration might be.)

She is intensely interested in everything I say, no matter how odd. In return, she tells me she lived on a farm out west somewhere, and it got too much for her. I want to ask her how she managed a farm by herself in a wheelchair, but my question is too urgent and too complicated, and slips from my grasp. She smiles though, as if I have asked it.

'I never married, and never had children,' she says. 'Never looked after anyone except myself and my animals.'

'I, too, have been an independent woman,' I say, 'though there have been—' The words scatter in all directions. Is it, *friends who shared certain things?* – no, too complicated to remember or explain. Is it, *moments of terror?* – ha, plenty of those.

'Yes?' Meredith says, encouraging.

'There have been times when I wished I'd taken my mother's advice!' Meredith laughs as if she understands perfectly, and explanations are unnecessary.

Pushing her wheelchair, I feel stronger straight away. My legs steady, my feet become firm. Only the question of direction remains difficult, as all the corridors look exactly the same, and seem always to return to the same vases of flowers and rows of chairs. But Meredith points confidently ahead, and I follow, all down the winding way to her room.

*

Now that Meredith is here, I have no need of my own room. I sit in her wooden rocking chair quietly, my hands folded in my lap, but I don't rock. I want no distraction. Sometimes, Meredith reclines on her bed, propped by many cushions, her bright eyes settled on me. Sometimes, she sits in front of me in the wheelchair. She has the air of a benign doctor, who is prepared to take the time to get to know her patient. She asks me questions, as if there is a great deal that she needs to understand. Was I ever married? Did I ever have children? What was my career? Did I travel? Did I ever live overseas?

Even if I had the words, my answers wouldn't matter. There is nothing to know about me that has any relevance. I laugh at some of her questions, and shake my head. I say, 'Ah well!' and 'I can tell you one thing for certain!' and she hangs on my words, waiting, and the silence stretches, balloons, mutates around us, changing its meaning a dozen times, until we are done with it, me with trying to find the words, and she with wanting to know the answers, and we just sit, nodding and smiling together, as two elderly women will do.

'Come on, Lillian, go back to your own room now!' Nina says, flicking her purple nails at me. 'You're disturbing Meredith.'

Meredith has fallen asleep on the bed. Her head has lolled to one side, and her lips are slightly apart.

'Come on!' Nina says again, so loudly I am afraid she will wake Meredith, so I follow her out of the room. On the way, I take the little wooden horse from the top of Meredith's chest of drawers so that I can look at it more closely back in my own room.

'It's afternoon tea down in the dining room!' Nina calls after me. 'Go down and have a cuppa!'

Is she going towards the dining room or away from it? I walk slowly to the end of the corridor where it branches three ways. There is a large fabric collage hanging on the wall here, of a midnight blue sky and bright yellow, gauzy stars. I gaze at it, holding the little horse deep inside my jacket pocket, and I think of the glittering stars in the black bowl of night above Meredith's farm.

'Has the plumber arrived yet?' an ancient gentleman enquires of me, passing slowly through this junction.

'I can't help you, I'm sorry,' I say. Meredith's corridor is empty again, so I turn and go back to her room. I close the door quietly behind me, and settle again in the rocking chair to wait for her to wake. Peace settles round me like an old shawl.

*

I'm in love, of course. It's unmistakeable, that flood of exhilaration and relief, which washes everything else away. It's like returning to a landscape I thought I'd never see again.

But as soon as I have it, I begin to dread that it will be taken away. I'll lose Meredith, she will leave again, or someone else will claim her. I can't risk a single moment away from her.

'Leave Meredith alone while she's got her visitor,' Nina says, hauling me from the chair, pulling me from the room. I am a house torn apart by a tornado and the wind howls through me. I must be with her. I stand outside the door, where I can just see the visitor, sitting in the rocking chair where I was sitting. She is a coarse-skinned woman with cropped orange hair. Nina opens a door into the courtyard, and taking my hand leads me through it and shuts the door behind me.

I lie on top of my bed, staring at the dark. If I had stood up to Suzie, and refused to be bullied into coming here, I would never have met Meredith. But if one idle day, out of so many indecisive weeks and desultory years, I had said to myself firmly, 'Come on, Lillian, what you need is a good old fashioned walk in the country,' I could have chosen the road to her farm, I could have seen her, by the pig pen perhaps, struggling with a bucket of kitchen peelings, and offered to help her. My arms would have been strong, my flesh young and firm, I could have lifted her from her wheelchair then.

Suzie rings me, but I have nothing to say.

'Who is Meredith?' she asks.

'I want you to know ... I want you to know ...' is all I can say, because my words have taken instant fright at the phone.

*

'Would you like to walk over to the park?' says Suzie.

'Ah!' I say, and I think of trees, and the wide empty spaces between them.

'Mum! Where are you going?' She stops me, blocks me rather. Her hand is on my arm. 'You've got everything you need, we don't need to go back to your room.' She scratches at the pumpkin-soup stain on my jacket with her fingernail.

In the absence of words and reason, I find my will, and it strengthens my body as nothing ever has before.

'Come on, Mum!' Suzie says, taking my hand. 'I don't have all afternoon.' Then she puts her arms around my resisting body. 'I didn't mean it to sound like that,' she says.

'Meredith,' I manage.

'Mum, for goodness sake, forget Meredith. Can't you just come for a walk with me for half an hour?' But she follows me down the corridor, rummaging in her bag for her phone and pressing the keys rapidly with her thumb. She always hated to walk slowly.

Meredith is sitting up in her wheelchair. She brightens when we come in, and invites Suzie to pull up a chair. Her good manners transform room 17 into a gracious lounge. When we go back to her farmhouse, this is what it will be like. She will preside over the arrangements, courteous and hospitable; she will make everything comfortable.

After Suzie has gone, with a promise to be back on Sunday, the room settles again. Meredith pulls the curtains shut and closes the door.

'I'm going to have a rest,' she says, 'but you are welcome to stay.'

I watch her manoeuvre herself onto the bed, and pull the bedcover over herself. She faces away from me, the shape of her body like rolling dunes under the cover. I go to the bed and touch her shoulder.

'It's alright,' she says, 'I'm still here.'

Gently, I climb onto the bed beside her, and lie down with my chest against her back. I reach my arm around her and feel for her hand. We breathe together, still and warm. There is no other place that I would wish death to take me from but here.

*

Meredith has had some money go missing from her room.

'You don't know anything about it?' she asks me.

'I would never ... I would never ...' The urgency of my denial sticks in my throat like rising dough, thick and claggy. Tears wet my cheeks. She reaches for my hand.

'I'm sorry,' she says, 'I had to ask.'

She says she is going to inform the authorities.

Anxiety billows down the corridors and into every room, like an epidemic. No one is spared. There are whisperings; there are agitated flutterings of hands. Those who normally pace have sat down in unlikely spots; those who normally sit have stood up with shaky purpose. Mr Chesterton, accompanied by Nina and the little Thai nurse, advance methodically. They shut each door behind them, there is a dark silence for about five minutes, then they emerge again. Poor old Mr Evans is brought from his nook in the garden, his mouth a shining purple hole in his head. They take him into his room and it's the same routine – five minutes' silence, then they emerge again.

I have been sat on the couch in the courtyard window, the ancient Greek crone with the hooked nose on one side of me, weaving her fingers together and moaning, and creamy fat Nora on the other side, sighing, 'Oh dear! Oh dear!'

Then it is my turn.

'It won't take long,' Nina says. 'We just need to check your room to make sure there is nothing there that shouldn't be there.'

I sit on the edge of my armchair and watch them. Mr Chesterton stands in the middle of the room, nodding, 'Just a formality, just a formality.' They open my drawers, they look through my handbag, they open my wardrobe and check the pockets of my jacket and slacks. Then Nina lifts the pillow on my bed and finds Meredith's horse.

She hands it to Mr Chesterton, who looks bemused. 'It belongs to Meredith,' she says to him. 'I knew it! We could have come straight here and saved ourselves the trouble.'

All three face me; the Thai nurse has her arms folded.

'Have you been taking things from Meredith's room?' says Mr Chesterton unhappily.

'Have you taken any money?' Nina asks, very loudly. 'Come on, Lillian, where have you put it? We know you've taken it.'

'Well,' says Mr Chesterton.

I am speechless, of course.

'We're going to find it,' says Nina, and pushes the mattress right off the bed. There, of course, is the brown envelope with the five hundred dollars, selotaped to the bed, where it always is.

I watch them counting the money, my hands fluttering up and back again like foolish little flags. They talk softly to each other, but then Mr Chesterton turns to me and says, 'Lillian, I'm sorry, but you're going to have to stay in your room now while we decide what we're going to do about this. You're not to go into Meredith's room again, do you understand?'

'We could just lock her door,' says Nina.

'We can't do that,' says Mr Chesterton. 'We will just have to keep a watch.'

'We haven't got the staff,' says Nina. 'Anyway, this is just the icing on the cake. She's very inappropriate and disinhibited around Meredith, it's a really unhealthy relationship, and it's upsetting the other residents.'

They leave at last. 'Don't come out until I say you can!' is Nina's parting shot.

*

Suzie has brought boxes, and squats on the floor, packing my things.

'They can't look after you properly here, Mum,' she says. 'I've had to find another place for you.' She is holding back her tears.

I don't even try to stop her. My will has dwindled to a memory, and my belly seems full of stones.

'Can't you just say one thing, Mum?' she pleads. 'Anything?'

If I could, I'd tell Meredith I'd have given her all my money. I'd tell her that if ever I'd known that she was in the world, I'd have taken the road west and found her. I'd tell her I can't bear to lose the sight of her.

Bats

John Kinsella

I don't believe you, she said to him, as the sun sat on the edge of the hill.

It's true, he said emphatically.

And you said this was a mountain and it's really a big hill.

It *is* a mountain, he said. It's over a thousand feet above sea level and that makes it a mountain.

She stared hard and suspiciously at him, not sure what to say, and finally out of instinct said, I don't think *that* can be right.

What would you know? he said, annoyed. You live in the city right near the beach. You live at sea level. What do *you* know about elevation?

She wasn't entirely sure what he was getting at, but she wasn't going to say so. Instead, she shook her gleaming blonde hair just because it was there to shake, and she thought it'd look special against the sunset.

He noticed. Your hair makes black lines against the sun.

It's not black. There's no black in it. It's a hundred percent blonde. She thought she should be as precise as possible with the boy. What's more, she continued, Mother says it's 'translucent.' She thought she had him with that word.

That may be true, he said, but with the sun like that your hair blocks the harsh rays and makes it look like a squiggle of black lines.

She was offended now, and no longer wanted to wait for the

purple he claimed would fill the sky around the mountain, going into the mountain itself, when the sun dipped below the horizon. She'd asked him why he'd called that *hill* a 'purple mountain' and he'd said, I'll show you before dinner. It turns purple most days, especially in summer.

Aware that he'd pushed things too far, he pulled back. He was delighted this girl was visiting from the city, and he tried to regain lost ground by distracting her, rekindling her interest.

At dusk there'll be bats in the sky, he enthused.

Bats? she cried. No!

Yes, bats, he said, pleased with her reaction.

Vampire bats? she asked, incredulous.

He wanted to say yes, to frighten her, but that wouldn't achieve anything. Well, it might in time – over days and weeks – if he had time, but she was there only for the afternoon and evening, so he didn't want to take the risk.

No, no, just plain ol' bats. Dad says they're called Western Freetailed Bats, he said. He respected facts.

They were both silent, and fell to watching the sunset with their own thoughts, their own intensities.

We watch sunsets at the beach all the time, she said. There are so many reds and oranges and purples in so many patterns, especially when it's cloudy. I didn't know the colours reached this far away from the sea.

Yes, it's wonderful, he said, and shortly the mountain will go purple. And then it will be grey and black like the sky. The bats will come in the grey, at dusk. If you throw a rock or a stick high up into the air they will go for it, thinking it's alive, something they might want to eat. And you can hear them the whole time. You can hear their wings flapping flapping flapping ...

Soon the two of them would be called into the house for dinner, and there were mosquitoes about, but they stood transfixed, caught in the stretching and contracting of time as the mountain went purple and loomed massive before them, loomed much greater than any hill could loom, then blackened as the sky went grey.

I think I can hear a squeaking sound, she said, though she thought she might be imagining it. She wanted there to be bats.

Bats echolocate, he said seriously, and moved ever so slightly closer to her. It's how they see in the dark, he confided. They see with their ears, because they are ...

Blind as a bat, she said, and they both laughed quietly.

They hear their own sounds come back, he added, after a moment. They send sounds out of their throats that bounce off things and come back and tell them the precise shape and movements. The boy felt his description was getting lost in the words, so he added, They can *see* an insect flying at night through their ears.

She believed him. It was truth, she was sure.

Throw a stone up in the air, she said suddenly.

And he did, immediately. In the half-light they saw a small black entity swoop out of the grey and twist about the stone as it reached its apogee, before flashing darkly away.

I think there are a lot of bats out this evening, he said proudly. There'll be heaps later tonight. It's all the Bogong moths about. They love eating Bogong moths.

This confirmed her growing belief in the boy. On arriving at the strange house she'd felt revolted to see the veranda lampshade filled with hundreds of dead moths. It's the Bogong moths, the boy's mother had said, when the boy was still down at the machine shed with his father.

Now the girl was really quite happy to be inland. It was warm and dry-smelling, and the mountain had been purple. The boy *had* told the truth and she trusted him in the thickening dark. He was bigger than her, and seemed someone she could lean on if she had to, though she'd never have to, she was sure. And there were bats. Best of all, there were bats. She wondered what they looked like, really looked like, up close. And then she shook her hair in the dark-light with excitement, thinking she'd light up the night with her blondeness. She did this for herself, but also for the boy, the mountain and the bats.

And at least one bat heard her. There was a pulling and a tangling and a clawing in her hair and she screamed a short, stifled scream.

There was a bat tangled in her hair. The boy knew straight away and took her arm and directed her towards the lights of the house. Keep calm, he said, bats often get caught in people's hair. Keep calm or it will tangle worse.

She was sobbing but his steady matter-of-fact voice kept her calm. She knew the bat must be confused and in terror – this knowledge overrode everything.

The boy was amazed at her 'self-control,' as his father would have said. *Get some self-control, son!* And here she was, terrified and in pain and in control. It was as if a spell had been cast. She wanted to tell him that she didn't normally swish her hair about, it's just that it was a special day. That it was because of him.

They reached the front door and he called inside for help. The adults rushed out, her mother instantly upset, her father looking sheepish. Somebody said, Calm, calm ... scissors, we need scissors. And the scissors were found. Leave plenty of hair around the bat or it will get hurt, the boy said. And the girl, gritting her teeth and fighting the ultimate hair fight, said the same.

Nasty bat, said one of the mothers. And such beautiful hair.

It looks repulsive. Looks like a dead hand. Watch its little claws. And those teeth!

I am sorry, darling, but you're going to be a sight by the time we've got this beastie out, said the boy's mother, all practicality and dexterity.

I don't care! I don't care! exclaimed the girl. I ... and then she paused to feel the bat clawing and making a distressed sound, maybe echolocating the scissors and her hair and her skin and the blood pumping warm beneath. I want to see it, she said.

Bats are dirty creatures, said the boy's mother. They carry disease. The boy's father squeezed the mother's arm and whispered, You'll frighten her more.

But the girl no longer cared. I want to see it!

And she did – caught in a hank of her hair. Entangled and frightened. She starred at it with wild eyes, then looked to the boy who had been closely watching the operation. Take it, she pleaded with him in a way that made the adults shrink back. Take it and let it go so it can fly back through the dark to reach tomorrow's sunset, to wake when the mountain is purple, to fly into the dusk, the night.

The bat was placed on the veranda, struggling under the moth-light in the net of translucent and blackening hair. It started a slow, agonising clawing towards the edge of the veranda.

The boy flew from the veranda, through the flywire door, to his room, where he retrieved an old shoebox. By the time he was back, the bat had almost plunged over the edge, watched by the stunned and possessed. Deftly, he scooped it into the box with the lid.

Be careful! his mother said as the boy gently pulled strands of hair away from claws and membranes between limbs, watching the sharp teeth, the tiny half-moon eyes, the veined ears, the fur.

Come inside now, said the girl's mum. You look a fright, darling. She kept saying this as if to soothe herself.

No, please, Mum. I want to see the bat fly free.

So the adults stepped gingerly inside, unsure about everything, watching through the window as the girl and the boy worked together to disentangle the bat.

And then it clawed its way up the wall of the box to the edge as the last strands were extracted, its heart visibly beating in the vein-work, through the fur, mouth open and panting. The boy said, It will remember you forever and it will tell the other bats of the light in the dark, how it really saw you.

She smiled, and reached without thinking to the bald spot on her head.

As the bat suddenly flew into the darkness, they grabbed for each other's hands, and the boy said, I like your hair like that. It looks cool.

Agni

A Neighbour's Photo

Mike Ladd

They appear suddenly in the dogbox flats behind us. Arwan and Niall, tall and slim and Sudan black. A generation ago they would have become 'Alan and Neil,' but now at least they can keep their names intact. Arwan is about thirteen. He meets our son on the school oval one evening. He says his older brother Niall is angry with him and he doesn't want to go back to the flat. Their mother is in a refugee camp in Kenya and their father is still in Sudan – doing what, we never find out. Niall, at eighteen, is Arwan's guardian. They walked thirty days from Sudan into Kenya and now here they are, stark against our horizon of cream brick flats, trying to learn a new language, trying to understand how this place works.

This place where dogs are fed fresh chicken breasts, and swimming pools are fenced off for the exclusive use of just two people. This place where the religious days are as mixed as the styles of food and it's all 'go easy, cruise along, don't take too much interest,' but then suddenly a minor traffic incident makes strangers explode into punch-throwing violence. These dead-quiet streets interrupted by hotted-up cars driven by men yelling out something savage as they go past. This place where the magpies sing and the eucalypts form silhouettes against the orange west and their bark clatters and falls to reveal new phosphorous green and mars-violet skins. In this strange world at evening, Arwan waits out on the oval.

Arwan stutters badly – he's in trouble with his brother because he went out all day without telling Niall where he was. Niall cuffed him about the head when he came home, so he ran out and has been wandering the suburb. Now that it's dark he's worried Niall will be even angrier. He shows us a bruise above his elbow, 'My … brother … he … hit … me.' His stutter is a series of gasps before each word, a gulping for air. We're not sure how much English he understands. When our son brings him into the house he doesn't react when we ask if he wants a lemon drink. He stands there observing. I am cooking dinner and he finds this funny, a man in the kitchen chopping vegetables, as odd as a horse in a tree.

We feed him. He's hungry though we can tell he doesn't like the chilli we use in the stir-fry. 'H … H … H … Hot,' he says, fanning his tongue. After dinner we go with him to the flat to tell Niall that Arwan has been with us. The front door opens straight into the lounge off a treeless pen of cement enclosed by a high metal fence. Inside there is almost nothing. Two plastic chairs. No television. A couple of beds in the next room.

Niall's English is much better – and he speaks another three languages, Swahili, Arabic and Dinka. He explains how hard it is to discipline Arwan. Niall must be the father now, but he's only a teenager himself, and the boy doesn't show him enough respect.

Arwan appears next evening in the middle of our lounge while we are watching a DVD. One of us turns around and he is simply there, standing quietly in the dark. We explain about knocking on doors and being invited in. Now he is at our front door almost every night. He would like a drink of water. Can he use the telephone? He needs a lift to his married sister's house. He would like to live with his sister but since he has reached puberty, their tradition prevents it. He wants to play with our son. Arwan likes basketball but dislikes the egg shape of Australian Rules footballs. Later, he appears with a half-wrecked pushbike donated by the local church. It has no brakes and its tyres are worn through. The front tyre is flat. I fix the brakes and repair the punctured tube, but tell him it will keep happening with such threadbare tyres. He comes two, three, four times to have punctures repaired. I should really buy him new tyres, but never get around to it. In the end, when our son gets a new bike for his birthday, Arwan inherits the old one.

Arwan's English improves, but his stammer does not. We often wonder what it's like for him in a foreign schoolyard with a stutter like that. He says Niall has 'girlfriends' at the flat and he has to go out. He picks the grapes from our vine without asking. He comes over so often our son says he's sick of him – he's too annoying.

One afternoon Arwan gives us a badly torn black and white photograph. The bottom left-hand corner is missing, and the whole picture is crushed and dog-eared. He asks if we could fix it for him. The image shows a young Sudanese woman in a Western tailored dress and an older Sudanese man in a Western suit. They stare seriously, unsmiling and slightly off-centre, at the camera. The stamp at the back of the image says 'Modern Photographers Khartoum.' We imagine the heat and the dusty light outside the studio walls – how sweat patches are hidden in the Western clothes by arms held formally at their sides. Arwan's mother and father in this family portrait are as impersonal as a mugshot. Nevertheless, this is Arwan's only picture of his mother and as it turns out, the only sight he will have of her for the next several years. We do not understand the delay in his mother's arrival from the Kenyan refugee camp – that is, if she is really there – and we see it causes him distress, so we stop asking him about it. He tells us the man in the photograph is not his father, but his uncle. Another aspect we don't really understand.

Arwan and his brother move out of the dogbox flats. Everything they own fits in one carload. Niall has a factory job and wants to be closer to it. Arwan continues to visit, turning up unannounced, having walked kilometres across the western suburbs. He never phones first. Sometimes our son is not home, and after a glass of water, Arwan walks away again. We had forgotten the photo. My wife pulls it out of a drawer and carefully repairs it with sticky tape and puts it into a spare frame. It waits on a side cupboard for Arwan to collect next time he walks here. Two strangers stare down our hallway, watching the front door.

The Adelaide Review

Still Here

Anna Krien

Enormous things are in the water now. Bull sharks roll below the surface and carp with whiskers like whips slip under the house. A great swatch of brown cloth, the water won't break – it just bulges and inhales as if it were a single living creature. Stuart and I make promises, like when the water gets this high – and we mark it on the stilts with blue Texta – we'll leave. But we've made eight blue marks, first from the ground in our gumboots, and the last three Stuart hung upside down from the veranda to draw them. Each blue mark disappears overnight, regular enough to make us paranoid that someone is floating past to rub them out, rather than the waters actually rising. And so, on account of our suspicion, we're still here. On his haunches, feet wrinkled and blue from the cold, Stuart spits at the water from the veranda. His phlegm clings to the stumps. The air rings with the tinnitus of mosquitoes. The lichen that grew on the shower curtain is spreading all over the walls like a pale-green flocking. The carpet squelches under my gumboots. In Beth's old bedroom, the pink paint is lifting off the walls, bubbling like a rash. Her single bed, neatly made with a colourful crocheted rug, stands solid in the water. The stilts at the back of the house have sunk lower than the front, so the rear of the house is filling with water and collecting in the belly of her old wardrobe. Tadpoles dart through the ground-floor rooms of her flooded dolls' house.

Each morning I get dressed in town clothes, as if the water might suddenly recede and I'll be able to do the errands. Stuart doesn't bother. He's been wearing the same shorts and T-shirt since the sky broke down. If Beth was here – not as the nineteen-year-old university student she is now, whose shoulders stiffen whenever we talk to her, but if she were eight again – she'd have insisted on staying in her room despite the water, and listened to the lap of tiny waves against the skirting boards. She'd have enjoyed the adventure of her bed slowly lifting and floating like a raft. She and the boys could make boats from Paddle-Pop sticks, and the sample perfume bottles I used to bring home from the chemist would wash up in the corridor with tiny notes inside them. But we haven't heard from Beth for months. Not since Stuart pulled out the internet cord in a rage and told her she wasn't welcome home until she took everything – her photos, her poems, *everything* – off the web. I didn't mind it so much. Some things she wrote were hurtful – but we don't know for sure that she was writing about us. I tried to tell Stuart that, remind him that she always did have a good imagination. But Stuart was furious. 'I am a goddamn English teacher,' he said.

Without telling him I used the computer at the library to look her up after he disconnected our internet. The photos aren't as slutty as he thinks they are. She looks like she is having fun. And she has hundreds of friends. I study all the boys in the pictures with her and wonder which one is her boyfriend. I opened a Hotmail account and emailed her a few times. I thought we were getting along, but her last email was too much. *Susie told me what happened. Tell Dad he is a hypocrite. No, actually, he's worse than that. He's disgusting. And you're an idiot for staying with him.* It was a cruel email to receive. I deleted it and shut down my account. As for the boys, I don't know if they know. They haven't said anything. I called them and asked them to help after the sandbags we laid out around the stumps kept getting nicked. But they were too busy and couldn't get time off work. I tried to speak to Beth but her housemate said he'd get her and then left me on the line. I don't know if he forgot about me or if she was home and refused to come to the phone, but I sat there for some time, listening to the sounds of our daughter's life. Eventually someone must have seen the phone off the hook and hung it up.

The rescue boats pass us everyday. Once we even saw our cat on it, sitting proudly on the bow. But we can't call out. Stuart says what's the point; they're just staying at the community centre, eating and shitting together. We may as well stay put and be civilised about it, he reckons. But it's more than that. No one on the boat even looks at us, let alone checks to see if we're okay. I'm surprised they let our cat aboard.

We can tell who's left. The hovering orange glows of cigarettes and drifts of smoke give them away. Eddie Rollins is in his place behind us; the Bertie sisters across the road; and further down the way Joe Feltham is still there. During the day the boat checks on all three households, trying to persuade them to leave. But so far they've stuck to their guns, probably convinced that if they go they'll never return. A couple days back, Eddie's wife went with the boat. She has emphysema. The poor woman never smoked a cigarette in her life but got it from Eddie's smoking. Their cockatoo, Frankie, got it too but died pretty quick. For the past three years, Narelle sat at the window with a plastic oxygen mask attached to her face. Eddie had a lit cigarette in his mouth as he helped her down to the boat.

The Bertie sisters must have a stockpile of cigarettes. They light their smokes off each other's, as if to keep some vigil going. A single orange glow leans in, blossoms and then after the brief flare separates into two pulsing lights. My grandpa used to always talk about cigarettes as the perk of serving in Papua New Guinea instead of Europe during the war. 'You could smoke at night because of the fireflies,' he'd say. 'The damn things were everywhere. They made us right jumpy at the start but after a while we stopped shooting at them. We didn't have enough ammunition to shoot at a million specks of orange just in case one of them was a Jap having a smoko.' He laughed as if he were the luckiest bastard in the world because he and his mates could smoke while knee-deep in mud and leeches. Even coming back with one arm couldn't dampen it for him. 'I can still smoke,' he'd say when we pointed this out, holding up a cigarette in his sole hand.

At night we can hear a canoe cutting the water near us, wooden paddles stirring the night. The whirr of fishing line is followed by the plonk of a sinker. Stuart and I hold our breath, staring hard at the black, trying to make out the shape of the boat. I rub my calves, using the last of the eucalyptus oil on my shin splints from netball. My muscles are locking up from the wet. Like the worms that showed up at the beginning of the storms, wriggling red all over the footpaths, the veins on my legs are swelling and rising to the surface. The lumpy feel of them makes me sick. Eventually in the black, a fish is jerked out and slaps against the surface of the flood, trying to get back under its wet covers but it is as if the river has hardened, leaving the fish to the metric clicking of a spinning reel.

The storms began a week and a half ago. Stuart kept saying, 'What's everyone complaining about? We *need* the rain.' But anyone who knows anything about farming knows that a flood after a drought is just as bad as no rain. Stuart is a typical city man like that. Thinks he knows everything. Or at least, that everything that can be seen can be known. There's something about how a flood can change all that. It has cloaked this town like a sheet over the dead. The spill of water as it coagulated around the cattle, muting the bleats of drowning sheep; the branches of ti-tree rubbing against each other sounding like rusty swings until their roots loosen, let go and tip over. And then silence. That's obvious, I suppose, but it's a different kind of silence to the one we had been getting used to.

Stuart emptied out the supermarket after it happened. He did the shopping anyway, all five aisles, including the toiletry aisle – which is a first for him – but at the checkout no one would serve him. They had turned off the lights above their registers and put the folded closed signs on their conveyor belts. Then, so they wouldn't have to look him in the eye, they stood outside on the street smoking. Not even Susie, Beth's best friend, served him. After that, Stuart didn't bother going back to the high school to clear out his desk. Said he didn't need to be told he was fired. When his graduating class got their marks back – the best final-year results in the history of the school – the local newspaper rewrote history by stating the Year 12s were taught by Mr Robbs. Which they are now.

To begin with, people were nice to me. I run – ran – the chemist, so I guess they had to be. It was Stuart who was the outsider, after all; I was born in this town. Fourth generation. Girls I'd babysat, braided their hair and coached at netball came into the chemist with their own children and mentioned in loud voices that their husbands had invested in the new units out next to the fake lake with black swans brought in from Adelaide. 'We're looking for tenants,' they said, eyebrows raised at me before enquiring if the costs of goods had gone up recently or had my prices gotten a little bold? When I took the week's takings to the bank Sally widened her eyes at my numbers, even though I'd been banking with her for fifteen years. She said a few times, loud enough so everyone could hear, 'It's not as if you're stuck for choices, Margaret,' banging the notes crisply against her desk, making neat stacks. People call me Margaret now. Sometimes it's Mrs *Cedar* for real emphasis.

I'd always wondered about the wives of men in court over some sex scandal, how they dealt with the newspapers and the television cameras, everyone knowing. I studied their expressions on the six o'clock news. Pointy chins jutted forward as they held their husband's hand. I always thought these women were weak, even when it was all over the news – they still believed their husbands. How could they have not known what these men really were?

When Stuart and I first met, before the children came along, he had wanted to have sex with me there. He tried a few times but I wouldn't let him. I thought – *I think* – it's unhygienic. Why didn't I know then? It's like Janice used to say: if you don't let them do what they want with you, they'll do it with someone else. But Stuart was different. He wasn't from here. He didn't force things like the boys we had grown up with. It's almost like a religion I think now, when I see images of women supporting their husbands. You can't just stop believing in them – especially after twenty-two years and three children. Soon the chain chemist the town had been so against for the past three years opened up in the arcade opposite me and I closed up that same month, arranging a deal with the chain to buy my stock at a loss.

In the evenings, when the rescue boats have left, I paddle out on the kids' old boogie board. I touch the marble heads of angels peering above the water line, the tips of their wings poking up like fins, trying to guess which granite curve is my parents' gravestone. I float under the houses of all the people I knew, their pocked dartboards half-submerged like sinking suns, the basketball hoops where the kids mucked around after dinner when it was daylight savings. In the main street I pull myself along by the parking meters until I reach the chemist. There is graffiti on the shop sign hanging over the footpath. Red paint scribbled over the mortar and pestle my father painted when I was a girl. Faded signs for hay-fever tablets and acne cures are still in the window. Stuart asks me what I do out here on these night paddles; he says it with fear, like I'm meeting with the rest of the town and conspiring against him. I don't say anything; let him think he's going to get tarred and hung from a tree. Dipping my arms into the water, I feel the odd flank of fish.

I used to tell the kids a great big carp lived in the river and it was his whiskers, not reeds, that lassoed their legs when they went swimming. This carp lived on children whose siblings had not kept an eye on them, because that was all it took, I told the boys, reminding them that Beth was the youngest. A glance at the sky or the small study of an insect, and the carp would rise up, gills full of mud, smacking its Botox lips, wet and hungry. All of our children managed to avoid the carp. They managed to avoid this small town altogether, escaping to the city as soon as they got their P-plates, except for Beth, who was so impatient she left on her learner's licence. The Felthams' little girl wasn't so lucky. Or Mrs Shaw's husband, who got drunk on a forty-degree day and drowned. There was Lucy Stone, who went to school with me. And now Jason. I never thought to tell Stuart about the river and its silent takings. It was just a silly story I told the kids to make sure they looked after each other. 'We had been drinking rum and coke but we weren't drunk,' Stuart had first insisted to me. 'The others had gone on to the pub to keep celebrating but I didn't join them. I was coming home. You *know* that – I *texted* you.'

He had texted me. At the station Stuart made me show the police the message, demanding they read it. Even the woman at the front desk had to read it. *Still celebrating w students be home in half hour,* it said. When the main sergeant shrugged and handed the phone back to me, Stuart went crazy. 'This is evidence – shouldn't this be filed somewhere?' In the end one of the policemen put it in a plastic bag and dropped it in a filing cabinet to shut him up. I hated Stuart for that. It was my phone.

'What if the kids are trying to call me?' I asked Stuart after we left the station.

'The kids don't call you. You call them,' he spat back at me.

The night it happened Geoff phoned me, telling me to bring some of Stuart's clothes down to Townsend Road, at the bridge. Geoff had been an outsider like Stuart – they bonded over it, Geoff the policeman and Stuart the teacher from the city. But this evening Geoff sounded different: not cold, but distant. I know now that, like everybody else, he was probably weighing up his loyalties. When I asked him what happened, if Stuart was okay, he said, 'He's okay … Look, you better get down here,' and hung up. The whole road was lit up when I got there, with searchlights and dogs, and I forgot to slow down, still doing eighty kilometres until a man I'd never seen before waved me down furiously.

'Can't you see we've a situation here?' he yelled when I wound down the window. 'If I had any time I'd fine you on the spot. Jesus.' He stormed off and I pulled the car over slowly onto the gravel. There were small groups of police I didn't recognise. The Townsends' house in the far corner of the paddock was lit up, and I could see the kids' faces pressed up against their windows. John was out the front, talking to a policewoman – I started to walk over but then he saw me and scowled. He said something to the woman and disappeared inside.

The policewoman came over to me, holding her hand out formally. 'Mrs Cedar?'

I was holding Stuart's clothes and by the time I had swapped hands to return the handshake, her arm was back by her side, hitched on her holster.

'What's happened?' I asked her. 'I've Stuart's clothes. Where is he?'

The policewoman gently tried to take the clothes from me. 'I'll make sure he gets them. We need to take him back to the station.'

I wouldn't let go. We both held on to the bundle until a T-shirt fell out of the pile onto the ground. I let go and picked it up, handing it over. 'What's happened? Where's Stuart? Can I see him?'

'We're not at a stage to know. A young man has disappeared and we need to talk to your husband about it.'

'Who – which young man? One of his students?' I looked around. 'Who?'

Torchlight was panning the gum trees; the trunks were like white spindly ghosts. Men in black wetsuits slipped in and out of the river, their headlights glowing under the water. Police wearing rubber gloves were picking things up with tongs and putting them into plastic bags, clothes I recognised as Stuart's. 'I'm sorry, we can't say who …' the policewoman started – but then I saw Marie Strand kneeling on the muddy banks, her mouth gulping silently. Two policemen were hovering around her, their hands splayed out as if spotting her.

'Jason? Is it Jason?'

Marie's head jerked up and stared at us. The policewoman noticed and tried to pull me away. 'Like I said, I can't say anything at this point.'

'But maybe he's at the pub? Has anyone checked the pub?' I was getting panicky. 'Didn't they all go to the pub?'

A slow howl rose up out of Marie, a guttural sound as she sprung from her haunches towards me. The police grabbed her, held her down. I stared at them. She was screaming. Quiet, meek Marie, who worked everyday at the canning factory, was screaming and swearing at me. The policewoman took my elbow and pulled me away. 'A police car will drop him home,' she was saying. 'Go home – get some rest. Things will be clearer in the morning.'

She left me at my car, satisfied after I pulled the car keys out of my handbag and put them in the door. It was then that I saw Stuart. He was in the back of the ambulance, the doors wide open – he was wrapped in brown blanket. He looked up and caught my eye. Without thinking my arm shot up and I waved. He stared at me and then looked away. I stood there for a long time, hand in the air.

Two weeks later Marie Strand went through Jason's English essays and photocopied Stuart's comments. Phrases like *You have such a beautiful way with words* and *This is penetrating stuff, Jason* and *Jason, I think you have real talent – I think if we work together we can get some of your writing published.* It all sounded so predatory. She ran off about fifty copies of his comments and did a letter drop around town. In thick black Texta she wrote at the top of each page, *Stuart Cedar hunted my son. He is a Killer.*

Things got worse when Jason's VCE external examination results came in. He just scraped a pass in the English exam. Mr Robbs wrote a piece for the local paper after Marie asked him to read Jason's short stories and essays. 'Nothing within these stories indicated to me that Jason had been an exceptional student, let alone a talented writer,' he stated. 'How Stuart Cedar had become so enthused over Jason's writing is a mystery to me. It would seem, to me, that he held no *genuine* literary aspirations for this young man, on the cusp of his adult life.'

The evening that was published a rock came through our window. The article was wrapped around the rock. It knocked over a clay vase Beth made in primary school when she was learning how to join coils. Stuart was furious. He went outside onto the veranda and yelled that everything this town did was a cliché, that throwing a goddamn rock through the window was a cliché and no one in this town could think of anything original and a goddamn rock through the window was a cliché. I collected the broken pieces of Beth's vase and carried them to her bedroom as he paced and yelled. I lay on her bed and cried. The next night someone threw a garden gnome through the kitchen window. Miraculously, nothing broke except the window, sending shattered glass all over my clean dishes. The gnome lay on the cork floor, nose chipped, staring at us. Stuart laughed. 'Well, at least they worked out what a cliché is,' he said proudly, as if he had educated the rock thrower. After that I slept in Beth's old room and Stuart in the boys' bunk bed. Neither of us wanted to sleep in our bed.

On the fifth night of the flooding I tied the boogie board to our stairs. I tested how many steps were underwater, counting four before clambering back up, my legs dripping and muddy. I'd paddled to the edge of town this time, looked up at the green highway sign pointing towards Adelaide. The roadhouse was ruined; through the windows I could see the tables and bar stools covered in a mould, the fridges and food counter ankle-deep. This was where we used to sit, us girls, and watch people leave town. Especially at graduation time, the place would be feverish with plans of escape, dreams of getting a job and a flat in the city. I'd met Stuart there. He was just a boy then. A writer, he said. Hitching his way around Australia. He stayed for a week, camping by the river at a spot I showed him. I went home only once, to pack a bag and leave a note. It was the wildest thing I'd ever done. I honestly thought I was never coming back.

I missed him then, under the highway sign and drowned roadhouse. I turned the board homewards and paddled. I crawled into the bottom bunk and saw his eyes were woven shut with salt. He'd been crying. He looked so young. I saw our two sons in his face. I put my face in his neck and kissed his skin. 'I'm sorry. I'm sorry,' I said, over and over, prying my arms around him. I lifted him off the mattress and held him. Tears, his and mine, ran down my neck and onto my breasts. 'I'm sorry, I'm sorry,' I kept saying. 'I love you.' And it's true. I still love him. We sunk into each other like we had been starved by the silence. Butting our heads hard. Like horses. For a moment I thought I felt the bunk beds lift, bobbing in the flood, until I cried out, a spasm going through me and into the empty town.

We lay together, on the bottom bunk, for the rest of the wet. Our bodies shifted into their habitual curve around one another, as if in sleep we knew no grudge.

Things will be different when the water recedes, as though sucked away with a straw. The crows will be the first to return. Picking at the bloated flesh of drowned dogs and sheep stuck in the mud, river shrimp and crabs coming out of their mouths. Pecking at the eyes of stranded fish, the silver gills fanned open. The hovering powerlines will return to the ground, and puddles will remain, like a great big mirror has been broken over the town, each reflecting pieces of the sky. They'll find him. Jason Strand. Blue like a swimming pool. Toes and fingers nibbled. Stuart's thumbprints all over him. The streets will fill up with new cars, tyres spinning in the bog. And our house will probably collapse, its knees rotten.

Griffith Review

Get Well Soon

Antonia Baldo

My sister Rebecca is fierce and has always carried something inside connecting her to a beat I can't hear. I'm the fusty one, ready with a stable hand and an aspirin. I can imagine myself standing at the gate, waving a little hankie to all my loved ones as they leave. It's true that I walk slowly in the hope that we'll all be kept safe.

At the fag-end of summer dogs piss up against letterboxes and then sniff around the twisted frames of bikes that the kids have dumped on front lawns. Fathers drag nets through backyard pools that are as blue as toilet bowls while mothers put their feet up and sigh. I can imagine those sighs coming together to form a single cloud that bounces down our road like a huge wobbly balloon, shaking hedges as it goes but unable to get off the ground.

Upstairs, Rebecca lies alone, throbbing with woe among a twist of Bo-Peep sheets. Time is very slow in her room. It moves backwards, a long way back, to a past before either of us was born. It crawls forward to a future where the whole race is dead or dying of our own malignant humanness. Sometimes, in that room which is full of things from a more joyful time, when objects were fingered and scrutinised, when her mind was a wonderful child that clasped onto everything that came near and squeezed, time doesn't move in any direction at all.

*

My grandmother Teresa left Malta in 1949. Over the years she's given us many reasons why her family migrated, none of them heroic. She bores her mates in the Italian café rigid with talk of a home more imagined than real.

'The most bewdiful place in the world,' Nana says over her coffee. 'And friends that know your family right back.'

'What the hell you know about Malta? What kinda history you got there anyway?' shouts Ugo from behind the counter. He's wiping grease off the plastic menus. 'I leave you to your memories, Teresa,' he says, and scratches a fat belly. 'Enjoy.'

'Don't get me started on history.' My Nana's mind is groping for some detail about Mussolini. She's trying to waggle her finger at Ugo but she's pointing at the cash register instead. Her joints, riddled with arthritis, are askew. And then Nana goes silent. Details have slipped.

*

My father, Frank, is home all day now. He sits at the desk in his office and scribbles. There's a line that he can't finish. He can't find the rhyme. He's been staring at it for nearly an hour and now he reaches for the whisky bottle beneath his chair, optimistic that one little drink will be the key to unlock his thorny arrangement of words.

All my father's drawers are bottom drawers, stuffed with reams of scrawled pages. Before he was a compulsive poet he was a teacher of ancient history, a specialist in oracles and divination. His walls are covered with certificates and postcards of eroding stone sites. But knowledge that has no market value, the dean of his old university told him, is difficult to fight for. Looking at Frank the dean didn't see a fighter.

My father likes to joke that ancient history is ancient history. He took his pay-out with a shrug and decided he'd be a poet instead.

*

And here's my mother, Helena, parking her shiny car and clacking her way up the garden path in silly shoes, the office laptop swinging at her side. She peeks in the door of Dad's study and kisses him somewhere between his eye and his ear. She can't find his mouth anymore, even though it's right where it's always been. His neck is stretched up, his own lips are parted, ready to give and receive.

'Where the hell is my mother?' asks Mum, disappearing. 'If she's gone off to that damn café again, I'll send her to a home. Don't think I won't. And I suppose you haven't made a start on the dinner.'

*

Outside, the gutters are clogged with leaves and the shrubbery needs a prune. My Nan's two goats gnaw the yellow grass. Ford looks at Holden and Holden turns his efficient head to Ford. They stare a while before returning to their meal. God, how simple it is to be a goat.

I spread out the vegetable peelings and watch them chew.

We're a disaster of a family; rootless, no religion or politics, no sense of a culture beyond the concrete buildings and the football fields we visit. Our past is a mishmash of Irish and Maltese. Migrants hunger after dining suites and qualifications and somewhere along the way something important gets lost.

I look up and see that Rebecca's curtains are drawn. She's depressed. Her cannibal mind is eating itself.

*

She got back from overseas a week ago. We celebrated her homecoming with wine and watermelon on the back lawn. Nana opened the windows wide to hear Juliette Greco on the record player and danced a two-step with the goats.

'When I was young,' began my mother, 'we thought we were lucky if we made it over to the beach. Fifteen miles was all we dreamed of.'

Rebecca didn't say, 'Mum, you should have dreamt more. If only you'd dreamt more.' Instead, she lolled against our father and started handing out presents. There was a bottle of brandy for Dad. For Nan, a crushed packet of biscuits. A watercolour of fishermen for Mum, who put it to one side with barely a glance. A T-shirt with an inane slogan for our little brother, Karl.

Karl, lying in the paddling-pool and glugging wine from a Vegemite glass, shouted, 'And I got this for you, Becs!' bashing the plastic pond with his still-hairless calves. 'I nicked it from K-mart!'

Nana chuckled but my mother looked away as she does when people spit in the street.

'There's nothing like the wide blue ocean!' laughed Karl.

'So, Rebecca, are you going back to uni?' asked Mum.

Rebecca took off her shoes and sat in the paddling pool with Karl, her jeans getting soaked through.

I was watching from the sidelines as usual, poised to fetch napkins or answer the phone should it ring. Looking back, I see that we were all trying to act normally but our humour was strained and we were cautious with our words. Tiptoeing, inching our way. Candour is impossible amongst us. We'd have to be at the end of the world, on the edge of a crisis bigger than any puddle of blood we've ever seen, and only then could we whisper what we really feel.

But there was no chance of honesty that day, with Rebecca's backpack still in the hall and the fear she wouldn't come home at all still present with us. So we smiled, tipping our heads back into the sunlight, and we didn't admit we were half-expecting her to break apart before our eyes. I think she understood all this and was happy to talk nonsense too, dipping her hand in the water to save another black beetle from drowning.

She gave me my present later; a little straw doll with wings to hang in my car. A little crackly angel to hover over my dashboard.

*

A week later, Rebecca has crept back under the covers and we fear it's all going to happen again; the silence, the tears, the horrible gnawing fear of her harming herself. She's decided not to eat or move, although *decide* is far too dynamic a word.

'I can't stand to hear her crying through the walls,' says Karl.

My father gives up trying to reason with her through the keyhole and goes to his study to write, the loops growing larger, the focus looser. To forgive him his dependency, we've tried to convince ourselves that he's a genius, that the whisky is as essential as his sharpened pencils. 'I'm a traditionalist!' he shouted once, lurching in the corridor. 'Longhand and booze!' We kept our alarm to ourselves. One casualty is enough.

My mother has turned on her laptop and spread her work out on the dining-room table. She puts together development proposals for dead areas of the city, spending her days walking up alleyways and taking snapshots of defunct factories. She conspires with architects and members of the local government. If she could, she'd see a shopping mall or a block of luxury high-rise apartments on every corner.

'I don't know what I can do about your sister,' she tells me. 'I have to finish this report by the morning.' Her face looks sickly in the glow of the computer screen. My poor mother. Her hopes for us have been thwarted; we are so plodding and mediocre.

*

On the first night after Rebecca's arrival, Nana pulled the disintegrating shoebox of photos from the back of her cupboard.

'This was your grandfather cutting cane up north,' she said.

Sitting either side of her on the bed, we gazed with adoration at the sun-blackened face of this man we never knew. We could smell the stink of working men and hear the flies buzzing round the amber cane as loud as helicopters.

Nana held out dog-eared photos of peeling weather-board houses we've never lived in and strangers with all manner of moustaches. The craggy coast of her flat island home.

I got up and gave Nana her medicine – steroids to keep her blood moving.

'Bloody asteroids,' she whined. 'They send me to outer-space.'

When I'd got her under the covers, she took Rebecca's chin between her fingers and said, 'Isn't she bewdiful, eh? When she was little, she'd cry to see a lost dog. Cry over nursery rhymes. Jack fell down and broke his crown! Owwwooohh!!'

Rebecca giggled and then Nana turned to me. 'And you were the one who was always thinking. All the time working it through in that computer you got in your head.'

It didn't seem so much of a compliment.

'We should go back to Malta,' she went on. 'You two wouldn't have a chance to float away. There'd be people, eh. Real family to hold on to.'

*

That night the sky seemed so very high above the tops of the swaying blue gums. Rebecca and I sat on the back lawn. Rebecca said she saw falling stars but I was looking the wrong way at the moment each one appeared.

'Going away did nothing at all,' she said later. 'It's with me. It's always with me.'

*

Karl's best friend, Paul, with his acne and prominent bones, is loitering in our kitchen like a stray dog round the tip. My mother is kind to him and I'm proud she remembers how to be warm.

He looks at her with some kind of devotion and says, 'Hey, Mrs O'Brien, I remember one morning when me and Karl got back here from drinking all night' – my mother does a comic frown, never sure of the part she should play – 'and you were in the kitchen in your dressing gown. You gave us a glass of pineapple juice to drink and that juice was the sweetest, most pineapply thing I've ever drunk in all my life. I always remember the taste of that drink, Mrs O'Brien.'

My mother is rendered oddly speechless. Perhaps she feels how strange it is that this boy has held on to a memory of her goodness.

But then Karl comes down and the boys crack fists. 'Let's get out of here,' they say and they're gone, loud and rude and taking with them any last trace of summer.

*

The dean was wrong. My father is a fighter. He brawls with any-one who opposes his truth of universal goodness. He battles pessimism, lack of communication, the hospital with their clinical diagnoses and my mother's inhuman composure. Most of all, he fights the part of Rebecca that's chewing up the other part. When he's drinking, he can fight with most vigour. Wildness floods his muscles. He rages against her doorframe.

But I'm the only one she lets inside her room. Once there, I sit by her skinny body offering sandwiches while she carps on to me about economic doom and rising oceans, about spiritual emptiness and the absence of an afterlife.

I want to tell her that if she doesn't move then neither can we, but instead I say, 'It's okay, Becs. I love you. I won't stop. I'll keep on giving you love.'

'And how will that help?' she asks, alarming me with the power in her two dead eyes.

*

I like to imagine a scenario where Rebecca and I are soldiers in a war. Wearing combat greens and rubber boots, we're sheltering in a trench while everyone around us fights. In my dream, the disease she lives with is a real wound with a real cause. I can see the gaping hole and the blood that seeps out. And in the dream, I know how to fix her. I have my needle and thread. I say, 'Stay still Rebecca. I'll do everything I can not to hurt you but you must be brave.' She cries out as I sew her up and tie the thread. The stitching doesn't look like it will hold – the raw skin puckering around it. Her eyes are squeezed shut but we wait while the war rages and soon the rawness begins to mend, the stitches dissolve and then we can run our hand over that wound, see the scar, but know that it's gone.

*

I have my own flat now. A tiny box floored with charmless lino. I have phone calls to make, bills to file and a boyfriend called Jack who needs to be held and inspected. Twenty-six last April, Jack reckons he's found grey hairs in his sideburns. I suspect he's feeling old for the first time in his life.

'I'm moving out,' I tell Rebecca.

'Good,' she says. 'Fuck off.'

An old song I hear in the car cracks open this nearly numb chest of mine and makes me long for those hot-blooded days when she and I lay on my bed, feet out the window, watching storms explode above the telegraph wires, or when we hypnotised possums with flashlights, or snuck into a hotel pool up the coast and swam, watching the shiny underside of bats fly above us.

Rebecca's disappointed that I don't live for these moments of rapture anymore. It's true. I'm ordinary. I've accepted the inadequacies of living. But I can't sit beside her forever and whisper that discovering the world is a matter of choice. I can't remind her of the smile on her face when she wore that strapless sea-green dress to her formal. I can't tell her she's so alive she just might have to die while I, half-dead, can afford to go on living. And so I leave her, a white frame twisted on a bed, those sharp-angled thoughts cutting into her brain.

*

I climb the stairs to the new flat and find Jack washing dirt from under his nails. He starts telling me about the native plants that have just arrived at his nursery and asks if I can help with planting the seeds on Sunday.

'I'm going grey,' he says, smiling at me in the bathroom mirror. 'Do you want to leave me?'

I come close and explore his scalp, my fingers creeping like pincers. I can't exactly remember but I think we've done this whole routine before. There's reassurance in our familiarity. Rebecca would say how dull we are but I soak him up.

'How is she?' he asks.

I won't say. Being here with him now is so healthy.

*

It's late. Karl and Paul are spinning pearly bottle tops in the park, talking about the engines of cars they don't own. My mum sits in bed alone, a travel magazine open on her lap. She's staring at an image of New York, thinking that perhaps she'll take a trip one day when Rebecca is strong. My dad, growing sober, is about to cry through her keyhole once more and Nana sleeps, galloping over fields that might exist in Elysium but certainly nowhere in Malta.

Rebecca rolls over and scratches a heel that's going tender from under-use. She stares at a smudge on her wall from a livelier time.

Listen, I tell her, there can be beauty in a rectangular house, in a slab of sky and a doorbell. There can be enchantment along hot carbon roads. There's dignity in all this, I promise her.

I can't sleep. I'm not used to the new place. And so here I am, wide awake and hoping that she'll come flying back to us through this husky summer air she thinks is dead. I'm sending Rebecca all my faith, this faith in life that hangs about like a vagrant in a doorway.

Island

I Forgot My Programme So I Went to Get It Back *or* 101 Reasons

Joshua Lobb

Reasons not to say anything:

1. You don't want to make a fuss.
2. You don't want to make this any more complicated than it is.
3. He won't remember anyway.
4. It's nice enough that the usher said she'd get the house manager. This is London, after all.
5. You don't want to have to buy another one. £3.50. Think of the exchange rate.
6. She didn't need to bother. The theatre was all locked and they were just about to go home. She could have said No or You'll have to buy a new one or You came all the way back up that long street for a stupid programme?
7. She could have stood there in that stolid stony-faced English way and frozen you out. Instead she said Oh let me see if – just wait there. And fetched the house manager.
8. You're standing there, sweaty from the sudden turn around and the rush back up the black-lit London street. Your Fortnum & Mason's carry bag filled to the brim with tourist detritus: postcards from the National Portrait Gallery and a refilled water bottle and an umbrella and a half-eaten Double Decker bar.
9. Nobody likes sweat.

10. She went that extra mile for you. And now the house manager's gone that extra mile for you. The least you can do is thank him politely and get out of there.

11. It's late.

12. The moment has passed to say anything.

13. You should have said it as soon as he came through the auditorium doors. What a thing to remember.

14. Let's face it: you don't have any proof that you bought one in the first place. And he's just unlocked the cupboard with all the programmes – all the £3.50 programmes – and he's handing it over to you.

15. He had to squat down to get to the cupboard. Cut him some slack.

16. You may have to get into a conversation about the play. The play was not really worth talking about. Not awful – not like some plays you remember – but not worth talking about.

17. He couldn't care less what you think, I'm sure.

18. Be grateful that he's not making you pay for a new programme.

19. He's probably heard it all before.

20. And – even now with your student days behind you – £3.50 is a lot of money.

21. You're in London, not Sydney.

22. You're grown men, not students.

23. You're fat now. You've got a beard.

24. He could say It's bad enough that I had to come all this way down the stairs through the auditorium doors down the access ramp and squat down in front of the programmes cupboard: now I have to engage in an awkward conversation?

25. What would you say, anyway?

26. The Fortnum & Mason's bag is heavy. You still have to lug it all the way back down that long street.

27. There's grey in your beard. You're fat.

28. Just take the damn programme.

29. He's handing you the programme. He's being friendly. Don't make this awkward.

30. There's awkward, and there's awkward. Don't go there.

31. Yes, you did say something when he came through the doors, but he may not have heard it.

32. He's busy. He's had a long night.

33. You said Oh I know you, and he didn't respond. Just leave it at that.

34. Oh I know you is not something that you want to hear when you're busy, when you've had a long night.

35. But he's had ample opportunity to notice me. He should recognise me.

36. It could be worse. Rather than handing me the programme, smiling politely, he could in fact have said Well! You claim to have left your programme in the auditorium but my ushers found no programme left behind. He could say My ushers have better things to do than to listen to the ravings of some fat grey-flecked beardie weirdie with a tatty Fortnum & Mason's bag. Take your Double Decker bar and get out of here.

37. It's unlikely that he would use the phrase My ushers, not from what I remember of him.

38. It's likely to rain. You still have to traipse back down that long street carrying your packed Fortnum & Mason's bag.

39. He could have recognised you and is choosing to ignore you.

40. More probably, he doesn't recognise you.

41. It was – Jesus – fifteen years ago?

42. It was in Sydney, not London.

43. We were students, not grown men.

44. He probably doesn't even remember. Why should he? It wasn't his moment. It was mine.

45. It's not like it was anything memorable. One song.

46. I don't even remember his name.

47. You can't say Oh I remember you but I don't remember your name.

48. Keep it clean and simple. Let him give you the programme and get out of there.

49. Blazey's boyfriend is all I have to say.

50. I wonder if Blazey remembers?

51. I can't say You were Blazey's boyfriend, weren't you?

52. Maybe he doesn't want to remember Blazey. What if the break-up was terrible? What if he spent fifteen years blotting Blazey out of his mind and now I come in with Oh I know you – you're Blazey's ex, aren't you?

53. It's stupid to say Oh I know you when you don't even remember his name.

54. And it's clear he doesn't remember me.

55. This is probably the least important moment of the day. The National Portrait Gallery and St Paul's the Actor's Church and a walk up to Islington and a night at the theatre. Don't dwell on moments.

56. He's giving you the programme. Just take the programme, you idiot.

57. What do you want to say anyway? Thank you? Thank you for what?

58. If it was important then he'd remember it.

59. It doesn't matter to him.

60. There's only so long he can squat there, his arm outstretched, offering you the programme.

61. It wasn't sexual if that's what you're thinking. Maybe he does remember and he's thinking that I was in love with him or something. It wasn't that.

62. It's too late. The moment has passed.

63. Let it go. You've got the programme in your hand now. You don't have to fork out another £3.50.

64. It was such a small moment anyway. You idiot.

65. You're an idiot. Fifteen years have passed and you still remember that tiny moment. Other people have let it drift away like the small moment that it was. Just one song in the night. Just one quiet moment after a horrible year.

66. It was an indulgent moment. Let it go, you idiot. One song can't save a life. One Blazey-boyfriend listening to one beardless student singing one song does not save a life.

67. It's not that I remembered it before tonight. I only remembered it when he came swinging through the auditorium doors. I'd completely forgotten about it. But it was an important moment for me.

68. He may not even remember Blazey. He may have moved to London, become a grown man, forgotten Sydney, forgotten Blazey. He may not have to hold little moments in his head. He may not need little moments to keep him moving forward, away from Sydney, from student life, from Blazey.

69. How would you even remind him? Oh I know you is all

you've come up with so far and that didn't really make an impact. Probably because you don't know him. He was just Blazey's boyfriend who happened to be in the right place at the right time.

70. It may not even have mattered who had been there. It could have been any one of Blazey's boyfriends who needed to be there. Or anyone's boyfriend. Or anyone at all. The important thing is that it had to be someone I didn't know. Someone outside the horribleness of that year.

71. How can you remind someone you don't know of a moment that will never be important to them?

72. The usher's locked up. They all want to go home.

73. Four o'clock in the morning after the cast party for that awful student play that Blazey and I were in and me wanting to kill myself.

74. A darkened bedroom in the cast-party house. The noise of the rest of the cast ripping through from the lounge room.

75. Me getting up to go home and thinking I'm going to go home and kill myself.

76. Me having planned to kill myself throughout that whole horrible year.

77. Me mentally running the bath and laying out the pills and wanting so much to have that horrible year over and done with.

78. I was a student after all. Melodrama comes easily.

79. We'd escaped from the ripping-air cast party of an awful play. The world's stupidest director and the world's most irritating lead actor and the world's most embarrassing stage fighting you have ever seen.

80. I've never been satisfied with theatre. If he was to say to me tonight Here's your programme, I hope you enjoyed your night, I'd end up saying The staging was great but I didn't like the representation of women.

81. It's statements like that which make people say That'll be £3.50, thank you.

82. We were sitting in the dark and Blazey was singing songs from *The Muppet Show* and I was talking about Gonzo's great song from *The Muppet Movie*.

83. And not just the awful play. My father being an arsehole and my mother being dead and 1994 being the world's most horrible

year and that fight with Amy and not knowing where that anger came from. The air ripping that whole year.

84. What a great song. Better than the ordinary play tonight and the awful play fifteen years ago. Better than dead mothers and heavy Fortnum & Mason's bags. Better than polite awkward exchanges between the house manager of the Almeida Theatre and a tourist from Australia.

85. And the room was still and quiet and the air did not rip. And Blazey singing Miss Piggy singing 'What Now, My Love?'

86. Me going on and on about Gonzo's song from *The Muppet Movie*.

87. And me almost not wanting to kill myself.

88. Me half-up off the floor and him – Blazey's boyfriend, who I never knew before that night and never saw again – saying Don't go, sing that song you like.

89. Him saying Here's a replacement programme. And then going back through the swinging doors into the auditorium.

90. It's silly. Maybe it was Blazey who said Don't go, sing that song. Maybe he couldn't even care less about Gonzo's song. Maybe he was thinking Dear God, you idiot, I'm with Blazey, get out of this darkened room and leave us alone. But that's not how I remember it.

91. The cast party and my arsehole father almost not mattering any more.

92. The ordinary play and the heavy bag and the almost-rain not figuring at all.

93. I'd be happy to pay the £3.50. I can claim it on tax if you give me a receipt.

94. You choosing to ignore the Oh I know you. Or perhaps not hearing it at all. Perhaps not seeing the flash of recognition in my face or perhaps thinking God it's late, can't I please just go home?

95. Of course I remembered that moment before I saw you again tonight. I remember it often. You let me sing that song in the dark and because of that I didn't go home and kill myself. Yes, I probably wasn't actually going to kill myself – I was a student after all – but you stopped me anyway. You said Don't go, sing that song you like. Blazey lay on the bed in the darkened bedroom, her head (I think) in your lap and you let me sing.

96. Gonzo's song from *The Muppet Movie*:

There's not a word yet for old friends who've just met
Part heaven, part space – or have I found my place?
You can just visit, but I plan to stay
I'm going to go back there some day
I'm going to go back there some day.

97. And it made me feel better. And I didn't go home and kill myself.

98. The usher's gone home.

99. And when I do want to kill myself I remember that moment: four o'clock in the morning during the worst, most horrible year of my life in the dark singing Gonzo's song for Blazey and Blazey's boyfriend who I never saw again until tonight. That moment has saved me many times and I want to thank you for that. I'm sorry it's late and you had to come down through the swinging doors and unlock the programme cupboard and squat down and get out another programme for a now-fat beardie weirdie but I thank you. I wish it were possible for me to thank you.

100. You left the theatre half an hour ago. You're now on the street, further down from where you turned, suddenly, after root-ling through your silly Fortnum & Mason's carry bag, shoved with your water bottle and your umbrella and a nostalgically half-eaten Double Decker bar and a book and some liquorice all-sorts and a stash of postcards from the National Portrait Gallery, and noticed that you must have left your programme behind. But that was ages ago now. Fifteen years and an infinitely paused moment of a grown man giving another grown man a programme to replace the one he left in the auditorium. Keep walking and put all that behind you.

Reasons to say something:
1. You saved my life once. And I thank you for that.

The Bridport Prize

Wildlife

Cory Taylor

'Hippy theatrics,' said Samuel.

He and Mr Jurss next door stood at the fence watching, while Steph held the hose on the garden beds up behind them. All week the protesters had been down the back, some on the ground in tents, others up in the tall trees flying pirate flags, shouting the police down with loud hailers, calling them fascists and Nazis, which made Mr Jurss laugh, since in his youth he had known real fascists and Nazis.

From here Steph could see right into the tree branches where a young man was staked out. He had built himself a platform so that he could lie flat to sleep and his friends had been ferrying in food and water, hoisting it up to him in a bucket. Twice Steph had left a bag of fresh fruit at the base of the tree hoping they would find it. She didn't agree with her husband. She didn't think it was just hippies. And even if it was she thought they had a point. The neighbourhood was losing its scrappy, untamed heart. But there was no point arguing with Samuel. He had made up his mind.

'The cops could be out there fighting real crime,' he said.

'What I'm always afraid for,' said Mr Jurss, 'is a fire. One strike of lightning and *whoosh*.'

Samuel cupped his hands around his face and yelled. 'Go home and have a bath!'

Stephanie looked at him then and felt a wave of sadness. She didn't know when it was that he had turned into this defender of developers and the rule of law. As a much younger man he would have been less sure of who was right and who was wrong, of what was real and what was just pie-in-the-sky wishful thinking.

'They're never going to win,' he pronounced later, while they watched the news footage of the day's events. 'It's private property. End of story.'

'Spoken like a true government lackey,' Steph replied, and was immediately sorry, because Samuel chuckled then, in the sour way he did whenever she brought up the subject of his job.

'Yeah well some of us don't have the luxury of choosing whether or not to work,' he said. 'Some of us actually like money.'

It wasn't true that she had chosen not to work. She'd been *let go*, making her sound like a dog on a leash. But Samuel seemed to blame her anyway, for that, and for a whole lot of other things, including what happened to the boy.

*

He broke his nose falling off the jungle bars at school. Actually he was pushed, he said, by a boy called Byron whom nobody liked. Steph knew him by sight, a brawny blond kid too big for his age, who had no father and two mothers. A typical son of West End, Samuel said, destined to develop a dope habit in grade seven and take up housebreaking as his vocation. Samuel wanted the boy to go to Churchie.

'At least book him for grade five,' he told Steph.

'You do it,' she said. 'If you're so keen.'

She thought the boy was fine at the state school. She also believed that it was better to learn how to stand up to bullies as early in life as possible.

'The world is full of Byrons,' she told her son. 'You can't give in to them.'

And then they had all stood by and watched while the police cleared the sitters out of the trees and dismantled the tents and arrested anyone who talked back. Since then the bushland out the back had gone quiet, like it was waiting for the next big thing.

'It's valuable land,' said Samuel.

'So you keep saying,' said Steph. It was as if he was trying to comfort her somehow with the thought that everything was about its cost. She couldn't even begin to explain to him how mournful it made her feel to listen to him.

*

The boy was asleep upstairs when it happened. Steph was sitting with him, trying to memorise his eight-year-old face. He was slipping out of childhood so fast it was like a tide going out. Only when he slept did it stop long enough for her to truly see him, and even then she was mystified by how foreign he was. In the deep part of him he was still untamed, an animal, some solitary and quick-witted thing.

*

Steph headed downstairs as soon as she heard Lily barking. Lily was Mr Jurss's dog, a lightweight little Jack Russell terrier he'd inherited from a nephew who stayed in his downstairs flat when he wasn't at Charters Towers working in the mines.

'She gives me the company,' Mr Jurss would say, while Lily stared up at him with her heartbroken eyes.

She was not a yappy dog unless she had reasonable grounds. Birds were a constant provocation, especially the owls that flew in on dark and ogled her from the low branches of Mr Jurss's jacaranda. But this was a full-throated alarm, coming from the back landing where Lily was confined whenever Mr Jurss was out.

Steph put the laundry basket down on the dining table and went outside onto the back deck. From here she could see the frantic dog, all its attention on a spot in the corner of the fence where Mr Jurss's yard bordered Steph's. Steph moved down onto the steps so she could see what was there.

A man stood in the garden bed, naked except for his shorts and ragged sandshoes. When Steph stared at them he started to knead the dirt under his feet like it was burning his soles. Sweat ran down his chest as though some private downpour had drenched him and left everyone else dry. She thought it strange that his skin was so pale except where a florid tattoo covered his narrow chest and spilled down his arms to the wrists. He wasn't a hippy. Steph thought of the real crime that Samuel had talked about to Mr Jurss. This must be what he meant. The fear came off the man like a sound only she and the dog could hear, making Steph tremble.

It was like this whenever snakes came up into the garden, which they did once in a while, fully grown carpet pythons with silken skin. All she could do was stare while her heart hammered against the walls of its cage, flailing wildly for as long as she had the snake in her sights, whipping up in her a kind of loathing that was also worship, because the snakes were so unreasonably beautiful.

'What are you doing in my yard?' she called out. Her voice sounded unnatural in her head, like it was someone else asking, not her.

That was when he slid his hand into the front of his shorts and kept it there. It occurred to Steph that he might have a weapon, except that then he had started to scratch himself almost pleasurably. As if he had fleas, she told the policeman later.

She shouted the question again, shaking with anger. How dare he come here, where he didn't belong. If Lily kept this noise up, she wanted to say, the boy would wake up.

'I'm trying to get out the back there,' he said, which was when she saw how green his eyes were, so lit up they were electric.

'What for?' she said.

He didn't answer. Instead he looked up at her with a kind of condescension, while at the same time his eyes seemed to burn brighter. She yelled at the dog to shut up but Lily, in her frenzy, was unreachable.

'The gate's behind the water tank,' said Steph, pointing to the opposite corner of the garden to where the man stood. He stepped out of the garden bed, crossed the lawn towards the water tank and disappeared. The gate opened then slammed shut on its hinge. He didn't bother to slip the latch. She would have to go down later and shut it properly or it would bang all night in the wind. There was a storm coming. Steph could already feel it building. The clouds at the back of Mt Cootha were gathering steam and starting to darken. In a few hours they would explode overhead like some huge blister had burst, and all the streets would turn to rivers and be washed clean.

*

'You did the right thing.' The policeman was dressed like a stormtrooper, in body-hugging blue fatigues. Steph could hear the rest of the squad down the back directing the dogs, two big German shepherds they'd brought with them in their van. It was parked out the front of Steph's place where the neighbours could all see it. A few of them were gathered on the street now trying to find out what was going on.

'The lunatic fringe,' the policeman said.

*

When Mr Jurss came home she told him the whole story. How Lily had raised the alarm and how, twenty minutes after the police dogs went down into the scrub, they'd cornered the man and he'd screamed and carried on and called them every name under the sun, all of which she could hear because the gully was like that. It amplified everything.

'When they build houses down there we're going to hear the neighbours breathing,' she said.

'It won't be so bad,' said Mr Jurss.

'It'll be terrible,' said Steph.

The boy said someone should come and find all the animals before they cut the trees down.

'It's not possible,' said Mr Jurss.

'Why not?' said the boy. He was stroking Lily's back with all the tenderness of a lover.

'It's a jungle,' said the old man.

Steph could see the boy swoon at the idea. He had just read a book on jungles and jungle animals and his head was full of green tangles and heat.

*

The storm came through at ten, after the boy had gone back to sleep again. He had been well enough to sit up for a couple of hours and watch some television. He had even managed to eat an egg mashed up with some buttered bread. Samuel wasn't home yet. He was doing a course two nights a week, something to do with wealth management and investments. He had asked Steph to do it with him but she had told him it wasn't her thing.

'What's that supposed to mean,' he said. 'Not your thing?'

'Sorry,' she said. 'I'll stay home and babysit.'

Which is what she did. For two nights a week she and the boy had the house to themselves. It was like they were on a holiday from Samuel. They ate together after he'd gone, and she never forced the boy to finish what was on his plate because that only seemed to confuse pleasure with suffering.

'You don't discipline him enough,' Samuel told her. 'You let him run wild.'

'How is he going to grow up if we're constantly on his case?' said Steph. 'He'll be too scared to risk anything.'

Samuel didn't agree. She could tell from the way he looked at the boy sometimes as if he wanted to tie him up and whip him, break him like a horse with too much pride.

*

At three in the morning Steph woke out of a dream about a man with Clive Owen looks whom she'd tailed down into the scrubland as far as his hide-out, at which point he'd spotted her and demanded a kiss. In exchange he offered her a coin-sized emerald-green stone. She knew it wasn't a thing of any value but she was willing anyway and let him unbutton her blouse and put his hands all over her, while the trees all around them whispered and the animals made their little scuffling noises in the dark.

She opened her eyes and struggled to climb out of the dream, checking that it was Samuel beside her in the bed and not Clive Owen. The sound from the dream was still there. Not a snake because snakes were soundless. Not a cat, because cats were stealthy. This was a lumbering, more awkward thing. It was in the garden outside their bedroom window. Steph was certain she knew it from the time before. She slid out of bed and padded out of the bedroom, making sure not to wake Samuel since he had never understood her excitement about anything at all unexpected.

After the violent beating the storm had given it the garden seemed abnormally still, like something that has stopped breathing. Once her eyes had adjusted to the dark Steph could see the way quite clearly in the starlight. She came round the corner of the bedroom and there was the echidna, probably the same one she and the boy had found the other time, when he'd been camping out the back in a tent.

'Hello there,' she whispered. The animal had already sensed her coming. Its spines were up and its head wedged between two boulders so that all it presented to her was its prickly back. As a defence system it was impenetrable. There was no part of the creature that was unprotected. Steph thought of what the boy had told her after he'd done his investigations. Echidnas, he said, roamed huge territories and navigated by some system that was barely understood but was probably tuned to magnetic lines in the earth.

It occurred to Steph to wake Samuel to ask him whether they should try to rescue the animal and take it to the RSPCA before it was run over by a bulldozer or buried alive under a ton of fill, but she was afraid of what he might do. The first time the echidna had come into the garden she had sent the boy into the bedroom to wake up his father but Samuel had refused to come.

'He said to let him sleep,' said the boy.

'He doesn't have a soul,' said Steph.

When she thought of that now, of what she had said, and of how she and the boy had sat together on the grass in the dark, the boy so wide awake and still so young, she wanted to howl out loud like a wolf or a bear protecting its cub from all the harm that would ever come to it.

One Book Many Brisbanes

The Tower

Meg Mundell

She found us a week ago, in the arts section of the newspaper. Or to be honest – and really, at this stage, what's the point in lying? – we found her.

'Listen to this!' Marianne's voice pricked a sharp hole through my sleepy Sunday afternoon. She read aloud from the paper: *'However you phrase it – disabled sculptor, artist with a disability – they're pointless labels. I am a sculptor. My physicality is irrelevant. Why automatically insert it before the art itself is appraised?'*

The journalist had used the word 'defiant,' Marianne reported, but I thought the artist, whoever they were, had a point. Eyes half-shut, I stroked the cat and felt almost content, waited for Marianne to finish her dramatic pause. I am interested in art, but the feeling is not mutual. Marianne is impasto, thick reds and dark greens and tobacco golds; I am the water in which the brush is rinsed.

She read on: *'But Alice Rowe's upbeat, assured personality may well have a darker side, if her art in any way reflects her life.'* I opened my eyes. Marianne stared at me over the newspaper and a sneaking unease crept between us. I tried to keep my voice neutral.

'I'd heard she had become successful. How much space did she get?' I asked.

'Half a page. That should piss her off. Extra space because she's a sculptor with a disability *and* an attitude.' Marianne doesn't really mean it when she talks like this. She only does it when she's frightened.

'Maybe she's good.' Distracted, I stroked the cat too vigorously and did not snatch my hand back in time – there's still a red scratch on my wrist. She's a pretty thing, but unpredictable.

As I sucked at the scratch Marianne got up to make coffee, but after announcing this plan and banging cupboard doors busily she just stood at the sink in a kind of dream. She left the tap running for a long time. I had to remind her that we're in the middle of a drought.

*

It happened down by the river. Summer would turn us into mosquitoes, quick and irritating, whining in our parents' ears until they shooed us out the back door and we all flew down to the water.

With each passing year memory blurs, another hazy layer of plastic wrap is laid over the senses, but at the age of eleven things are still as clear as the water, solid as the river stones. The world existed around us in a bright, clear bubble and nothing beyond the immediate horizon counted.

The water tower loomed over a bend in the river near the train tracks, a squat cement cylinder stained with lichen and faded graffiti. It cast its shadow over our swimming hole, darkening a rectangle of water that shifted slowly with the path of the sun.

Daniel was the first to conquer the tower. One still afternoon, after weeks of brutal heat, he climbed the worn metal ladder and stood on the tower's crumbling edge, peering down at our upturned faces. Before anyone could yell out 'Chicken!' he'd done the unthinkable. Those skinny bird legs pedalled the air like Roadrunner suspended over a cliff, his eyes and mouth three black circles in his pale face; the drop of his scrawny body seemed endless.

Water exploded everywhere like glass. The swimming hole rocked and slapped against its banks. We waited.

Finally Daniel surfaced, eyes huge above the choppy water, the shock in his face already turning to pride. He strutted ashore, chest pushed out like a pigeon, face split by a grin, to shake his wet hair all over us.

But the hero shrank in status as, one by one, we followed. Marianne was first; my turn came later. But by the weekend, all but two of us had jumped off the tower. John, who was only seven and deemed too small, looked relieved when we forbade him.

But Alice didn't get off so lightly.

*

Children are not, by nature, kind. They know that a group is made stronger by the presence of an outsider, that someone has to be the runt of the litter. Perhaps they know this instinctively; or perhaps they learn it from their elders.

That summer Alice had already been made to pay for many crimes: chickening out of our stick-fight tournaments, running home crying when a rubber tarantula landed in her hair, telling her mum about Marianne's strip show, with us selling tickets at twenty cents a head. Alice who went to church every Sunday, who once wet her pants in assembly, who stared at the ground when teased. Alice the bag carrier, the moneylender, the punchline; the one whose clothes got hidden after swimming. Alice the lonely, and I later realised (hindsight being an inferior source of knowledge), the harmless and helpless.

The water tower waited for her like a judge.

Cajoled, enticed, bullied – I am still not sure how she got up there. From below I could see her crouching near the edge, the panicky flutter of breath in her ribs; it brought to mind a tiny mouse I once found cornered by our cat. It was easy enough to save the mouse.

*

The rest is blurred in my memory – a deliberate haze, I suspect. But Marianne and I have always agreed that it was Sarah and Dean's fault.

Nasty little Sarah with her beautiful hair shimmering, her sharp stick prodding. Mean Dean with his goblin teeth, laughing too high and too loud. They scampered up the ladder after her. I don't remember what the rest of us were doing – just watching silently, I hope. It was a long time ago.

Hot mixed-up air, the sounds ugly and jumbled: Alice's jagged sobs, Dean's wild laughter, the swish of Sarah's stick cutting through the air. Five children staring up at three children.

And then there were two.

I am certain she was meant to land in the water. If she had fallen into the river, rather than landing on the bank, one of us could have pulled her out before panic swallowed her – Alice couldn't really swim.

But after the sickening sound of flesh on solid earth there was only silence. The sun smiled down on seven tanned children standing very still. Only the river moved.

*

I refused to go with Mum to visit Alice in the hospital. This didn't rouse suspicions: I'd always been petrified of anything even vaguely medicinal.

Anyway, it was an accident. We were all fooling around on top of the water tower and Alice slipped and fell – didn't she, Helena? Right, Daniel? That's what happened – remember, John? *That's what happened.* We all knew the drill.

And, incredibly, Alice's story was no different. To my knowledge it never has been.

I cried that first day she came to school in a wheelchair. I contracted a mysterious illness, thoughtfully passing it on to the others, and we all spent the week in bed.

Eventually we had to go back to school. At first, Sarah and Marianne would bring Alice Redskins, sherbet bombs, Wizz Fizz. But Alice never said thank you. Alice didn't say much at all. And after a few weeks we came to an unspoken agreement: it had never happened. Alice got no more lollies. We used the stairs instead of the corridors. When the bell rang we'd head for the back of the field, far out of reach of the smooth asphalt, on the rough grass where wheels could not travel.

At first, parental concern forced token visits. But after a few months the dreaded questions ('Helena, why don't you go and visit Alice and lend her your new book?') became less frequent, then ceased altogether. I guess Alice made new friends. We went to the movies, hung out at the mall or played quietly in our bedrooms. We stayed away from the river. Our parents said the current was too strong.

*

Marianne flicked a chocolate into the air, catching it in her mouth. I've never seen her miss yet. Like she says, maybe if her hand-eye co-ordination wasn't so good, her jeans would still fit.

'So, Hells. Want to go and have a look?'

'No,' I answered.

*

Friday lunch hour. The gallery doors flick shut behind me. The woman behind the counter hands me a catalogue without glancing up.

The room is all-white, long and narrow, the sculptures set along its length. The first one I come to is a black cauldron filled with cement feet; further along I find an ornate life-sized window frame, carved entirely from a block of soap, hung with a black lace curtain; then a three-course meal for one, hewn from white marble and set on bone china. The titles, written in the language of art, make no sense to me.

And then I see it.

It is more of a scale model than a sculpture: a cement temple, an icon of the rural landscape. A monument cut down to size. Below it, on the rocks, lies a tiny broken doll. The title card reads '*Birth.*'

*

The next weekend is my mother's birthday and I must make the rare trip out to the country. The train-ride is hushed, each stranger wrapped in their own silence, and the landscape is parched and singed. Cheek laid against the synthetic fabric of the seat, I retreat into my own quiet bubble.

With me I take Alice's black-and-white smile from the gallery catalogue. It's not a posed smile, and there is nothing modest about it. She is smiling just like Daniel was when he walked out of the water.

An hour into the journey, by the time the train clatters out of the burnt trees and past the gorge, I have fallen into a gentle half-sleep. I don't see that grey concrete mass standing sentry over the river. I tell myself that on the train-ride back, if I keep my eyes shut tight, I can pretend that it was never there at all.

To the Other Side of the World

Sherryl Clark

Tell me a story, the boy said every night. So I did. Every night, a different story. Fairytales, Dr Seuss, favourite picture books. But always he wanted more, as if something was missing. I wouldn't tell him the old stories. The ones that keep you awake in the dark.

*

The back lawn is a rectangle of green. I clean the spade, sand smooth the handle, sharpen the blade. I choose a spot in the far corner, thump the spade down, feel the blade bite. The ground is harder than I thought – we haven't had much rain lately. I lift the turf, lay it aside in small patches, widen the square of plain dirt.

'What are you doing?'

My wife of twenty-three years has crept up behind me in her red velvet slippers. I wipe sweat from my forehead.

'I'm digging a hole.'

'What for?'

She eyes the dirt, the marred surface of her perfectly mowed lawn. We spent last weekend planting a neat border of mondo grass. Her garden now looks like a gaudy beach umbrella with a brown fringe.

'I thought I might put in a pond.'

'Here?'

'Why not?' There are lots of things I could say to convince her.

I could talk about rocks, pond plants, ground covers, darting tiny goldfish.

'I suppose …' She waits and watches.

'It's getting a bit hot. I'll do some more later.' I lay down the spade and walk inside to get a glass of water. When she has gone, I return and carefully dig up some more grass. After about an hour, I stop. I load the grass clods into a wheelbarrow and put them in the compost.

The lawn now has a neat rectangle of dirt etched into it. It seems about the right size to me.

*

At dinner, my wife seems edgy. She fiddles with her wine glass, turns the music up and down, spreads crumbs on the table and then sweeps them up with her hand. Her rings glint in the candlelight.

*

Every Sunday I visit my mother. She is in a rest home, one of those almost-luxurious residences that use thick carpet and lined curtains and central heating to disguise the fact that they are prisons.

My mother is not allowed outside. Not even in the back garden. Once she climbed the gum tree beside the fence and escaped. They found her in Myer, putting on lipstick from the sample display. Four colours at once, maybe more if they hadn't stopped her. They laughed and said how 'spritely' she was. Her carers were hoping I wouldn't sue, and I didn't.

Every Sunday, I sit beside my mother and she asks, 'Who are you?'

I am tempted to say, 'I don't know. Who do you think I am?' But I don't. I say, 'I am your son, Charles.'

'I don't have a son,' she says. 'I'm not married. How can I have a son? That would be a sin.'

Sometimes I talk to her about my family but she doesn't remember them either. She lives back in the past somewhere, a place that holds sharp moments, people who are long since dead but still vividly alive to her.

So mostly I listen. I listen to other visitors trying to get their mothers and fathers to talk to them. It seems sad that all those words go to waste.

*

During the week we have normal dinners, my wife and I. Normal means that we eat at the kitchen table with the small television on. We try to talk.

'How was work today?' she says.

'The same as usual. Dobbs is going on long service leave next week. They've got a replacement in for him. Young man with earrings.'

'Won't that mean more work for you?'

'I don't think so.' She knows that I have been shoved sideways, that I have a managerial job with nothing to manage. On a good day, I finish the crosswords in the newspaper by 11 a.m. I have six more years before retirement. I spend a lot of time wondering why they haven't downsized me.

'I had lunch with Mary today, then I went to the library and helped out with the book sale.'

I watch my wife's mouth move as she tells her story. She never deviates much from the plot. Someone must have told her it is safer to stick with familiar details. That way you don't get caught out.

She is still an attractive woman. At business functions, I see other men, both old and young, watch her move, smile when she laughs, offer to get her a drink. I stand with my back to the wall. I wait for the moment when her eyes will meet his. I imagine a spark leaping across the room, just for an instant, before they both turn away.

That's how I know who it is she has been sleeping with, making love with, fucking. Everyone else gets her full attention, including me.

*

I clean the spade again, test the blade. It is time to cut into the earth. I press down on the handle, use my foot to dig deeper, force the spade to carve bricks of dirt.

The hole slowly deepens. Soon it is a trench that widens, brick by brick, into a rectangle again.

'How deep are you going to make it?' She is there again, a line creasing between her eyebrows. Her mouth is tight.

'I'm not sure.'

'You're not planning this very well,' she says.

No, I'm not. But I am doing it very neatly and precisely. Is it possible to be precise without having a plan?

*

I decide to tell my mother about the hole. She listens intently, nodding. 'Is it a pond?' she asks.

'I don't know. Maybe,' I say. I feel a thrill of happiness at her interest, even though she probably thinks I am the gardener at her father's huge, columned house.

'How deep will it be?'

'I haven't decided yet. I thought I might dig until it seems perfect.'

'Perfect?' She frowns. 'Can a hole be perfect?'

I can't answer. I want to say yes but I'm not sure where that would take us.

'You shouldn't dig a hole for no reason,' she says. 'Someone might fall down into it.'

For a moment I'm angry with her, then she says, 'Who are you?' and I laugh.

*

It is Friday morning of an ordinary week. I have just finished the crossword when I'm summoned to the director's office. He is fifteen years younger than me and he has never been able to grow a proper moustache, although he's been trying for as long as I have known him.

His secretary makes us real coffee and I know something is wrong. I know what he is going to say before he says it. All I'm waiting for is the amount of money they will offer to get rid of me. It is larger than I expected but not as much as I'd hoped for.

His face reddens as I sit in silence. I want to say something that he will remember but my mind is blank. Except that I think about the hole and suddenly I can't wait to get home and pick up the spade again.

*

I tell my wife over a Saturday-night dinner of candles, burnt lamb chops and peas.

I've never seen anyone literally go white before. It makes her eyes darken and glitter, and her mouth thins out to nothing. I realise she is biting the inside of her lips. I think I see a tiny smear of blood.

'So what are you going to do?' she says. 'Are you going to find another job at your age?'

'Probably not.' I think about her Chanel perfume, her designer clothes, her last pair of shoes, which cost eight hundred dollars. Maybe she's worried that she'll have to buy things at Kmart now. 'I think we'll be okay financially. I've made good investments, the house is paid off …'

'But – what will you do all day?' she says wildly.

No, she's worried that if I'm home she won't be able to see her lover. I smile at her. 'I have a hole to dig.' I push my plate aside. 'I think I'll make myself a sandwich and watch TV.'

On the way to the kitchen I turn off her classical music.

*

On Monday morning, I don't go to work. I can't endure the last two weeks they offered me. I can do the crossword at home. But straight after breakfast, I can't wait to get back to the hole.

When I dig down deeper, I discover a new layer of earth of a different colour. Instead of dark, rich brown, this layer is caramel. When I was a boy, we used to joke about digging to the other side of the world, right through the middle.

My wife comes to stare at the hole. Her face is stony but I can't work out if it's the hole or my being at home on a Monday that upsets her most. I take a break for lunch; the house is empty.

When I return to the hole, I realise that it looks like I am digging a grave. I sit by the hole for a while. Maybe my mother is right – a hole should have a purpose and even if I don't know what it is yet, I know it's not for a coffin or a body.

I widen the hole until it is a square.

*

One night, after a long, stressful day, when the boy asked me to tell him a real story, I gave in. I shouldn't have but by the time I realised, it was too late.

I told him the story my father told me when I was very young, a story about black creatures who lived under the ground and came up through the drains and slipped into people's houses via their pipes and plugholes. In the story, the people managed to fight off the creatures because only small ones could fit in the pipes. Until one day a man digging a garden accidentally opened up one of their nests. And that was the end of the humans.

The boy had nightmares for weeks, and refused to enter the bathroom or the kitchen unless someone put plugs tightly in the various holes. Finally, I had to tell him a new story, one I made up myself, about how the humans conquered the creatures with a mix of bleach and water in spray bottles. The boy carried his bottle around for years before he finally threw it away.

*

By the next weekend, my wife is almost beside herself. She says she can't bear seeing the ugly mess I have made of her lawn. The angrier she gets, the more patient I become. I am waiting for something but I'm not sure what.

On Sunday, I visit my mother. I take her two goldfish in a small tank, set it up for her with filter and plants, and leave fish food with her carers. She is entranced by the fish and sits staring into the tank while I watch her.

'What are their names?' she asks.

'They don't have any yet,' I say. 'I thought you might like to name them.'

'I think I'll call them Charles and Bernard,' she says. 'I always liked those names. I would have called my children Charles and Bernard, if I'd had any.'

I open my mouth to tell her she did have two sons, and she did call them Charles and Bernard, but I don't want to upset her. It's the first time she's mentioned Bernard in thirty years.

Maybe her dementia is not such a burden after all.

*

On Monday, the sun shines brightly and by eleven o'clock the whole garden looks full of colour and happiness. All except for my hole. I haven't worked on it for several days. It seemed pointless to go any deeper.

At midday I fetch the small ladder and climb down into the hole. I lie on the bottom, gazing up, seeing nothing but blue. I wonder what to do with the hole now. In California there is an underground garden connected by a series of tunnels and rooms, one of which holds a pond with a glass bottom. There is a room under the pond. The man who built the complex used to sit under the pond and watch the fish through the glass.

I think about how to create this in my hole, but it doesn't seem right. I climb out of the hole and put the ladder away.

*

My wife has left me a note, not on the kitchen table where I might find it immediately, but in the lounge room under the remote control. I waited until my stomach was grumbling loudly before I heated up some canned tomato soup and made half-a-dozen pieces of thickly buttered toast. I thought briefly about my wife's lectures on cholesterol and then forgot them again.

When I carry my dinner into the lounge on a tray, there is the note. I don't open it at first. I pour myself some wine, eat my soup and toast and watch TV. After I've had another glass of wine and tidied up, I open the note and read: *I am leaving you. I think you need help. I will be in touch. Alyssa.*

She never was very accurate. She has already left; what exactly do I need help with? (I will be able to do the housework myself now I am unemployed); and she hasn't been in touch with me for years.

I laugh. Then I go to bed and read several books at once, dipping into each one, taking turns. I find myself smiling every now and then.

*

The next day, I fill in some of the hole and drive to a garden centre that specialises in ponds and water features. I come home with several hundred dollars' worth of equipment and materials, and a book about ponds and waterfalls.

By the end of the week, I have built a four-foot-high waterfall using a load of rocks, and finished the pond, installing eight large goldfish.

I decide to bring my mother home for a visit. My wife would never allow me to take Mum out before. She said it wasn't 'safe.'

*

My wife phones and leaves messages on the answering machine. I can't work out whether her tone is apologetic or annoyed. I don't return her calls. Instead I dress in my suit and tie, for the first time in several weeks, and visit my bank manager and then my solicitor.

At night, I read into the small hours then fall asleep and dream vividly of my son. He appears as a boy of about ten, happy and boisterous, playing in the garden with a friend while I watch through the window. I can't hear them although I know they are shouting and screaming with laughter. I wake with tears on my cheeks.

For the first time, I investigate what my wife has taken with her and what she has left behind. All of her clothes, shoes and jewellery have gone, and when I notice lighter patches on the walls, I realise she has also taken some paintings and photos but I have no idea which ones.

In a cupboard in my study, I find an old framed photograph of Bernard and myself, after a muddy football game. We are grinning, victorious no doubt, covered in splatters of mud and grass. I hang the photo in the lounge on one of the empty hooks.

*

On Sunday, I bring my mother back to my house for lunch. She doesn't want to leave her fish at first, until I assure her they will be fine and I have some of my own.

When she sees my pond and waterfall, she claps her hands. I fetch a chair and a hat for her and she sits by the pond for half an hour, feeding the fish and watching them dart around.

After lunch, she walks around the house, admiring the furniture. In the lounge room, she stops in front of the photo. I panic. I should have hidden it from her. Then I think that she probably won't know who it is.

But her face shows differently. Tears fall silently down her face and she whispers, 'Bernard was such a lovely boy.' She turns to me. 'What happened to him? Why doesn't he come and see me any more?'

I don't know where to start. I say, 'He can't, Mum. He's ...' The word won't come. I search around for an alternative. Gone to God? Passed away? Left us?

She leans towards me and brushes a speck off my shirt. 'How about a cup of tea?' she says. 'Will the owner mind?'

'Mind what?'

'Us being in his nice house. We'd best not stay too long.' And she walks into the kitchen.

'I'm sure he won't mind,' I say to her back. She just nods.

*

That night I finally find what I hadn't known I was looking for. The family address book. In it is the current address and phone number of my son. He is living in London. The other side of the world.

I wonder if he is married. I might be a grandfather. I pick up the phone and put it down again.

Bernard never was a very good swimmer. He told me once that he was scared of the water, especially at the beach where he couldn't see the bottom. But he was more scared of our father. Otherwise he would never have attempted to swim out to the buoy that day. No boy likes to be called a 'gutless wimp,' least of all by his dad.

I pick up the phone again and dial. It will be breakfast time in London.

Griffith Review

The Wife and the Child

Louise D'Arcy

Lately Hugh had taken a liking to nursery food: crumpets, jelly, sausage rolls. Alex caught him in the pantry, his tongue in the palm of his hand, dabbing up hundreds-and-thousands.

'Let's have rice pudding tonight,' he said, as if offering her a real treat, as if that explained his presence in the pantry. So she re-arranged her expression to indicate appreciation, already dreading the maggot slither down her throat. He took the rice down from the shelf and bore it to the kitchen bench.

And he made it with his usual single-minded focus on the task at hand. When she first saw him, he'd been bent over her essay in just the same way, as if her words were the most absorbing thing he'd ever seen. He'd made her blush then, blush for the sheer pleasure of his attention.

Now that focus was turned away like the passing of a searchlight that left her invisible. She'd had her hair cut. Nothing drastic, but different enough for the woman at the milk bar to notice. After two days he ran his hand through her hair,

'We've got nearly the same haircut,' he said and she went out the next day and had it razored close to her skull.

'Lesbian chic,' he said and went to bed without her.

Ten years together didn't feel so long. But when she looked in the mirror she saw a woman. She'd been waiting for it to happen, through all those 'girl bride' jibes that made Hugh laugh and her clench her teeth. Now her eyes had become shrewd. They met her reflection frankly. So this is how we look, they said. She held a hand over her belly for a second and found herself imagining the swell, the queasy roll under her hand she'd felt on faculty wives' bellies.

'You're too young to have babies,' they'd told her, boasting comfortably of thinning hair and wobbly teeth. They'd seemed like comic-book crones then, but now, ten years on, she wanted nothing more than to be one, too.

Hugh went to bed as soon as they'd finished eating. 'I need my beauty sleep,' he'd said. But at sixty he needed less sleep than ever and was up at four every morning, reading and writing up notes. She scraped the remains of the rice pudding into the bin and remembered what she'd said in reply.

'You'll be a shoo-in for early morning feeds.'

Hugh's face had closed over and she saw for the first time how his nose would become a beak, his forehead an immense portico presiding over the ruins below. She'd changed the subject, lightly and swiftly.

The next morning he woke her at four and they made love. It was the first time in weeks and she smothered her surprise.

'You're all I'll ever need,' he whispered, holding her face, covering her ears with his palms. She read his lips and smiled but found herself unable to return the words as they were no longer true. He stared at her and she felt the old intentness of his gaze. He was holding her neck at an awkward angle and she shifted slightly. He rolled off her and left the bed without a word. When she woke up it was eight o'clock and the bed was cold.

The early nights became a routine. In defence she decided to go to bed early with him. It put him out, she could see. In a few weeks his routines had become set and she tripped over them, bringing tea where none was needed, turning on lights that should be left off.

'I might use the spare room,' he said one evening, pausing at the door to give her one of his Patrician stares, the one that said 'I am not to be countermanded on this issue.' She had to duck her head to hide the smile, remembering how it had impressed her at first. He could reduce her to silence mid-sentence with a turn of his head then.

Sex at least was safe. Their coupling was just that, the smooth interlocking of bodies. He cried out and clutched her and then slept, one hand on his chest, inviolable and quite separate. Alex lay beside him, willing his sperm along the way, cheering them on like a coach on the sidelines. Her pill packet lay on the bathroom shelf. Not to fool him, she told herself. Yes, to fool him in actual fact – the packet was empty. But he never asked, did he? He'd always assumed it was her job. Well, it was time to take a bit of long service.

Then the lovemaking stopped. Custard appeared on the menu but sex went out of season. His belly flourished and hers remained flat. When she tried to seduce him he looked at her, just looked.

'That's not your style at all,' he said eventually. But it was his style that it wasn't, she realised. He had always initiated sex and that was the way he wanted it.

Her period came and she cried. She shut herself in the bathroom and sobbed silently while he watched television with a bowl of ice-cream in his lap. She heard his companionable comments to the newsreader and doubled over the pain in her gut.

The next morning he brought her breakfast in bed and sat beside her like a hospital visitor.

'How are you feeling?' he asked and she wanted to cry again. He'd noticed last night, he'd felt her distress, she reached her arms for him and the breakfast ended up on the carpet. For the next four days he was insatiable. He looked exhausted but she was light-headed with the power of it all. They'd make a baby in no time, and he'd come round to the idea. He was such a young sixty, after all.

But the lovemaking stopped. She lay in bed beside him but received a kiss as chaste as a nun's before he rolled over and slept. She held the alarm clock over his face and studied him in its bilious glow. The lips were just closed, fluttering a little. The eyelids papery and pulsing slightly. Hair sprouted from his nostrils, dark and thick, in contrast to the moustache, now more white than black. His ear was a plasticine creation that gaped, the hole deep and wide. She put the clock back on the bedside table and lay stiff and still beside him, banishing the unloyal thoughts, overlaying them with memories of the man, the oh-so-masculine man she'd fallen for, the alpha male among the pale willowy students in her tutorials.

They had bread-and-butter pudding that night when she came home from work. He met her at the door with news of it and she had to hide the carrier bag behind her back, with its guilty hoard of lace and elastic straps. She stuffed it behind the giant vase that served as an umbrella stand. They ate the pudding in silence. He took second helpings and she slipped the remains of her first to the dog. She rescued the carrier bag and dressed herself later but he was fast asleep before she emerged, awkward and stiff. It was a relief to strip off and put on her nightie.

Three weeks on he laid siege again. There were flowers, jewellery even. It confused her. They'd never had that kind of relationship, had they? She'd never been a woman to price her affection. It was insulting and furthermore, his timing was off. Ovulation was long past. They eyed each other for a long second over their glasses of wine.

'More trifle?' he asked, delving the spoon into what looked to her like a car smash. When he leaned across to serve her his new belly knocked his glass over and the wine was a blood splash on the white linen. She felt a tingle in her belly and took his hand.

It turned out Hugh did like stockings and teddies. He liked them very much. He kept them in his drawer and brought them out every now and again, handing them to her with the quiet dignity of a ruler bestowing a great honour. She wanted to laugh and had to turn her face away but the sex was so good it took her mind off the joke.

Hugh made jam tarts that weekend. He was wearing her apron, the apron he'd bought her for a joke the Christmas before. It had frills around the edge and a big pocket at the front. He looked ridiculous.

'All you need is a pair of pompom slippers with kitten heels and you'd be perfect,' she said, leaning on the kitchen bench behind him.

'You're a naughty girl,' he said and turned round with a wooden spoon in his hand, 'and you know what daddy does with naughty girls ...'

There was bile in her throat and in her mouth and she backed away from him, flapping a hand in distress to fend him off. At the door she turned and ran, ducking into the bathroom and just reaching the toilet in time. She tried to retch away the memory of his face, his grandfather face set in the wrong lascivious smile.

She went to bed before him that night. He was staying up to watch the football. Or was it soccer? Or cricket? He'd never shown any interest in sport before. She didn't want sex with him anyway. Possibly not ever again. She rolled on her side and curled tight, her hand tucked under her chin, thinking. From the lounge came the sound of an over-excited commentator. She lay awake until the sound stopped and he crept in to join her. She feigned sleep then, holding herself still as he stroked a hand down her back. Then the bed rocked until silence fell again, briefly, before he began to snore. It felt like the start of eternity.

Of course she fell pregnant. She didn't even bother with the pregnancy test: she knew. When had they made love? When she looked back, she could see a cycle of feast and famine, based on a calendar of Hugh's reckoning. Perhaps one he'd read in one of his thousand-year-old texts, the ones he had to read with white gloves on, the ones he kept in airtight boxes, the ones she wasn't allowed to touch.

She didn't tell him, not for weeks. The lovemaking cycle continued and Hugh became more and more loving, more attentive. She wasn't sick and he noticed nothing. He was away on a conference when her first period was due. When the time for the next one came she feigned a temperature and slept in the spare room, hiding his proffered painkillers under her pillow. When at five months she began to show it was winter and she wore baggy jumpers. In bed at night she kept the light off.

Hugh brought Candice round one Friday night when tiredness threatened to overwhelm her. In the bathroom where she fled to brush her hair she noticed a white hair in her eyebrow and the start of creases beside her nose.

Candice was twenty and one of Hugh's star students. She was peachy and perfumed with small, high breasts. Alex looked down at hers, bigger now, somehow acquiring a life of their own. Candice didn't say much and nor did Alex, and when she walked into the kitchen later to find Hugh with one hand cupping a hard high breast, the other clutching a tea towel, she simply backed out again without a word.

Nor did she want to discuss it later, when Candice had been driven back to her student house and Hugh had come to bed after showering.

In the morning she told him, as simply as she could. He cried. Her heart was moved until she heard the anger in his sobs. He slapped her ineffectually and turned his back. She patted it quietly and waited for the storm to subside.

'I'll make jelly for supper tonight, shall I?' she asked.

Really, it was going to be so easy. She couldn't think why she'd been worried.

The Sleepers Almanac

Can't Take the Country Out of the Boy

Joanne Riccioni

The next time I saw her she was on the train, looking out of the window. Her eyes flicked at the scenery gathering speed, catching on something now and then – the back door of a grubby terrace, kicked in and hanging on one hinge, a strawberry-red billboard promising something *Longer Lasting*, a carriage derelict on the sidings, burnt out and skeletal like the carcass of some long-dead animal. She watched the junk of the city surging away. And I watched her.

She didn't remember me. She'd looked up from her book and I'd seen the green of her eyes, waited for them to stall on me and flare with recognition. But they didn't. They just passed aimlessly over my boots, across my chest, rigid with held breath, and over to the opposite window.

She didn't remember me. Couldn't forget her, though, even if I'd wanted to. Here it was again, my life aligning to hers, swinging away and re-aligning, like a needle to the pole. Huh. In Mingindiri I'd have been laughed out of the pub for that one. Fate, destiny, all that stuff – no one has the time of day for it where I come from. In Mingindiri, people are born in their boots and die in their boots, and their boots don't go very far in between. In a place where you wake up to the empty sky yearning above the long slow curve of the earth, you'd think a man would have room for a bit of philosophy. Not in Mingindiri. Livestock diseases, feed prices, new fertilizers, GPS rigs – they were the realities that marked the years. Despite that great flare of blue above, there wasn't room for anything else.

We rocked across the aisle from each other for fifteen minutes out of St Pancras. The gentle sway of her shoulders and knees in the wheelchair marked out the seconds, as I charted the lines of scars on her cheek and neck and on her hands holding the book. White ridges of skin like puckered sealant, closing her up where the windshield had shattered in on her; one long track gathering her top lip right up to her nose where she'd split her mouth on the steering wheel. But it was the eyes that made me sure. The green eyes and that skin, so white she should have had milk flowing through her veins instead of blood.

After I found her, that's what my mind kept sticking on: how wrong the blood had seemed on her face, filling her ears, wandering slowly down her neck and pooling between her pale breasts, as wrong as a red-bellied black coiling in the warm white sheets of an unmade bed. For years afterwards when I was with a woman, I'd be getting off more on remembering the even blanch of that skin than from anything they were doing. Perverted, I know, and I tried to shake it from my head. But, you see, she went inside me like nothing else had for a long time. Funny how being close to death can do that – I mean, make you feel more alive, jump-start part of your brain that had gone flat long ago and make you urgent with thoughts.

I'd first seen her at the Carlisle. I was filthy from dipping and weary with the prospect of another whole week of it ahead of me. And that day I'd seen the years filing out before me as predictable and mindless as the long line of sheep through the channels. She was new behind the bar and there were quite a few of us giving her more than the once-over. She wasn't local, not even Australian, or at least hadn't been for very long. Christ, that red hair and the marble skin and those eyes like some shady pasture seemed exotic out there where everything was degrees of brown, sapped and desiccated with drought. Even the women in Mingindiri have skin as tanned and creased as an old pair of Baxters from the neck up, cuff down. Some mornings in bed with Dee I'd see her hand on the pillow, furrowed and mottled like the bark of a red gum. So she went through us like rain, this girl, and we were sucking her back more greedily than our beers.

'Hard day?' she asked me when she saw my fingers in my hair loosening dust and bits of dry grass onto the bar. I nodded.

'Where you from?' I said.

'Ireland. Waterford.'

'What do you want here, then?' I asked her. She looked a bit indignant, so I said, 'I mean, why would you leave a place called Waterford for a dust bowl like this?' She laughed.

'Ah, ya know. See what's out there,' she said, and even the rise and fall of her voice stirred me up inside like a breeze scuffing through an old shed. Right then, all I wanted to tell her was, 'Just keep talking.'

*

A week later I found her on the back road to Mundee, all bloodied up and the ute mangled round her, trapping her in from the waist down. And while we waited for the ambos on the hour-long drive from Moree, I got to tell her that. 'Keep talking, okay? You need to keep talking to me.' Through the open window I held my T-shirt to her face and watched those green eyes rolling up into her head and flicking back again.

*

'And what is out there?' I'd asked her, elbow up towards the pub windows behind me.

She'd cupped her chin in her white hands on the bar and tapped her cheek with translucent nails, and she'd said, 'A lot of feckin' chickpeas, for sure.'

I'd laughed. I'd laughed a lot, because no one had made the truth funny for a long time.

'What? I'm only telling it like it is,' she said.

'Yeah, you are,' I said.

Then she asked me, 'Is it true one of the farms up here is half the size of Ireland?

*

The road where I found her ran through that property. My father had managed part of it when I was a kid and the tree she'd run into marked the entrance to the homestead, still over a kilometre away. I'd bike to that tree in summer and climb it to look down the road, a shimmering line of mercury through fields of sorghum and wheat as far as the horizon on 360 degrees. In the holidays I'd scout the perimeters of the stock farm for lost sheep. Sometimes I'd find one or two in the bush, legs skinned to the bone straining on fox traps. Or sometimes there were shivering ewes that had been attacked by feral dogs, their glossy innards seething about them as if they had a life of their own. I'd shoot them with the rifle and sling them in the back of the ute, as mindlessly as taking garbage out to the skip bins down on the sealed road.

*

When I found her she was panting the way those sheep did when they were too far gone for bleating, when the automatic reactions of the body, the suck of the diaphragm or the squeeze of the heart, have become conscious and are all that can be managed. I looked down at the casing of metal crimped about her legs and knew that even if she got out of it alive, she'd never use them again. I could so easily have covered her bloody mouth and broken nose with my shirt, pressed gently and just waited for the paltry remnants of life to let go of her.

*

'Have you never wanted to see what's out there, then?' she'd asked me while she was stacking the glass washer behind the bar.

'No,' I'd said. But I'd wanted to say, 'Not until now.'

She told me about her travels, her plans, how she wanted to see every last bit of the world, her voice lithe and contagious as a child's laughter, until she stopped and snatched her breath.

'Shit,' she said, holding up a finger pumping blood.

I grabbed a napkin from the bar and wound it about her hand.

'Broken glass in the washer. Sorry.'

'What for?' I asked.

'I got blood on you.' I saw the drops on my shirt where the grimy cuffs were rolled back but I kept my fingers pressed on the napkin around hers until she laughed, 'You can let go now.'

*

'Talk to me,' I told her and her eyes twitched and her tongue clicked on her dry mouth like she was about to say something.

'Can you hear me?' I said. The scratch of the cicadas stopped in unison and I held my breath, listening. Her fingers fluttered in my hand like the wings of an insect.

*

I talked to her. I didn't know what else to do. I told her anything: the rain forecast for the month; the price of feed at auction; how Harrisons had spread flu through their stud pigs so they could monopolise the market with other immune stock. I told her how I hadn't loved Dee, but couldn't leave when she'd got pregnant and anyway where was there to go? I told her how the baby had tested positive for some chromosome defect and I'd convinced her to abort it. I told her how she'd left eventually because she said I treated people no better than fucking sheep. And I asked her again why she'd really come to this hole of a place. Then I ran out of things to say.

*

Her breathing had become shallower, but her eyes under their bloody lids still twitched and her fingers still had the tremble of life in my hand. And then she whispered to me. She tried to say something. Her lips moved in the shape of words but no sound came out. I leant further through the window of the jammed door and put my ear up close to her mouth. I felt her breath on me.

'Do,' she seemed to exhale.

'What?' I asked.

'Do it,' she tapped the words from the roof of her dry mouth like code.

I pulled away to look at her. Her green eyes were half open but as lucid as when she'd leaned across the bar to me and asked my name.

'Do it,' she mouthed again. Then in a long hiss, suddenly alive and violent, she breathed, 'Don't save me for this shit.' And she was looking at the bloody shirt in my hand.

*

I yanked away from the car then and stood up too quickly, the blood banging in my head like fireworks.

'Ah, Jesus,' I said, reeling. 'Christ.' And I meant it as a prayer of sorts, as much as I've ever managed anyway, not because of what she wanted me to do, but because she'd nailed me. In those few tragic minutes when our paths had crossed again she'd nailed me exactly for who I was: a fucking brutal no-hoper, a hard-arse country boy who might take her out like wounded stock.

*

When the stars cleared from my eyes, the ambos and the firies were there and I sat in the ditch and watched them cut her out with chainsaws and get her in the van. Afterwards one of them checked me over. He took the bloody shirt off me and looked down at my bare feet.

'Where are your boots, Dean?' It was Johnny Sands, the paramedic from Moree who drank at the Carlisle. He pulled his chin in, scanning me over like I was naked.

'Dunno,' I said, waving him away and walking barefoot through the dust to my ute.

'You know you should come back with us. You might be in shock, mate.'

'Yep,' I said and drove away. And I kept driving for ten hours, until I got to Sydney.

*

I called Johnny two weeks later to ask about the girl.

'Deano. Where are you?'

'Construction site. Coogee,' I told him.

'Look, Dean. She was in a bad way. They had to airlift her to Brissie and she was on a machine. Don't hold your breath. But you did everything you could, right?'

'Right-o.'

'And Dean?'

'Yeah?'

'Got your Baxters, mate. You left 'em in the ditch.'

'You keep them for a bit, Johnny, okay?'

*

So you see, I knew it was her the moment I saw her. You never forget something like that, someone like that, even six years later, on the other side of the world. Of course I'd seen her plenty of times before, in my dreams, sucking her finger at the bar or bloodied up and whispering at me from behind the wheel of the ute, her eyes rolling back in her head. And I'd seen her on buses, in shops, passing building sites all over the world. But she always walked away and turned into someone else. Now I was raw with the certainty of it, shaking so much I couldn't sit still and had to lean my arms on my knees just to breathe. The memory of her and the reality of her fused and came at me like a knee to the stomach, until I had to swallow back vomit. When I'd caught my breath and pulled myself together I just stared at her down the carriage, watching her turning pages, rocking with the train, her withered legs rubbery-looking and perfectly aligned as only nerveless limbs can be. I watched every movement as if it was a revelation, like a father with a newborn: the biting of a thumb-nail, the stroke of a hand under the fine hair of her neck as she stretched, the roll of her wrist unscrewing a water bottle, the flash of her teeth as she swallowed, and the settling back to the book. All the unconscious, inconsequential movements of a life.

*

As the train pulled into Luton, a steward came to wheel her off. He flicked the brake and rolled her chair backwards, and she caught my eye and held it all the long length of the carriage to the door.

'Thanks,' she said, 'thanks for your help,' without looking at the steward behind her.

I pulled my eyes off hers then, away from that green that could break a drought and for a long time I looked at the deep wet creases of my boots.

The Age

Beckett & Son

A.S. Patric

Devon's father had a heart attack. Devon was at home with him when it happened. They were having breakfast and Roland's eyes blinked and blinked as his mouth opened wide. He tumbled as he tried to find a hold on the kitchen bench. He hit the ground but he looked like he was falling on down through the floor, even though he was still there; back to the tiles, his mouth open, working with soundless air. His legs moved spastically and his arms reached out for something to stop his fall. Their eyes met with everything that was part of the complicated sum of Devon and Roland Beckett.

Devon went to the phone. He stood there, then bent down to take a hold of the phone jack and carefully pulled it from the wall. He walked to the front door and made sure it was locked. He went to the back door and made sure it was locked. He walked around their large family house and checked every window, making sure they were all closed. He pulled the curtains. He could faintly hear his father struggling in the kitchen when he came to the stairs that led up to his bedroom. He climbed the stairs and then he turned on his stereo. A band called Fireside Bellows played a song called 'I Ain't Gonna Fall.'

*

Devon had already showered and shaved. He and his father both had. The rule was to come to the kitchen table already prepared for work. So Roland was dressed in his crisp white shirt when his heart faltered and failed. The only concession to comfort was he hadn't put on his tie and his top button was left undone.

Roland's hand had tugged open that shirt and popped two perfectly white buttons out onto the tiles. They'd reminded Devon of teeth. There was a little white thread bound within the holes of one of those buttons. Nothing in the other. Those buttons had looked lovely lying on the spotless off-white tiles. He had paid attention to them as he listened to his father's body writhe – the backs of his shoes squeaking as they moved uselessly on the kitchen floor. He'd made himself look at those two buttons on the tiles, and at nothing else.

Devon listened to Fireside Bellows play another song, and for a few moments considered not going into work. But that choice was so distant it didn't feel like a possibility. It felt like the idea of suicide. He couldn't imagine calling Mr Waterston in the mail-room to tell him he wasn't coming in. The problem was Devon couldn't lie very well. And the truth was another kind of suicide.

*

He was almost late getting to Brighton train station. He was usually five minutes early. Today the train was waiting for him at the platform like it was there just for him. He stepped inside the cabin and had the pleasant smell of aftershave and perfume wash over him.

There weren't many seats available. He looked at his choices and saw a group of three, dressed in business clothes. There was one seat among them, though there was barely any space to get into it. They shifted their briefcases and moved only the most minimal distance they could to accommodate him. Devon didn't mind. He wanted to be as close to them as possible. He always chose men like these to sit near if he could. He could see their faces had just been shaved. They looked so smooth and clean, all of them. They smelled of shampoo and deodorant, dry-cleaned clothes and shoe polish.

Devon had his iPod playing and couldn't hear what they were saying. He listened to Ian Curtis sing 'Twenty-four Hours.' It amazed him how many times he could listen to a song and not really hear parts of it. It was like all those parts had to find a way to fit into his mind. Like they had to wait for him to be ready before they could enter him and leave their gifts. The next song on the album was 'The Eternal.' He didn't like it and turned down the volume to nothing. He wanted to hear what the three men were talking about.

He'd watched them become more animated. They were a few years older than Devon – maybe in their mid-twenties. It was possible they were even older but the gusto with which they went at each other in their arguments made them seem just out of high school. Men that worked in his father's firm would rarely show this kind of excitement in public. And they would certainly not allow themselves to look this earnest.

The one with perfect teeth in front of Devon was saying, '… and of course you're going to go and lay it all at the feet of Greenspan. Doesn't matter I suppose that he tugged the US economy through the '87 Crash and post 9/11. That means shit. He was supposed to predict that the banks would start playing fast and loose. That's what he should have known, hey? That they'd want to screw their own shareholders—'

'What? He wasn't warned? Is that what you want to believe? That you have to be a prophet to see how this was going to play out—' The man with glossy black hair sitting next to Devon had cut in and now the third man was forcing his way in with his views.

'But that's what they called him – the fucking oracle. The fucking maestro. Did he tell anyone he'd decided on a fucking funeral march?' The swearing barely marred the elegant voice. The use of the word fuck was just something to give his soft voice bones. 'A fucking elegy,' he said in conclusion, but the one with perfect teeth began talking a torrent again.

Devon thought they were more interesting when the volume was up on his music. His father talked enough about all of this. Men like George Soros and Warren Buffett felt like uncles. Ones you never enjoyed coming over. Ones that took over the house, changing the music to what they wanted to listen to, the television to programs they needed to see. He picked a song called 'Wolf Like Me' by TV on the Radio.

The train vibrated and swayed. It rocked and let Devon touch the man next to him at the hip, the knee and the shoulder. He felt his warmth. The commuter's face was so smooth it made Devon want to run the back of his hand across the man's cheek.

All three of the young men wore wedding rings. Devon liked the idea of wearing one of those gold bands but knew that wasn't likely to happen because he was probably gay. He never thought about making love with men. Didn't dream about them or fantasise about men in elaborate sexual positions. Problem was, that was true for women as well. He didn't know what he was, but women didn't really exist, so he was most likely gay. Secretly he probably wanted all three of these men to stick themselves into him even if the thought frightened him. That was the thing, you never knew what was behind the fear.

As the train vibrated and swayed he felt the suffocating presence of his father very near him as well. But he knew how to push his father away so that even when he was very close, like now, he was somewhere else. In science fiction they called it a different dimension. The world was the same here, but in *this* dimension, his father had never existed. And if Devon had never existed as well, that was also fine. You couldn't be unhappy about never being born. You couldn't be anything.

When the song 'Wolf Like Me' finished the band played another song, which was all right, but he switched to Built to Spill and played his favourite song by them, 'I Would Hurt a Fly.'

The three men rode into the city with Devon and they got off at the same time. It looked like they were all friends. Devon was delighted to be able to follow them under the station to where it came out, onto Degraves Street.

They didn't stop debating the whole way. To Devon they looked like glorious heroes of a noble capitalism. Their hands and arms suggesting traffic could be directed through any and all confusion. Their forceful group stride that forward momentum would carry the day. Stepping up the slumping tired stairs and out into the city's busy morning light, three strident visionaries.

Devon knew he needed to have his headphones turned up with 'Black Steel' by Tricky playing for the illusion to work, but he allowed himself these illusions when he could find them. If there was no truth in an illusion then there was nothing at all that would catch your eye. The rabbit had to disappear, not necessarily into thin air, but it did have to vanish.

Devon wondered whether it was even possible that these three men might possess the secret to the causes and solutions of the Global Financial Crisis. They moved through hundreds of people pushing past on their ways to wherever they were working. All part of the problem. All part of the solution. And these three like seers, looking into their complex interweaving and intermingling, trying to discover a way to understand it all and solve it for them. The people of Melbourne just went on into their own discrete worlds.

Devon was going out of his way now, following these three men. The thought of being late finally pulled him out of the thrall he was in. He turned down Collins Street and headed towards King.

His dad talked about the GFC a lot as well, and despite having understood the markets for over thirty years, he didn't have an easy solution either. He didn't go in for blaming people like Greenspan or Bush, Senator Phil Gramm, Abby Cohen or Kathleen Corbet.

Roland Beckett blamed a lack of discipline. The principle Devon had been hearing about since he could crawl. That the world only had one true motivation – survival. The two sides of that one principle were fear and force. The only two valid responses – discipline and drive. All the talk of love in Devon's songs was nothing more than folly. A lack of discipline. A waste of drive. When Devon focused on his own survival, he didn't feel the *force* Roland liked to emphasise. All Devon really saw around him was fear.

Devon played a song called '100%' by Sonic Youth and got to work only a minute before he was supposed to start. Usually he liked to be at least ten minutes early.

*

Devon was asked to help out with the sorting today. There were other jobs he preferred but Warwick had called in sick again. He called in sick almost every week. He was already past his allotted sick leave and his colleagues in the mailroom had gone from thinking the guy was skating on thin ice to wondering why he hadn't been given the sack already.

Roland Beckett could have got Devon a job pretty much anywhere in the tower but he wanted Devon to work his way up from the mailroom. Said you only appreciate the top when you've been at the bottom. Devon didn't mind. Soon he'd be going back to uni anyway. He should have gone last year but Devon had taken a bottle of pills and that ruined a whole semester; derailed him for a while in general. Roland thought he'd be ready for it after a year in the mailroom. If not, then there were ways and means of getting up into those offices on floors in the twenties and thirties. Roland would make that happen but first Devon had to show some grit.

The sorting was mind numbing. Devon could allow himself to drift free and let his hands just throw the letters out into their appropriate destinations. He could ease away the pressure of holding down his thoughts. He could let his father come close again without worrying about the suffocation and crush. Devon looked only at the letters and let a few hours pass. The paper cuts were distant events he didn't need to worry about.

His music played into his ears and he didn't have to hear the people talking around him. He listened to two albums by Jane's Addiction, replaying 'Three Days' and 'Ocean Size.' He loved it when Perry Farrell sang in the second song about how he was born with a heart of stone, how he seemed to pause for the briefest moment, allowing that image to settle in Devon's mind, and then went on singing about how this heart of stone wasn't just hard like a rock but could be shattered into fragments.

It wasn't what had happened to Devon's father this morning. Roland had a normal heart and it just got worn down with time and in the end it just spluttered and stuttered. Finally stopped working, like an old toaster. One last flash of heat, and that was it.

Devon didn't know what Perry Farrell meant but Devon wondered if he had a heart of stone too, because there were fragments and pieces, broken shards in his brain, and somehow this might explain why most of the time he felt nothing – but when he did – it tore through him into places that could only gasp and tremble.

*

Mr Waterston found Devon in the toilet. Devon sometimes went into a cubicle and sat there reading the walls and listening to his music. Often he sat there for as long as fifteen minutes. No one said anything about it, but Mr Waterston knocked on the toilet door like it was Devon's office and told him Mr Cornell wanted to see him. Devon could see Mr Waterston's shoes below the door so he couldn't pretend he didn't hear him.

Devon had been trying to think about what happened this morning, what he'd done and what it would mean now that Roland was dead, and what that would feel like when the numbness and confusion lifted. But Devon had been living numb and confused a long time. His dad alive had driven so much distortion through his ears that his death didn't change the distortion still roaring in his head.

Through the door, Mr Waterston told Devon he was to go up to Mr Cornell's office, now, and he didn't go away until Devon told him he'd go up as soon as he was done. On the toilet wall someone had written what was probably the name of a band – Perils of Paradise. It reminded Devon of a song he'd heard with the lyrics *that pain in paradise is a pleasure in hell.* Devon got up and flushed the toilet even though he hadn't used it.

*

From the toilet to the elevator he'd kept repeating a phrase in his head. Sometimes this could go on for days. The same word, or a sentence, going through his skull again and again. He wished he could stop it. From the toilet to the elevator he had been repeating the two words – Studiously Aloof. It just didn't sound right. Was studiously even a word? Even though he knew it was, the final f in aloof made him think it should be Studio-fly. Which was wrong. Aloof also sounded false. What kind of word was that? So it kept going through his mind as he caught the elevator that would ascend only up above floor seventeen. Studiously Aloof. Over and again.

And then it got worse. Looking at the numbers scroll through one to seventeen, without the possibility of stopping, he got a feeling of déjà vu. It seemed pleasant to most people but to Devon it came with the fear that it wouldn't stop. The déjà vu could start repeating as well until everything he was looking at and everything he was thinking came with the feeling of déjà vu. The stain in the carpet in the corner of the lift. *Noticing* the stain in the carpet. The déjà vu itself. This trembling feeling he had going through his whole body. The vibration of the lift as it rose and finally broke the seventeenth floor and kept rising now towards the twentieth. The slight pause as though the lift wanted to stop at the twentieth but kept going. All of it, something that had happened before. Even the thought of his father at home in the kitchen, pulling open his business shirt and popping out those two buttons. Déjà vu in those two buttons.

Devon tried to push his thoughts away to something else. He thought about the birds his mother had bought him for his tenth birthday. The déjà vu followed him there but he couldn't help it. Now he was thinking about how his mother wanted to buy the cage full of brightly coloured Dutch frilled canaries because he'd begged for so long, even against Roland's wishes. A big, wonderful cage that was meant to go in his room but when he got them home he found that they were noisy and he couldn't sleep with them in his bedroom. So they went downstairs. They were too noisy for Roland as well and they were moved to the back porch. Roland told Devon they were Devon's birds, so it was Devon's duty to feed them. But he forgot and Rose began feeding them.

His mother's medication affected her memory, though, and all the birds starved to death a few weeks later. No one removed them from the ornate bamboo cage because Roland said they were still Devon's responsibility and they just made Rose cry when she saw them. Then one day, Devon came home and climbed the stairs to his bedroom and found that Roland had taken the long jar that the Becketts normally used for spaghetti and filled it with the ten brightly coloured canaries. It was sitting on Devon's school desk like it was a present for him. No one threw it away and Devon watched them begin to decay. Maybe he was supposed to throw them out but he just couldn't touch the glass and they started to seem pretty in that long, airtight glass jar. Eventually they disappeared as Roland had to finally deal with the birds he'd insisted were a bad idea from the start.

The lift got to the top of the elevator shaft and released Devon. He turned Tindersticks off because they weren't helping him with his déjà vu or the memory. He put on Mogwai's album *Come on Die Young*. Skipped it to the song 'May Nothing But Happiness Come Through Your Door.'

*

The office had a breathtaking view of Melbourne but Mr Cornell wouldn't have been able to tell Devon if it was raining without turning around to check.

On one of the walls was a portrait of Hyman Minsky. An economist Mr Cornell particularly liked to quote. Roland had told Devon the repetitions over the last six months, of the same mantra, were maddening. 'Extended periods of healthy growth convince people to take ever larger risks, and eventually, when enough people have enough risky bets on the table, the smallest trouble can have catastrophic results.' In short, it was all about cycles, but at the moment Mr Cornell wasn't thinking about his mantra or Minsky. He was talking on the phone, giving someone harried directions regarding a meeting. As soon as he hung up the phone he was speaking to Devon.

'Get those white things out of your ears.'

'Oh, sorry.' Devon turned his iPod off and took out the headphones.

Mr Cornell was in his late fifties but he looked older. It took energy to talk as aggressively as he wanted to, but he took a deep breath. 'Where's Roland?'

'He's not here?'

'Don't be an idiot, son.'

'I thought he was here. He's not here?'

'Don't be a fucking idiot, Devon! What's happening?'

'I left for work. I always leave like twenty minutes before him.'

'What? What do you mean before him?'

'What?'

'Basic question, son. Basic! The answer is …'

'Well … I've got to get to the train on time. And he drives. So he leaves later.'

'But you work in the same building. How do you not come in together?'

'He says it teaches me discipline. To use timetables and trains. If he drives me, then it's luxury I haven't earned. He …'

'Son, I'm asking you where your father is.'

'Mr Cornell, I'm trying to explain. I thought he was here.'

Mr Cornell stood up. He opened his arms and looked under his armpit. 'Well, he's not here, Devon. You understand. And it's not a day he can miss. I mean it's impossible that he wouldn't be here today, yet I'm looking around, and it seems like the impossible is my reality. Those clients in the meeting room just waiting for Santa Claus six months before Christmas. I mean ... this is impossible. This is, in fact, inconceivable. And no phone call. Not even a phone call. I can't go down there. What am I going to say to them? This was your father's whole deal. The tough explanations. The visionary spiel. What am I supposed to do?' His voice had become a roar but the statements had become childlike and the question didn't seem rhetorical.

Mr Cornell closed his eyes. He leaned heavily on the desk with his arms before him instead of slumping back into his office chair like he wanted to. He murmured sotto voce like he had forgotten his partner's son was in the room. 'And he knows I've got cancer.' He swallowed but held himself up at his desk. 'That I'm going. That there's nothing I can do to stop it.' He opened his eyes and looked at Devon.

Mr Cornell said, 'I'm sorry. I know it must be hard for you to even think about cancer.' Cancer meant almost as little to Devon as Sagittarius. He didn't say anything, though.

Mr Cornell asked, 'Was it long? Her suffering? Sorry to ask ...'

'What do you mean? Who?'

'Rose. Dying of cancer. Leukaemia ...'

'My mother didn't die of cancer.' Devon shook his head. Couldn't really imagine that Roland had maintained a lie like that for almost ten years.

Devon said, 'A bathtub full of blood. That's what it looked like. Blood on the bathroom floor. Blood down the hall. Down the stairs. Blood on all the handles. Because he carried her out to the street crying like a woman.' Devon fumbled with his iPod. Managed to get the earphones into his head. Sometimes he thought of them as plugs. And sometimes he wished he never had to pull them out at all. 'I don't know what leukaemia is,' he told Mr Cornell.

*

Devon didn't want to go home. He sat on a bench outside the tower and thought about places he could go. He listened to the whole album *Ma Fleur* by The Cinematic Orchestra. Eventually some young guns from the firm spotted him and recognised him as Roland Beckett's son. Pulled him along with them, down the road to a bar for a drink. Devon said yes but he followed them with his earphones on. He walked into the bar listening to 'Suds & Soda' by Deus.

Of course they yanked out his earphones but they let him put them back in after a few minutes and motioned sign language at him occasionally. Making fun of him but unable to make him respond. They left him to drift into his numb paralysis.

He watched them mock and torment a young waitress by dropping things for her to pick up, like cigarettes and beer bottles. When they got even more drunk they let a glass break and made her clean it up. She was too pretty and removed. She wasn't impressed by them. Maybe that's what it was, but Devon didn't feel sorry for her. He didn't hate the hot shots. He listened to another song by Deus called 'Jigsaw You.'

If he was honest with himself he wasn't numb at all really. He wasn't quiet and still because he had nothing to say or nothing he felt like doing. He kept imagining what they would do, these young men in their lovely attire, if they saw him start screaming and flailing his arms around. He skipped to the next song. Mouthed, *Not yet. Not yet. Just a few more moments.* And knew it would pass. That it could pass like a song. That it had passed. If he gave it another few seconds.

*

The young men from his father's firm began to leave and he left with them but they each went to cars or piled into taxis and he still couldn't go home. He walked a few steps as though he would go somewhere but then turned down the first alley and found a place beside a dumpster full of wine bottles, beer bottles and bottles for spirits. Other dumpsters were full of other kinds of rubbish. He listened to an album by a band called Lamb.

The waitress came out of a side door crying. She lit a cigarette even though her face was getting warped by the crying. She took a puff and didn't move. She tried to get the hurt out but new waves kept breaking over her. She took a few more breaths and then noticed Devon beside the dumpster.

It would have been natural for her to flick her cigarette at him or shout something and leave, but she walked over to him and motioned with just her palm opening and closing to stand up. He got to his feet and took a step towards her wondering whether she wanted to kick him for what the men he was with did to her.

She stepped closer to him and took one of his earphones and put it in her ear. 'Gorecki' was playing. She listened for a few moments.

'I got fired,' she said.

'That sucks.'

'Didn't want the job really.'

'Maybe you should be happy.'

'I should have quit though.'

'Maybe you did. Just reversed the way it happened.'

'I like this song,' she said and Devon nodded at her. 'I was wondering what you were listening to all night.'

'Just music,' he said.

'It didn't make sense – you with those arseholes.'

'I'm an arsehole as well. I'm worse.'

She smiled like she didn't believe him and leaned in to kiss. She was still wearing her name badge. It said Nadia. It took a while for Devon to feel her lips. He had a lot of thoughts about what it might be like. It felt like nothing until he closed his eyes. There was tobacco on her breath and there was the taste of tears because her face was still wet. Nadia was the first person Devon had kissed. They listened to Lamb play a song called 'Gabriel.'

When the déjà vu started this time it brought with it the phrase Studiously Aloof and the words Perils of Paradise he'd seen on the toilet door. Déjà vu about kissing Nadia and the feeling of suffocation, like both of them were stuffed in a long airtight glass tube. Déjà vu about being in this alleyway surrounded by the bottles. Déjà vu in the taste of tears and tobacco. Devon thought about *pain in paradise being a pleasure in hell,* and didn't know where Nadia's kiss came from.

*

He walked to Flinders Street Station. Let two trains go before he caught one. He listened to Primal Scream. He got to Brighton station on the last train. Got off and walked home slowly. Turned up the volume on his iPod until he could barely think. Unlocked the front door. The air in the house seemed vast and dead. Like it had been a tomb for a decade instead of a day. Everything perfectly placed and immaculately clean. As always. As though Roland and Devon Beckett had been living in a museum instead of a home.

He walked to the phone and plugged it into the wall. He turned his iPod off and pulled out the white plugs. He dialled the number for the police. He hung up. Took a breath and tried again. He told them he'd found the body of his father on the kitchen floor. That Roland Beckett was dead. He said it a few times before they accepted the information and asked him for his name and address and then told him they were sending a car over. They would have continued talking to him but Devon hung up and pulled the phone out of the wall again. He picked up his iPod. Put it down again. The light was still on in the kitchen from the morning.

Devon walked towards the kitchen and its body. When he got there he sucked in a hiss of air. The two perfect white buttons from his father's shirt were still on the pristine off-white tiles. One with thread in it and the other without thread. But the body wasn't where it had fallen. The body wasn't there.

Devon couldn't think. He looked around like it might materialise suddenly. He listened to the house and couldn't hear a thing. He wasn't sure if it was silent. His ears were roaring with sound. He wasn't sure his eyes were working properly either. He kept blinking, trying to see the body of his father. But it wasn't there and now he thought he could hear the sound of footsteps climbing down the stairs.

Overland

Publication Details

Antonia Baldo's 'Get Well Soon' was first published in *Island*, issue 117, Winter 2009.

Sherryl Clark's 'The Other Side of the World' was first published in *Griffith Review 26: Stories for Today*, Text Publishing, November 2009.

Louise D'Arcy's 'The Wife and the Child' was first published in *The Sleepers Almanac No. 6*, Sleepers Publishing, Melbourne, 2010.

Robert Drewe's 'Paleface and the Panther' was first published in *Brothers and Sisters*, edited by Charlotte Wood, Allen & Unwin, Sydney, 2009. Reprinted by permission.

David Francis's 'Once Removed' was first published in *Harvard Review*, issue 38, Spring/Summer 2010.

Karen Hitchcock's 'Little White Slip' was first published in *Little White Slips*, Picador, Sydney, 2009. Reprinted by permission of Pan MacMillan Australia Pty Ltd.

John Kinsella's 'Bats' was published in *Agni Online* in November 2010.

Anna Krien's 'Still Here' was first published in *Griffith Review 28: Still the Lucky Country?*, Text Publishing, May 2010.

Mike Ladd's 'A Neighbour's Photo' was first published in the *Adelaide Review*, issue 360, February 2010.

Nam Le's 'The Yarra' was first published in *Brothers and Sisters*, edited by Charlotte Wood, Allen & Unwin, Sydney, 2009. Reprinted by permission.

Joshua Lobb's 'I Forgot My Programme So I Went to Get It Back' was first published in *The Bridport Prize 2009: Poetry and Short Stories*, edited by Jackie Kay and Ali Smith, Redcliffe Press, Bristol, 2009.

Michael McGirr's 'The Great Philosophers' was first published in *Readings and Writings: Forty Years of Books*, edited by Jason Cotter and Michael Williams, Readings, Melbourne, 2009.

Suvi Mahonen's 'Bobby' was first published in *Island*, issue 118, Spring 2009. It has since been reprinted in *Shalla Magazine* (USA) and in *All Rights Reserved* (Canada). It was the winner of the 2009 Laura Literary Awards, Open Section.

Ryan O'Neill's 'The Eunuch in the Harem' was first published in *Harvest*, issue 5, Winter 2010.

Paddy O'Reilly's 'Salesman' was first published in *Griffith Review 29: Prosper or Perish*, Text Publishing, August 2010.

A.S. Patric's 'Beckett & Son' was first published in *Overland 199*, Winter 2010.

Joanne Riccioni's 'Can't Take the Country Out of the Boy' was first published in the *Age*, 9 January 2010.

Josephine Rowe's 'Brisbane' was first published in *Small Room*, issue 1, November 2009.

Michael Sala's 'Outside' was first published in *Harvest*, issue 4, Summer 2009–2010.

Cory Taylor's 'Wildlife' was first published in *One Book Many Brisbanes 5*, Brisbane City Council, 2010.

Chris Womersley's 'The Age of Terror' was first published in *Readings and Writings: Forty Years of Books,* edited by Jason Cotter and Michael Williams, Readings, Melbourne, 2009.

Notes on Contributors

The Editor:

Cate Kennedy is the author of the critically acclaimed short-story collection *Dark Roots* and the novel *The World Beneath* (both published by Scribe), as well as poetry collections and a travel memoir. Her work has appeared in many publications and anthologies, including *The Best Australian Stories*, the *Harvard Review* and the *New Yorker*. She works as a mentor, editor and judge when not at work on her own writing. She lives in north-east Victoria.

The Authors:

Antonia Baldo is a writer of screenplays and fiction. Her short stories have appeared in *Southerly, Ulitarra, Island* and *New Writer* (UK). She is working on her first novel.

Stephanie Buckle lives in Canberra, where she works as a counsellor. Her writing has won numerous awards and several of her short stories have appeared in the literary journal *Island*. She has written two novels and is currently working on a third.

Sherryl Clark's poetry and short fiction have appeared in many Australian magazines and journals. She has published over forty children's and young-adult books and two collections of poetry. She teaches in the Diploma of Professional Writing and Editing at Victoria University TAFE, and is a co-editor of *Poetrix* magazine. (www.sherrylclark.com)

Louise D'Arcy is a writer from Yackandandah in north-east Victoria. She has had more than thirty stories published in magazines and anthologies including *The Sleepers Almanac, Overland* and *Imago*. She won the *Age* Short Story Competition in 2010.

Robert Drewe was born in Melbourne and grew up on the West Australian coast. His many novels and short stories and his prize-winning memoir, *The Shark Net*, have been widely translated, won national and international awards, and been adapted for film, television, radio and theatre around the world.

Gillian Essex has been a teacher, a principal, an educational consultant, an author and a bureaucrat. She now freelances as a writer and editor and teaches corporate writing at the Centre for Adult Education. She is also working on a novel and two non-fiction books. 'One of the Girls' won the local section of the 2010 Alan Marshall Short Story Award.

David Francis is the author of two novels, *Agapanthus Tango* (published in the USA as *The Great Inland Sea*) and *Stray Dog Winter*. *Stray Dog Winter* was named Australian Novel of the Year in the *Australian Literary Review*, and won the 2010 American Library Association Award for Fiction. His short stories have appeared in the *Harvard Review*, the *Sydney Morning Herald*, the *Age*, *Wet Ink* and elsewhere. David currently lives in Los Angeles but spends part of each year on his family's farm in West Gippsland, Victoria.

Tim Herbert is the author of *Angel Tails* and co-editor of the collection *Love Cries*. His work has appeared in *The Oxford Australian Love Stories*, *The Best Australian Essays 2005* and most recently at gay-ebooks.com.au in the anthology *Catching On*.

Karen Hitchcock is a writer and doctor. Her collection of short stories, *Little White Slips*, won the 2010 Queensland Premier's Steele-Rudd Award and was shortlisted for the New South Wales Premier's Literary Awards and the Dobbie Award for women writers. Her first novel, *Read My Lips*, will be published by Picador in 2012.

David Kelly studies and teaches creative writing at the University of Newcastle. His first novel, *Fantastic Street*, was published by Picador in 2003.

John Kinsella's most recent volume of poetry is *Divine Comedy: Journeys Through a Regional Geography* (UQP, 2008). His *Activist Poetics: Anarchy in the Avon Valley* (ed. Lucy Niall) was recently published by the University of Liverpool Press. He has just completed a new collection of stories.

Anna Krien is a writer of journalism, essays, fiction and poetry. She has been published in the *Big Issue*, the *Monthly*, the *Age*, *The Best Australian Essays 2005* and *2006*, *The Best Australian Stories 2008*, *The Best Australian Poems 2010*, *Griffith Review*, *Going Down Swinging*, *COLORS* and *frankie* magazine. Her poem 'The Last Broadcasters' won the 2008 Val Vallis Poetry Award. Her first book, *Into the Woods: The Battle for Tasmania's Forests*, was published by Black Inc. in 2010.

Mike Ladd lives and writes in Adelaide. He presents *Poetica* each week on ABC Radio National. His most recent book of poems is *Transit*, published by Five Islands Press. His stories have appeared in *Famous Reporter*, *Island* and the *Adelaide Review*.

Nam Le is the author of *The Boat*, which won over a dozen major awards and was selected for over thirty 'best books of the year' lists internationally. He is the fiction editor of the *Harvard Review* and divides his time between Melbourne and overseas. (www.namleonline.com)

Joshua Lobb's writing has primarily been for the theatre. Between 2003 and 2007 he was writer-in-residence for State of Play Theatre Company. This produced the plays *Still at Aulis* and *Wilde Tales*, which was selected as part of the Belvoir B Sharp season in 2004 and toured New South Wales in 2007. Joshua is a lecturer in creative writing at the University of Wollongong.

Fiona McFarlane was born in Sydney. Her work has been published in *Southerly*, *Zoetrope: All-Story* and the *Missouri Review*, and she has received fellowships from the Fine Arts Work Center in Provincetown and Phillips Exeter Academy. Fiona is currently a student at the Michener Center for Writers in Austin, Texas.

Michael McGirr is the author of three books of non-fiction: *The Lost Art of Sleep, Bypass: The Story of a Road* and *Things You Get for Free,* all published by Picador. His short fiction has appeared in numerous periodicals, books and anthologies, both in Australia and overseas. He was formerly the fiction editor of *Meanjin* and publisher of *Eureka Street.* He teaches at St Kevin's College in Melbourne, where he lives with his wife and their three children.

Suvi Mahonen is completing a Master of Arts in writing and literature at Deakin University. She has previously been employed as a journalist in Australia and Canada but her focus is now on fiction. She has published short stories in various literary magazines in Australia and overseas and is currently concentrating on a longer work.

David Mence is a writer, director and dramaturge. As artistic director of White Whale Theatre his credits include *Macbeth Re-Arisen, Convict 002, Melburnalia, Melburnalia No. 2, Othello* (Bell Shakespeare) and *Blackbird* (MTC). David has been a creative fellow at the State Library of Victoria and is currently completing a PhD at the University of Melbourne.

Meg Mundell was born in New Zealand and lives in Melbourne. She has published journalism in the *Age,* the *Monthly,* the *Big Issue* and the *Sydney Morning Herald,* and creative writing in *Meanjin, The Sleepers Almanac, Harvest* and *New Australian Stories.* She is now working on a PhD about sense of place in literature. Her first novel, *Black Glass,* will be published in March 2011 by Scribe.

Ryan O'Neill's work has appeared in numerous journals and anthologies. His short-story collections *Six Tenses* and *A Famine in Newcastle* are published by Ginninderra Press. The latter was shortlisted for the 2007 Queensland Premier's Literary Awards. He lives in Newcastle, New South Wales with his wife and daughters.

Paddy O'Reilly is the author of a short-story collection, *The End of the World*, a novel, *The Factory*, and a novella, 'Deep Water.' Her stories have won national and international awards and been widely published and broadcast.

Alec (A.S.) Patric writes in Melbourne and is a St Kilda bookseller. His *Music for Broken Instruments* was recently published by Black Rider Press. He was shortlisted in the Lord Mayor's Awards, and his poetry and prose have appeared in literary journals such as *Going Down Swinging*, *Wet Ink*, *Etchings*, *Quadrant*, *Blue Dog* and *Overland*.

Joanne Riccioni's stories have won the Yeovil Prize (UK), the Banjo Paterson Award, the Wells Prize (UK), the Katherine Susannah Pritchard Award and the E.J. Brady Award, and have been published in *Stylus*, *Taralla*, *Westerly*, the *Momaya Review* and the anthology *Her Story* (ed. Indi Zeleny, Adams Media, USA). 'Can't Take the Country Out of the Boy' received second prize in the *Age* Short Story Competition in 2010. Joanne lives in Sydney and is working on a collection of short stories.

Josephine Rowe's poetry and short fiction have been widely published and broadcast. She is the poetry editor for the independent literary magazine *Harvest*, and her collection of short stories, *How a Moth Becomes a Boat*, was published earlier this year by Hunter Publishers. (www.josephinerowe.com)

Michael Sala spent his childhood moving between Holland and Australia. He currently teaches and studies in the creative writing department at the University of Newcastle, and is working on a novel and short-story collection. He was shortlisted for the 2007 *Australian*/Vogel Literary Award and has been published in *HEAT*, *Brothers and Sisters* (Allen & Unwin, 2009), *Harvest* and *The Best Australian Stories 2009*.

Dorothy (Dotti) Simmons grew up in Northern Ireland and came to Australia after graduating from Edinburgh University. She is an English teacher and the author of a play, *Night Exercise*, and four young-adult novels (published by Lothian books), and has had various short stories and poems published in literary journals. She is currently studying for a PhD in creative writing at the University of Melbourne.

Cory Taylor was born in Queensland in 1955 and grew up in various places including Fiji and Kenya. She is an award-winning screenwriter, and her non-fiction has appeared in *Griffith Review* and the *Courier-Mail*. She is married to the artist Shin Koyama and divides her time between Brisbane and Fukuoka, Japan. Her first novel, *Me and Mr Booker*, is scheduled for release in March 2011.

Chris Womersley is a Melbourne-based author. He won the 2007 Josephine Ulrick Prize for Literature for his short story 'The Possibility of Water,' and the 2008 Ned Kelly Award for Best First Fiction for his novel *The Low Road*. His second novel, *Bereft*, was published by Scribe in October 2010. (www.chriswomersley.com)